KOETHI ZAN

Koethi Zan was born and raised in rural Alabama. She attended Yale Law School and currently lives in an old farmhouse in upstate New York. Her first novel *The Never List* was a bestseller and a Richard and Judy Book Club pick.

ALSO BY KOETHI ZAN

The Never List

KOETHI ZAN

The Follower

VINTAGE

3 5 7 9 10 8 6 4 2

Vintage
20 Vauxhall Bridge Road,
London SW1V 2SA

Vintage is part of the Penguin Random House group of companies whose
addresses can be found at global.penguinrandomhouse.com

Penguin
Random House
UK

First published in Vintage in 2017

penguin.co.uk/vintage

A CIP catalogue record for this book is available from the British Library

ISBN 9781784702335

Printed and bound in Great Britain by Clays Ltd, St Ives PLC

Penguin Random House is committed to a sustainable future for our business,
our readers and our planet. This book is made from Forest Stewardship
Council® certified paper.

MIX
Paper from
responsible sources
FSC® C018179

. . . Save yourself; others you cannot save.

Adrienne Rich,
'Snapshots of a Daughter-in-Law'

CHAPTER 1

Julie Brookman's life was absolutely fucking perfect. She turned the rearview mirror of her brother's car toward her face and wiped a stray smudge of mascara from the corner of her eye. Admiring her long reddish-gold hair, she smiled at herself the way she knew made her green eyes sparkle.

She'd finished her paper on the transcendental poets four days early and would turn it in to her professor in the morning. Professor Greenfield was her favorite. She may have even had a slight crush on him, but that had nothing to do with it. Julie always did things ahead of schedule, always made sure her work was better than anyone else's.

For this paper, she'd stayed up at her parents' place in Westchester because she believed she wrote best in her childhood bedroom. Routine was crucial to success. That was one of her maxims. She'd decided to take the late train back, and give her essay a final proofread first thing in the morning before hitting send.

Ryan pulled into the station parking lot.

'Okay, kiddo,' Julie said, turning to the backseat to grab her computer bag. 'This will be just fine.'

'I can wait with you,' he said, but only after a conspicuous hesitation.

Julie took out her phone.

'We got here early. It would be silly for you to stay. I got it.' She nodded toward the train station. 'Look, Kurt's in there. You go meet Janie.'

He looked at her uncertainly, but it was obvious he wanted to go.

'Come on. It's totally fine.' She rubbed her hand over his hair, so long it would have hidden his eyes but for the natural upward sweep it took at the ends. He was adorable. 'You've got good cover now. Mom won't even ask where you've been. Get your precious time in before they ground you again.'

Ryan rolled his eyes.

'Listen –' he paused, still looking unsure – 'just wait inside, okay?'

Julie nodded as she slung the strap of her bag over her shoulder and pulled twice on the tiny silver heart medallion hanging from the clasp. Her good-luck charm.

'Yep. Me and Kurt, best buds.'

Julie got out of the car and peered through the window into the station. Kurt's outline was just visible as he stood behind the counter going through the receipts. She knew he'd be there until one a.m. She'd taken this late train a hundred times.

She glanced back as Ryan was pulling his car onto the road, his tires spinning out in the gravel at the edge of the turn. She waved half-heartedly but knew he wouldn't even look back. Kids today. She smiled.

It was a beautiful late-September night. The air was still warm. The stars, such as they were this close to the city, shone with full force. She took out a pack of cigarettes and knocked it against the post of the wooden porch that encircled the building. Instead of going in, she sat on the bench just under the windows, lit a cigarette, and took a long slow drag. Her parents disapproved of the habit and she agreed with them technically, but, this, her first cigarette in two days, was going down beautifully.

She blew out a long puff of smoke and absentmindedly rubbed the zipper of her bag. This paper was better than anything she'd done last year. She wondered if she should submit it for publication. Professor Greenfield would know the best places for it. Even if she didn't publish it, this was one more step toward the J. Burden Senior English Award next year.

She stood up and walked over to the steps that led to the tracks, took a final hit on the cigarette, and dropped it on the sidewalk. She rubbed it out with her shoe and then lifted her foot to check underneath. She had this thing about cigarette stubs. Bad luck if they stuck to you. But her sole was clean. She laughed to herself. Yes, she thought, her soul was clean.

She took out her phone, checked the time. Twelve minutes until the train would arrive. She opened Instagram, scrolled through some posts, liked a couple. Boring. She checked the *New York Times*. Sent a text to Mark. *Luv u.*

She waited. He didn't text back. Must not have his phone on him. She watched for a couple more seconds waiting for the dots to appear. Nothing.

Eleven minutes.

Should she read on the train or try to doze off? It was always a gamble as to whether she could sleep on the Metro North seats. She was so sensitive to smells and that horrid faux leather stuck to her skin whenever she moved. She could always read that *New Yorker* article she'd emailed herself.

Suddenly, the lights inside dimmed. She turned around, puzzled. Was Kurt leaving early? She leaned in toward the glass, but the interior office door was closed. She walked over to the side door and pulled hard but it was stuck fast. Locked. He'd gone home. She would have expected him to have said goodnight before he left or even to have waited with her. Unless he hadn't noticed her out there. She glanced at the parking-lot exit, and, sure enough, a car was turning out onto the road. But why would he leave now? Did they change the train schedules?

Damn it. This had happened to her once before. She took a step toward the board to check the timetable, but suddenly felt the eerie sensation that she was not alone.

She turned to see who it was, but before she'd gone full circle, a leather-gloved hand smothered her face and forced her head back.

All she thought of at first was the pain.

That fucking hurts.

She was too disoriented to understand what was happening until he was dragging her by her head and neck across the parking lot. Her feet struggled to keep up, to stay planted on the ground; otherwise the arm squeezing her throat would strangle her.

She couldn't breathe. Her mind buzzed with confusion. She had to get some air into her lungs *right now.*

Her assailant loosened his grip slightly, just in time. She gasped at the air in great gulps while trying to get her bearings as her eyes darted around for an escape route. In a split second, she took it all in. They were in the parking lot on the far side of the station, not a soul in sight. Headlights flashed by from the highway through the trees – too far away to make a difference.

Then suddenly her body was airborne. She landed – hard – in the back of a semi-truck trailer. It knocked the wind out of her. She tried to scream, but nothing came out. A metal roll-up door slammed down behind her, cutting her off from the world. It clanked shut. The locks turned and the engine roared to a start.

As it did, her voice returned and she yelled with all her might. At first only a foreign, guttural sound she'd never heard before, didn't even know she could make. Then the useless words came.

'What the fuck is this? Let me out!'

She scrambled her way along the empty, cold floor of the trailer. The truck lurched and she flew sideways, slamming into the sidewall, which was covered in thick Styrofoam padding. She clawed at it with her fingernails. Little bits came off in her hands and stuck to her fingers.

'What is this shit?'

She wiped them off on her jeans and dropped down, crawling her way in the pitch black to the end of the container, searching for a handle.

She finally found one on the far right edge and struggled with it, pulling with all her strength. The door creaked loudly but went up only half an inch. Through that tiny crevice she could see the road passing swiftly beneath her in the moonlight. They were going fast, but not fast enough to draw anyone else's attention.

Julie let go and the door latched shut again. She beat her fists on it.

'Help me, please. I'm in here! I'm in here,' she screamed until her throat went raw, but she could tell from the way the sound refused to bounce that the foam was doing its job. She stepped away from the door, balancing with one hand on the sidewall as the truck bumped along the road.

'Okay, Julie, keep it together. Think.'

Except she couldn't think. Her mind flew from one thought to another, none of them helpful.

'This is not happening. This is not happening,' she moaned as she felt around in the vast emptiness of the space, trying to focus, trying to get a grip. She patted herself up and down searching for anything that might help.

Her phone must have gone flying when he grabbed her. They'd find that tomorrow. At least that would raise an alarm.

Her computer bag. Gone. She didn't remember losing it in the struggle, but he must have ripped it off her shoulder. The thought of her paper flitted across her mind.

'Come on, that's the least of your problems,' she muttered, rubbing her face with her hands in frustration.

She thrust her hands into her jacket pockets looking for something – anything – to use as a weapon. She pulled out a gel pen. It wasn't much, but she could go for the eyes or the groin. All the soft spots she knew were vulnerable. She wouldn't go down easy.

She crouched in the corner, clutching her pen, her heart pounding in her chest. She was as ready as she could be, but her breathing was too loud in her ears. It was impossible to concentrate. Impossible to keep the panic from taking over.

It was a long time before anything else happened. Hours sitting in that truck, imagining every possible scenario that could occur when that door was raised up. Hours trying to focus her jumbled thoughts, to sort out the shock from the anger and fear, to force herself to accept that she had to face this horror utterly alone.

'I want my mommy,' she whimpered to herself. 'I want Mark. I want to go back in time and make Ryan wait with me. I'm such an idiot. No, I can't think like that. No crying.

'Come on, Julie. Come on. No one will realize you're missing until tomorrow and tomorrow might be too late. You have to get out of here as soon as he stops. Come on, you can do it, buck the fuck up.'

Then without warning, her body was thrown again hard to one side. They were turning. It must have been a tight one because the truck struggled to make it, lurching back and forth as the driver changed gears to get it up the hill. Eventually it reached level ground and then slowed to a stop.

Julie stood up and ran her hands along the side of the trailer until she reached the end. She hugged the right wall, hoping he wouldn't see her at first and she could jump out, get past him, and make a break for it.

As he hoisted the door open, she saw his form in shadow, a bright light shining from behind as his outline was revealed to her inch by horrible inch. His face was familiar, but she had no time to puzzle it out. She screwed up her courage, hunched over, and launched herself out of the truck bed.

She bolted sideways, determined to slip around the side of the truck and back down that hill. He'd anticipated that, of course, and he was fast. She never had a chance.

He grabbed her by the arm and yanked her around to face him. Her eyes met his – his squinting, terrifying, pale eyes, full of suppressed rage. She went for them, jabbing at his face with her pen but he pried it effortlessly from her hand. She tried to twist out of his grip, to kick him in the groin. He shook her so hard her feet came off the ground and her head whipped back and forth.

He pushed a pistol to her face.

She froze, staring at the barrel, at his hands clutching it. '*Please*,' was all she could muster up to say.

She'd never seen one this close up, didn't even know anyone who owned a gun. She stood there, in the cold, in the dark, shivering with fear and blinking back tears. Her mind had gone entirely blank when she saw that hunk of metal. No one had ever prepared her for this.

'Please let me go. I know it was just a mistake. I won't tell anyone. I'll tell them I ran away. I swear I won't tell them if you'll just let me go right now.'

He didn't even appear to register her words.

Then she heard a door slam and turned toward the sound. Her heart leapt, though she could hardly believe what she saw. For there, just a few hundred yards away, was a farmhouse all lit up. A plump, middle-aged woman headed straight toward them. She looked like someone's favorite aunt, wearing a loose-fitting housedress, her wispy brown hair pinned up messily.

It was surreal, unfathomable, yet there she was, walking across the moonlit yard filled with scrubby brush, past an overturned wheelbarrow and a clothesline where shirts twisted precariously in the wind, the cuffs of the sleeves nearly touching the ground.

Julie thought at first it was a hallucination, but no, she was real. Hope welled up in her. It's so hard to kill hope.

Her abductor still had her by the arm, with the nose of the gun now pushed into her back, but she took a chance that he wouldn't kill her in front of a witness.

'Help me! This man kidnapped me. Call the police. Run! He's dangerous. He has a gun!'

In that moment she felt a rush of relief. Help was here. Maybe there were even others inside who had heard her scream.

But the woman didn't react. She just walked toward them, calm and unhurried.

'Do you hear me? This man abducted me! I need help!'

Everything began to unfold in slow motion. The woman's lips were pressed tightly together, her eyes fixed steadily on

Julie's captor. There could be no mistaking the situation. She had to get it. But her expression wasn't right.

If anything, the woman's eyes glistened with a kind of adoration. She ignored Julie, who stood there frozen. Julie realized at that moment that this woman was not appalled or outraged or terrified. She wouldn't be her savior, delivering her from evil.

No, she wouldn't help her.

She was in on it.

CHAPTER 2

The basement of the Stillwater public library was always deserted and that suited Adam just fine. He'd been down there for three hours already and hadn't seen a single person except the assistant librarian who checked on him religiously every forty-five minutes. She pretended, without much success, that she had some administrative task involving the abandoned card catalogue shoved over in the corner. He must have looked suspicious, but he didn't owe her an explanation.

Adam turned the knob on the microfilm machine, watching the front pages of the *Stillwater Herald* spin past him. He wondered if the time would come when even these documents would be online and he'd be able do this work from the sanctity of an impersonal hotel room. He doubted it would ever happen for these stories. Not these leftover bits of history, important to no one. Forgotten tragedies, blips in time. Not worth uploading.

'Finding everything okay?'

Adam jumped.

'Fine, just fine.' The screen was too big to cover with his hands. It sat there in front of them, the words blown up to twenty-four point. She leaned toward it, squinting despite her bright blue-rimmed glasses.

'Oh, the Fairmont Street murders. Wow, haven't thought about that in a long time.'

Adam flipped the knob to change the page. It landed on a Sears advertisement for riding lawnmowers.

She glanced down at the small white boxes he'd pulled from the drawers.

'You're looking at the wrong years though.'

'I know. I've read all the original reports a thousand times over. Trust me. Now I'm looking for follow-up stories. Thought maybe there'd be an anniversary piece. You know –' he picked up one box – 'ten years later.' Then the other – 'Twenty.' He noticed for the first time that she was kind of pretty. She was about his age, late twenties, and her long hair was a little darker brown than his.

'Writing a book?'

'Nope. Investigating.' He couldn't help but say it with a hint of pride.

She sat down next to him, clearly intrigued, and rolled her chair close to his.

'You don't look like a cop. You look more like the bad guys.' She winked. Was she flirting with him?

'I do a lot of undercover.' Used to, anyway.

'As what? A grad student? Look at you, jeans, hoodie, what is that, four-day stubble? You don't look like you've slept in days.' Definitely flirting. Adam suddenly felt uncomfortable. He'd been so focused on this case for so long that he'd forgotten what normal human contact was like.

'You've been here every day this week. Working hard, I guess?'

He glanced up at her. So she had been checking up on him.

She blushed. 'Not a lot of people our age in here. You stand out.'

'Are you from Stillwater?' he asked, mostly to break the awkward silence.

'Born and raised.' She didn't seem too thrilled by the fact.

'Maybe you can help me out then. I could use some local insight. You know, where do the kids hang out – that sort of thing.'

'Sure, I'd love to.' She cleared her throat. 'Actually, Tuesday nights we close early. You wouldn't want to grab a bite to eat later, would you? Savoy isn't half bad. It's just a few doors down. I could give you the rundown over dinner.'

He glanced back at the microfilm machine, thinking of all those articles he'd yet to search, then looked over at her shiny red lips curled up into a half-smile. He was tempted to go, he had to admit.

But that's what a lesser man would do. Someone without a mission. It might not seem like it, but he knew he was getting closer. He felt it. He couldn't stop now, not even for a minute.

'Maybe next week?' He started gathering up the pages he'd printed out. 'I'm close to a breakthrough and I'll probably have to work all night tonight.' Just like most nights.

'All night, huh? Your dedication is admirable. It must be awfully important.' She pointed to the boxes. 'Do you think it's a serial killer? That always happens, right? Like, the guy was in jail for twenty years and then when he gets out the same kind of murders start happening again.' She shivered, playing it up. 'There's not a serial killer around here, is there? If that's the case, you should definitely walk me home.' She grinned.

'I think you're probably pretty safe.' He smiled back. 'Really though, I have to get through this.' He pointed to the stack of papers. 'I've been working on this for a long time and I finally have a lead.'

'Does that mean you'll be here in Stillwater for a while?'

'Maybe. I'm searching for a man and a woman who passed through this town twenty years ago. That's going to take some digging. I don't know where they went from here. Disappeared without a trace.'

She shrugged.

'Oh, you'll find them. People don't really disappear without a trace. You should know that, officer. Humans leave their marks on things. You just have to look . . .' She rolled her chair toward him until their knees were touching. He could smell her floral scent. 'Really. Close. Up.'

He pulled back. Now he was the one blushing.

'Bye for now,' she said, standing up. 'Maybe I'll see you tomorrow. And be sure to put that microfilm in the return tray, will you? The yellow one, by the copier.' She smiled.

Slightly dazed, he watched her sashay away from him, thinking only, 'She's right. I just have to look harder.'

CHAPTER 3

Cora hauled a black garbage bag out of the pantry and went back to the kitchen. One by one, she withdrew the contents and carefully placed each item on the rickety wooden table. James had done well to collect her belongings.

There they were: the tiny black T-shirt and dark skinny jeans, the light brown leather jacket, size two, brand new hi-top sneakers, size seven and a half. Cora didn't bother folding anything, but she paused to stroke the smooth leather on top of the pile.

She dug around in the bottom of the bag again, fished out a smashed iPhone, and laid it next to the clothes, then took out a heavy black case and balanced it on its edge as she unzipped it. Hanging from a metal beaded chain was a silver medallion in the shape of a heart. She unclasped it and slipped it into her pocket. There couldn't be any harm in keeping such a small thing.

She lifted the slim computer out of its snug padded compartment. She'd never held such a beautiful object. What must it have cost? Rubbing her flattened palm across its cold surface, she imagined that it belonged to her and felt the envy flare up inside. She must keep her mind clean as James had taught her, must focus on her duty. Yes, she must take heart, be strong and purposeful. She would reap her rewards.

She flipped it open and ran her fingers across the keyboard. Even this had to go. It was part of the plan.

Under the front flap of the computer case was a shimmering pink wallet, jammed with credit cards and worn receipts. Cora unsnapped it, pulled the cash out of the fold, and counted. Nearly thirty dollars. She tucked the bills into her dress pocket. Perhaps James hadn't bothered to check it. She'd store it in her cash box until he asked for it and maybe he never would. He didn't understand the household expenses.

She sighed again, more deeply this time, and lined up the girl's effects in a neat row, her fingers tickling over each one. From the drawer by the sink, she withdrew her latex gloves, slid them on, and took out a clean towel to wipe everything down.

When she had finished, she opened the garbage bag and threw everything back in, then lugged it out into the yard behind the barn. The skies were mostly blue, but storm clouds were brewing off to the west. She'd better get this job done before the rain came. Leaning the bag against the wall, she built a fire in the pit a few feet away and soon enough had it roaring.

She took the computer out, set it on the ground, and went to the barn for her safety goggles and a sledgehammer.

It would be good to obliterate this thing she so coveted. Coveting was evil.

The fire grew hot behind her, flickering and spitting out sparks. The wind picked up. She raised the hammer, preparing to throw her whole weight into it, to dash this object of temptation into a thousand pieces and then burn them in the pit with all the rest.

But something stopped her.

She didn't want to do it.

She took a deep breath. There was no choice, obviously. James had been very clear in his instructions, and there would be hell to pay if she didn't heed them.

Why was she plagued with these urges to disobey? They were going to get her in trouble.

She put down the sledgehammer and paced a few feet away, glancing over at the boarded-up window of the house. She hated the way it marred the building, like an eye poked out. She bit her lip absentmindedly as she thought hard about what to do.

Walking back to the hammer, she lifted it up a second time. It felt heavier than before.

She swallowed. Then, without thinking – as if her body were not under her complete control – she flung the tool away. It clanged against the side of the tractor, the sound echoing across the valley.

She rushed over to check the damage, terrified that she'd broken something else, but it had only made a tiny dent. James wouldn't notice such a thing.

She let out her breath with relief.

Everything was fine. It was all fine.

She glanced around as if someone could be watching her, ready to report to James. Moving fast, she shoved the computer back into the garbage bag and bunched up its edges in her hand. Running full tilt, she flung open the kitchen door and flew up the stairs to her bedroom. On her knees in the closet, she pushed aside a heavy clump of camphor-smelling dresses and shoved the bag all the way to the back.

James would never look there.

She sat down on the bed, panting, and slowly lifted her eyes to her reflection in the mirror above the bureau. She was flushed, shocked by what she'd done. She'd never disobeyed him so directly before.

But she had to have these things, these treasures from a different world. She knew it was a sin to keep them, but it seemed so insignificant. As long as no one ever found them.

Especially not James.

CHAPTER 4

Julie adapted quickly to the routines of captivity. Initially, she'd considered her abduction to be an event, a single dot, a point in time and space. Not a new life.

Luckily, she'd always been a fast learner.

Her room – that's how she thought of it now – held a single bed with a lumpy mattress rank with sweat and other unthinkable bodily fluids. They'd left her with a sad little excuse for a blanket, an old matted fleece thing with the image of Winnie-the-Pooh spread across it.

There was old Pooh, sitting there innocently with a dopey grin on his face, his hand dipping into the honey pot on his lap. Julie had spent endless hours looking at that sweet, dim-witted bear, imagining the taste of honey on her tongue. She would cry, remembering her mother reading A. A. Milne to her at bedtime when she was six. Some days, however, the memory hurt too much and she only wanted to shred his adorable face into a million tiny threads.

Truth be told though, she talked to him. He was the only friend she had anymore and at some level she was thankful he was there. He didn't hurt her. He didn't call her terrible names. He didn't starve her and then feed her revolting inedible garbage.

Julie knew it wasn't his fault, but he smelled too, just as bad as the mattress, and no matter what she did she couldn't scrape that last bit of flaky detritus off his face. Nevertheless, she'd curl up in a corner of the bed and stroke his cheery little face, hugging it to her, looking for solace, commiseration, love. Any poor pittance.

This room, the only space she'd laid eyes on for weeks, was entirely devoid of warmth, a stark white cube either flooded with the harsh bright light of the uncovered bulb or enveloped in total darkness. The top edge of each wall was covered in arcane symbols crudely painted in black, with a row of crazy text beneath them: 'Behold the death-keeper.' 'The impure shall be purified in blood.' 'Those who question must sacrifice.' She avoided looking at them now, but the words already ran on repeat in her brain.

Shoved against one wall was a blond wood console from a million years ago, with a built-in radio and gray bulbous television screen. It taunted her with the prospect of diversion, but didn't work.

Her only distraction was attempting to detect the sub-tlest noises in that house, to identify and categorize them, so she could anticipate to some degree the arrival of food, water, or pain. Her senses were heightened from depriv-ation, and every smell and sound provided a coordinate, a detail, a piece of the puzzle of life down below. She'd learned to interpret the particular language of the building itself, the irregular clank of the radiators, the sudden rush of water through pipes above her head, the creak of rusty door hinges, the slam of cupboards.

She knew at all times who was home and exactly where they were located below her. She'd memorized their daily routines and their repertoire of tics and gestures. He cleared his throat out of habit and groaned when he yawned; she was clumsy, dropping the silverware, her toothbrush, the bucket she was filling in the sink. She heard his wild rages and her muffled cries when he let them out on her. This small mastery over their physical dimensions was her survival map, her only power over them. But it earned her very little.

Nothing in her stifling cell of a bedroom could help her either. In one corner, a couple of cheap plastic lawn chairs were stacked haphazardly. Julie had assessed that neither of them was heavy enough to do any damage to his skull. In the opposite corner, there was a portable toilet and sink, though she'd learned her lesson about drinking the fetid brown water that flowed from the faucet. She'd examined every inch of them, hoping for some pipe or wire she could pull off to stab into his beady eyes. Not one bolt was loose, not one hinge needed oil. He'd been so very careful.

What she missed most were light and fresh air. The space shriveled up on her day after day, the walls appearing at times to undulate before her, closing in tighter and tighter. Yet her captors had threatened her with death if she tried to break off a single fragment of the rough-sawn boards over the window. She believed them. She was fungible. He'd gotten her easily enough, hadn't he? She was terrified to be here, but even more terrified at the thought of being discarded and replaced.

It didn't matter what they said though, she spent hours trying to pry off bits of wood. Her nails bore the evidence, broken down to the quick. The pads of her fingertips were rubbed raw and her hands were covered with splinters, the tiny prickles edged in burning red flesh. Some days she hardly noticed it and on others she berated herself for her stupidity. She couldn't afford to have an infection. That was no way to die. She didn't want to make it that easy for them to kill her when he was finished with her.

Eventually, she gave up trying to claw her way out and would spend the days lying there listlessly on the bed, half-covered with the grimy blanket, staring at the cracks in the thick layers of paint, thinking about how she'd had *everything* before this had happened. It was funny how she hadn't realized it until now. Her perfect family, perfect boyfriend, perfect tiny West Village apartment. Perfect, perfect, perfect. And these gruesome lowlifes – these nobodies she wouldn't have even noticed on the street – had been able to steal it from her. Just. Like. That.

The first few days in there she'd thought they'd never get away with it. Then she'd been convinced that the police would bust in at any moment. She'd *known* it. As awful as it was, she just had to have faith and wait it out until her parents found her. They always took care of her. *Surely* they would notice that one of the three men on the construction job didn't show up after she disappeared. They would realize that couldn't be a coincidence, that he was her abductor.

It was killing her to know that her parents were so physically close to the key to finding her. His fingerprints must be everywhere, covering the house. Surely he had a police record and they could identify him. Or had he always worn gloves? She'd never noticed, never paid any attention when she'd gone home for the weekend to visit. Those guys worked on Saturdays until two. She would occasionally take lemonade out to them. She was sure he'd taken his gloves off then – check the glassware!

Then the most chilling possibility had occurred to her: maybe he *did* keep showing up. What if he was there, in those first days after she was gone, finishing the build out on her parents' new three-season room, wondering when they would discover she was missing? Then he could peer through those freshly installed Marvin windows to see their most private pain. He must have felt so powerful, in charge, as though he were the puppet master, watching the results of his actions play out in horrible order, just as he'd planned.

But she tried not to think about her parents. She knew how they'd be suffering and she couldn't bear that on top of everything else. They must have found her phone, must be organizing search parties and making heartfelt pleas on the news. Her mother would never let anyone rest until they found her. But what if they never did?

She closed her eyes as tight as she could. She couldn't focus on that now, because the truth was she'd been reduced to a near-animal state, worrying more about how to wrangle food out of these beasts than anything else. So here she was, on day thirty-eight, lying on the bed wallowing in her misery, when she heard the familiar step on the stairs.

She would have recognized the rhythm of her walk even if she hadn't been the only one around for the last week. The sad truth was, Julie was eager to see her today. Even if she was a pathetic excuse for a human being, she was at least a human being. And she wasn't *him*. Better to see her than be locked up alone surrounded by these four walls for yet another twenty-four-hour stretch. Better than just having Pooh.

Julie watched the door as she counted off her usual fifteen steps up the stairs and six light footfalls down the carpeted hall. The door creaked open on cue and she entered carrying the tray with Julie's meager rations for the day.

Julie knew the drill. She sat perfectly still on the bed with her hands up in the air and her legs crossed at the ankles, just as they'd instructed. She knew now that if she made one tiny mistake, veered from the ritual one iota, all sustenance would be swiftly removed and she'd have the rest of that day to reflect on her disobedience.

As the woman put today's paltry provisions down on the floor in front of her, Julie's salivary glands came alive. It didn't matter what was on that plate. The first few days she'd been disgusted by the slop they fed her, but now she found it disgusting only in theory. Her body responded otherwise.

The woman twitched her finger up, the signal to begin, and Julie dove first for the paper cup. She knew she shouldn't drink it all at once, but she couldn't help it. The days of the automatic gallon jug had ended when she'd attempted to escape after her first week there. Now she had to earn it with absolute compliance and she usually managed to fall short.

When she'd gulped down the water, she lunged at the bowl, shoving the scraps into her mouth with her fingers. She couldn't help it, didn't care how it looked. Decorum was the least of her concerns. When she'd devoured the last morsel, she scraped at the microscopic bits of bread and the glistening smear of chicken fat at the bottom of the dish. She was still ravenous but at least she wouldn't die.

The woman moved forward in that bored rote way of hers to clear away the things and go, but Julie couldn't stand to be left alone again so quickly. She would do anything to stop her.

'Request permission to speak,' she said meekly, eyes downcast as per the required protocol.

The woman put her hands on her hips and stared at her stupidly.

'What is it?' She was usually impatient to get out of there, apparently not eager to linger in this room which must smell horrible to anyone not perpetually inhabiting it.

'Would you . . . I was wondering if you would consider staying. For a minute or two.'

The woman stared at her, obviously perplexed by her audacity. She may as well have been one of the farm animals who'd suddenly acquired the gift of speech.

The woman turned to go, but Julie thought she saw her hesitate. Could she be considering it?

'I'm begging you. *Please*.' Julie could hear the whine in her voice, but she couldn't help it. 'I'm going crazy in here. Please. I've been alone for weeks And I can tell he's gone. Can't you spare a few minutes? Just to talk to me.'

The woman's heavy-lidded eyes met Julie's. For a second Julie wondered if she was dense, a mental defective he kept around to handle the drudgery. Did she even understand what Julie was saying? Should she repeat herself, louder this time and more slowly?

The woman took a step back and wiped her hands on her dirty apron. She opened her eyes wider and for a split second Julie thought she detected a spark of intelligence in there. Now if it could only be conjured up to the surface.

'I guess you *are* desperate, if you're looking to talk to me,' the woman finally replied. She laughed a hard little laugh that Julie counted as progress.

Julie wiped her face with the front collar of her sweatshirt in an attempt to show some dignity before she propelled herself forward.

'So then, what is it? Are you trying out a little game on me? Some trick you have in mind? Give up. I've seen them all.'

Julie shivered. What did she mean by that?

'No games. No, no. I'm . . . I'm just lonely. Really, really lonely. I swear. I won't do anything. Won't try anything. I'll sit here, like this. In position.' Julie got back on the bed, held up her hands, and crossed her ankles. 'I won't even move.'

The woman stood studying her a minute longer, narrowing her eyes as she edged toward the door. Then she shrugged her shoulders.

'Fine, fine. One minute.' She walked backwards slowly over to the corner, her eyes still fixed on Julie, and dragged a lawn chair over, letting its legs screech across the floor.

She took no chances even then. As soon as she sat down, she reached into the front pocket of her apron and brought out a switchblade. She clicked it open and balanced it on the narrow plastic arm of the chair.

'Don't try anything. I mean it,' she said, glancing down at the knife to emphasize her point.

Julie was determined to ignore it. The threat of violence seemed a small price to pay at that moment.

'Thank you,' she whispered, elated by this victory. Having been without human companionship for so long, she didn't know where to begin. It occurred to her that the two of them were in the same boat on that front. Maybe she'd help her, even if only in little ways.

'What are you smiling at?' the woman said, mistaking Julie's hope for slyness.

'I'm just . . . glad to have this chance to talk to you. I appreciate it,' she replied tentatively.

The woman took out a shiny miniature object from her other pocket, turning it over between her fingers like a Chinese medicine ball.

Julie took a deep breath, or tried to.

'Do you find it kind of hard to breathe in here?'

The woman only stared at her.

'I guess not. Okay, then.' More silence. 'I wonder if you'd consider taking me downstairs – not outside or anything. I don't mean that. Just somewhere I could sit next to an open window for a few minutes? I swear I won't try to run away. It's just I feel like I can't breathe in here sometimes.'

The woman sniffed.

'James would never allow that.'

'Oh, right. Well, I mean, like now, while he's away. I wouldn't tell.'

She jerked back her head, clearly appalled.

'Oh, no. I would never go against his wishes. Never.'

'So are you saying I'll never leave this room?'

The woman blinked once. Twice.

'What's going to happen to me?' She hadn't meant to ask so bluntly and wasn't entirely sure she wanted to know.

The woman turned away. Was she ashamed? Did she even know?

'I shouldn't be talking to you,' she finally answered, looking back at Julie. 'But you want my advice?'

Julie nodded. She was almost sure she didn't, but at least it would keep the woman there a few minutes more.

'You're focusing on your pain and suffering. That's not going to get you anywhere. Accept the Word and follow the Path of Righteousness. Your past self is dead and you have been resurrected. The sooner you give yourself over fully to the Path, the easier it will be.'

Julie stiffened. This wasn't what she wanted to hear.

'I understand what you're used to. A girl like you with such a sweet face and pretty little figure, provoking lust and sin. You must have enjoyed your role as temptress.' She shook her head wearily. 'Now you will be redeemed here with us.'

Julie could feel the color draining from her face. Then she felt her heart harden a little bit.

'Can I ask you a personal question?'

The woman shrugged, put the trinket she was holding back in her pocket.

'You can ask. Doesn't mean I'll answer.'

'Why do you stay with him? I mean, I don't understand –'

The woman's face froze, but Julie couldn't stop herself.

'How did you end up here? Is it because you really believe all that crazy religious stuff?' That didn't come out quite right, she knew.

The woman rose slowly from her chair.

'What did you say?' Her face went red.

Bad idea, Julie.

'I'm sorry, I didn't mean that. It's really – it's none of my business. I'm sorry.'

When Julie saw the knife in the woman's hand, she realized what a mistake she'd made and a wave of nausea passed through her.

'I swear I didn't mean anything by it. I just meant that, you know, I just wanted to get to know you—'

'Stop talking your blasphemy,' the woman interrupted. Julie stopped talking.

But it was too late.

The woman came closer until Julie could feel her hot breath on her face and smell her strange mix of earth and sweat and soap.

What had she done?

'Look at you with those long lashes, the tears always delicately balanced on the edges. Oh, so pretty,' she said, squinting at her. 'You think that gives you the right to say something like that?'

Julie felt the tears spring into her eyes, as if on command.

'Everyone's always done whatever you wanted, haven't they? You've never had to show anyone else any respect.'

Julie tried not to react, but inside she quaked. She swallowed. Her arms were aching from being held up so long. A drip of sweat slid slowly down her back. Terrified, she stayed still though, would stay like this as long as she was told.

'You must have been given so much to achieve what you have. A life of free time, healthy food, and paid lessons.' She paused, like a storm gathering. 'And now you think you have the right to criticize things you know nothing about?'

Julie regretted asking her to stay more than anything in the world. She'd thought the woman couldn't be as evil as him, had to have a heart. She'd been horribly wrong.

'You don't get it, do you?' The woman's voice dropped to a whisper. 'You think you have something over on me, don't you?'

Julie hardly dared to look up. She held her breath, afraid to speak, not wanting to say something to tip the balance.

'You think you have a right to judge me? If so, then you need to learn your place.'

At this she grabbed Julie's hair with her free hand and pulled as hard as she could, forcing Julie's face upward, where she had no choice but to meet the woman's dark, empty eyes.

She leaned in, enunciating the words carefully: 'You have to understand, girl, some people are just pawns in the universe's overarching plans. It looks like you're one of them.'

She released Julie's hair with a final jerk.

Julie couldn't hold back the tears at that point, but knew better than to break the rules by putting her hands down. No matter how much her arms hurt, she held them in place. No matter how wet her face, she didn't dare wipe it. All she could do was sit still and watch the woman angrily gather up the tray to leave, her only consolation the way that miserable loser fumbled with everything she touched, dropping the spoon, tripping over nothing on her way out.

Idiot woman. Cruel witch.

When the door finally slammed behind her, Julie let the sobs explode so that it felt as if her chest might heave open from them. How had she ever thought that woman was anything but a monster? She hadn't wanted to accept it. In her state of denial, she had tried to bear her circumstances day to day, hoping her parents would find her or her abductors would come to their senses and let her go.

Now she knew for certain there was no time to wait for help. If she didn't figure out something fast on her own, she'd never make it out alive.

CHAPTER 5

James had been away for nearly a month and Cora was beginning to worry. The last time he'd been gone this long it turned out they'd arrested him in Arizona and he'd spent ninety days in jail for some stupid thing. They'd gotten the indictment but the prosecutor let him take a plea. No evidence, James said. They were playing cat and mouse with him and he'd won with such a short sentence on what would have been a felony conviction. He knew how to play the system, for sure.

But she knew he'd be back as soon as he could get here. The girl guaranteed that. That awful girl.

Cora should never have talked to her. So what if she was lonely? Cora was lonely too. What had she been thinking? She'd been immune to the other one – that one had been docile at first and even in the last days she'd been quiet except for the crying. But this time Cora had been lured in.

Things were different with this girl. The other one had come to them willingly, a Follower who was undergoing the preparations to join the Divine Family. But then the plan had gone wrong. It wasn't James's fault. The Dark Spirits had taken over by then, and he wasn't himself.

They'd been forced to build the cell after that first incident. It had been for her own good, to keep her safe. It wasn't their fault she died before she accepted her destiny. She shouldn't have pushed James like that.

This new girl worried her, though. Could she truly be the one sent to fulfill the Revelation? Was this as the prophecy had declared? *A Servant at Hand, one who arrives in Darkness, to bring the Light.*

Even if she was the Servant at Hand, Cora was meant to keep her place – that much was clear. It was also written: *The Wife shall suffer, but in suffering shall find her Great Reward.*

After all, Cora had found them the farm in the first place. They'd done what they'd had to do to get it, and after years of waiting it out and dreaming of it, it was theirs. Seventy-five acres of prime soil in upstate New York, rolling hills, deep green fields of rye, a fine garden, three outbuildings, twenty head of cattle, and seventeen chickens. She had a view of the Catskills from the backyard, a formal dining room, and a six-burner stove. It was all she'd ever wanted. A home.

She would take long solitary walks over the fields regardless of the weather. The wind would whip up her hair and she would laugh the way she should have done as a child. She would run through the pastures and throw herself down into the grass, feeling its softness tickling her face and neck. In those moments, she could make herself believe that everything had happened for a reason.

Sometimes when she was lying out there in those fields, looking up at the clouds drifting by in a pure cerulean sky, she'd indulge in her other world. If she squeezed her eyes shut tight enough, she could block out so many things and pretend she had the child after all. A little golden-haired daughter with a pixie face and his eyes, who would have loved her mother more than anything in the world. Everything would have been different.

Now she just wanted to hold onto what she had. Her mind was ticking all right. Strange things were brewing in her head. She felt uneasy, unsettled. It wasn't her place to question, but still.

She knew what was the matter: she hated this girl.

James had made a mistake. This girl was not the Servant at Hand. She knew it deep down in her bones. Cora would have to be the one to reveal this disappointing truth to him, but she wasn't sure how. She must be clever about it, lest he think it was merely jealousy. It wasn't that at all.

She stood up, her course of action decided. She would be doing it for him, not herself. One day he would understand the sacrifices she'd made and risks she'd taken for his sake.

She went to her closet and reached far in the back until her hands met the crumpled plastic. After hauling the sack out into the middle of the room, she turned it upside down and dumped the contents onto the floor.

First rule of thumb: know thine enemy.

She started with the computer case, sliding her hand in the front pocket and along the bottom of the inner compartment. She brought out handfuls of yellowed receipts, rainbow-colored Post-it notes stuck to one another, a couple of parking tickets. A box of Altoids that proved to be empty.

Well, there was one thing she knew: this girl was a disgusting slob.

Then there was the wallet. Cora unsnapped the small tab that struggled to contain everything and dumped all the dirty slips of paper onto the floor. She sifted through them, a scowl on her face. She took out the credit cards one by one and tossed them aside.

Platinum Visa, Gold Mastercard, American Express.

Rich girl. That made her nervous. The other one had been a straggler. She'd been a runaway and a prostitute who was looking for shelter, and she'd found it. That girl would have slipped through the cracks one way or another.

But they'd be searching for this one.

Next was her driver's license and behind it a student ID, bright purple, from NYU. She lifted them to the light. Julie Brookman. So the thing had a name. It made her feel queasy to see it. She dug her fingers deep into the remaining pockets, pulling out several more cards: health insurance, Staples Rewards, the Mamaroneck public library.

And then, wedged far back into a slit someone had specially made for it was a small square of cut-out cardboard. She grabbed it with the tips of her fingers and slid it toward her. Written on one side was a series of letters and numbers jammed tightly together in nearly microscopic script.

Passwords. Six of them in all, unlabeled. They were the formulations of a child: Bumbl3b3321, MissFancy911, Bab33doll. And yet in truth these were the keys to a kingdom, Cora would bet, including the girl's bank account.

It was awfully tempting – she could only imagine the luxuries she could afford with this kind of financial access – but she knew better. The cops would be on her in a second. There'd be alarms set on the account and video footage to convict her. It was all so inviting, but she'd better forget it.

Then it dawned on her: the computer. Of course.

Her heart beat faster as she carried it over to the bed, plugged in the cord, and flipped it open. The screen flashed up with a small box for a password.

One of these had to be right but she knew if she tried and failed too many times, she'd be locked out for good. She ran her finger down the list and first typed in JulieB999.

Not it.

Cora started to sweat. She didn't know how many chances she'd get before the device would freeze up. She studied each combination on the list. There had to be some rhyme or reason to it.

How would this ridiculous girl think? Perhaps she'd gotten this as a gift for high-school graduation. Yes, her college computer. If so, then there was one obvious choice, something she'd tossed off in the haste of her excitement about school: NYUNYU111. Just the sort of thing she'd do.

She typed it in, her hands trembling, pausing before finally taking a deep breath and hitting the last digit.

The screen blinked.

She was in. Stupid girl.

Seven tabs were open across the top, and below them an inbox of 3,329 undeleted emails, 251 of them unread. It was all there for Cora to peruse at her leisure.

She eagerly clicked on the top one from someone named Mark Battersby. Instead of his note, however, a new box appeared with the message 'Unable to Connect to the Internet'.

Of course, what was she thinking? This machine was useless here in their remote, disconnected world. Her only option was to take it to the library in town and sign onto their Wi-Fi. A place where anyone could look over her shoulder, could wonder what she, of all people, was doing with a gleaming thousand-dollar laptop.

It would be dangerous. It would be foolish. But she couldn't help herself. She'd already broken James's trust. What difference would it make to take one more small step?

CHAPTER 6

Three years ago, Adam had made his first major career mistake: he'd spoken to the staff psychologist. To be honest, he hadn't had much of a choice. He'd been drinking on the job and had gotten caught. It was so unfair though. The situation had been completely under control. No one need ever have known except that his partner wasn't a detective for nothing. He'd found the empties and thought Adam needed help.

That first visit to the shrink had ruined everything. She sat there – so sure of herself – with her professional hairdo and a cloud of sweet scent filling the air around her. Her office oozed calculated warmth with its sophisticated dark gray walls, a leather couch as soft as butter, and a framed diploma on the wall covered in swirls of illegible calligraphy. Everything seemed specially designed to disempower the patient.

They sat in silence just looking at each other as Adam nervously tapped his fingers on the armrest. He was determined not to go first.

'What brings you here today, Adam?' she finally asked.

At first he considered refusing to speak, but that was a fast train to a long-term disability leave. He would co-operate just enough to keep his job, but he didn't intend to make it easy.

'You tell me, Dr. Lyle. I'm reasonably sure you've got it written down right there in your file.'

She nodded calmly. He could see her recalibrating her initial assessment of him. She jotted something on her note-pad that he imagined to be 'Difficult' or maybe 'Resistant'.

'Okay, fine. Let's try this again.'

She took a sip of coffee from the oversized mug that had been sitting on the low table between them.

'We're here because you're having a bit of a tough time. You've been drinking. Why don't you tell me about that? What's happening?'

He took a deep breath.

'I guess you'd say I was having some . . . trouble deal-ing with the Sloan case. I didn't get there in time. A few hours sooner and that kid would still be alive. And we still don't even have a suspect.' His voice cracked. He cleared his throat to cover it.

She calmly wrote in her notebook, then lifted her eyes to meet his, waiting for him to go on.

'Well, I said it. Isn't that enough?'

Dr. Lyle leaned back in the chair, obviously enjoying lording her power over him.

'I understand. That's hard. Really hard,' she said.

He shifted in his seat and looked through the frosted privacy glass of the narrow window onto the street where he could see the outline of his car. He wished he could get in it and drive until he hit some border. Any one would do.

'Homicide is a tough beat.' Her voice came out of nowhere, summoning him back to the room. 'Not everything can be solved,' she continued. 'People get away with terrible crimes sometimes. It's often very hard for police officers to accept that.'

'Yeah, well, I *won't* accept it.' He studied his shoes. They could use a good polish. Maybe he'd get to that this afternoon.

They sat in silence.

He knew she already had the details. She had Google, didn't she? It was the third hit when his name was searched.

'It's because of my sister. That's why it was so bad for me,' he said, finally raising his head to look her in the eye.

She put her coffee cup down. Oh sure, now she was interested.

'Yes?'

'She's dead too.'

Dr. Lyle didn't flinch. So he was right. She probably knew every gritty detail but she wanted to force him to say the actual words, maybe burst out in tears and have some cathartic emotional breakthrough right here in her office. Wouldn't that just complete the picture?

'I see. I'm sorry to hear that. Perhaps you'd like to tell me what happened?'

Adam propped his elbows on his thighs and rubbed his face. He needed a drink, that's what he needed. Not this bullshit. But fine, he'd give her the gory details. Just put it out there and be done with it. See what she'd think of *that*.

'She was abducted,' he said flatly. 'Seven years old. Out riding her bike and then, whoosh. Gone. Four feet tall. Long blond hair, blue eyes. Last seen in pink terry-cloth shorts and a white T-shirt with sparkles. Shoes that lit up.'

Dr. Lyle said nothing. Her pencil was still.

'How old were you when this happened, Adam?' She asked it very quietly.

'I was nothing.'

'Excuse me?'

'I mean, I wasn't born yet.'

'So you never knew her?'

Adam looked up at her sideways. 'Obviously.'

Silence again. He sighed.

'I know what you want me to say.'

She gave him a questioning glance but said nothing. He could hear the clock ticking off a minute, then another. He couldn't stand just sitting there like that.

'Yes, Dr. Lyle, I feel like I knew her. Yes, even though she was gone. They never took anything down: all her school pictures, her drawings taped to the fridge, those little gold trophies everybody gets for participating. Her bedroom is still exactly as it was, a pink, fluffy shrine. Why, yes, Dr. Lyle, if you're asking, she *is* still more real to my mother than I am.'

He inhaled sharply. He hadn't meant to say so much and didn't know why it came out that way.

'What do you mean by that?'

He took another deep breath and let it out slowly.

'I guess what I mean is that there wasn't much of a mother left for me when I came along. My dad worked all the time, avoiding us all. My mom holed up in her room for years with the TV blaring. Just stayed in bed with a whole lot of wadded-up tissues around her, crying and watching soaps and stuff. She'd come out every now and then and practically crawl to Abigail's room.'

In his mind he saw the image flash of her hands, covered in blue veins even then, hanging on to Abigail's lacy curtains, shaking as she cried.

'She would, you know, fold and re-fold Abigail's clothes. Then she'd just sit there –' he stopped, wiped his face with his hands – 'smelling them.'

Dr. Lyle handed him a tissue. He blew his nose, closed his eyes, and then tried to lean back nonchalantly.

'There. Satisfied? Deep dark secret right there out on the table for you to dissect. What have you got?'

He sat up straight again, kind of interested to see how she'd respond.

'I think it's too early to—'

'Oh, come on, Dr. Lyle. You can do it. Lay it on me. I know what you're thinking.'

'You do?'

'Yeah, I can just imagine what words you've jotted down on that piece of paper. Something about my mother, right? Maybe something Oedipal?'

'No, not Oedipal. I think your mother went through a terrible tragedy and that may have impeded her ability to emotionally bond with her second child, but—'

'You're thinking attachment disorder, aren't you?'

'I didn't say that. I don't think we need to be talking about disorders. We don't need to label anything at this point. Let's just talk. See where it takes us.'

Adam didn't want to see where it would take him. He didn't want to go back to that room again. It was bad enough that he'd spilled his guts about his sister in that first session. And why had he sounded so angry? That wasn't how he felt at all.

Imagine what he might say if he kept going. All those thoughts, all those stories that would live in some official file in the police building. Confidential, sure, that's what they said, but nothing was safe when somebody up the chain had some so-called compelling reason to see it.

No therapist would make him stray from his mission anyway. He knew in his heart he'd been given life specifically for this purpose, to restore karmic balance to the world. He'd slipped this time, he'd let his emotions get carried away. But he'd get back on track. His sister might be gone – he'd given up any hope for her return – but he could save someone else's. He would right the wrongs. He would find lost girls or at least solve their murders. He would punish every man like the one who had so brazenly dared to take his sister. These men. These killers. Stealers of children and innocence. He would sacrifice his entire life to this cause, and if he could save just one girl, it would make it all worthwhile.

CHAPTER 7

Cora sat at a small metal table beside the stacks with her contraband open in front of her and in her hand a little slip of paper with the Wi-Fi code. She hunched over the laptop under the hum of the fluorescent lights, glancing around now and then to make sure no one was watching.

Her knowledge of computers was limited. She'd used the library's occasionally to look something up for the farm, but didn't have an email account and had only the faintest idea about social media. Luckily, as soon as she entered the code, the computer located the library's Internet service. Once she was connected, new emails flooded in, the computer pinging quietly with each one. She scrolled to the one farthest down in bold, dated September 23. Like so many of them, it was from this Mark person.

Where r u? Why didn't you call last night? Worrying here.

It was followed by several more, each progressively more frantic. Cora understood. These were from the day after Julie had gone missing.

She scanned the list. There were dozens of names on emails received over the course of the following days, mixed in with plenty of others announcing 50-percent-off sales with special coupon codes and the like.

The personal ones started off confused, but not desperate. No one seemed willing to accept at first that things had gone quite as horribly wrong as Cora knew they had. Then they escalated.

Julie, why aren't you answering texts? Did you lose your phone?

Hey girl, did you forget our lunch date?

Honey, please call us. Wondering where you are. Need to talk about travel dates.

If you're getting this, Julie, please know that we are looking for you with the police and FBI. We will find you, wherever you are. Hold tight, honey. We're coming to get you.

Darling Julie, NO STONE WILL BE LEFT UNTURNED. We're ALL looking for you. We love you and will never give up on you. Never. WE WILL FIND YOU.

And then, as her friends and family appeared to accept that there'd be no response, the personal emails drifted off, leaving only those from the Gap or West Elm or Zulily, promising the best buys of fall.

Cora shivered. Even though they seemed to be looking in the wrong places – Westchester, New York City – it scared her to imagine all those official forces out combing the earth, looking for the girl in her upstairs bedroom. She pictured uniformed officers with guns drawn, scaling the walls of the house, bashing in through the windows to rescue her. She'd never imagined anything like that before. Not for that other girl. But this one? They'd do anything for her.

Cora forced herself to breathe more slowly. The emails terrified her, but she couldn't stop reading them, one after the other. So many people cared so much about this girl. People loved her in ALL CAPS. No one had ever loved Cora like that.

Next she went to Facebook, where she was greeted with a startling close-up of the girl, her name in bold letters underneath. The text below the header was bright red:

This page is now administered by Friends of Julie Brookman, a non-profit formed by the Brookman family to bring her home. Julie was last seen just before midnight on September 22 at the Mamaroneck Metro North Station, southbound track, wearing a brown leather jacket, black T-shirt and jeans. Julie has reddish-blond hair, green eyes, is 5' 7" and weighs 120 pounds. She has a small scar on her left inner thigh, just above her knee, and a dark birthmark about an inch and a half long on her right shoulder. Please notify the Mamaroneck Police Department if you have any information, no matter how small or insignificant it may seem. Julie, we love you!!! And to the hundreds of people who have come together to help us and pray with us and donated their time, energy and funds to the cause, we thank you with all our hearts.

The picture was not a good likeness, her face fuller and happier, her eyes shining with warmth. She didn't look like that anymore.

Someone had posted links to news accounts and provided regular updates on the search. Cora read through a few and it calmed her down. They knew nothing. No one had spotted James or his truck. She sighed with relief at their useless efforts, but the feeling of reassurance trailed off into a creeping sense of foreboding. They might not know anything yet, but they wouldn't give up easily. There'd always be a shadow over her life now because of this girl.

She clicked the photos and the screen filled with a wall of images that made her feel lightheaded. She leaned in closer. They were incredible. She'd never realized regular people got to have a life like that.

Many of them showed the girl with her arms around an attractive young man with brown hair and light eyes. He was tanned, broad-shouldered and his teeth blared out at her, impossibly white. Mark, apparently.

There were pictures of the two of them on white sandy beaches, on a gleaming sailboat in the Caribbean, on a red lit-up carousel, at a stylish bar with sparklers glowing on a cake held between them. Pictures with hordes of entitled young people hanging on to each other possessively, all as attractive and wealthy-looking as her, mocking Cora with their collective gaze.

There she was in a cap and gown, her parents beaming at her on either side. There was one of her on stage under a spotlight in a gauzy pink tutu, en pointe, with one leg lifted up straight as an arrow behind her. In the next she appeared thoughtful, gazing out at the ocean from her perch on a jagged rock, her face delicately framed by the final golden streaks of the day's sunlight.

Cora touched the screen, tracing Julie's image with her fingertip. This privileged and precious creature. This person who mattered and counted.

One image struck her particularly hard. It was Julie alone, standing on a cliff that loomed out over a lush tropical rainforest. It must have been taken within the last year; the caption told her it was in Costa Rica. Julie wore khaki hiking shorts, a pale blue T-shirt, and a backpack. A black bandana held back her hair and her arms were lifted up over her head in a giant V for victory. Of course that's how she felt. Victorious.

Cora wouldn't know about that, now would she?

She had an overwhelming impulse to print this one and take it home with her as a small token of her power over this girl. A symbol of how the universe restored its balance.

It wasn't a good idea. It was far too risky. If someone saw it, how could she explain printing out this picture of a girl whose face must surely be plastered over newspapers, Internet boards, missing posters, and milk cartons?

She couldn't. There was no explaining any of it.

But still.

The printer was less than ten feet away in its purpose-built nook. She could see the output tray from where she sat. It wouldn't be all that dangerous.

It took her a while to figure out how to print, but she managed it. Her plan was simple: hit return and then discreetly gather her spoils. Two seconds and it would be done. Nevertheless, she sat there, unmoving, her finger hovering over the enter key, thinking how James would kill her if he found out.

But no, it wasn't a big deal. She shouldn't be such a coward.

She took a deep breath, let her finger drop, and watched the printer for signs of life.

Nothing happened.

She waited a few seconds more and then pressed the enter key again. She silently counted to ten. Still nothing.

Annoyed, she held the key down with her thumb, listening for its inner mechanism to engage. The computer told her the job had been sent, but the printer sat there taunting her with its implacable silence.

Why was it taking so long?

She had no choice. She'd have to ask.

Cora closed the computer and gathered up the cord, clutching them to her chest, and went to stand in line behind two others at the circulation desk. It felt like hours waiting for those imbeciles to ask their inane questions about some John Grisham novel and the Saturday reading program for tweens, while she kept her eyes on that god-forsaken printer that remained as unresponsive as ever.

Finally, it was her turn.

'Excuse me, but I sent something to the printer and it doesn't seem to be working.'

The pasty-faced girl with glasses gave her a vacant stare – where did they find these people? – until slowly the situation seemed to dawn on her.

'That printer?' she asked, pointing to the beast in the nook.

'Yes, that one.'

'Ohhhh.' The word came out long and slow. 'Yeah, did you see the sign?'

'The sign?'

'There's a sign on top of it. Maybe it fell off. That printer's out of order and all print jobs are being rerouted to the one upstairs. In the Social Sciences section.'

Cora felt all the blood drain from her face. The girl stared at her, looking confused.

'There's an elevator.' She pointed to the right.

'Thank you,' Cora whispered.

She somehow managed not to run.

How many times had she sent that document to the printer? That face, repeated over and over, would be implanted in some stranger's mind as they paged through the print jobs in frustration.

Cora reached the elevator and hit the button hard. It took forever but finally lurched forward and rattled its way up to the second floor. She hit the door with her palm and finally, after several agonizing seconds, the elevator bell dinged and the door slid aside.

She raced through the stacks into the reading area. There stood an even row of oak tables, each with four matching wooden chairs and two bankers' lamps. Half a dozen people were scattered about the room, books open, papers askew, seemingly engrossed in their own business, but how could she be sure of that?

She spotted the printer in a small alcove tucked in the corner and held her breath as she approached it. It was twice as big as the one downstairs. It could have churned out a hundred copies of the girl's wretched face by now.

But there was nothing in the output tray.

She went numb. Did someone take it?

She glanced around the room again. One of these people must know. One of them must be watching and waiting to see who came to that machine to retrieve the pictures of the missing girl from Mamaroneck.

There was a small table with a wire basket on the far side of the printer that she hadn't noticed at first. A piece of paper was taped to the wall: '10 cents per copy. Pay at circulation desk.' The sign next to it, the one that hung over the basket, read: 'Place found print jobs here.'

She swallowed and took a step toward it, the fear lodged in her throat like a stone. Her mind almost would not accept what she saw, for there, on top of the stack of papers, directly under the sign's arrow, was Julie's beaming face.

Someone had seen it.

Cora glanced around furtively. Maybe they were watching her, but if so, they were being sly about it. She flipped through the documents. Julie's face appeared and reappeared in between spreadsheets, a lost-dog poster with pre-drawn tabs for tearing, and a specials menu with a crab-cake appetizer at the top. She sorted through the pile, checking and double-checking it for stray copies, slipping them into a new stack. She counted sixteen.

Confident she had them all, she picked them up and quickly shoved them into her bag.

She wanted to walk away as if nothing had happened, but she was having trouble breathing and her face felt hot. She needed air. She had to get out of there, had to go straight to the exit. The library would survive without its ten cents per copy.

As she headed for the elevator, it seemed as though a woman with short graying brown hair and smudged lipstick was walking purposely toward her. Surely not. She looked vaguely familiar. Perhaps she was mistaking her for someone else. God willing.

No, she *was* coming toward her, waving some papers at Cora to get her attention.

Cora froze. Even from a few feet away she could see they were copies of Julie's picture.

'Here you go,' the woman said quietly, her arm extended toward Cora, offering them up. 'These got mixed in with my documents.'

Cora took them without thinking, instantly wishing she'd denied they were hers. The woman looked right at them, studying the girl's face. It would be weird to yank them away at that point. She was stuck there.

'Pretty girl.' She smiled at Cora, clearly waiting to be told all about her.

Cora nodded, trying to force a smile.

She couldn't turn this into a big production, couldn't look flustered. Better to come out with something ordinary.

'My niece,' she stammered. 'She lives in California.'

'Ah.' This seemed to satisfy the woman. 'Well, you must be so proud. You know how sometimes you can just tell from a picture that someone is a lovely person? She seems like that.'

Cora's stomach turned. She hoped she was nodding her head as she watched the woman pat her on the shoulder and walk away. As if nothing momentous had happened.

All Cora could do was hope for the best. Hope that she'd managed to make her lie sound plausible and forgettable. Hope that she'd never see that woman again.

She deserved this fright. She deserved to be punished. She should never have disobeyed James. He knew best and this experience only proved what she already understood at a deeper level. She resolved then and there to set herself back on the Path of Righteousness. She would follow his guidance and his rules to the letter. From now on, she would listen to James.

As soon as she got home, Cora went behind the barn and smashed the computer to bits.

CHAPTER 8

Cora worked herself to the bone on that farm, but it was what she wanted. Her goal was to throw every fiber of her being into it, to end each day so exhausted that sleep would take over before her thoughts did. The trouble was that her daily life consisted of a series of mindless repetitions: weeding the garden, slicing up onions, folding the laundry, feeding the animals, taking food to the girl. Efforts that could only occupy her body. Her mind still strayed.

She wanted more than anything to take her own advice, to remember that the past was dead. She said it to herself over and over, but it wouldn't stick. Especially now that she felt so mixed up. That stupid girl and those stupid pictures of her fairy-tale life had unleashed a tidal wave of memories. She couldn't help but compare and contrast.

James had warned her not to indulge in this weakness.

'Your memories are unclean,' he'd said. 'Remembering is a fall from grace.'

She truly wanted to obey him, but these thoughts were too powerful now. They kept flaring up like a sickness, dwarfing every other reality, making it hard to get her work done, hard to follow the rules.

No matter how she tried she couldn't forget that poor mousy girl she'd been, sitting shotgun in a half-rusted-out, beat-up pickup truck bouncing along the dusty roads, crisscrossing the whole United States of America who knows how many times over.

She and her father would drive through deserts, wheat fields, miles and miles of strip malls, every lowdown, dirty piece of America. Later, she figured out why they were on the run, but as a child, all she thought about was the way the sun would glint in the rearview mirror as she cupped her hand to catch the breeze outside the window, singing softly to herself so he wouldn't hear. She tried not to draw his attention. She was just a little twig of a nothing running after him at pit stops, keeping her eyes on the ground, making herself small.

Her most prized possession back then was the *Rand McNally Deluxe Atlas of the United States*, its oversized pages withered and hardened, the evidence of a dried spill that had earned her a slap across the face at the time. Grid page after grid page, the long thin lines traced out the routes to some truck stop, some dead-end road where they would park for the night, or some gritty construction site where her father could work for a day or two.

That atlas gave her life its structure with graphic specificity: E4 on page 97, H5 on page 134, R5 on 176. She would circle their destinations with a red marker she'd found buried deep in the crack of the seat, the lines scratchy from the dried-out ink, the barrel of the pen covered with a sticky substance she could never entirely wash off.

At night, Cora would look out of the grimy camper window at the glittering stars, the leaves dipping down from the trees, the flashing neon lights of a strip club, whatever was out there, and she'd feel her heart clench.

Even then, she understood that to survive she couldn't let herself be vulnerable. She had to push all those feelings away. But at some level, some horrible deep level, she knew what she was losing.

Her father never knew where they'd go next. He was driven by some inner demon that wouldn't let him rest and every day depended on how much he could keep that demon under control, and for how long.

For Cora that meant new schools at least three times a year. Sometimes they didn't stay in one place long enough to enroll, and he'd drop her off at the public library instead while he went looking for work. She'd spend those days in between the stacks evading the librarians, who were quick to call the authorities on a truant child. She learned to stay quiet for hours, lying on the cold floor silently turning the pages of the *Children's World Atlas* or *Jane Eyre* or *Knights of the Round Table*, keeping watch out of the corner of her eye. That's where she got her real education.

School was a different matter. All the adults – even the nicest teachers, the bedraggled school counselors, the plastic-capped lunch ladies behind the steamed glass – ignored her for the most part. It might have been better had the kids done the same. They were cruel sometimes – so cruel – but she couldn't exactly blame them. She was dirty and uncommunicative, a feral child who'd landed among them from out of nowhere. She didn't try to make friends.

In truth, she kept quiet because it was safer to say nothing than to say the wrong thing. After that first time in a police station, she'd learned her lesson. Her father would kill her if it happened again.

They'd kept them apart for hours that day, questioning her in that dull gray interview room with the single bright light. Those officers loomed over her, just mildly threatening, as if they knew they couldn't push a child too far.

She wouldn't have blamed her father if he had left her behind that time. It *was* her fault, she'd thought then, crying quietly with her cheek pressed against the cold metal table, refusing to speak.

Eventually they sent in someone without a uniform, one Ms. Martinez, a nice enough lady in a proper suit with smooth soft brown hair swirled into a low bun at the back. Her lipstick was a shocking shade of coral that edged out just past the line of her lip – the only flaw in her otherwise solid perfection. Cora focused on that tiny bit of wayward color, fascinated by it. It was that crack in the woman's armor that led her to believe she could wriggle her way out of this situation after all.

Ms. Martinez sat down beside her with her clipboard in hand, smiling her best warm smile. She obviously didn't realize that Cora wouldn't be taken in by something as unreliable as kindness. She knew full well that the niceties never lasted long.

She had to give credit to this one though, she tried.

She reached out her hand to Cora, who steadily ignored it, letting the woman's long slender fingers with their bright pink polish hang in the air between them. Luckily she gave up quickly.

'First,' Ms. Martinez began somewhat timidly, 'let me apologize for the others. I don't think they're used to being around children.'

She scooted her chair closer to Cora's. For a second, Cora thought she might actually touch her, but she had the good sense to have second thoughts and instead she turned her attention to her files.

Cora, on the other hand, stared at the wall, her elbows propped up on the table, her face leaning against her balled-up fists. Her own nails were dirty and bitten to the quick.

'You said something in there that we need to talk about. I know they were a little harsh, but we just need to know the truth. We want to help you.'

Cora didn't move, didn't even look at her.

'They're lying,' she finally said. 'I never said anything. Don't you dare say that I said anything.'

That last part came out with more force than she'd intended. She needed to save her fire.

'I know you must be frightened about what will happen if you talk about it, but—'

'There is no "it". There's nothing. They're lying. People lie, you know.' Cora folded her arms, leaned back in her chair, and studied the frayed edge of her sweater as if it were the most intriguing thing in the world.

The beleaguered social worker nodded, checked the file once more, and cleared her throat, preparing to go in again.

Cora continued to gaze blankly at the table, blinking slowly. She was counting it out, waiting for the woman to break the silence.

'Okay.' Ms. Martinez glanced back down at some scribbled notes in her file. 'How long have you been on the road with . . . your father?'

Still Cora stared, her face empty. Her heart pounded in her ears but she was determined to hide her fear at any cost.

The woman tried another angle.

'Okay, then, let's start with school. You are currently attending . . .?'

No harm in that one, but Cora couldn't remember the name of the place. Thornhill, Thornton, Thornville?

She took a guess. 'Thornton.'

The woman nodded and made a little check on one of her precious documents.

'And before that?'

Cora saw where this was going and sensed this line of inquiry would end up getting her in some big-time trouble. She had to put a stop to it right now. By whatever means necessary.

She burst out of her chair, sending it crashing to the floor, and ran to the most shadowy corner of the room. She slid her back down the wall. Since actual tears wouldn't come, she shook her shoulders deliberately and faked it as best she could, clandestinely pinching her cheeks to draw out a convincing crimson flush.

'I just want my father,' she said, peeking one eye out from under her arm to see how this was going down. 'I want my daddy. Why are you keeping me from him?' She was no fool. They'd never make her tell them.

'But you said—' the woman began.

'No, I never said anything.' Cora kept her small body tucked in that crevice, sniffling. 'I want to go now. Can I go?'

Then the woman surprised Cora. She left her papers behind and got down on her hands and knees to be at Cora's eye level. She disregarded her fine wool skirt and her delicate stockings and crawled slowly across the filthy floor over to Cora, approaching her as if she were a starved cat abandoned in a dark alley.

This was a new one.

When she reached the corner, she twisted around to sit next to Cora, leaning against the same wall. She tipped her head back and closed her eyes for a moment, as if she were considering what in the world to do next. It frightened Cora to think she might not know. Adults were supposed to know.

Finally, she opened her eyes. Their faces were inches apart. Ms. Martinez was studying Cora with – was it curiosity? Contempt? Cora couldn't tell.

'I have a lot of cases, you know,' she said, her frustration showing through, but only a little.

Cora nodded, sniffling again.

'A lot,' she repeated as if Cora might not understand such a sophisticated term. Cora blinked.

They sat in silence for a full minute.

'You know, I could force the issue here. Order up more records, tests, get other divisions involved. I could really make a push for you, but if you aren't going to cooperate – if you're just going to tell endless lies and then run away at the first chance when I put you somewhere safe – I wish you'd just . . .' She seemed at a loss for words for a moment. 'I wish you'd just tell me that now and save us both a lot of heartache. Because honestly, I've been through this plenty of times. I can't help you if you don't want help.'

Cora sat there stunned. She licked her chapped lips, thinking.

'And then I can go?' she said finally.

Ms. Martinez sighed.

'Yes, I suppose so. If that's how it is.'

Cora wasn't sure what to say. She figured social workers were like this. Overworked, pushed to the brink. She'd drawn a lucky card here.

Or had she?

Something in Cora knew this was her do-or-die moment. For a fleeting second she thought, what if everything *was* different? What if her life changed entirely, just like that?

Cora couldn't quite formulate the words her brain was trying to force her to say. She simply couldn't speak. No one had put it to her so starkly before.

Eventually, the woman took her silence as an answer.

'Fine, then. Go.'

Ms. Martinez shook her head in defeat, her eyes sad and withdrawn. She slowly got to her feet and left the room, her heels clicking in the void she left behind.

Cora stayed there a few minutes. She wasn't sure, she just didn't know. Should she follow her back down the hall, crying out for her to wait, to save her, to take her someplace else?

She was paralyzed with indecision. It was too much. Too confusing.

After a moment, an officer came in and told her he would walk her out. She got up and followed him, pulling at the string hanging off her sweater, unraveling it nervously as they went down the hall under the fluorescent lights. Apparently she'd let the choice be made for her.

Reunited with her father again in the hallway, Cora felt a rush of complicated emotions. He stood there, flanked by uniformed officers, but he wasn't cuffed. Happiness and relief flooded over her. They were free. They could go.

Then came the fear rising rapidly up inside her. She'd seen her father's clenched fist and the way his eyes had gone black and impenetrable. Couldn't anyone else see it? Nausea rose up in her throat at the thought of what was coming.

Cora knew then, as she knew now, that she could never get anything right.

CHAPTER 9

Adam sat at the tiny veneer-covered desk in his motel room, listening to the cars whizzing by on the highway just outside the dirt-caked window. The slight rain on the asphalt swished under their tires tonight, making them louder than ever. Their lights swept across the back wall over the bed every few seconds, just before the sound hit his ears. It didn't bother Adam. The regular noise helped keep his thoughts in rhythm.

His cell phone rang, buzzing and half spinning on its back on the corner of the bureau. He got up, glanced at the number, and sat back down. His mother. Again. He couldn't talk to her about this tonight. He didn't have the energy.

He sighed as he picked it up.

'Mom.'

'Adam, where are you?'

'In Stillwater, but I'm leaving tomorrow.'

'Are you coming home?' She couldn't leave well enough alone.

'I've told you a thousand times. There's no reason for me to go back to St. Paul. That's a wasted plane ticket that I can't afford.'

'Adam, you're burning through your savings on this . . . this obsession. It isn't healthy. And for what? You aren't a police officer anymore. You don't have the right to go around pretending to be one. You could end up in jail.'

He didn't answer. Her worry spread across the airwaves and seeped into his chest. He took a deep breath.

'Do you hear what I'm saying?' she asked with a hint of irritation.

He sighed.

'I've told you, I'm not coming back until it's over.' This would get her going, but it had to be said.

'Over? It's already over. It's been over for years. You will never be able to solve this, not on your own. Adam, I know why you're doing it. And it isn't worth it. That's over too. She isn't coming back.'

'Mom, I can't talk about this right now. I'm so close. Closer than I've ever been.'

'You've been saying that for years. Exactly those words.'

'I have to go.'

'Call me tomorrow. Okay? Adam? Adam?'

He pressed end without saying good-bye. She couldn't understand, but she would once he achieved his goal. Then she'd see.

He walked back over to the other side of the desk and squatted down. There, lined up against the wall on the faded brown carpet were four cardboard boxes of tabbed files, each labeled with a different name: 'Elsa Sanders', 'Phoebe Ranson', 'Isabel Davis'. . . Fourteen names in all, but only one thread.

He was working his way through them again, still hoping to find something new. His mother's words echoed in his head, but he had to brush them aside. He pulled out one file and put it on the corner of the desk, sat back down, and continued with his work. He ran his pencil under the line of text in front of him to stay focused. The words were so familiar they wouldn't sink in anymore. He knew them by heart, but he kept hoping to trip some new wire in his brain.

Three years. Three years he'd been on this hunt. And he *was* closing in. He could feel it.

His mother was right about some things though. He couldn't afford to make another mistake. If the department found out he'd stolen the official files and the physical evidence, he'd never be able to go back. Luckily, the case was cold and the department woefully understaffed. And to be safe, he'd been sure to make friends with the file clerk. He'd spent six months buying that guy drinks at the Mighty Pint's happy hour. After all that Guinness, he wouldn't turn him in as long as the situation didn't blow up too much.

Adam slid his hand under the papers in the file and took out the photographs, paper-clipped together. He pulled them apart and flipped through them again, staring at each of the three in turn. The crime-scene photos. Three bodies, lying together in a pool of mixed blood, limbs sprawled in different directions.

He was numb to it now. It might as well have been on television.

He carefully replaced the paper clip and put the photos back in the file, closed it, and set it on the edge of the desk. He picked up the next one he'd laid out and gingerly placed it on the desk in front of him: 'Laura Martin-1'. It was thick. His hands always shook a little when he handled this file in particular. This one brought him closest to the truth. This one had provided his first real lead two years ago. It was his Bible, his Rosetta Stone. He lifted it out of the file. The faded pages crackled as he turned them. The *Rand McNally Deluxe Atlas of the United States*.

CHAPTER 10

James was back.

Cora could hardly believe it had happened at last. Thank goodness everything was in order. The house was clean, his usual meal ready just as though she'd known he was coming. Animals fed. Girl calm.

Cora never left much to chance, though. When he was gone, she had a settled routine to prepare things for him the way he liked. Just in case. Because he expected everything to be ready when he was.

Just as she had every evening he'd been away, that night she'd set out the best china on the Chantilly lace placemats she'd found in the dining room. She'd taken out the silver from the velvet-lined chest on the sideboard and given it a touch-up polish. On warm nights like this one, she laid everything out on the table in the gazebo out back. The previous owner had left it strung with festive lights that gave the scene a magical air. It always put James in a better mood.

Despite her relief at being sufficiently prepared, the instant she heard his truck roaring up the drive she'd felt the panic rise in her throat. She would have denied that had anyone asked. She would have smiled right past the question. These were her secret trials and she must bear them. Faith did not always follow the easy path.

She knew she'd been bad while he was away. She'd sinned against him. How had she ever thought she could keep secrets from James? He'd see the guilt on her face right away, would surely read her mind where she harbored those unclean thoughts.

Meanwhile, the heart medallion was in her left pocket, a lucky charm she'd been carrying against her better judgment. The rest of the girl's things were still in her closet. All the evidence of her transgressions he'd ever need.

Her glance swept the room. It was too late to hide anything now.

At the sound of his engine revving for the final hill, she ran to the window. Even through the dirty glass of his windshield, his face told her everything. His dark brows were pressed together, his full lips twisted into an angry scowl. He got out of the truck and slammed the door hard behind him.

Her eyes traveled immediately to his hands. Even in the dim light of dusk she could see it. The right one, sure enough, clutched that old bowie knife. She knew what that meant. He'd had trouble on his trip and she'd be the one to pay for it.

As expected, he came straight toward her when he walked into the house, banging the door behind him so that the window rattled in its sash. He grabbed her left arm and pulled her whole body to him, putting the knife's edge up to the flesh of her neck, and running it gently along the skin. Her heart thudded but she knew better than to move.

'Who's here?' He yanked her even closer to him as he said it and the blade sank into the flesh of her neck, just shy of penetrating it. She dared not resist him.

Searching his glassy eyes, she tried to determine if he was in the grip of the Dark Spirits. They sometimes drove him to temptation, leading him to take things, to drink or to ingest those diabolical pills.

'Answer me, damn it. Is there anyone else in this fucking house?'

He gripped her arm harder. She felt it burn. There'd be a mark there tomorrow.

Cora trembled, wanting to answer exactly right. The wrong words could increase the Dark Spirits' hold.

'Just me.' She swallowed. 'And the girl upstairs.'

For a moment, he seemed to be unable to remember just who 'the girl' was. Cora knew this was not a good sign. He was in the grip of an evil force and she must be patient.

He pulled away, his mouth going slack, a vague flash of confusion across his face. He mumbled something under his breath and stumbled backward, reeling slightly. He blinked, perhaps trying to focus, but he didn't look directly at her. Instead, he pulled at his jeans that were held up by a worn leather belt that Cora had experienced intimately against her skin. She flinched from the memory.

'I'm not asking about the girl. I mean the dark ones, the interlopers. The demon forces that seek to destroy me.'

'No. No one else.' She stepped back cautiously, taking advantage of the fact that his eyes had begun to swirl around the room. She hoped he might not notice her tentative retreat as she backed toward the door that led to the dining room, thinking about the knives in the top drawer of the sideboard. She would never hurt him, but might need to slow him down if it came to that, if this situation got entirely out of control.

Her calculations were for nothing. He slid toward her and pulled her close, twisting the knife slowly before her eyes. She couldn't help but close them.

'Is somebody hiding out up there? They've been tracking my spirit across the land. They thought I wouldn't know but I can feel them.' His eyes scanned the ceiling. He was still, his head cocked to the side as though that would improve his hearing.

'No, no.' She shook her head a fraction of an inch. She opened her eyes despite her fear, and kept them fixed on him, her face as far from the knife as she dared.

'Are you in league with them? Don't think I won't kill you too. Don't think I'd spare you.' He wasn't looking at her. This wasn't for her benefit.

Cora shook her head. The word wouldn't come out.

Putting both hands on her shoulders, he pushed her down into a chair. The heart medallion made a tiny thud against the seat through the fabric. She tensed up, waiting for him to notice.

'Swear it,' he said, holding the knife up to her face again. He stepped back, looking around the room. 'Wait, wait.'

He grabbed the Book from on top of the refrigerator and placed it on the center of the table. It was jammed full of loose papers covered in his messy scrawl. The edges were yellowed, some stained and torn. It was a life's work, the Book.

'Swear it,' he said through his teeth and then turned in a circle as if expecting to find his enemies surrounding him.

Cora placed her hand on the Book and swore. Her voice was a whisper at first but he pounded on the table again and again until she was finally screaming it right along with him.

'I swear there is no one else in this house. I swear it.'

'You would never lie to me, would you, Cora? If you lie to me, the penalty is eternal damnation. It is written.' His fist hit the table.

'No, no.'

'Say it,' he commanded.

'I would never lie to you.'

She lifted her hand to stroke his cheek to soothe him, her heart plagued with guilt. She *was* lying to him about the girl's things. She should just tell him everything.

He grabbed her hand and slammed it back on the table.

'Say it again.' It was not the right moment to confess.

In a shaking voice she pleaded, 'James, James, please. I love you. Our souls are as one, just as it has been revealed. I will protect you until death.'

He studied her, his eyes bulging out of his face, then finally let loose her hand. Her head sank down onto the table as she watched him walk slowly around the kitchen, listening.

'Maybe you weren't guarding the house the way you should. Anyone could have slipped in here. Maybe that's what you wanted. Is that what you secretly wanted?'

Cora said nothing. She knew better. He would make his way slowly through every room of the house until he was satisfied. She trembled, suddenly afraid that she hadn't been paying attention, that there *were* intruders hiding out up there waiting to jump him.

She watched him turn the corner and heard his slow, stealthy steps up the stairs. Now she was the one with her eyes to the ceiling, listening to his footsteps on the floorboards above her head creaking as he crossed their bedroom.

Panic washed over her. Had she shoved the black garbage bag far enough into the closet? She should have told him while she had the chance, before he found it on his own.

Then there was a crash from above. The house shook.

'What is *this*?' he yelled.

She jumped up in terror, rushing toward the stairs. He'd found the bag. Now she'd pay for her betrayal.

She found him sitting on the floor next to the bed, a small braided area rug twisted around his ankle. He'd only tripped.

She was saved.

'Who put this here?' he said, holding the tattered cloth up between his fingers, a look of disgust on his face. He'd fallen in an awkward position and for a moment looked weak. She wanted to rush to his aid, but held back, waiting for his signal.

'I did,' she said, trembling, but knowing the answer was obvious. He just wanted to hear her confession, as usual. 'That was wrong of me.'

'Have you let a conflicting spirit possess you? One who plots to overthrow my kingdom?'

He wadded the rug into a ball and threw it at her as hard as he could. It unraveled in the air, landing on the floor between them, which only infuriated him more.

His face went red and his hands folded slowly and deliberately into tight fists. He stood up with some effort, regained his balance, then shoved her back against the wall with a brute force that surprised her, even after all these years.

'You must be punished for your waywardness.'

He snatched up the rug with one hand, whipped it into a thin, hard roll, and then slammed it across her chest, over and over. Each fresh hit stung and then throbbed. Cora took it as best she could, whimpering but not loudly enough to provoke him further.

Finally, he stopped. Sweat poured down his beet-red face. He panted quietly, staring into her eyes.

She didn't move, trying not to blink. The pain meant nothing to her anymore, but her body tingled with fear and her muscles twitched slightly as she held them rigid, determined not to move. She watched him, waiting, hoping to keep her face clear of any expression that might set him off again. The Dark Spirits were powerful that day. Their wrath must not be triggered further.

'Now you will know not to stray from the Path,' he said. His voice had lost its energy though and she felt relief spread out over her.

'As it is written,' she said, bowing her head.

He threw the rug down at her feet. She put it back in its proper place by the bureau, and then followed him meekly out of the room. It could have been so much worse.

They could have dinner now.

CHAPTER 11

Cora had been a daydreamer since she was a child. Because of that, they'd thought she was stupid and had always put her in the remedial classes. After a while, she'd gone along with it. What difference did it make? She couldn't get a diploma anyway because her name changed with each move and her records mysteriously never transferred from one school to the next.

Now it was worse, though, because her mind was not clean. She couldn't concentrate. It was that girl – that girl stirred everything up. For years, she'd managed to keep her sinful memories at bay, but in these last few days she couldn't purge the thought of the months they'd spent in Minnesota. The year she turned fourteen. The worst of her life.

It was the first time she'd had something like friends her own age. She'd realized only too late how they'd taken advantage of her. She hadn't known anything about real life back then. Johnny Mavis, Reed Lassiter, Joy Marcione. They'd manipulated her. Tricked her.

The first day of school she stood in front of the crowded classroom.

'I'd like you all to welcome Laura Martin,' Ms. Thompson said. Cora winced slightly upon hearing the name her father had picked that time. It took her a few weeks to get used to each new one.

Most of the students didn't look up from their notebooks, so Cora felt enormous relief when a girl in the far back corner with long curly dark hair, dyed with streaks of pink, blue and green, fluttered her fingerless-gloved hand at her and winked. There was an empty desk and she leaned her head toward it. Cora's heart flooded with gratitude as she made her way over.

'Where'd you come from, Laura?' The girl scooted her desk closer to Cora's.

'Around,' Cora said. She knew better than to give too many details. 'We move a lot.'

The boy next to her, with coppery hair, a tiny silver nose ring, and a tattered leather jacket, put out his hand.

'Reed.' She took it. Shook his hand. Sealed her fate.

Three weeks later the four of them, Joy, Reed, Cora and their friend Johnny, who had left school the previous year, sat on a beat-up couch in the basement of a run-down building on the edge of town. This dingy apartment belonged to Joy's father. He'd tried to rent it out but it had stayed vacant now for years. The rats had taken it over, and so had the kids.

Smoke filled the air and an old Sonic Youth album blasted on the stereo as Johnny lit the joint Cora held. She took a long, slow hit, just the way they'd shown her, and then passed it along to Joy.

She'd never felt better, never felt that she'd *belonged* anywhere like this. She hoped it would last. That her father would let them stay put here, if only for a little while. A few months. Maybe even a full semester of school.

She glanced over at Reed, who was staring at her, a tiny half-smile on his face. He made her nervous.

'What?' She tucked her knees up under her chin, eyeing him watchfully.

'Nothing. Just thinking.' He leaned over, grabbed her toe and pinched it harder than was strictly necessary. She swallowed her cry, pulled it back, and tucked her foot under her uncertainly.

'About what?'

'The Shakers.'

'Here we go again,' Joy said, rolling her eyes.

'I mean,' Reed leaned in, whispering ominously, 'Laura, what do you really know about the Shakers?'

She laughed, unsure of herself. 'I'm going to have to go with "nothing".'

He was always coming up with these wild ideas.

'Surely you know *something*. Come on.' He looked serious now.

'Um, they make furniture?' She paused. 'They don't use electricity?'

'Yes to the first, no to the second. Failing grade, Laura. But what about the important stuff? I'm talking Mother. Ann. Lee. One bad-ass bitch.'

'Never heard of her,' Cora said, smiling up at him.

'This was like, I don't know, two, three hundred years ago. This girl had one major fear. No, not the devil. Don't say the devil. I know that's what you were thinking. I can read your mind.' He leaned over and put the fingertips of both hands on either side of her head, pushed in hard, and then let go.

'No, *sex,* Laura, sex. She was, like, totally phobic. Then lo and behold, her dad was like, yo, you're going to marry this dude. Probably some creepy old bastard friend of his. Then she had four kids. Boom, boom, boom, boom.' He punched the air each time. 'One right after the other.'

'Yeah?' Cora hung on his every word. He was like a snake charmer.

'Well, they all died. Every one of them died as babies. So what did that crazy bitch think? Did she think, hey, antibiotics haven't been invented yet, so child mortality is, like, really high? No. No, Laura, she did not think that.'

'Can't imagine what then,' Cora said, trying to mimic his playful tone.

'You are so fucking sick, Reed,' Joy said without looking up from the *Us Weekly* she was flipping through.

'No,' he went on, 'she thought it was *punishment* for *having sex*. Kind of fucked-up logic, now isn't it?'

'Nuts,' agreed Cora obediently.

'Anyway, that just makes the bitch crazier. She gets all wild with that religious shit and claims to be the Second Coming of Jesus Fucking Christ.'

He paused for effect.

'How do you like that for *cojones*? Downside, they threw her ass into an insane asylum. That worked out for her in the end though, because in there she had these, like, intense fucking visions. Like, better than acid. And guess what they told her?'

'No idea. What did they say?'

'That the only way to be rid of sin is to *avoid sex*. Like completely. Those Shakers, man.' He paused, watching Johnny pass the joint to Joy.

Then he leaned toward her conspiratorially, whispering, 'You know why they're called Shakers?'

Cora shook her head, wondering if he was putting the whole thing on, waiting for the punchline.

'Because they would shake when they were praying, like dancing but shaking, you know, *shaking the sin out of them*.' He bounced up and down, his arms and hands flailing, his head bobbing from side to side.

'Well, that's a lot more interesting than I might have guessed,' Cora said hesitantly, not sure what he was getting at or why he was telling them all this.

'Yeah, wild, man. Not many Shakers left, obviously.' He grinned. 'There's something to it, though. Something to her vision, don't you think? That all sex is sin?'

'Jesus, Reed.' Joy shook her head. 'Freak.'

Reed ignored Joy and moved over closer to Cora. He got down on one knee on the matted shag rug and took her hand in his, stroking it slowly and deftly down the middle with one finger. Her skin tingled.

'We need to do something, Laura,' Reed continued quietly. His smile was gone and now he stared intently into her eyes, further casting his spell. 'Something fun. I'm so fucking bored. Are *you* bored, Laura?'

Cora shook her head. She didn't like the strange look on his face, didn't understand where he was going with this.

'Nope. I'm happy at the moment. Let's just chill out. Smoke some more.' Leaning her head back, she somehow managed to drag her eyes away from his. She closed them, trying to look relaxed and unconcerned. She wanted to play it cool.

Reed dropped her hand and sat down on the floor, legs crossed, perhaps giving up on her but she avoided the temptation to open her eyes to check.

'What about the caves?' Joy said, handing Reed the joint.

Johnny stood up, turned down the volume on the stereo.

'The cops have blocked off the good ones. After those two kids died down there last spring,' he said with a shrug.

'Oh, yeah, we could never get in there,' Reed said facetiously. 'What with all that big bad police tape across the entrances.'

Cora glanced at her watch. Nine ten.

She stood up in a panic.

'Listen, sounds fun and all, but actually I gotta go.'

'Why? You claustrophobic?' Joy said, then blew out a long stream of smoke. 'Afraid of a little carbon-monoxide poisoning? Or afraid Reed will make us all do a charismatic dance of sexual shame?' She laughed, one hand twisting her hair around her fingers, glancing up at Reed.

'Relax, Laura, it'll be fun.' She leaned over and squeezed Cora's arm. 'You'll see. A sort of welcome party for you.'

'I'm not worried about the caves. I'm afraid of my father. I told him I'd be back by nine.'

'Oh, shit,' Joy said, bolting upright. 'You'd better get your ass outta here then. From what I hear around town, I do not want that motherfucker coming here to find you.' She said it jokingly, but Cora could tell she was sincere.

Reed stood up.

'Okay, tomorrow then,' he said decisively, still staring at Cora, his arms crossed and one eyebrow raised.

'Tomorrow what?' asked Cora as she slung on her jacket and leaned down for her book bag. Her hand was already on the door. She hated to leave. Hated to stop staring into his blue eyes.

'The caves. Tomorrow after school. We'll go to the caves. See what happens down in the dark.' He grabbed her around the waist and pulled her to him lasciviously, but whipped his head back just before his lips reached hers. He laughed.

'Just fucking with you.'

She knew that. He was so strange. No matter how weird he was, she secretly wished he was interested in her that way, but he didn't seem to have those kinds of feelings for anyone. It only made her want him more, this delicious temptation that was out of her reach.

No one offered Cora a ride home. She was disappointed and yet relieved, almost happy to hitch her way back to the RV camp just outside of town. She had, after all, worked particularly hard to keep it a secret from this new crowd. It would be difficult for her to get back home in winter when people didn't like to stop, but still she was grateful her father had finally put together enough money for a trailer with its very own propane heater. Before that they'd had to move south for the winter. Now they might be able to stay here. Here, where she had friends. Where she wasn't such a freak anymore. Here, where there was Reed Lassiter.

CHAPTER 12

Adam's alarm was blasting out radio static, but he couldn't open his eyes. What had hit him? His head pounded and his face felt hot and sticky. He smashed the snooze button with his left hand and flung his right over to the other side of the bed where it landed on warm flesh.

Now he remembered exactly what had hit him. He bolted upright in bed. There was Deirdre, the assistant librarian, sprawled out over two thirds of the mattress, unaffected by the sound spewing out of the clock. Her white skin glowed in the half-light of the room, pure and smooth against the orange-and-gold plaid comforter.

He covered her, stood up, and slid on his pants.

They'd gotten carried away last night and he'd brought her back to his place for the first time. That's what happened when he drank and he knew better. He'd always been able to leave her apartment when he was ready, but he couldn't just throw her out of here. Not after two months of seeing each other almost every day.

She was beautiful there though, wasn't she? He sighed. In another life, things might have been different. He might have let this fling get serious.

He went into the bathroom and ran the water at a trickle. If she woke up, she'd expect things from him. He knew her well enough by now. She'd want to spend the day together – it was Sunday after all. She'd want to read the paper in bed, have brunch, and discuss geo-politics or the latest in light literary fiction.

That's why he avoided this type of thing. No one else ever understood the urgency of his task. Everyone else moved forward with their mundane lives at a tedious pace, watching television, taking classes, carpooling, filling out paperwork, searching for décor ideas. All as if there weren't people in danger, people who needed saving. Every second he wasted on his own dreary personal life was a second someone could be suffering.

People were out there, waiting for him.

She shifted in her sleep. Adam stood still for a moment, holding his breath.

'Adam,' she mumbled. His heart sank. Now he'd be stuck. She sat up groggily, with a suggestive smirk on her face. 'Well, hello there.'

'Oh, hi. Good morning.'

'You sleep okay? You were having some kind of nightmare last night. Remember it?'

Oh, he remembered. They started the same way every time. He watched from the womb, seeing everything in wide angle, cat's eye, through flesh and pulsating blood vessels. His tiny baby hands reached out to save her but they were blocked by his mother's abdominal wall, a red transparent barrier of veins.

'Hm. No idea. That's weird.'

She shrugged and leaned over the side of the bed, grabbed her shirt from yesterday off the floor and slipped it over her shoulders. She stood up, stretched her arms, and yawned, then surveyed the room in awe.

'What's all this?' He followed her gaze, seeing the room as if for the first time through her eyes.

She stared at the bulletin board he'd installed over the dresser, which was covered in cut-out newspaper articles, blown-up photos of a bloodied eye, a stitched torso, a hand splayed open in a sea of garbage, copies of map sections with his notes in tiny letters on the side, bright blue string connecting them all in an intricate web only he could understand.

Maybe he shouldn't have brought her here.

'Whoa, this is totally *psycho*.' She shivered and crossed her arms, glancing at the stacked boxes of files. She spun around and studied the pictures above the bed. He cringed inwardly. He couldn't explain those to her. They were copies of family photos of his sister, at two, at four, at seven, on her bike, in the snow, blowing out birthday candles.

She was obviously perplexed.

'This is normal protocol,' he said, shrugging. 'How else do you think cases get solved?'

'Why is it here? Don't you have an office somewhere? Like at the police station?'

'My office is in St. Paul.' The fingers of his left hand twitched ever so slightly.

'Why wouldn't the local police give you space?'

He wiped his face, hoping to hide his discomfort.

'Because no one cares about a cold case, especially one that's twenty-one years old. I'm on my own.'

She looked at him doubtfully.

'How'd you draw the short straw?'

A thousand voices were jumbled in his head, attempting to give order to the myriad complexities involved in the situation.

'Long story.' He felt a sweat break out on his back.

Before he could stop her, she dropped to her knees and started rifling through one of the boxes, finally lifting up a plastic bag of bloodied fabric samples.

'Don't touch that,' he said, pulling it out of her hands.

'Shouldn't that be locked up? Chain of custody and all? I've seen crime shows, you know.' She sat back on her heels, brow furrowed. 'Adam, what's going on here? Why are there evidence bags in your motel room?'

He didn't answer, couldn't think of anything to say.

'Adam? You'd better tell me or I'll assume something is seriously wrong and start screaming.' Her wide eyes darted to the door. He saw what she was planning. He couldn't let her leave, couldn't let her tell people. Either he'd have to come clean and hope she could keep a secret, or do something dire, though he didn't know what. He'd have to take a chance.

'Okay, okay, let me explain. Sit down.'

She found her pants on the floor, pulled them on, and sat down, twisting at her shirt nervously.

'I had a little trouble on the force a few years ago, so they gave me this cold case. A triple homicide. They thought of it as a sort of paid leave of absence frankly. No one can solve these kinds of cases. Witnesses are gone, evidence is locked away, missing or mislabeled, relatives want to move on. That sort of thing. It still matters though. It matters a lot.'

She nodded hesitantly.

'What kind of trouble?'

'Nothing. Well, nothing big. A little drinking on the job.'

'Okay, okay. I can handle that.' She let out her breath. 'So then what? They give you the case. And then they send you out on the road with the evidence? That doesn't seem right.'

'Not exactly. No. You see, I made a . . . mistake on this case the first time around. I thought I knew who did it. A janitor at the school. Eugene Woodlawn. I tracked him for months and I was *sure*. I couldn't prove it though.'

She looked at him expectantly, so he went on.

'They found a ton of narcotics in that apartment – cocaine, ecstasy – you name it. We all assumed these murders were connected to drugs. So when I heard a rumor that the janitor had been dealing to kids at school, I put two and two together. And then when I examined the evidence one last time, I found a note in the lining of the jacket of one of the victims. It was from the other murdered boy arranging to meet up at an apartment the day of the killings. I checked the record and no one had logged it. It gave me an idea.'

She winced.

'And was it a good idea, Adam?'

He blushed.

'No, it was a bad one. I . . . Everything I did, I did in good faith, Deirdre. I didn't mean for anyone to get hurt.'

'What did you do?'

Neither of them moved a muscle.

He was surprised how much he wanted to tell her what he'd never told anyone before. Not his lawyer, not his chief, not his mother. He'd tried to forget it had happened, but he needed to get it off his chest and something about her drew him in, made him feel safe. He needed this, though even thinking about saying the words made him feel like vomiting.

'I helped things along.'

Her eyes widened.

'Helped?'

'I was sure he'd done it. Positive. But I couldn't prove it. I had to connect Eugene to the scene of the crime.' He took a deep breath. 'So I planted the note.'

He saw the shock on her face, but it was too late to stop now.

'It gets worse.' He swallowed.

'I led a raid into his apartment. Full-on SWAT team. I'll never forget it. The guy was sitting there, on this tattered green couch, eating microwaved chicken nuggets in front of the television. We burst in, and then there were gunshots. Three of them. So I fired back.'

'And?'

'The gunshots were from the television.'

She winced.

'And Eugene?'

'Dead.'

'Oh.'

'Then a few weeks later, exonerated.'

'Oh, Adam.'

'Yeah, iron-clad alibi.'

She shook her head slowly.

'It was a mistake. You thought there'd be a trial. That he'd only go to jail, right?'

He nodded.

'Exactly. But they put me on medical leave. Indefinitely. They were more worried about a riot than my mental health, I can tell you that.'

'But you didn't stop investigating.'

'No.'

'And you took the evidence. Stole it.'

'Yes.'

'Oh, Adam. This is bad.' She buried her face in her hands.

'I know.'

'What do you think you can accomplish here? The evidence is tainted even if you do solve it.'

Her luminous eyes studied his face. She was losing faith, he could tell.

'I'll put it back. Trust me, no one will notice. I'll re-interview witnesses. I'll do everything by the book once I know who did it. It will be fine. The ends justify the means sometimes.'

'And if you solve it, you think they'll reinstate you?'

'Of course they will. No one thinks this case can be solved. It's a write-off. If I can do it – well, it's my only chance.' He looked at her, unable to read her expression.

'So, are you going to turn me in?'

They stared at each other for a long time. He could see the doubts flickering across her face, but in the end, she let out a sigh.

'Maybe I'm a fool, but I'm not going to turn you in, Adam. I believe you're a good person, I really do. And the victims deserve justice.' She paused. 'I just don't know how I can fit in to all of this.' She waved an arm toward the bulletin board.

'And there's still one thing I don't understand,' she said.

'What?'

She pointed to the wall over the bed.

'Who's the little girl?'

CHAPTER 13

Julie had been wrong to get her hopes up. The Evil One had come back even more terrible than before. She didn't know what he'd been up to while he was away but there was a row of badly done stitches over his ribs encrusted with blood. That couldn't be healthy.

Julie hoped it was some girl who fought back hard, did him some damage. If only she'd managed to kill him – but no woman could fight that brute and win. Perhaps someone's boyfriend or father caught him in the act, ripped him off her, had a weapon.

She was glad he was hurt, even if he'd taken it out on her this morning. Even if she had a busted lip and a bruised eye, and had to put her cheek against the floor, unable to move for what must have been two hours, it was worth it to savor his fresh wounds. She decided to imagine that whoever did that to him, did it for her. An act of revenge without even knowing it.

She was sure his old lady would take care of him though. It was like she was under a fucking spell. It couldn't be his looks, not with his greasy hair hanging down over those watery, red-rimmed eyes, the right one twitching when he got excited. He looked like the losers Julie used to see begging for drug money on St. Mark's Place.

And whatever came out of his mouth was crazy, blithering mumbo jumbo. His fucking prophesies, his 'whithers' and 'thous'. A giant load of crap. A desperation move – this religious tripe – because he sure wasn't winning anyone over with his sense of humor and charm. A real world-class loser. Both of them, really. Birds of a feather.

She had to face it though, the evidence did not bode well for her. She'd noticed the dark brown stains between the linoleum tiles. And the forethought that had gone into the room. The toilet and sink, the four locks on the outside of the door. It was pretty obvious they'd done this before and most likely intended to do it again.

After she was gone.

If she weren't smart, really fucking smart, she would die in this room. And that would be only after he had done more unspeakable things to her. She didn't cry as often now, which was a shame because that was the one activity that brought her relief. Once the tears had dried up, she was left with nothing but her spinning regrets. She hadn't been brought up to deal with this kind of situation. She hadn't been raised for disaster. She had to learn it all the hard way.

It kept hitting her that – after everything, after building her life so carefully, after working so hard toward all her goals, the years of late nights studying to make all As, the dance rehearsals, the long nights talking with Mark – this would be how it all ends. In this stupid, senseless nightmare. Something she'd barely considered, something she'd thought was statistically impossible. A horror story made-for-TV. Only now she was the star.

She was so caught up in self-pity that she didn't hear the footsteps on the stairs until it was almost too late. Both sets. They were together this time, which was a first. Julie didn't like any change to the routine. It could mean anything. It could mean they were finally coming to kill her.

She wiped her eyes quickly with the backs of her hands and rushed to get into position, expecting the worst. When they entered though, they were obviously distracted, barely glancing at her. What a pair they were. Harmless-looking life rejects. The lowest of the low. He with his baggy clothes and darting eyes, she with her head hung down, like a ship sinking slowly to the bottom of the sea. No one would have guessed the evil they were capable of.

The woman locked the three of them in, the beasts with the prey, and Julie felt another wave of panic coming on. They continued to ignore her. It made no sense, but neither did anything else in that house.

'Don't move. Don't even look at us,' he said suddenly, jabbing his fat finger in her face.

She nodded though she fully intended to disregard his instructions. Such small acts of defiance bolstered her up, kept her going.

The Evil One carried a bright orange plastic toolbox and the woman followed a few dutiful steps behind, staring straight ahead. He crouched down by the sink and pulled away the cheap plywood box that housed its pipes, running his hand along them slowly as if looking for a leak.

So that was it.

'Wrench,' he said flatly. The woman dug around in the toolbox and handed it over. She tilted her whole body toward him, eyes locked on his face, waiting expectantly for his next command.

They carried on like that for some time until eventually Julie stopped watching, disgusted by the woman's subservience.

Then he paused in his work and Julie snapped to attention, all systems on high alert. There was a problem. Something wouldn't turn, some nut or valve or gasket, some accursed part whose failure to cooperate could cause a calamity of gargantuan proportions.

He strained against whatever it was with all his might, cursing quietly under his breath.

Julie's whole body tensed in automatic response. His frustration was not a thing to be taken lightly. Anything could happen, especially with a box of heavy metal objects within his grasp.

The woman was thinking the same thing, she could tell. They didn't need the words between them. They were battling the same demon, day after day, learning to manage the same beast. The unspoken energy of dread was a link that bound them together whether they wanted to acknowledge it or not.

The woman furtively glanced over and their eyes met for a fraction of a second. They understood each other perfectly. It was a treacherous bond.

The room fell silent but for the occasional clink of metal against metal.

He shifted his weight. Grabbed a hammer.

Apparently, the thing that needed turning still wouldn't turn because a long low growl escaped from him. Suddenly, he picked up a pair of pliers and slung them hard against the far wall, leaving a dent.

Julie and the woman stifled the same shriek and afterwards Julie held her breath, studying his slightest movements for any sign of what might be coming next. The woman edged away from him. Julie could tell she was poised to run, and watched as, without looking, the woman fumbled for a screwdriver that she then deftly tucked under her thigh out of sight.

He seemed calmer after his outburst though. He picked up the wrench and went back to the job. A triangle of sweat dotted the back of his hole-pocked white T-shirt.

After several minutes he made one decisive twist of the wrench and sat back on his heels, surveying his work.

'There,' he said, wiping his brow. 'The Star-Power within has blessed me on this day with the will and the knowledge, and it is done.'

'Amen,' the woman whispered.

At last. The thing had turned.

Julie let out a long slow breath, thanking all the forces of the universe, even his crazy fucked-up deities.

He stood up slowly, supporting himself with his hand on one knee as his other arm swung into the air for balance. It was obvious his injuries were bothering him, which gave

Julie a tiny jolt of pleasure as she watched him limp across the floor. The 'star-power' wasn't doing much to heal his wounds at any rate.

The woman, meanwhile, slunk to the far side of the room to collect the pliers he'd thrown. She placed the tool in the box, clicked shut the locks, and hauled it up off the ground. It must have been heavy for she showed the strain, both hands clutching the handle for support.

Julie tried to make eye contact with her again, but her eyes were riveted to his loping form ahead of her. Her god, her idol, her guiding light. It made Julie sick.

He stopped briefly in front of her and reached out to touch her cheek, stroking it possessively. It took everything in her power not to flinch. She, for one, hated his fucking guts.

'Good girl. Staying put when I tell you,' he grinned, self-satisfaction smattered across his face.

The woman glanced over at her, eyes flashing.

'Like a dog,' she muttered under her breath.

The Evil One whirled around to face the woman, and, without warning, lifted his hand up behind him, and delivered a hard slap across her face.

Julie winced instinctively but the woman, obviously trained to endure, barely registered it.

'You're no better,' he bellowed, leaning in close to her, his thick lips puckering out from his splotchy red face. 'You have no right to judge the Servant at Hand.'

The woman merely closed her eyes as if anticipating the next blow, but he shook his head with disgust instead and walked toward the door.

The woman stared at his back with fury in her eyes but exercised, in Julie's estimation, extraordinary restraint.

She didn't get it. The woman had the opportunity to do it right then if she wanted, with the screwdriver or the hammer. Poke out his eyes, bash his skull.

Why didn't she? Why did she tolerate this? She'd seen her rage and knew her strength. She was capable of it.

Julie felt the woman's gaze on her at last, but now she was the one who wouldn't meet her eyes. She knew better. Acknowledging her humiliation wouldn't make things any easier between them. For now, she would save the woman from her shame and pretend she hadn't seen a thing.

She was learning, slowly but surely, the internal logic of psychosis. If she had any chance of getting out of there, she must be the excellent student she always had been, practicing vigilance and care, studying them as subjects in the bizarre laboratory of fate. To stay alive, she had to be smarter than they were, mapping the patterns of their insanity and memorizing the intricacies of their dysfunction. She'd been given a gift on this day, reams of data to study and manipulate.

She was watching and thinking and waiting. They would make a mistake. And she would be there, ready to take advantage of it, ready to destroy.

CHAPTER 14

They did go down to the caves the next day after school. Johnny had brought the weed as usual and Joy had shoplifted a six-pack. With great ceremony, Reed handed out flashlights to each of them; his father had been a miner before the operations had shut down and had managed to sock away several boxes of company equipment.

The timing of their little adventure had worked out perfectly for Cora. Her father had started out the day with straight vodka, and she hadn't dissuaded him. She knew his bender would last until he passed out mid-afternoon, and he wouldn't wake up until the following morning when she'd be safely ensconced in her first-period social studies class.

She was free for now. And she'd never been happier.

She tucked the flashlight into her belt, threw her backpack over her shoulder, and joyfully followed Reed across the giant slabs of rock down the hill toward the old mine entrance. The day was quite spectacular, warm for fall, with the wind blowing softly through the white pine needles and orange-tipped oak leaves that swayed overhead.

From a short distance away, Cora could see the cave opening, a black hole in the rock face lined with huge timbers that looked on the verge of collapse. Sure enough, there was the yellow police tape flapping in the breeze, and a few yards up from the mine, the official danger sign – plastered with the obligatory skull-and-bones symbol – outlining the many perils of entry: rock slide, carbon-monoxide asphyxiation, flooded tunnels, snakes, ceiling collapse. The list went on.

They huddled in front of the notice. Cora's heart pounded; she wasn't sure if it was fear of entering such a death trap or just excitement from standing this close to Reed. The warnings seemed convincing, but she would never be the one to say it. She'd risk everything for Reed's attention.

'Pretty lame,' Reed said, making the pronouncement on behalf of the group. 'They have to say stuff like that, so if we die, they don't have any liability.'

'If we die,' said Joy, 'I'm not really going to care whose "liability" it is. But hey, no risk, no reward. And let's face it, we've done stupider things and lived.'

Johnny led the way. He'd clearly already had a joint or two so seemed reasonably mellow when it came to the idea of his own death.

The small flat rocks closer to the entrance had been broken up by repeated landslides and had never thoroughly settled, so the going was trickier. Cora slipped and came close to falling, but Reed grabbed her arm in the nick of time and dragged her up the slope to where he stood.

'Whoa there, young lady. Looks like you need a big strong man to lean on.' He lifted her face tauntingly close to his, but then, as usual, tossed his head back, cracking himself up.

Nevertheless, when he drew back he smiled and offered her a hand. He looked so hot in his leather jacket, and today he'd added a long, wine-colored scarf that went almost to his knees. Only he could pull that off.

Her fingers were tingling from his touch as they made their way across the uneven terrain, hands still clasped. She'd never felt so utterly elated. For a moment she'd forgotten her fear, forgotten the danger they were approaching. At the actual entrance, however, she stared into the gaping hole of the mine shaft with trepidation, wondering what the hell they were thinking. It didn't look safe in there by any estimation and even with their flashlights they couldn't see much more than a few feet ahead into the penetrating darkness.

Joy ran her beam along the iron tracks that started a few feet outside the cave.

'Here, let's follow this. It'll be like our breadcrumbs,' she said.

They stepped carefully between the crossbars of the mine railway, some of which jutted up randomly out of the ground, as if disturbed by an extraordinary seismic event. One that, Cora reminded herself, could repeat itself at any moment.

Not even ten feet in, she scraped her arm against something in the dark. It turned out to be a piece of rusted rebar poking out of the earth that left a long, thin scratch on her orange dust-streaked skin. This was already not a good idea.

Unfortunately, the tracks ended abruptly after about two hundred feet, and the cave split off in three different directions.

'Eeny, meeny, miney, moe,' said Johnny. 'I pick this one.' He pointed to the far right.

The others shrugged and Joy led them down it. After a few feet, the path narrowed so that sections of it were less than a foot wide. Cora felt claustrophobic.

She closed her eyes and counted to ten, reminding herself it was worth it to be a part of this group.

Their bodies barely fit through the passageway and her jeans and T-shirt were covered in rock dust.

She coughed. Was it her imagination or was the air much thinner down here?

She lifted her flashlight higher, hoping to cast a wider circle of light. There were no other signs of human life in here. No more railway, no left-behind tools, no abandoned carts. Maybe this shaft had been closed off early on because it was too hazardous even for the professionals. Jesus, what were they doing?

'You think there are bats down here?' came Johnny's voice from behind her. 'I fucking hate bats.'

'Shut up, man,' said Reed. 'You're going to freak the ladies out.'

'Fuck you,' Joy yelled back at him. 'You'd be more afraid of them than I would. You can pretend otherwise, but I know what a little bitch you are.'

He caught up to her and gave her a playful shove, then kept his hands wrapped possessively around her neck as he trudged behind her. Joy kept glancing back at him, giving him her dazzling smile. They walked like that for a few paces, during which Cora thought she might die. Was there something going on between them? Had she missed that?

They continued along a path of constricted tunnels, each of which forked into several more. They randomly chose their direction as they went until finally one led them into a large open cavern.

'Whoa,' said Johnny, gaping at the giant space. 'This place is awesome. We should totally have a party here in the spring.'

'*If* we can find our way out,' Reed said with a chuckle.

'Shh. Listen. Water,' Joy said.

Cora stopped. She could hear it. Shining her flashlight around the space, she settled it on a dark horizontal split in the rock about two feet wide. She crossed over to it and slid her arm into the hole, pointing the light toward the bottom.

'Guys, look, an underground pool,' she said.

They peered down, but didn't seem that impressed. Embarrassed for expressing such childish enthusiasm, she quickly moved on.

She opened her backpack and took out the camp blanket her father had stolen in Nevada last year.

'Shall we sit? Have a smoke?' she said, trying to sound cool. Reed shrugged his assent and she softly let out a breath. She was one of them now, surely.

Johnny had gathered a few pieces of wood on the way down that he'd shoved into his backpack. He built a little pile of them and then extracted one of his old school notebooks. He ripped out a wad of pages and shoved them under the sticks.

'Algebra I,' he said gleefully.

Then he struck a match, got the fire going, and took out a small plastic bag that held three joints. He lifted one out, sparked it up, and handed it over to Joy with a flourish. They passed it around and Joy brought out the beers.

'This,' said Reed, holding up his can, 'is living.' The flames lit up his face, his beautiful face. It held so much life, so much challenge in his every glance. It was as if he was saying to her, *Come on, life ain't so bad, join us out here in the real world.*

For the first time, she wanted to. She thought there might be something more to her existence than protecting her secrets, barely keeping herself fed and clear of her father's fists. It occurred to her now, in this revelatory moment, that she could actually be out on her own one day, away from him, out from under his control. Maybe she could even be with Reed.

She could stay here when her father split town next time. He wouldn't like it, but if she ran away and hid out for a while somewhere up in these mountains, in the wilderness, he'd get sick of looking. He sure wouldn't go to the cops.

She leaned back on her elbows, half fading away into a fantasy of a cabin in the woods.

Suddenly Reed jumped up. Pot always gave him a lot of energy, unlike the others, who had settled into a languorous stupor around the fire.

'Look where we are, dear friends. Plato's cave,' he said with faux-menace as he touched his fingertips to one another in the style of a mad scientist. He walked over to the wall, spreading out his hands over his head to touch the highest spot where his shadow fell.

'So fucking obvious, Reed,' said Joy. She turned over on her side and lay down. 'Wake me up when he's done,' she mumbled.

Johnny snickered, always ready for a show. Cora sat up, crossing her legs.

Then Reed seemed to have another thought, a different idea. He dropped his hands and made his way back over to Cora. He knelt down, gently lifting her foot and cradling it in his lap. He slid down her sock an inch and ran his finger around her ankle, very slowly and in ever smaller concentric circles.

Don't stop, she thought. *Don't ever stop.*

She nevertheless managed to keep her features perfectly still. Poker-faced.

'You know the story, yes?'

She thrilled to his touch and could barely concentrate on his words, but she forced herself out of it and pushed him away by the top of his head. She had to play it cool. Just a little.

'Yes, you moron, I get it. I'm guessing I'm the prisoner?' She rolled her eyes, following Joy's lead.

Johnny snorted and Cora turned toward him. He was hunched over, laughing the noiseless, slow-motion laugh of the very stoned.

'Yes, Laura, yes, you are the prisoner. You are staring at shadows all day. The shadows rule you. You are ruled by shadows. You can never see the truth. Not until you are well and truly blinded by it.'

He removed the scarf from around his neck. Took her two hands in his.

She felt dazed with her physical desire for him. Her hands went limp.

He pressed her wrists together, opened up her hands, palms up. He looked into her eyes and then bent down slowly over her hands, kissing the center of each one.

Cora closed her eyes, soaking in the pleasure of his soft lips on her skin. She opened them to see him wrapping the scarf around her wrists slowly, his hands lifting over and under. He pulled them tighter and held the remaining length of fabric in one hand.

Then he reached down to her feet, removed first one shoe and then the other. He carefully lined them up beside her. He slipped off her socks, slowly, seductively, one at a time.

She didn't know where things were headed, but even this would have been enough to last her a lifetime.

Johnny stifled his laughter behind his hand. Joy, apparently hearing him, sat up and peered over, curious. Cora didn't dare take her eyes off Reed long enough to see how she was reacting to this odd tableau.

Reed gingerly wrapped the rest of the scarf around her ankles, weaving it in and out between her legs. He was still staring at her, smiling his dirty smile. His eyes were so enticing to her in that moment, so sly and bold. They suggested that something unfathomably erotic was about to happen. She smiled back at him with what she hoped contained a measure of coyness, but also let him know she was up for anything.

Still gazing up at Reed, captivated, she could see in her peripheral vision that the other two had quietly gotten up and gathered their things. They were leaving, giving them some privacy.

Her heart surged. She couldn't believe her luck. She wondered if Reed had been planning this all along just to get her alone with him. The blood thudded in her ears.

He leaned over her, even closer. She could smell him, an undercurrent of musk under the sweet marijuana smoke. She opened her mouth to speak but he held his fingers in front of his perfectly formed lips.

'Shhh. Shh.' He smiled reassuringly.

'But—' He put his hand gently over her mouth and rubbed her lower lip ever so lightly with the tip of his finger. She nearly fainted.

'Shh. Shhh. I'll be right back,' he whispered into her ear. His tongue traced the inner edge of her lobe as he drew back.

Then he tiptoed out of the cavern silently, leaving her there, bound up, waiting for, longing for, his touch.

He never came back.

CHAPTER 15

Cora had finished her lemon cake and swallowed down three coffee refills, and could tell the waitress was getting antsy to turn over the table. She'd have to go back home eventually. She couldn't stay away from the sounds coming from the room forever. If James was still locked up with the girl, she could start pickling some of the vegetables she'd just harvested. Maybe clean out the closets. Start going through the remaining boxes.

As she stood at the counter waiting to pay, though, she felt a strange sensation. Someone was looking at her. She turned her head swiftly and for an instant her eyes met those of a man sitting in the booth across from her. He looked away immediately, embarrassed perhaps to be caught staring, and pretended to read the newspaper in front of him. He was a young ad-executive type in suit and tie, blandly good-looking. Ordinarily, Cora would have simply turned away and forgotten him, but for one detail: his eyes were the same electric shade of blue that *he*'d had.

Her stomach sank as a host of memories rushed into her head. What would *he* have thought of her now? What would he have made of her life with James? He wouldn't have understood. He would have laughed that wicked laugh of his and called her a fool.

Well, no one could have predicted things would turn out like this. She'd been an insecure nobody back then, and now? Now she was above such trifles. She was part of something sacred. She turned her back on this kid, away from his uninformed judgments. Those eyes of his had never seen anything, after all. What did he know? He had no right to judge the Spectacular.

'How's Mrs. Johnson?'

The voice startled Cora. She twisted around to come face to face with the woman from the library, the one who'd given back her pictures of Julie. Cora had to grab hold of the cash register to keep her balance. So this was where she'd seen her before. She knew her after all.

This was a catastrophe.

The woman, however, didn't seem to notice that anything was amiss. She just sat there, smiling at Cora, waiting expectantly for an answer. Cora stood there mutely, shocked by the question, just long enough for both of them to feel awkward.

The waitress cleared her throat.

'Six forty-seven,' she said, clearly repeating herself as she nodded toward Cora's bag.

'Oh, yes, I'm so sorry.' Cora pulled out her battered wallet and unfolded a small pile of cash. She handed over a crumpled ten-dollar bill.

'And Mrs. Johnson? How's she doing?' the waitress asked again.

Cora snapped back into the present. This was important. She had to focus. Her heart beat fast. She had to get it right.

'She's, um, doing better these days. Awake a little more of the time.' Cora forced a smile.

'I know that line of work isn't easy.' The waitress shook her head as she counted out the change and handed it over to Cora.

'My sister-in-law does home health too. Tough job. My hat's off to you.'

'Well, it has its own rewards,' Cora mumbled, unable to meet the woman's eyes. She shoved her wallet back in her bag and turned to leave.

But this woman wouldn't let well enough alone.

'That lovely niece of yours doing well?'

So she had recognized her. Cora couldn't formulate words, only managing to nod.

'And your husband, I've seen him around. He's a trucker, right? Gone a lot, huh?'

Why was she asking these questions? Did she suspect something? Cora tried not to panic. She'd always known this might happen and James had taught her how to handle it. In the moment, however, it was more frightening than she'd expected.

Everyone seemed to be looking at her. The fireman at the counter, was he turning around to hear Cora's answer? The Mexican short-order cook, was his head cocked to the side as he let the eggs scorch on the griddle? The farmers having their coffee by the window, were they all staring? Did they all know? Was this one big trap?

'He comes and goes. I'm used to it by now.' Always be vague, she'd learned from James. Never let them pin you down with facts.

'Oh, honey, I know exactly how you feel. I was married to one myself for thirty years.'

Cora was confused. Does she mean—? No, of course not. She doesn't mean *that*.

'Turns out he had a girl in every port, as they say,' she continued. 'Divorced him three years ago.' Then she was the one blushing. 'Oh, sweetie, I'm not suggesting . . .'

'No, no, I didn't think you were. I understand.' She turned to leave again, taking advantage of the woman's discomfort. It wasn't enough to shut her up apparently.

'You know, Mrs. Johnson took care of me and my sister when we were kids. Such a nice lady. I'd love to pay her a visit. Tuesdays are my day off. Maybe I could stop by one of these days? Bring over some chicken soup?'

A chill went up Cora's spine. She knew she'd paused a second too long, that it didn't look good, but she couldn't help it. She had to force out the words.

'Of course, of course,' she hesitated, 'only please do call first. In case she's having a bad day. I wouldn't want you to drive all the way out there for nothing.'

'Okay, sure. I'll do that.' Finally a couple stepped up behind Cora ready to pay. Thank God, Cora thought. The waitress's eyes looked past her at last.

'Why, how's that baby, Tanya?' Then she glanced back at Cora briefly.

'You have a good day now. I'll be giving you a call.' She waved good-bye, crinkling up her nose as she smiled, apparently oblivious to Cora's distress.

Cora took the opportunity to hurry out of there, berating herself all the way home for going out. She should have stayed at the house, shouldn't risk these kinds of encounters. What would she do if this woman became persistent? What if she insisted on seeing Mrs. Johnson? Started getting nosy, called the police?

The house was dark. She'd noticed James's truck was gone, but that didn't mean anything. He might have parked it behind the barn and be lying in wait for her inside, ready to pounce if she didn't do exactly as she was supposed to. It used to be one of the ways he would test her faith, but she wondered if she even mattered enough to him now for him to bother. He had more important concerns.

She stepped into the house, alert, listening. All was silent. She put her keys back on the hook, and walked quietly through the kitchen, peering down the hallway into the dining room, then creaking open the parlor door. Nothing. It was perfectly still.

He might be upstairs, though, maybe in the bath. She pictured for a second his face, blue and swollen, inches below the surface of the water. She shivered, shook off the image. What was wrong with her?

Suddenly, there was a loud knock. Cora jumped, all her muscles tensed.

Had the waitress followed her here after all? Was she bound and determined to pay that visit to Mrs. Johnson? Had she called in the state troopers? Or had the Mamaroneck police and the FBI finally tracked them down?

Then she understood. It was just the girl, banging on the floor. Cora relaxed and let her shoulders fall. The girl would know if James were here. She would never make a sound unless she was sure he was gone. Now that he was out of the house, she probably expected to be fed, probably wanted to ask Cora for things: a pillow, a toothbrush, or another blanket. When James was gone she turned into a real beggar.

Cora sighed and looked toward the stairs, ready to face her destiny, the endless, melancholy days from then on. Slave to the master. Servant to the slave.

CHAPTER 16

In her darkest hours, Julie would think things she didn't want to think. Things like, this should not have happened to *her*. If it truly had to happen, if the universe had to find its balance with this sort of evil, it should have happened to someone with less to lose.

Julie was so pretty, so smart. Everyone said so. And she worked so hard at everything she did. Meanwhile, there was a long list of messed-up, good-for-nothing girls from her high school – Jenny Vargas, Elaine Terrence, Maggie Sullivan, to name a few – who were going to waste their lives anyway. Why not them instead?

'Julie, you're disgusting,' she whispered to herself.

Sometimes she couldn't help it. It was so hard to keep all the bad stuff out. Like the memory of that first time he'd touched her, when he'd come into the room the night of her abduction. There they were, lodged in her brain: his burning hands on her cold flesh, while he laughed right at her the whole time, grabbing her face so she couldn't look away.

She tried to bury that image deep down, but it was the one that always came back first. No matter how much

degradation she'd suffered – and by then, she'd accumulated lifetimes of it – that memory hurt the worst. It had
simply been so shocking, so unlike anything she'd ever
imagined for herself. How dare he do this to her? How
dare he?

But she was past the initial panic and useless incredulity.
Now she was just so *angry*. And angry was better. It felt
good burning there in her heart, on her face, and in her
eyes.

'This is how I will survive,' she told herself. She stoked
it, worked herself up into a fine wrath as she paced around
the room, feeling the energy uncoil within her body, flow
into her hands, and steel her mind.

It had already helped her formulate a plan. She'd thought
about it continually since that last disastrous conversation
with the woman. She hadn't been prepared for the way
that turned out, obviously, but now she had a better sense
of what she was dealing with.

And she would put it into action soon. The rumblings
in her stomach told her to expect the woman any minute.
The man had been gone for a couple of days and without him around, life followed a predictable routine. So she
waited, like a spider to catch her prey.

'This is fucking war.' This time she was ready.

A few minutes later, sure enough, the locks turned.
Julie assumed her position, hands up, ankles crossed.
The woman came in, put the tray on the floor, and stood
there impatiently jangling her keys, looking off into the air
behind Julie. She must be embarrassed about the slap.

There on the plate were a bit of half-eaten toast, the yolk of an egg, and a handful of green beans. Julie drank and ate quickly so nothing would appear out of the ordinary, but also because her body demanded it. Then she returned to the bed, ready to deliver the speeches she'd prepared.

'Request permission to speak,' she said submissively.

'Yes?' Her tone was abrupt.

'I wanted to say that I've been thinking about what you said. And you're right.' She spoke earnestly and it sounded reasonably convincing. It should, considering how much she'd practiced.

The woman looked at her blankly.

'What did I say?'

'About how everything was easy for me growing up. That I didn't know anything about how the world really is. That I have a lot to learn.' Julie was barely breathing, hoping she could entice the woman into conversation without endangering her life this time. The knife bulged in her apron pocket and Julie wanted it to stay there.

The woman shifted her weight to her other foot, put one hand on her hip, and turned her head half to the side.

'Glad to hear it,' she said noncommittally. She was trying not to show it, but she obviously liked the sound of Julie's contrition. Julie knew it. She could reel her in.

'I was thinking – you see, my birthday is coming up.'

'Oh, well, I guess congratulations are in order,' she interrupted, throwing up her hands in mock surprise. Julie wished she could leap across the room and wipe that barely repressed smile right off her face. Instead she took a deep breath.

Eyes on the prize.

'And I was thinking about my last birthday. I'm realizing things about myself I might never have thought if you hadn't said that.'

More stony silence.

'It was a surprise party. My boyfriend, Mark –' She stopped for a second. Julie found it hard to say the name in her presence. The two parts of her life were so disconnected, her life cleaved in two by the abduction.

'He threw me a surprise party.' She thought of him pausing outside the door of the restaurant, his blue eyes sparkling as he leaned down to kiss her before going in to where her friends were crouching under tabletops. He'd slid his hand under her chin in that way he did, one finger pulling her face up to his.

She shook her head to brush the memory away. It was too painful, but she had to stay with the story. She'd had to pick something real to introduce this woman to her life. To prove to her she was a real person ripped out of her own narrative, not just an object in their fucked-up game.

'All my friends were there. Some of them had traveled from colleges across the country for that one night. I'd known most of them my whole life. Sarah, Theo, Beatrice, Chloe, Sampson.' She stopped again, her voice catching in her throat as she said their names.

'We grew up together, played on the playground out by Mitchum Park as toddlers, practiced our multiplication tables in third grade, studied for Ms. Vaughn's Algebra II tests in eighth.'

The woman's face had gone pale and the corner of her mouth twitched. Julie must be overplaying it. Better tone it down.

'Yeah, so?' the woman prompted.

'Well, I ruined everything that night. Was I happy to see my friends? I guess so. I took it all for granted though. I was such a baby. I spent half the party tearing up a paper napkin into tiny bits while I sipped a Long Island iced tea.' She paused. 'Not even a dignified drink.' She did regret this.

'I left early.' She could see in her mind's eye Mark standing there dumbfounded, trying to cover up her behavior, brush it off, and return to the crowd, laughing uncomfortably over the whole thing. 'I don't even remember why I did it. Some petty thing. Most likely people weren't paying enough attention to me. And it was my party. I was so stupid and vain. So childish.'

'What's your point?' The woman kept glancing at the door. Julie couldn't let her leave. Not yet.

'You see, I've always done things like that. That's what I'm realizing. I mean, now that I might not ever even *have* another birthday party, it's sinking in how I took everything for granted. I had always been confident that I could pull it off, push everyone right to the limits of frustration, and then with my big smile and a few flutters of my eyelashes, I'd be forgiven, embraced, and set right back on track. So I'm thinking, well, the world has taught me a thing or two this time. I get the message. And I want to change.'

Something simmered beneath the woman's expression that Julie couldn't read. Wouldn't she be gratified by Julie's mea culpa? Glad that Julie was suffering for the very vices the woman seemed to hate the most?

'You think that's why you're here? As karmic punishment for misbehaving at a party? You see, that's your problem. You're still putting yourself at the center of everything. The past doesn't matter. The person you were then doesn't matter. Your experiences don't matter. The beaches and the carousels and the ballet performances. The people who loved you. None of it matters.' She stood up. 'It's too late for you to change. What's the point? Your destiny is set.'

Julie swallowed hard. She was sure she'd never talked about any of that. How did this woman know those things?

Focus, she thought, *just focus*. Her original game plan wasn't working, so she'd try another tactic. She'd play dirty this time.

She gathered up her courage and looked right at her.

'What about *you*? Is it too late for you to change?'

She saw the scary look bubble up in the woman's eyes. But now? She didn't care.

'I don't need to change. I have found the Path.'

This set something off inside Julie.

'Oh, really? This is the Path? Married to a psychopath? I see how he treats you. That's okay with you?'

Julie's heart picked up its pace. She was pushing it.

'You should shut up now.' The woman's eyes were slits.

'I don't care. You think my life is worth living? Go ahead. Do what you want. Kill me. But first tell me because I'd really like to know – what happened to you? What kind of awful, horrible trauma got you to this hellhole? Something must have fucked you up pretty badly.' She paused for effect. 'Because you don't even fight back.'

The woman's face turned red and her nostrils flared.

'How dare you?' Her hand flew to her pocket.

'You really should, you know. Fight back. Me, I'm a dead man walking. But not you. You have every chance in the world. You have all the power. You can save yourself.' She fell silent, watching the woman, serious now.

'And you could save me,' she finished.

A shadow passed over the woman's face, her skin suddenly ashen.

Julie realized with disgust that she felt a tiny bit sorry for this hateful woman just then. She must be losing her mind.

Neither of them moved, until finally the woman picked up the tray, and, with the heels of her old-fashioned Mary Janes clicking on the floor, she left the room, slamming the door behind her.

She'd gotten to her at last. Now the idea needed to sink in for a while, brew up in her head like a potion. Julie was sure she'd be thinking about that as she fell asleep at night, when she did her chores, when she stumbled clumsily up the stairs the next morning.

Julie sat still on the bed for a long time after she left. That woman was wrong though. It wasn't too late for her to change. She'd never accept that.

If she had one more chance, just one more precious chance at life, she *would* be an entirely different person. She'd make up for every insensitive or ungrateful thing she'd ever done. She would tell Mark every day how wonderful he was and how much she appreciated him. She'd call her parents religiously every night at eight p.m. and would never be bothered again by their prying questions. She'd do her roommate's laundry and keep her shit off the floor. She'd do the dishes every night.

She'd be the fucking light in everyone's fucking life.

CHAPTER 17

Twenty miles outside of Stillwater, Adam squeezed into the breakfast nook of a fastidiously kept suburban kitchen across from Melissa Kruger, née Lassiter. Twelve when her brother had been killed, her hair had turned dark since then and her features had developed what one might call character. She was barely recognizable from the pictures he'd seen on the microfilm. Two years ago, she'd sent him the atlas with a letter urging him to follow this lead, but had refused to meet or even speak on the phone. She'd called him this time though. For some reason, she'd changed her mind and was ready to talk.

'I have something for you,' she'd said on the phone and Adam had rushed over.

Now he shaded his eyes from the morning sun streaking across the walnut tabletop, hoping for a new lead at last.

'I'd like my name kept out of it, okay? You know, the kids are in school. I don't want this story starting up again.'

Adam nodded. 'I'll do the best I can.'

This had to be good.

She lifted a box from the floor beneath the bay window and set it between them on the table.

'Go ahead,' she said, obviously happy to relinquish this treasure. 'All yours.'

Trying to look calmer than he was, Adam slowly lifted the lid and set it aside. Wrapped in turquoise tissue paper was a pink-and-white striped backpack.

'I found the atlas in that bag. I thought that would be enough for you. But I guess not, since the case is still open.'

Adam ignored her thinly veiled criticism and pulled a pair of latex gloves out of his pocket. If they could still manage to lift a print it would be the first one he had. He didn't even have a photograph of her. This would be an actual physical link. It could mean everything.

'Oh, you won't need those,' she said somewhat sheepishly. 'When I found it, I washed it in the machine and wiped down every single thing in it. I know that makes it a lot less useful to you. I'm sorry.'

Adam rested his hands back on the table, feeling the blood drain out of his face. He could not catch a break, could he?

'Why did you do that?'

'I thought . . . well, at first I'd planned to throw it in the dumpster behind the mini-mart, but something made me keep it. I wasn't thinking about proving who'd killed him – I didn't suspect her then. I just didn't want it traced back to my brother. Some things had happened between the two of them that I wanted to stay secret.'

'Melissa, I hate to remind you, but it wasn't going to make any difference to him by then.'

'It would have made a big difference to my parents though. If the full truth about Reed had come out it would have tarnished their memories. I knew he would have wanted me to keep this to myself. That girl was already long gone anyway, and no one seriously believed she could be involved back then, especially not the cops. A sweet young girl like that? It was only years later that I decided I'd been naïve.'

'What did your parents think?'

'They thought it was drug-related like everyone else. They blamed Joy. Thought Reed was in the wrong place at the wrong time. I knew better.'

'No one was suspicious when she left town?'

She shrugged.

'We all knew she was moving. A couple of kids at school joked about the timing, but that's about it.'

'So why are you giving me the backpack now?'

'My mom died three months ago and my dad has Alzheimer's. Reed didn't care what anyone else thought. This is the only lead that was never followed up on. It's my last hope.'

'I see. Where'd you find it?'

'In his room, under the bed. When they first found the bodies, I was so upset that I crawled under there to hide. We'd always done that as kids when our parents fought or if we were afraid of a thunderstorm or whatever. It was our safe place together. And there it was. I recognized it, took a look inside. That's when I understood the situation.'

She took a deep breath.

'The two of them had come here a couple of times and I'd watched them together. I got the picture. Listen, my brother was the absolute king of the bad seeds, but he didn't deserve to die.'

'Of course not.' He paused. 'My gut tells me you're right about her. But I've gone down the wrong path before. I have to be sure this time.'

She nodded in the direction of the backpack.

'You'll see. It doesn't exactly prove she did it, but it explains why she might have.' She paused. 'Just promise me no matter what you find out about him, you'll keep in mind that he was just a young kid who got mixed up with a bad crowd. Whatever it is he did, she still deserves to be punished.'

Her face wrinkled up. She was on the verge of tears but managed to hold them back.

'I'm sorry,' Adam whispered.

'No one else has seen that letter. I hope it helps.'

Adam lifted the backpack off the table and set it between his legs. He unzipped the pink plastic zipper – it was a cheap bag but made of the kind of vinyl material that would be filling landfills long after humans were obliterated. In it were a couple of schoolbooks – a math textbook and a copy of *A Separate Peace* – and a red plastic wallet.

He took out the wallet first. There was no money or ID, just a worn-out library card from Reno.

He took out the math book and flipped through it. Tucked in the front cover was an envelope.

He looked up at Melissa. She nodded. It was addressed to Reed and was in her handwriting, which he recognized from samples he'd collected from other towns, other schools, and her scribblings in the margins of the atlas. The envelope had been torn open.

'Did he read this? Or did you?' he asked.

'It was opened already. I think it will help you understand.'

He clutched the letter to his chest, forgetting for a moment about the woman in front of him. Here at last he held something significant. He took it out and read silently.

Dear Reed,
Since you won't talk to me, I'm writing this letter. You deserve to know the truth.

It went on for two pages in her loopy scrawl. When he finished, his hands twitched as he slid the letter back into the envelope.

Now he knew Laura's secret. And he knew that Reed Lassiter had known it too.

CHAPTER 18

That night Cora lay in bed alone, listening to the fallen leaves rustling outside her window. The air blew gently over her skin, crisp and invigorating. It was her favorite time of year but there was no one to share it with. James had been gone for five days.

As she drifted into sleep, she heard the girl stirring. Why was she making noise at this hour?

Cora sighed. The girl was an irritant, driving her crazy of late. Of course she *would* cause a problem just as Cora settled into bed after a long day. She flipped over and covered her head with her pillow, but the noise grew louder. No way to ignore it. Giving in, she tossed her covers aside, slid her feet into her slippers, and wrapped her robe around her.

The hallway was dark as she tiptoed to the spare room between them and turned the doorknob. It smelled of talcum powder and rubbing alcohol in there. They hadn't yet removed the oxygen tank, the hospital bed, or the spare canisters that lined the far wall. There was hardly space to listen in next door.

Cora found a spot though and, gathering up her nightgown beneath her, sank to the floor closest to where the sounds emanated. The girl was just on the other side, crying.

Spreading her fingers slowly, Cora lifted both hands to the thin wall. So little separated them physically, and yet they were worlds apart.

Yes, there she was: that beast, that animal, that nuisance.

How had everything gone so wrong?

Cora sighed. She'd have to deal with this. She stood up, walked out to the hallway, and banged on the girl's door.

'Quiet down in there!'

But the sobbing continued.

Exasperated, Cora slid open the slot they'd cut in at eye level and took a look. The girl's wild eyes stared back at her through the hard clear plastic.

'I'm sorry,' the girl whined. 'I can't help it.'

Cora muttered angrily to herself as she unbolted the locks and stepped inside the room. The girl sat on the bed, not bothering to get into position, sobbing into her knees. She wouldn't have dared do that with James.

Cora would have to be stern.

'You have to stop this nonsense. It's been long enough. Accept your destiny, girl.'

'I'll never accept this,' she spat out. 'I might as well be dead.'

If only. Cora looked at her thin neck, the pulse beating hard inside it. She could so easily squeeze it and stop that infernal *thud, thud, thud.*

'Watch out or you will be. You live at his mercy and under his protection. *He* thinks you're part of the Revelation. I'm not so sure. You'd better hope and pray he's right this time.'

The girl turned pale. Cora thought for a minute she might faint, but instead she clutched the folds of Cora's nightgown for support. Cora rolled her eyes but let her keep holding it. She was weak today.

'You can't believe any of this,' the girl said. 'You must see that he's manipulating you to do his bidding. You're nothing but a slave.'

Cora put her hand on the girl's arm, reached up and touched her tangled hair, pulled a strand out to its full length. Pretty, even like this.

'Not a slave. A Follower. I'm the only one now, but it wasn't always like that. There were many of us at Stover, more than twenty at one time. I have seen the paradise at the end of the Path. I have seen it. And we will have it again. We will rebuild the Kingdom.'

The girl shrank away from her, but Cora wanted her to understand. Cora wasn't a fool and she wouldn't be mistaken for one. She paused, wondering how much she should explain, then she took the girl's hands in her own. They were soft and delicate like a child's.

'It was wonderful. We all gave what we had to the Divine Family. We lived side by side, toiling together in peace, in service to the Chosen One. He gave us strength and spiritual sustenance.'

Cora remembered James's face, glowing with love in those days. They were as one when he handed her the golden cup of forgiveness at evening circle, or took the plow to lighten her load under the beating sun.

'James and I led the others in glory, guiding them to righteousness, in perfect communion with one another. He did not need to speak, I knew his thoughts, his wishes, his every desire, as he knew mine. We had created a heaven on earth.'

The girl had stopped crying and was staring at Cora, her eyes rimmed with red.

'If it was so great, why aren't the Followers here with you now?'

'Hush, girl.'

'They left, didn't they?'

'Shut up.'

Cora dropped her hands and rose to stand.

'They got away, didn't they? They saw how he was and they ran.'

'Be quiet, girl. You don't understand. The devil took their souls.'

'If they could escape, then so can you. We can get out of here together.'

'Heretics. Blasphemers. They were overcome by doubt and sin.'

'They came to their senses.'

'They were evil. They wrote things on the walls of our trailer. Insults, threats – oh, the perverse things they wrote. They called him . . . I will not say it.' Cora felt her great passion for him returning, slipping through her body like electricity.

'All we worked for, all we sacrificed.' She turned to the girl, as if she could ever understand. 'That's when the Dark Spirits came and the Great Struggle began, when they left us. They're to blame.'

'You mean that's when he started drinking? Taking drugs? Went insane? Because he's not in his right mind. You see that, don't you?'

'Liar! Blasphemer!' Cora raised her hand to strike, but stopped in mid-air, forcing herself to regain her composure. The girl must not judge him for his ways now. 'What do you think will happen if I tell him what you said?'

The girl looked directly into her eyes.

'I don't think you will. I think there's good in you yet.'

Cora turned away, a stab of regret shooting through her heart. This girl must have been sent to test her.

'You don't understand. The Dark Spirits force him to do things he would find shameful – that he *will* find shameful when his senses are restored. We have to believe. I wish I could express to you the great beauty that is in store for us both when the Revelation is fulfilled.'

Cora looked sorrowfully at this girl.

'I was like you once. It takes time to process the Word. You waste your time parsing over the past, the regrets and the blame, trying to find meaning in them. There is no meaning there, only useless pain. There is another Path. Empty your mind of those things and be free.'

She felt powerless, unable to express what she needed to make her understand. Of course, the girl couldn't appreciate that her current suffering was merely a bridge to a greater world. It was hard enough for Cora to remember that all the time herself.

Indeed, she saw suddenly with perfect clarity how she had been failing. Failing James, failing the Revelation, failing herself. How she'd let the little things – her own desires, her wishes, her petty grievances – overcome what she knew in her heart to be right and just. In thinking those unclean thoughts, she'd let herself become diverted from the Path. She resolved to be better, stronger.

Cora reached out and touched the girl's soft cheek, tracing a sunken line with her fingertip.

'It's going to be magical, when the Revelation comes to pass. Wait and see. You will learn to embrace your destiny. You will see the golden sunrise and the fury of a thousand stars shall light the Path.'

The girl just shook her head, her eyes squeezed shut. Why was she so determined to resist the Word?

Cora stood up.

'You have helped me to renew my strength tonight. I see things more clearly than ever. Perhaps you have another purpose that was not revealed to us before. It is a good thing. It is a gift.'

The girl just sat there in silence, her chest rising and falling, her lips quivering. Cora deigned to give her a slight smile as she left the room and bolted the door behind her. She walked steadily back to her own room, elated, inspired, her heart pounding with her own restored fervor.

Perhaps all was not lost. Maybe this was a new beginning after all.

CHAPTER 19

Reed was waiting by her locker before first period, but she ignored him, refusing to look up. She would never speak to him again. Maybe she'd stop going to school, convince her father it was time to move on.

He leaned over her open locker door and lifted a finger to her cheek, brushing it lightly.

'That wasn't nice of me, was it?' He smiled in that way he had that said everything in life was one big joke.

She didn't say a word. She wanted him to twist there in the wind.

'Aw, come on, Laura. Yes, it was mean, but I couldn't help it. It was a spur-of-the-moment decision. I kept thinking, what would happen if I just left? That would be ridiculous – an existentialist act of will. It was so fucking *wrong*, I couldn't not do it, now could I?'

He grabbed her arm, pulling her closer to him. She was furious with herself for being sucked in, but she couldn't help the way her body responded to him.

'It was really – you really hurt me, Reed. I can't – I don't think we can be friends anymore.' Even as she said it she knew it wasn't true.

'Let's go out tonight. Just you and me this time. I know a place under a bridge. It's even scarier.' He leaned over her, whispered in her ear while he tugged at a piece of her hair with one hand. 'I'll tie you up and leave you there.'

'That's not funny.' But she was looking up at him, already wondering whether it was too soon to forgive him and still keep her dignity intact.

'I know. It's not,' he said, wrapping his arm around her waist. She held herself stiffly against him. He pulled back from her, studying her with those soulful blue eyes of his, looking serious for once.

'Laura, I mean it. I'm sorry. That was a shitty thing to do. I always – I just do stupid stuff. Showing off or whatever. I mess everything up.'

He squinted his eyes shut and held the bridge of his nose between his thumb and forefinger, shaking his head.

'Can you forgive me? I didn't mean to hurt you.'

Cora didn't reply. A knot had formed in her stomach. She couldn't help but feel sorry for him because she knew what that was like. She messed everything up too.

'Meet me at Joy's apartment at ten? After your father passes out?'

She nodded slightly, still unsure of him. He smiled, gave her a delicate kiss on the cheek, and walked off to class.

She couldn't take her eyes off him as he swaggered down the hall. He was surely wicked, but it was a wickedness she could not resist. Her brain told her to stay away, leave him alone, but she knew she'd follow him to the ends of the earth if he wanted.

And on that night, she followed him to Joy's apartment, just as he'd asked. He was late, of course, and at first she thought he was standing her up. She was putting on her coat to leave, cursing her own stupidity, when he walked in with his usual sly grin on his face. He held out a bag of chips. His mouth was full and he crunched loudly, smelling of booze.

No respect whatsoever. Her heart sank.

'No, thanks,' she said. What was he thinking? She was an idiot for coming here. Yet when he sat down on the couch to tie his shoe, she started to take her coat off again.

'Leave it on, we're not staying here,' he said with a mischievous grin.

They went out into the night. It wasn't the kind of neighborhood where anyone went on midnight strolls. There were no sidewalks, just ditches off the verge. The brick ranch houses were mostly dark by now, except for a couple where the flickering televisions could be seen through front windows.

'Where are we going? Am I allowed to ask?' she said, her heart beating pretty hard by then. She was not going to fall for his bullshit this time.

'Under a bridge. I told you.'

She stopped. Stood still.

'And what about the rest of it? Are you setting me up again?' He tugged on her arm, but she didn't budge. 'I mean it, Reed. I need to know what's going on.'

'I swear. I swear I will not leave you. Come on. There's a dam on the lake. And I know how to get into the tunnels underneath. That's all.' He paused. 'You've spoiled my surprise.' He looked genuinely hurt, but she didn't believe it for a minute.

They walked around the block to where he'd parked a beat-up silver Honda.

'You have a car now? You're too young to drive, Reed. Where'd you get this?' She hoped against hope that it wasn't stolen. She could not end up in a police station again.

'I borrowed it. Relax, I have my brother's license with me. Works every time.' He opened the door for her with an exaggerated show of gallantry.

Against her better judgment, she got in and he drove along a twisted maze of roads. Cora had no idea where they were, which would make it somewhat complicated to get back home if he did pull something on her.

Finally, he drove into an empty parking lot and they got out. They stood at the railing by the edge of the lake, watching the water plummet majestically over the side of the dam. The even row of lights set within each cement archway bounced its rays back into the spray.

'Beautiful, isn't it? I mean, for a public-works project. Anyway, the tunnels are fucking awesome.'

He led her down several levels of cement steps. It smelled like mildew down there, as if the lock had been full of water until right that second. Ever more elaborate formations of green muck clung to the sides of the dam's infrastructure the lower they went.

She shivered.

'You cold?' He took off his jacket and put it around her shoulders. The smell of it was intoxicating. His smell.

They came to a rusted metal door that was partially wedged open. A red sign read 'Danger: Do Not Enter'.

'Here. Step carefully. We can only get it open about eight inches. I hope no one else is in here tonight.'

He was taunting her again.

She wondered for a moment whether Joy and Johnny would be waiting there, laughing in that way they did, the way that told her that she was still and maybe always would be an outsider. Anything could be in store for her down there. So far from anything else, they'd be able to do what they wanted. She shuddered to herself, hoping that wasn't the plan.

Yet even then she was willing to risk it.

As she pushed her body through the small opening she saw with relief that the dismal room was empty after all. A dim yellow industrial light shone from one side of the doorway. On the other side of the space a copper pipe ran from floor to ceiling, hissing softly. A red indicator light glowed from a metal panel mounted on the center of the wall.

'How charming,' Cora said with a laugh.

He smiled and without a word set down the backpack he was carrying.

'Hold, please,' he said as he took out a blanket, a small lantern, and some matches. He lit the wick and spread out the blanket with a flourish.

'Romantic, right?' He indicated for her to sit.

She smiled and sat down, leaning back against the cold hard wall. She just wanted to touch him.

'Did you bring any weed?' She needed it to calm her nerves.

'Nope, but I have beer.' He handed her a can and took out a second one for himself. They popped them open and each took a sip, then sat in silence for a minute or two. Cora wanted him to go first. He owed her that much.

He finally turned toward her.

'I've brought you here tonight for a reason, Laura Martin.' He touched her nose softly as he said it and inched over closer to her. Her skin tingled. He took out a pack of cigarettes, tilted it toward her. She shook her head, so he put it back in his bag.

'You're a mystery,' he began. 'A very strange mystery. That won't do. I want to know the truth about you.'

Cora tensed up. Honestly, she thought, couldn't they just make out?

'The truth? You're the last person to believe there's any such thing,' she said, hoping to deflect his questions.

'Yeah, well, all kidding aside –' He stopped, grabbed her hand, held it up to the light, flipped it over and studied her palm. 'Where did you come from? Where do you live now? Why isn't there a nice mother looking after a wayward girl like you?'

She pulled her hand away, as if he could read the secrets in the lines of her flesh.

'That's really none of your business, now is it?'

'Oh.' His interest was piqued. 'Sounds like there's a story. What happened?'

She didn't answer, just sat staring at her palm, wondering for a moment if the answers were there after all.

'Hello? Laura? What happened?'

She looked into his eyes. Maybe if she opened up to him, he'd be nice to her. Maybe it would bring them close. Or maybe he wouldn't like what he heard.

She lay down, straightened a corner of the blanket, and turned over on her side. 'I mean, really.' She unbuttoned her top button and smiled. She felt brave for doing it.

'Nice play, Laura Martin, but I really want to know.'

She sighed.

'To tell you the truth, I'm not sure. I have a pretty good guess, though, given how we're on the run all the time.' She paused, deciding whether to say it. She took a deep breath.

'I think my father took me from her. You know, like one of those custody cases you hear about on the news. Sometimes I imagine that she's out there, frantically searching for me. I like the thought that someone really wants me like that. You know, with all their heart.' Maybe he'd take the hint.

'You think you were kidnapped? Whoa, that's huge. That's like, Amber Alert. Why don't you go to the police?' For the first time, he dropped his cool demeanor. He seemed genuinely interested in her answer.

'Because I could be wrong. What if my father's telling the truth? What if she doesn't want me and gave me up to him? Then what? Then my father's pissed and I end up homeless and alone? No, thank you.' She shivered and pulled away from him.

'I don't know. Maybe I'll find her when I'm older. Until then, can we skip the family drama?'

She sat up and buttoned her shirt. Then something dawned on her. Of course. It was a set-up after all. She was starting to get the picture.

'Is that why you brought me here? Did those two send you to get secrets out of me? Something the three of you could use to humiliate me? I guess I delivered. Now you can post a big sign at the school pep rally. Or maybe announce it over the loudspeaker. Is that what this is about?' She stood up. She'd find her way back somehow.

'Whoa, whoa, wait a minute. I'm not going to tell anyone. Relax.' He grabbed her hand, eased her back down to the ground.

'I'm not out to get you, Laura. I just want to know you better, that's all. That's what people do, you know – they ask other people about their lives, their circumstances –' he leaned in close to her face – 'about their burning desires that will ultimately drive them into madness.' He picked up her hand again and put it against his heart. 'Feel that.'

She felt his heartbeat, the firm muscles of his chest. Nothing else mattered all of a sudden. This time he unbuttoned his shirt and slid her hand underneath it onto his hot, smooth skin.

With the other hand he started slowly unbuttoning her shirt, tugging at the fabric gently each time, sliding his finger delicately along the inside edge of her bra.

'Just relax. We won't talk about anything now.'

He leaned toward her and their lips met.

CHAPTER 20

Julie lay on the bed staring at the window, too tired to bother picking at the boards today. Her limbs were weak with exhaustion because sleep was another luxury she'd been robbed of lately. No matter what her body wanted, her mind kept her awake. All night long panic alternated with despair as she churned through her options, or rather, the dearth thereof.

Today was Monday, at least it was in the calendar she'd created. Keeping track of the days helped her feel ordered, even if she'd had to randomly assign a place to start. On 'Mondays', 'Wednesdays', and 'Fridays' she exercised. Stretching, sit-ups, jumping jacks. Her muscles were deteriorating and even though it was hard to muster up the energy on so little food, she knew her legs had to be able to run if she ever got the chance.

Today, however, she was too depleted. The woman was feeding her less and less, it was true, but mostly she was emotionally drained. She felt like giving up, except she wasn't even sure what that meant, since she wasn't putting up much of a fight to begin with.

She turned over and shifted her gaze to the ceiling. Nothing like a new view to liven things up.

She reached down absentmindedly to scratch a small tickle on her forearm. That's when she felt something weird. She glanced down and then bolted upright, holding up her hands in horror.

They were covered in spiders.

'Oh, my God,' she screamed, jumping up off the bed.

There must have been a hundred of them crawling on her palms, on the backs of her hands, out to the ends of her fingertips. Tiny black creatures with red eyes, tickling her skin all over, marching in unison up her arms, obviously determined to cover her, to fill her nose and eyes and mouth with their furry little bodies.

No, not hundreds, it must be thousands. Soon they would cover every inch of her.

'Jesus Fucking Christ. What the hell is this?'

She frantically brushed them off onto the floor as she tried not to scream again. Her captors might do anything – might try to kill them by dousing her with bleach or setting her on fire. Better to deal with it alone.

The creeping black specks had reached her clothes now and were disappearing into the folds of her shirt, slipping down under the elastic of her sweatpants. When she got them off one arm, there were more, another unit sent in for battle, climbing in between her fingers.

'I swear, I'm going to kill every one of you fuckers. I swear to God.'

She stripped off her clothes, her hands moving as fast as they could, and flung her shirt at the bed, beating it hard against the iron headboard. Spiders flew everywhere.

The house must have an infestation. She must have been lying on a nest of them.

With her hands shaking, she picked up her sweatpants and threw them into the sink in the corner of the room. She turned on the tap, drowning the little beasts and watching dozens of their tightly curled dead bodies float to the top of the water.

'Die, you little bastards. Die. Die.'

But just as soon as she'd killed one batch, there were more. She looked down at her bare feet. Oh, God, they were between her toes now, making their way up her legs. They were almost to her knees already. She slapped at her thighs as hard as she could, wiping their tiny smeared cadavers onto the floor.

'How can there be so many of them?'

She shut her eyes tight, wishing she could erase herself from planet earth. Then she opened them.

They were gone. Just as suddenly as they'd appeared, they had disappeared. It was like magic. There was nothing on her skin, nothing on the floor.

She stood there in the middle of the room, naked, her mind reeling.

'What the—? This makes no sense.'

In a panic, she inspected under her arms, the backs of her legs, and held up her hands in front of her face. She swallowed hard and took a deep breath, leaned down and squinted at the linoleum tiles, searching for any sign of them. She walked over to the sink, barely daring to look in it. She lifted her soaking-wet pants and held them up, dripping, to the light. Nothing.

'You're kidding me. No way, no.'

This was worse than an infestation. Worse than a million spiders.

This could not be true.

Suddenly it was imperative for her to find those bloody spiders. She would not accept for a single fucking second that she had imagined them.

'No, Julie, calm down. They were real. They had to be real.' It was the most important thing in the universe at that moment that she find those horrible bugs.

She threw herself down on her hands and knees, scouring the floor for signs of their dead bodies, looking for the survivors that must surely be scurrying back to their nest. She walked to the bed and ripped off the sheets, studying each filthy inch.

There was not a single sign of them.

She sat down hard on the stripped mattress.

'I'm fucked,' she said, shaking her head.

Picking them up off the floor, she pulled the sheets to her cheek and her face melted into tears.

'There's no arguing against it now. I'm going insane. This is it. Totally, completely insane. They win. They've turned me into a mental case. Hallucinations are probably only the beginning. It'll only get worse from here.'

She stood up to pace the room, running her fingers through her tangled hair, squeezing her head between her hands so hard she thought it might smash her ears together through her brain.

'So this is how it starts. I'll be like one of those kid-napped girls on television who walk around in public in robes, never even thinking of escape, proselytizing some fucked-up religion while they smile pitifully, their far-away eyes all glistening and shit. So this is how that happens.'

What if she started believing his bullshit about mysti-cal spirits in the forgotten universe? Started speaking in tongues or something?

Then she stopped, nearly knocked down by the force of her realization. She clutched the rail of the bed.

'Jesus Fucking Christ. What if I become *like her*?'

She was running out of time. She had to get out of that room.

Right now though, she had to lie down and think. There was only one possibility. She had to kill these people. Yes, somehow she had to kill them. She pictured his face before her and thought of the exquisite pleasure of slashing a thousand bloody cuts across it, of smashing it in, or no, better yet, of burying him alive, watching his hands claw up at her through the dirt as he panicked. As *he* felt that kind of fear she felt every day.

Her too. That bitch.

'I'll kick her to death and rip the skin right off her pudgy face. I'll . . . I'll . . .'

Julie was panting. She sat up. She had to stop. *She had to stop this right now.*

She picked up her sweatshirt from the floor and slipped it over her shoulders.

What was happening to her? Look what she was turning into. She was letting the darkness take over. Where did these thoughts come from? These violent desires, these sickening images? She had to resist these feelings because if she lost her mind in here – if she did become his religious zombie, his follower – she'd never know how these urges might manifest themselves. This was how he would defeat her in the end. He'd make her an animal like himself.

And then another far worse thought occurred to her. What if – she hated to think it – what if she'd *always been like this underneath*?

What if this was her true character coming out when she didn't have all the comforts of home: her plush bedroom, her gadgets, keys to the car, designer clothes? When she wasn't walled into her suburban paradise. When the chips were down, is this what happened to her? Was this the truth then?

In the face of hardship, would she just *turn evil*?

Julie had always assumed she was a good girl. She'd done everything right, followed all the rules. She never hurt anybody. But look at her now. Was this what it meant to be a human being? That there was no such thing as 'evil', only circumstance? A roll of the dice and we think it's character, but that's not the case.

All her smug ideals were in question now. She didn't even know who she was anymore. And this, now, when she had to be strong, had to hold it together.

She lay back down and stared at the ceiling, taking deep breaths as she clutched the sides of the mattress until her fingers hurt. She slid her hand down in the space between the bed and the wall and retrieved Pooh from where he'd fallen.

'Sweet Pooh.' She buried her face in the fleece and cried. 'Where are they? Where are the police? Where are my parents? Where's Mark? Has everyone given up on me?'

Where were her SWAT teams, like she'd seen on TV, the ones dressed in riot gear, who would burst through the doors and carry her out of the house? There she would be then, a half-clothed, pale, ruined woman. Just a degenerate with scraggly hair and enough trauma to last a lifetime. Someone who would do anything to survive. Kill anyone, hurt anyone. A brutal damaged shell of a person who would never get over it.

She stood up, her legs and hands shaking, and then fell back to her knees.

They did this to her. They had taken everything away from her, even her innermost self. She wouldn't let them get away with it. Even if they killed her and buried her a thousand feet underground.

She crawled over to what she called the 'south wall'. She had to impose an orientation simply to believe she existed in the regular physical world, to believe that this room was not a box floating in space on its own, in its own universe disconnected from everything else. No, that's not what it was. It was connected to the rest of the house, which was connected to the ground, which ran around the earth to wherever her parents were now. To Mark. To her apartment. To her own bed with her own books piled beside it, waiting for her return.

She came to the wall and put her hands on it, pressed her fingertips onto one spot and then another. She let the tears run down her face as she raced around the room, touching every object, pushing her fingers against them as hard as she could. She stood up and whirled in circles around the room, spitting on the floor, on the lawn chairs, on the bed, on her hands, wiping it everywhere.

If they killed her, if she didn't make it out of this room, goddamn it, she'd leave behind her prints, her saliva, her DNA on every possible surface. She spun in wild circles, touching everything.

'There it is, that's me, that's me, you fuckers. I haven't disappeared. I'm physical. I'm real.

'And I fucking leave traces.'

CHAPTER 21

They'd stayed on through that winter in Minnesota just as Cora had hoped and now spring was finally beginning to break. Cora didn't shed the bulky sweaters though. For good reason. No one knew her secret yet but everyone would soon enough.

That wasn't her immediate concern. This morning she was hunched over the portable stove in the trailer trying to get the burner to light for her father's coffee. He was passed out on the filthy mattress in the back, one arm thrown over his face. His clothes were wrinkled and dirty and the stale smell of beer reeked in the small space.

She'd just washed that shirt, she thought, sighing with frustration. If he'd been careful he could have worn it at least a couple of days.

There was a smear of blood across his elbow and a large bruise bulging out underneath it. He must have a cut somewhere she couldn't see. She'd help him clean up later. He needed to go out to find work today and he couldn't do it looking like a homeless bum.

The situation was getting urgent. They were lower on funds than they had been in months and she was in dire need of some cash. Usually she could make do. No one could stretch the money further than she could, but this time they'd tested the limits of her ingenuity.

He rolled over, muttered in his sleep.

The flame lit suddenly and she blew on it gently, put the pot on top of the coils. She pulled her sweater tighter around her shoulders, then rubbed her ice-cold hands together, still suffering from the lingering effects of a brutal winter she'd thought would never end.

She stood watching the burner, making sure the flame stayed on.

'Cora, are you here?'

'I'm here, Father,' she said quietly as she folded their one clean kitchen towel and put it on the counter by the sink. She turned toward him, anger and tenderness mixed up in a strange brew inside her. 'Are you feeling okay?'

'I'll live.' He sat up, put his head in his hands, rubbed his eyes. 'But I'm going to fucking kill that bastard. Rip his fucking eyes out of their sockets.'

'No, no, don't say that. I'm sure he didn't mean it.' She didn't know what he was talking about, but she'd learned it didn't matter. It was always the same story. Luckily, he didn't have great visual recall the next day so he wouldn't even know who it was he aimed to kill.

'Maybe it's time to cut back on the drinking. You need to get back to work anyway. We're down to seventy-three dollars, which will only get us through about a week and a half and that's if we're careful.'

He ignored her.

'I'm hungry. What do we have?' he asked without moving. She went over to their small refrigerator.

'Not much here.' The fridge was completely bare except for an open container of yogurt. She lifted up the lid and closed it again quickly when she saw the surface was covered with bright blue spots. She tossed it in the garbage, tied up the bag, and lifted it out of the can. 'I can get you something tonight, but I'll be late. I have a project after school.'

He grunted at her.

'Enough with the school. What you need is a job. Just lie about your stupid age.'

It was her turn to ignore him.

She'd noticed that he looked worse today than usual and the shakes had already started. She felt a mild pang of fear. What would happen if he were truly sick this time? What if he *died*? She knew that, whatever else was true, he was all she had.

'Maybe it's time to move on,' he said. 'This town disgusts me. Fucking podunk backwoods ass of America. We've been here too fucking long.'

Cora's stomach sank at his words. She wasn't ready for this. It didn't really matter though because until she told Reed, there was no decision to be made. Her whole future would be at his feet. This was it. Her fork in the road.

He tried to sit up, threw off the blanket, and heaved over onto his back like a beached whale. Cora rolled her eyes and turned away from him. It was a shameful display.

His eyes opened to a squint and she could feel them following her movements from across the trailer.

The coffee was ready so she poured him a cup first. They didn't have any milk. She knew he didn't like it black but there was no choice in times like these. She carried it over to him and gently set it down on the small table next to the mattress. She helped him get adjusted, to sit up and lean back against the pillows.

The blood from his elbow smeared onto the sheet. She'd have to deal with that later.

He didn't move so she handed him the coffee, but he was so weak he couldn't even hold the cup. She took it back from him before it spilled, then watched him drop his head back onto the pillow and close his eyes again.

She stood there for a minute or two observing his prone, bloated body. The thought occurred to her, unbidden, that she could kill him right then if she wanted. The opportunities became apparent instantly: she could smother him with the pillow, grab his neck with her bare hands and squeeze like the devil, or stab him with the butcher knife she'd hidden away in a drawer so he couldn't find it when he was drunk. He barely had the strength to move right now, he'd never be able to fight back. And it would solve so many problems.

She shook her head. *Stop it. Just stop.*

Instead, she lifted the coffee cup to his lips and he took a loud slurp.

'That's too hot,' he scowled, pulling his head away from it.

Instinctively, he raised a hand to strike, but then, perhaps realizing his vulnerable position at that moment, he dropped it and said plaintively, 'Oh, Cora, what would I do without you? You're all I have. Everyone else can go to hell.'

She winced, feeling guilty for her earlier thoughts. Of course she would never do anything to harm him. He needed her. He was her only family in the world.

Only then did she realize he was crying, shedding actual tears. She hadn't seen that in a while and it broke her heart, even if she should have known this would happen eventually.

'I'm alone, Cora. I was always alone until you came along. Don't leave me. Don't ever leave me.' His voice was a pitiful whine. He got like this sometimes when he was drunk, but never when sober. He reached out to her like a blind man, his fingers shaking.

Against her better judgment, Cora was overwhelmed with emotion. She threw her arms around him and felt her eyes fill with tears too. She'd been struggling with so much all winter and it had been such a long time since he'd been like this, so subdued, almost loving in his own way. If only he would do this when she needed it, not just when he was in this morning-after state, feeling sorry for himself. This was the father she loved. It didn't take much to make her happy. Here he was, back here with her, if only until it was time for the next drink.

After this pronouncement, he lay back down and waved her off. She took the coffee cup back to the sink and turned on the tap, waiting for the hot water to come on.

It didn't take long for him to drift off back to sleep, a state she was sure he'd continue in for most of the day.

She put his mug away, went outside, and sat on the swing-down front step with her own cup of coffee. She stared out at the woods filled with new-growth pines, dotted here and there with RVs and a couple of Airstreams. Morning fires were going and strings of laundry hung out of every vehicle. Tattered clothes, washed to the point of colorlessness, waved in the chilly breeze.

A gray-haired woman with long braids was scrubbing some towels in a bucket out in front of the trailer next to them. She glanced up and waved, gave Cora a big friendly smile. Nothing fazed these aging hippies. Cora returned the greeting, careful to be cordial but distant. They didn't want to stand out but they didn't want to make any friends here either. Sometimes the camps developed too much of a community atmosphere and people started getting nosy. They couldn't have that.

Cora took a sip of coffee. She wished she could remember her mother. She had only a few threads, a few stray memories here and there. She recalled her thin fingers, buttoning up her winter jacket. Her own small hands dropping a toy boat in a stream and screaming as it floated away. Barnacles growing on the side of a dock while she struggled to keep her head above the water as a woman's voice called from far away. Bits and pieces of time that slipped away when she tried to retrace them.

Her father refused to talk about anything from her early years. He would only tell her she shouldn't waste her time thinking about her anymore.

What was it he was hiding from her?

It was useless to search through their possessions looking for answers. He'd burned every piece of paper except the maps. It was as if she'd sprouted fully grown from his head, the rotten fruit from the rotten tree.

How could she bring a child into this?

She'd brought this all down on her own head though, hadn't she? Forced her own hand by getting herself into something she couldn't get out of. She hadn't done it on purpose, exactly, but she hadn't thought about the consequences either. Something in her obviously wanted to turn everything into a catastrophe. Blow everything up.

And today she would break the news to Reed. She would do it right after school, meet him at Joy's if he would even do that. She'd written him a letter explaining everything in case he refused. She looked it over one last time before shoving it into her backpack.

Since you won't talk to me, I'm writing this letter. You deserve to know the truth.

She wasn't sure how he would react, wasn't sure how she felt about it herself either. All she knew was that she was afraid of almost every possible outcome.

She wasn't stupid. There'd been times when she thought she and Reed were close, when he'd made her believe he might even love her. Like that time he'd chased her across the parking lot in the pouring rain just to tell her good-bye. Or when he'd stayed with her in the library, distracting her from her homework with kisses between the stacks.

Then he'd gone AWOL for several weeks over the winter, staring off into space, not talking to her, refusing to make plans. She was never sure of him, never sure whether he truly wanted to be with her. But she took what she could get.

At first she'd wanted that baby the way a child wants a scruffy puppy it finds in the street. It was something she and Reed made together, not exactly out of love. No, perhaps not love but out of this strange energy that existed between them. In her heart of hearts though, she knew it wouldn't work. And if it didn't, she couldn't bring that child into her life and have it sleep in that tiny trailer with her and her father, scraping together this pathetic existence with them. Her father would kill her anyway when he found out.

She simply couldn't let bad things happen to this baby the way they always happened to her. If that were the only option, she'd have an abortion and save it that way. Maybe people were right about reincarnation and that child could roll the dice again, have better luck, and land on a safe square.

She didn't know. She just didn't know. She went back inside, grabbed her backpack, and headed out to the road toward town.

Today was the day everything would be decided.

CHAPTER 22

Adam pulled up in front of the charmless cinderblock building and turned off the engine. He sat staring at the glass doors, formulating his thoughts. He didn't have any right to be here. Even if they had reinstated him – which they hadn't – he was out of his jurisdiction. They could make an issue of it if they wanted. Call up his precinct. Double-check his badge number. He could be arrested for impersonating a police officer. Or worse.

He picked up his briefcase and took out his fake badge. He'd had to pull in some contacts from his undercover days to get his hands on one that looked this legit. He comforted himself by thinking that would help his cover later if they sent him back to vice.

Today he was counting on the social worker to bend the rules a bit. Hoping she wouldn't ask him too many questions. She would surely want to do some good, regardless of the formalities. Wouldn't she?

A Google search hadn't turned up that much useful information about her. She'd won a service award from the state a couple of years ago and they'd written up a basic bio. Angela Martinez. Nice local girl, straight-A student. She'd gone away to college on the east coast, spent a year and a half in New York City, then come back home. Probably with her tail between her legs. Last year, she'd come in second place in the agency's 'fun run'. Not exactly what he needed to work up a complex psychological profile.

However, even from those facts, she sounded like someone who'd be a real stickler for details and that's why he was sweating under the collar about this encounter.

But if she did help him – if she only would, he was certain she could help him fill in the gaps of Laura Martin's story. And if he were especially lucky, maybe there'd be a picture or a print in the file.

He screwed up his courage and opened the car door.

Inside, one look at the reception desk made it clear he'd been naïve about the administrative hurdles he would have to overcome. This place was a fortress of records and interview rooms. It was almost enough to make him walk out and run. But he couldn't turn back now.

'Angela Martinez,' he said with a crack in his voice. 'I have an appointment. Name's Adam Wilson.' A fake last name, even. What was he coming to?

Sitting at the front desk, slowly chewing her corn chips, the matronly woman with frosted hair and a name tag that said 'Hilda' apparently felt his request was an unconscionable burden on her. She sighed deeply and then swiveled in her chair, rolling it over so she could reach an appointment book on the other desk. She lifted up the glasses hanging from a bejeweled chain around her neck and held the book far from her face, squinting.

'Yes, here it is. Okay, have a seat. We'll call you.'

Adam sat down on one of a long row of plastic chairs joined together underneath by a rusted metal bar. He picked up a newspaper, the *Austin Messenger*, an artsy weekly, and flipped through it. Not much news in it, mostly ads for bands. Adam smiled to himself. Before he'd met Deirdre, he'd gone nearly three years without seeing a show or a movie or attending any event unconnected to his search. Loyalty to a cause, that's what the trainees were missing these days.

By the time his name was called, Adam was feeling confident. He'd gotten in, hadn't he? He brushed off his khakis and checked for his fake badge in his breast pocket. He could do this.

Hilda directed him to the third door on the right along a long bright white corridor. He knocked timidly and a tall brunette in her early fifties wearing a snug-fitting tweed suit and freshly applied lipstick opened the door.

She didn't invite him in. Flustered already, he pulled out his badge and gave the name that matched it. She gave it a cursory once-over and stepped back inside, motioning for him to follow her.

Only when she sat down facing him did she offer up a perfunctory half-smile. A professional courtesy only. Definitely a stickler.

'So, Officer Wilson, I pulled the file you asked about. You're lucky. Files that old are usually shipped to our warehouse in Marfa, but I kept that one in my personal filing cabinet.' She brushed back her already-smooth brown hair.

Things were off to a great start.

'Why did you keep it?'

'First things first. Why are you interested in that case?'

Fair enough. He would tell her the truth, more or less.

'That incident may have a connection to a crime that happened four years later in Minnesota.'

'And how exactly did you find out about this . . . incident?'

He was ready for this one too.

'I can't compromise our criminal investigation, but I can tell you how my search led to you. I traced the girl – this Elsa Sanders – to Austin, where she attended Thornton Middle School. Then I tracked down the school counselor, Wanda Munro, now retired, at her home outside of Austin. She remembered that you'd called her – I guess you'd worked together pretty often on cases originating at the school – and this was an unusual situation, she said, so it stuck out. She didn't give me any details though.'

'Is Elsa Sanders a suspect in your case?'

He shook his head.

'A person of interest. For now.'

Ms. Martinez nodded but said nothing. She drummed her fingers on her desk, her long nails clicking on the metal. She picked up a pile of papers and straightened them.

'Officer –'

'Wilson,' he provided helpfully.

'Officer Wilson. As I'm sure you're aware, I can't just turn over files to a police officer from Minnesota for a juvenile case from over twenty years ago. Those records are sealed and . . .'

'I know that. I understand it's a difficult situation.'

'Not "difficult". I simply can't do it.' She leaned back in her chair and closed her eyes, rubbing them with the palms of her hands.

'Listen,' she began again, 'there *is* a reason I kept that file. That case stood out for me too. I always thought – well, maybe I'd rushed that one through, given up on that girl too soon. Regardless, my hands are tied now.'

'Ma'am, I understand your obligations, but this is a matter of life and death. Your information could—'

'I can't. No way.'

They sat staring at each other. Adam knew he should accept defeat and just be grateful he wasn't leaving in cuffs. He was about to rise and thank her for her time when she cleared her throat and spoke again.

'Can you tell me though, what happened to her? Is she okay?'

Now they were getting somewhere. He suddenly realized that she might work with him on it. If she felt guilty enough. If she didn't have to be implicated.

'Honestly, I don't know. That's part of what I want to find out. If I'm going to understand what happened, I need to know about her criminal history.'

'Criminal history? I see. Officer Wilson, this case was not—'

Then she stopped.

'Again, I wish I could help you with your investigation, but without a court order, I can't do a thing.' She was chewing on her lip now, not happy. She wanted to tell him.

Adam had an idea.

'You have the file there. Let me ask you this. When I called, did you check it? To refresh your memory?'

She sat up straight and adjusted her jacket. Her hand went up to her hair again. She was nervous. Disturbed. Ripe for this.

Without taking her eyes from his, she slid her hand under a stack of papers and pulled out a yellowed file with worn edges, putting it on top.

'I did, as a matter of fact.'

'And that's the one?'

'It might be.'

'Could I have some coffee, Ms. Martinez? I thought I smelled some when I was walking down the hall.' She didn't move a muscle. Adam was afraid to breathe. They understood each other perfectly.

She stood up slowly, not looking at him now.

'Of course. Excuse me. I'll be right back.'

She left the office, careful to close the door behind her. Without a second's hesitation, he grabbed the manila folder and flipped it open.

Adam sat there for a moment, stunned by what he saw. He couldn't move, but finally remembered himself, picked up his phone, and took a picture of each of the report's three pages. He rifled through it, expecting more. There'd been no arrest so unfortunately there were no photos and no prints. He closed the file and placed it back on her desk exactly where she'd left it.

She returned a few minutes later and slipped back behind the desk. She hadn't brought any coffee.

Adam's eyes watered. He hoped she wouldn't notice but she handed him a box of tissues, looking at him quizzically.

'Pretty sensitive for a police officer, aren't you?'

'Why'd you let her go?'

'I told you. I had to. I couldn't prove anything. The cops weren't interested. In the end I had to take her word for it when she recanted.'

She stopped, stared off in space for a few seconds, perhaps deciding whether to tell him something more.

'Honestly, it was one of the biggest mistakes of my career. I felt it in my gut, and yet I let her slip away.'

She paused.

'I hope you find her. And I hope she's okay.'

Adam stood up abruptly.

'Well, thank you for your time. I'll let you get back to it.'

He left without shaking her hand. He couldn't somehow. If that woman had done something then, right then – gone with her instincts, even just followed the absolutely standard protocol for chrissakes – none of the rest of it would have happened. Everything would be different.

He walked out, clutching his phone so hard his fingers were white, trying to process the ramifications of what he'd just learned, if it was even true.

Elsa Sanders, Laura Martin – whatever her name actually was – claimed she'd been abducted. She'd told another girl at school who had in turn told her parents. She'd changed her story later, yes, and then had obviously slipped through the cracks of the social services system. But what if she'd been telling the truth?

He'd seen in her file that she was born the same year as Abigail. It made him think. Their stories could have easily been the same. That could only mean that Laura's case had come to him for a reason. It suddenly made him see the facts through a different lens. She might be a murderer, but she was also a victim, and his past made him uniquely suited to parse through these complicated dynamics.

If it was true – if she *had* been abducted – then this case was more than a coincidence. It was his destiny.

CHAPTER 23

He was late, but that didn't surprise her. He'd been avoiding her again at school so she'd had to resort to leaving him notes in his locker. On this one she'd underlined 'important' three times and followed it with a line of exclamation marks. He'd left a note taped to hers the next day with just two letters: 'OK'.

These circumstances didn't bode well for a warm reception.

She'd let herself into Joy's apartment using the key they kept under the mat, and she sat on the couch with her shoes off and her feet tucked up beneath her. Finally the knob turned and in walked Reed, his expression inscrutable, detached. Despite herself, Cora felt her heart melt at the sight of him. Suddenly she felt she had to keep this baby no matter what, had to get more of his genetic material out into the world.

His attitude was so cold though, that her heart was sinking deeper by the minute. This was a fool's errand. She should have gone straight to the abortion clinic, kept him out of this. The news wouldn't change anything between them. She thought about running out the door. Keeping this her secret like everything else.

Still, there was a tiny part of her that held out hope that the fantasy would miraculously come true.

She smiled at him tentatively, testing the waters.

'Thanks for coming,' she said, gesturing for him to sit down beside her.

He dropped his backpack onto the floor with a thud and took off his jacket, threw it down beside her. He remained standing.

'What's this all about?' he said, taking out a pack of cigarettes. He didn't offer any to her, but lit one for himself. He blew the smoke toward her without bothering to apologize or even wave it off in another direction. It wasn't good for the baby, so she moved to the other part of the couch, out of its way.

'I have something important to tell you,' she said.

'Yeah, that's what I gathered from your note. Not just "important" but IMPORTANT. So, out with it.' He finally sat down, but on the other half of the sectional. He studied his fingernails and took another puff of his cigarette.

'I'm pregnant,' she blurted out. It wasn't the way she'd planned to tell him. She swallowed hard, terrified of his response. Her eyes began to hurt from not blinking.

He looked at her seriously for the first time.

'What? What are you saying?'

She just stared back at him. There wasn't much to explain. He sniffed.

'Are you claiming it's mine?' Oh, he was cold. So cold.

'Of course it's yours. What do you think I am?'

'I have no idea. I don't keep tabs on you. I don't even know where you live. What you do. For all I know, that's your father's kid.'

It was worse than a slap in the face. Worse than anything she might have imagined him saying.

'Well, trust me, it's yours.'

Reed's hands were jittery as he mashed the cigarette stub into an overflowing ashtray on the floor.

'I don't see how you could let this happen, Laura. I mean, that's pretty fucking stupid. What are you going to do about it?'

'Reed, I –' She moved toward him, tried to stroke his cheek, but he caught her wrist in his hand.

'Laura, this is serious.'

'Of course it's serious.'

'I mean, no more fucking around here. You have to deal with this now. How much money do you have?'

'Not a lot. Not enough.' She was starting to panic. What *was* she going to do now? She thought of what her father's face would look like when he heard this news. She didn't even know whether or not it was too late to have an abortion. She'd waited too long to deal with this situation and now everything was crumbling around her.

He ran his fingers through his hair. She'd never seen him like this.

'Jesus, Laura, you are making it impossible.' He stared at her for a minute. She couldn't read his expression. He sighed.

The door clicked open and Joy and Johnny sauntered in. Joy was obviously on speed, her fingers twitching as she twirled that infernal hair of hers. Johnny looked agitated, barely able to stand still. His face was flushed and his pupils dilated. Cora couldn't believe it. The worst timing ever.

'Why so serious?' Joy asked, a half-smile playing at her lips. No one said anything until the silence became awkward.

'She's pregnant,' Reed finally murmured.

Joy's eyes locked on his.

'Yours?' she asked through clenched teeth.

Reed shrugged.

Joy took a deep breath.

'You fucking asshole. You told me nothing was going on. And you –' she turned to Cora, her eyes two slits – 'who do you think you are?'

With a grunt of rage, Joy grabbed Cora by the collar of her shirt and yanked her up off the couch. She expertly dug her nails into the back of Cora's neck at some sort of pressure point, and with the other hand took hold of her ear, twisting it back. Pain shot through Cora's head with unexpected force. Cora picked up her backpack and tried to pull away, intending to run for it, but there was no getting loose. Joy had her in a death grip.

'Jesus, Joy, what are you doing? Hey, guys, come on, let's talk about this,' Cora screamed. She was used to violence, but she usually knew when to expect it. The disorientation was what shocked her now.

'Nothing to talk about, Laura. This won't do. It won't do at all. We'll have to take care of it.'

Reed and Joy looked at one another across the room until he nodded at her ever so slightly.

Joy led the way out the door with Cora in tow as the other two trailed behind. Cora struggled to pull away, but the more she moved, the more pain Joy inflicted on her ear. Cora flung her backpack at Joy's head in desperation, but Reed intercepted it. He yanked it out of her hands and slung it over his shoulder.

'Reed, what are you doing? Help me!' But he wouldn't look at her.

Johnny caught up to them and pinned her arms behind her back. She had no chance against the three of them, she realized, as she staggered along, trying to keep up the pace enough to stay upright.

They went through a wooden gate behind the apartment complex into a deserted, fenced-in yard. Even if the neighbors had been around, they'd never notice what was going on. This space was built for privacy, the tightly set boards of the fence at least six feet high.

Off in the distance somewhere a dog was barking. Cora heard a car drive past the front of the building.

In a panic, Cora's eyes scanned the windows across the back of the building hoping to find someone to pay attention. The curtains were all closed, except for a flutter of fabric on the third floor. As soon as she noticed it though, those too were hurriedly drawn. 'Someone' wanted to stay out of it.

She wondered if anyone would help her if she yelled loud and long enough. Not in this neighborhood. Maybe not anywhere.

She looked right and left, searching for another exit, a direction to run if she could break free. The backyard was scrubby, with patches of newly sprouted grass trying to poke through here and there between expanses of mud and rock. In one corner, there was a small pile of gravel and a stack of cement blocks, half of them broken. The only way out was the way they'd come in.

It was the absolute end of the world.

Joy pushed Cora down onto the ground on her stomach. Cora fleetingly thought of the baby's safety, but then she knew it was true: there wasn't going to be any baby. They'd make sure of that.

Johnny kneeled down beside her, pushed her face into the wet mud and held it there. She thought she might suffocate – she couldn't get any air – but he released her head just as she started to black out.

Reed leaned down on one knee and whispered into her ear soft and close the way he used to. But this time there were no sweet nothings.

'You should have listened to me about sex, Laura. You dirty, filthy whore,' he hissed.

And then he walked away, still carrying her backpack, leaving Joy and Johnny alone with her in the back lot.

CHAPTER 24

Cora counted the steps in a whisper as she carried the tray up to the girl's room. For weeks she had held on to her resolve to stay on the Path of Righteousness, but without James there to reinforce the message, she'd felt it gradually slipping away. She hated herself for her weakness, but she could not keep her thoughts clean. James insisted that the girl had been sent for a divine purpose, yet Cora couldn't help but feel bitter serving her day in and day out.

The morning's rations consisted of a bowl of scraps from Cora's meals over the last two days. Fat she'd cut off from the bone and fried in a pan with her leftover spinach. Oatmeal that was hardened into a dry chewy mound. A cup of water she'd taken from the rain barrel, two tiny fruit flies drowned and floating on top. It was her one solace: she'd make sure the girl was never given any special treatment, would never rise above the animals in the barn. They at least provided sustenance. This girl only took from her, confused her, and messed with her mind.

Cora rapped on the door to get the girl's attention as she peered in through the window in the door. She waited for her to get into position, but the girl was still lying on the bed, her sheets wadded up on the floor next to it. Cora knocked again. She'd move. She knew better than to ignore her.

Finally, she saw the girl slowly drag herself upright, looking dazed.

True, it was awfully early in the morning but why should this girl get to sleep in? This wasn't a Hilton or some fancy day spa. The girl had probably seen plenty of those places during her pampered young life and didn't know anything different. Well, now her horizons were expanded.

Cora swung open the door with one forceful push. Immediately, the smell of vomit hit her full in the face. She covered her nose and mouth with her apron, got out of there fast, and slammed the door behind her.

Disgusting animal, she thought, as she bolted the locks back again.

'What have you done, girl?' she yelled through the slot.

'I . . . think I'm sick,' she barely managed to choke out.

Cora gritted her teeth. There was always something to slow her down around here.

She set the tray on the floor, kicking it over into the corner, and started back downstairs to get a bucket and some rags, muttering to herself the whole way.

This girl was up to something but Cora Jenkins would not fall for any chicanery. She knew how conniving girls could be.

Returning with the bucket and a pile of tattered rags, Cora hauled them over to the bed and plunked them down on the floor, splashing water everywhere. She wasn't stupid enough to bring in chemical cleaning products though. That's probably just what the girl wanted. She'd try to dash them into Cora's eyes so she could steal the keys and her knife. She probably intended to turn the tables on Cora and leave *her* locked in the vomit-filled room. Cora wouldn't fall for that though. She was much too smart for this know-nothing kid.

She stood towering over the girl hunched on the bed, staring down at her near-lifeless, shivering form.

She did look awfully pale. But still.

'Clean it up,' Cora said over her shoulder as she turned abruptly and walked away.

Leaning against the wall in the hallway, Cora counted once again. She didn't want to look. This was the last thing she would be able to deal with when she had so many chores to do. No time for this nonsense.

On the count of thirty, though, she forced herself to check in through the window again.

The girl was trying, she'd give her that. She'd rolled off the bed onto the floor and was wiping up the dull greyish liquid, dry-heaving all the while. Cora rolled her eyes, but even still she felt a fleeting pang of – what was it – pity?

No, she'd push that away if that's what it was, coming back on her again. This girl was faking it.

Then suddenly a different thought occurred to Cora. She felt the blood drain out of her face as she tightened her crossed arms, digging her nails into their fleshiest parts. Her head spun.

Perhaps it had happened. The Revelation.

The girl swiped half-heartedly at the floor, obviously pretending to be too weak for this task, but Cora would make her finish it before she went in. She'd wait outside until she was done, even if it meant postponing her own relief.

She pounded on the door again.

'Hurry up. And get it done right. Clean up every last bit.' Cora's voice was unexpectedly shaky.

The girl tried to hurry, but then, with one great spasm, she opened her mouth and a torrent of fresh vomit spewed across the room.

Cora winced. *There was so much of it.*

She shook her head with exasperation, clenching her teeth.

At this rate she'd be cleaning all day. This girl would never finish the job before the vomit dried and Cora would be forced to take over. She'd have to tie the girl to the bed and soak it up with rags right in front of her. What a victory for the girl, watching Cora scrub the floor at her feet.

Her patience was running out. She had to go in. She had to know.

She went back in, locking the door behind her. She reminded herself to be careful, that she had a live one on her hands. Cora grasped her switchblade in her pocket. She was skilled with it, so the girl better not get any ideas.

As their eyes met across the room, Cora saw the fear flash in the girl's face. Oh, yes, she'd better be afraid. That showed good sense at least.

Cora approached her slowly, watching her continue to wipe up the wet mess around her, but Cora couldn't wait. She grabbed the girl off the floor by her stick-thin arm and shoved her onto the bed, ignoring the slippery tiles beneath her feet. She held her down easily with one arm and yanked up her sweatshirt. The girl fought her with her last waning bit of strength, kicking and struggling to sit up, but Cora was stronger and nearly twice her size. She overpowered her with little effort.

Yet it was Cora who shrank back in horror when she saw the skeletal structure beneath the baggy shirt. No longer the healthy specimen James had brought in, she was now skin and bones, her pale flesh marked with cuts and bruises.

And there it was. Exactly what Cora had dreaded to find. She had been lazy, had not done enough to save James from his mistake. It was all wrong. Between the jutting hipbones was a tiny bulge in the girl's abdomen: she was pregnant. The Revelation had come to pass. So she *was* the one after all.

Cora's thoughts flashed to Reed's blue eyes, her own bulging belly that her sweater didn't quite cover, the imaginary child of her daydreams. *She* was the one who was supposed to have the child. Not this girl. She pushed it all out of her mind before those memories took over.

The girl had given up the fight. She lay there, her lungs laboring heavily, staring up at Cora in sheer terror. So she understood the situation.

Without thinking, Cora hauled her arm back and slapped the girl's face with all her might. A red mark flamed up on her cheek instantly and the girl's hand flew to the spot. Her face wrinkled up in pain and then there they were, those inevitable tears. Could she never stop crying?

Cora ignored the waterworks and leaned in close. Their eyes locked. So this was it. They were bound together now.

The girl buried her face in her hands, sobbing hysterically. Then she stood up suddenly, positioning herself to retch again. Cora jumped out of the way, but the girl managed to swallow it back.

She was a mess. Her hair was tangled in the tears and snot on her face. Her eyes were like those of a feral animal, trapped and ready to attack. Cora knew what was coming if she didn't handle it just right. If she got too frantic, she wouldn't be rational, and wouldn't act in her own best interests. She might take risks that were stupid and that would make her dangerous.

Cora had to calm this girl down, for her own safety. She pulled her to the bed and sat beside her.

'Shh. Try to relax. Breathe.' It disgusted her to use such soothing tones on someone she hated so much. It nearly killed her, but she knew what she had to do. She gently pulled the long strands of golden hair off the girl's sticky face, until slowly her sobbing subsided to an intermittent sniffle.

This girl was usually such a mouthy one, talking at her every chance she got. Trying to 'make friends', or win her over or whatever senseless ineffectual ploy the witchy thing was trying to accomplish. But look at her now. Now she didn't have much to say for herself. Cora couldn't help but feel a small triumph, even in the midst of this disaster.

Cora was at a loss though. She'd held the Revelation so dear for so long. Two years ago, James had woken her in the middle of the night and dragged her out under the stars. His eyes ablaze, he'd explained that he'd had a vision of their Divine Child, that he understood how it would all come to pass. He'd gripped her shoulders and gotten down on his knees before her. He said it would be a heavy burden, but he knew she had the strength to bear it. She had been in awe then, impressed that he believed in her. She had thought only of the Divine Family, of the new community they would build there at the farm. She'd imagined how she and James would sit at the head of the table, a heavenly king and queen presiding over a new paradise like the one that once was. Her spirit had soared.

But now that it had come to pass – now that the Revelation was fulfilled – she didn't feel the way she was supposed to feel. She felt no joy. Her spirit was not uplifted. Her heart was as unclean as it had ever been.

She only knew she could not let this girl replace her. She would never be her servant, letting her take her man, her house, and her place at the head of the table.

The girl leaned toward Cora, apparently mistaking her insincere gestures for true compassion. She rested her smelly head on Cora's shoulder and wrapped her limp arm around Cora's neck. She sobbed into Cora's dress, clutching it in desperation.

'Help me,' she said in a whisper. 'Please help me.'

Cora stiffened.

She would kill this girl. She would kill her and her little bastard brat.

Nevertheless, ever so slowly, Cora slipped her arm around the girl and held her close, the tears gathering in her own eyes as she rocked her back and forth, back and forth.

They stayed like that for a long time.

CHAPTER 25

Adam sat stiffly in a plastic chair that barely felt capable of holding his weight. He shifted, feeling the molded seat bend precariously, never taking his eyes off the lock-up. He expected the bars to slide open at any minute. It was noisy in there, the background a near-constant clanging of metal against metal punctuated by intermittent loud buzzes that rang out as soon as he stopped expecting them. Laughter, prodigious weeping, and hollow screams of frustration echoed down the hall. This place seemed more like a madhouse than what it was: the Connecticut Women's Correctional Facility.

Finally he saw a flash of tan sleeve with her maimed hand jutting out from the end. He'd read about it in the newspaper accounts of her trial. Something to do with machinery her victim had set in motion when groveling for his life. The poor sod had gotten that small revenge on her. According to the forensic expert's testimony, he'd almost certainly managed to witness the damage before he bled out.

At last, she sat down before him on the other side of the bars and pulled a cigarette out of her pocket with her twisted hand.

Joy Marcione. In the wasted, worn-out flesh.

Her hair burst from her head in uneven patches, each spiky protuberance dyed a different color of the rainbow. Her bugged-out eyes were ringed with red, and the left one was black and blue.

'Got these,' she said, lifting the pack of cigarettes he'd sent her. 'Thanks for that. Now gotta light?' Her twisted smile curled up over the side of her scarred cheek as she leaned back in the chair, propping one foot up under her. He knew he wasn't supposed to reach through the white-painted bars between them, but as he glanced around he saw that this rule was widely disregarded. One seat over, a heavily tattooed gangbanger with bulging arms put his lighter through the bars to the woman across from him. Adam followed suit.

Once they were settled in, he took out his notebook and wrote her name and the date in careful block letters at the top of the page. He looked up at her, holding back his smile. She hardly seemed the girl Laura Martin had described in her letter, the intimidating, tough girl who showed no mercy. He had to remind himself that she'd pulled down a life sentence for a notoriously gruesome homicide. Looks were obviously deceiving.

In all her police interviews, she'd insisted she knew nothing. But after reading Laura's letter, he knew that couldn't be the case. They'd all been so close. She had to know more.

'Thanks for agreeing to talk to me,' he began. 'As I mentioned in my letter – well, letters – I've been investigating the Stillwater murders and it's of vital importance that I track down Laura Martin.' He shifted in his chair, watching to see if her face changed when she heard the name.

She laughed.

'Well, yeah, I guess you are. Obviously. Laura Martin. How I miss that bitch.' She blew out the smoke over her shoulder behind her, her useless pinky twitching as she flicked the cigarette ash onto the linoleum tiles. 'If you find her, please tell her I said hi. And that I wish she'd visit me some time. Of course –' she laughed gruffly as she blew out more smoke, this time forgetting to aim it away from him – 'I guess if *you* find her, Mr. Cop-man, it will mean she might be joining me in here and I can say hi myself.'

Adam suddenly pictured himself sitting there, waiting for Abigail to take the seat across from him through the bars. He imagined how his mother would have felt if that's how her story ended, in jail, her moral path diverted by a one-in-a-million tragedy. He pushed the notion away. Why was he thinking like that?

'Are you being facetious?' he asked, staring at her long nails painted pitch black.

'Facetious. Now isn't that a fancy word?' She smiled, rubbing her upper teeth with her tongue, then licking her lips slowly. 'Dude, I'm totally giving you a hard time. How could I like someone who killed my best friends?' She leaned forward. 'I fucking hate her.'

'You think she killed your friends?'

'I know she did.'

'How?'

She smiled.

'Now for that I'm going to have to hear what's on offer. I'm not a snitch. I've kept my mouth shut this long. What makes you think I'd tell you now?'

Adam shifted in his seat. He was in no position to offer anything, but she didn't have to know that. And besides, all that would change if he solved the crime.

'If you tell me what happened now and agree to testify in court, I'll talk to the D.A. and the parole board. I can't promise anything, but I think I can get them to give you another hearing. I understand it didn't go so well last time.'

She blew a ring of smoke in the air.

'Yeah, they don't exactly like me there.'

She appeared to be weighing her options.

'Listen, I'll tell you what you want to know, Mr. Cop-man, but I won't testify in court without a written deal on the table.'

He nodded. 'Good enough.'

She sat up straight and looked him in the eye.

'The thing is I *saw* her, right after. She was so naïve. She thought I'd help her in spite of everything. She didn't have anywhere else to go, I guess.' She stubbed out her cigarette but left it on the shelf to cool for later.

Adam's heart raced. She really did know something. Finally, he might have real evidence that would be admissible in court. She wasn't the most reliable witness, but combined with what else he'd gathered, he could cinch this case. Still, he didn't feel as happy as he'd expected at the idea of locking up some poor abducted girl who'd been hauled around the country by a madman. It wasn't the victory he'd been imagining all these years.

'Why don't you tell me exactly what happened?'

'Well, you see, I got lucky. I was supposed to be at the apartment that day with Reed and Johnny. We were meeting there right after school. But what do you figure, I got detention – I, uh, set Misty Runyon's hair on fire during third period. Aw, come on,' she said, seeing his look. 'Not very much, just the ends. Turns out it was the best juvenile act I ever committed in my life. So, anyway, I sent Lila over there to let them know, to tell them to wait for me, and then we'd go down to the dam to meet Stokes.'

'Lila McIntyre, you mean?'

'There but for the grace of God. Boy, do I feel guilty about that one. Pure victim of circumstance. Wrong place, wrong time. She didn't even *know* Laura.' She took another drag on her cigarette, not seeming sorry at all.

'And Stokes?'

Joy froze.

'Did I say Stokes? I don't think I said that.'

'First name?'

'Um, no. I think you misunderstood.' She glared at Adam pointedly, but he wrote the name down and underlined it three times. That name didn't appear in any of the case files. He'd find him one way or another.

'So *anyway*, right after detention, I headed straight for the apartment like I'd planned. If only you could have seen my face when I opened that door.' She tried to laugh, but nothing came out except a coughing fit. She waved the smoke away from her face.

'You could barely even see any skin, there was so much blood everywhere. Just lumps of stuff – like tissue and guts and, and *innards* – strewn all over the room. The blood had soaked into the carpet, under all that trash – we hadn't kept the place so neat, you know? There was a big pile of Mars bar wrappers and a couple of rats were . . . Well, I'll spare you,' she said, looking at Adam's puckered face.

'I always thought of myself as ready for anything, but to be honest, I kinda freaked, you know? Like, I mean, the smell.' She wrinkled up her nose. 'But then I thought, damn, this is my apartment and I, um, at the time, had a little bit of a juvie record. I didn't want to get roped into that shit. And those guys, I mean, they were goners. They didn't, like, need an ambulance or anything. So I ran home and stayed put.'

'And what about Laura?'

'Like I said, she came by the house after, asking for my help. She could barely talk she was so freaked out – but I mean, come on, she had blood all over her. It was a fucking mess.'

'How did she think you could help her?'

'She said she was running away from her father. She wanted me to hide her or give her some money or something. She didn't exactly have a plan.'

Adam nodded, encouraging her to go on.

'We were both completely wigging out. I mean, for real. Those were the first dead bodies I'd ever seen. And you know, I *knew* them. They were my *friends*. Who knows, everything might have turned out differently for me if I hadn't been so, you know, traumatized.' She winked. 'I tried that at the parole hearing. Got nowhere.'

'Did you help her?'

'No way.'

'Why didn't you call the cops?'

'Listen, with my record, the cops would have assumed I was involved, especially if they found that blood all over my house. That was kind of a brilliant move on her part, now that I think about it.'

'So what happened then? She just left?'

'Yeah. I never saw her again. She was lucky because it happened right before spring break. By the time we got back to school, the cops had some other theory. A drug deal gone bad or something. I was just relieved no one was pointing the finger at me.'

'Why do you think she did it?'

Joy shrugged.

'Couldn't say. Although to be honest, the girl was totally obsessed with Reed. Always following us around, throwing herself at him like a damn fool. She totally *stalked* him.'

'And he wasn't interested?'

'No way. I mean, he liked the attention, sure. But he would never go for a girl like her. Never. He was something special and she was just a nobody. I guess she finally figured that out and snapped.' She paused. 'Such a fucking waste.'

At that, a buzzer went off and the inmates stood to go. Joy picked up the end of her other cigarette and shoved it in her pocket.

'See ya, Mr. Cop-man. Good luck finding my old friend.' She leaned down close to the bars. 'I suggest you look in hell.'

CHAPTER 26

Julie could no longer smell the vomit and if she had, she wouldn't have cared. All she thought about was the abomination growing in her belly. She paced the room, wearing down the layer of dirt on the dingy tiles with her bare feet as she crossed and re-crossed the floor, muttering to herself. She held a hand over her stomach, not protectively, but to convince herself it was really happening.

She'd folded up the Pooh blanket and shoved it under the pillow. Poor Pooh shouldn't have to hear this.

'Okay, okay, Julie, it's time to face facts. You are finally in hell. You thought it was bad before but what did you do to deserve *this*?'

Maybe she could have handled the rest, adapted, made do. Maybe she could have learned to live with their grotesque routine, become some kind of mindless zombie going slowly insane upstairs in this decrepit house. But this. This was too much.

She couldn't even think of it as a real baby. She could only picture it as *him*. A monster, a scary fetus-beast with claw hands and his laughing, apelike face. Oh, yes, the devil was inside her.

What made it worse was that Julie had always wanted children, but it wasn't supposed to be like this. She should have been thinking about vitamins and pre-natal yoga, reading *What to Expect*. It wasn't supposed to be this excrescence, nothing more than a tumor spreading poison within her.

'Wait a minute, Julie. Just wait. Can you use this situation to your advantage? What if this is what he wanted from you all along?' She shuddered with disgust. 'What if you're some sort of vessel for his tainted seed and now you've succeeded in your mission?' The thought made her want to throw up. She ran her hands up and down her face, rubbing her skin hard.

'Julie, stay tough. You have to think about this.'

She needed her parents here to talk her through it. She wanted someone to help her decide: a friend, a therapist, a guidance counselor. But no, she had to take this one on her own.

'So okay, think. What if you pretend to go along with it? Tell him you feel different now that the pregnancy has changed everything and the power of his words, of his – what does he call them, damn it – his "ecstatic lunar prophecies" hit you all at once, full-force, and you are honored to be carrying the heir to his heavenly kingdom. Is that the play here?'

But what if she was wrong? What if this was part of some ritual sacrifice?

Or maybe this is why there was blood between the tiles. What if, in this room, pregnancy was a death sentence?

Should she threaten or plead? Fight or accept? Her mind was spinning too much to know which tack to take.

'Okay then, play it out. Say everything fails. Say the child is born. It isn't going to live in this room, is it? They wouldn't let you keep it, would they?' She choked up. No, they would most certainly take it.

She hated to imagine what would happen to a baby raised by those two. After all, this child was half her. No matter what, they'd surely torture it in their own sick manner. Whatever good spirit was left from her DNA would be twisted out and turned into something evil. And then a part of her would be out there in the world, a little satellite self, committing atrocities alongside them.

'No, no, they must never take the child. I can't let them take it.' His line could not be allowed to continue.

She knew in her heart there was only one conclusion. She hadn't wanted to allow herself to think it, but the time had come. She sat down on the bed, chilled to the bone by the realization. If she couldn't get out in time, there was only one Plan B. She'd have to kill it.

The concept couldn't be abstract either. She had to plan the logistics. It had to happen the instant it was born, so there'd be no time for feelings, no time to second-guess. She'd snap its neck or smother it with a pillow. She'd seen newborns before. They were so fragile that she was afraid to hold them. It couldn't be hard to do but she would have to practice the act in her mind every day so that when the time came, she could do it without thinking.

'Come on, Julie, it will be *his* neck, his baby mouth and nose to be stopped up.'

She'd tell them it was stillborn. And then let come what may. If they killed her in turn, well, she would deserve it. She'd willingly put her head on the block. The act was wrong, but it must be completed.

'I'll be a murderer,' she whispered. The word made her feel sick.

She lay on the floor in the dark in the middle of her room, with one cheek pressed to the tiles, sobbing.

Her mind was settled though. There was no alternative. No going back.

With that decision, a sort of calm descended over her. She understood then the feeling of the executioner who knows that though his task is horrific, it is the only lawful and moral path. The killing would be a sacrifice to the gods of justice. It would be against nature, but it must be done.

Death was growing inside her. Death, not life.

'And so it is written,' she whispered.

CHAPTER 27

'Car accident,' Cora said, not meeting anyone's eyes back at school three weeks later. 'Just got out of the hospital.' They didn't ask questions. One look at her face and the admin staff had stamped her hall pass with 'Excused' in red ink and sent her on her merry way.

If she'd been anyone else, someone friendly and popular, someone who belonged to the history club or the marching band, she'd surely be getting warm hugs, tender consolations in the halls, and get-well notes taped to her locker door, just like Millie Mason when she'd broken her arm in a cheerleading fall or Cy Parsons when his older brother had died in a small-plane crash.

But that wasn't the case for her. She was invisible for the most part and if she got any notice at all, it wasn't the welcome kind. Sometimes a couple of sophomore girls would brush past her, walking close together like Siamese twins, their hands joined over their faces as they murmured to one another.

Once a football player got really close, and whispered in her ear.

'Slut,' he hissed and then high-fived his grinning buddies who'd watched him fulfill their dare.

Maybe they all knew the truth, maybe they didn't. Either way, Cora had lost her thin sheen of social cover when she'd been so forcibly and literally kicked out of her wayward little clique.

Now she had to get out of Stillwater.

'You said yourself it was time to leave,' she pleaded with her father at breakfast.

'I did. And we will. Soon enough.' He swigged down his second beer of the morning. He hadn't touched his eggs.

'What about Florida?' she pushed. 'You always said you wanted to live somewhere warm. We can camp at a National Park.'

He leaned toward her, smiling.

'We'll go when I'm good and ready.' He was enjoying this.

She knew how his mind worked. She'd made a mistake letting him see what she wanted. Now he could torment her with it, play his little games.

She stood up to clear the table, brooding over how he'd barely remarked on her bruises or her hobbling gait. He was oblivious to her situation. She'd have to up the ante or they'd stay there forever.

She threw the plates into the sink and jerked the faucet handle to full blast.

She knew what she had to do. She would tell him. That was how it worked sometimes. She had to blow everything up and climb out of the ashes, born anew. It was the only power she had.

She sat back down across from him. When he cracked open the third beer, she took a deep breath and gripped the edge of her seat, her heart thudding out of control. She had to do it before she lost her nerve.

Say it.

'You don't understand,' she forced out. 'They killed my baby.'

There. She'd done it.

But when his cold eyes flicked over to her, she experienced a moment of sheer panic. She watched his face, waiting for the explosion, ready to raise her hands up in defense against him.

But he said nothing, did nothing. He only drummed his fingers slowly on the table as his gaze drifted off into the distance behind her. She couldn't read the thoughts that must be swirling behind his blank eyes and that terrified her a million times more than his usual temper tantrums. She'd never seen him so somber, so controlled.

'Explain,' he said at last.

With a shaking voice, she told him the whole story, bit by horrible bit. She begged for forgiveness. She cried. She swore she'd never do anything wrong again. She'd be dutiful. She'd be good. If they could just leave Stillwater and pretend nothing had happened, everything would be okay.

Finally, he'd had enough. He held up his hand to stop her.

'I have some things to take care of. Then we'll go. We'll head east. To Virginia.'

Cora sighed with relief and wiped the sweat from her brow with the edge of her sleeve. She closed her eyes and gave a silent prayer of thanks. He hadn't even hit her. Maybe he had pity for her after all. Maybe he really loved her.

That day she started packing her things.

Then two weeks later, everything came crashing down.

As she walked home from school, she noticed a light glowing from the trailer window. She slowed her pace. Who was in there? Her father usually didn't stick around during the day. Had someone broken in?

Why now, when they were so close to leaving town? Couldn't they make it those last few days without more drama?

She went around the back to peer through the dirty window over the bed. She heard glasses clink. Putting the plastic bag she used now for her books under the back tire, she returned to the door, ready to fight. Everything she owned was in there.

She swung open the door, fists up.

It was her father. He stood there, expressionless, dressed in dingy work overalls with a beat-up satchel slung over his shoulder. This couldn't be good.

'You're late,' he said. 'We have things to do.'

He grabbed her by the arm and dragged her out front to the truck. He'd already disconnected it from the trailer and put the keys in the ignition.

'Get in,' he said, not looking up. He threw the truck into gear and they bumped along the rocky road out to the highway.

'Where are we going?' She was terrified. He had that dead look in his eye.

'You'll see.'

He drove relatively steadily, considering the amount of booze she could smell coming off him.

They crossed the bridge into town and made their way down Main Street. It had rained earlier that day so the streets were slick and dark and drops clung to the trees dotting the sidewalks. The brick buildings of downtown huddled protectively over her. She felt that as long as they stayed there, in the comfort of the bustling commercial district, she was safe.

They passed the enormous cinderblock edifice of the Stillwater High School. In a way, she hated to leave all this behind. Everything could have been different if things had not gone so wrong with Reed. She wouldn't have to be a nomad anymore. She could have put down roots.

Then her father turned left and Cora's heart began to pound. This was the way to Joy's apartment. But her father didn't know about that, did he? How could he? Unless that's how he'd been spending his time recently. He was smarter than he seemed and his petty criminal mind sometimes yielded results.

Why had she told him their names? Had she been angrier than she'd realized? Was she secretly hoping he'd exact his revenge? Whatever she'd felt at the time, she did not want this to happen.

'Father? Where are we going? Please tell me.' She felt desperate.

They were coming up on the right turn, but he was going too fast to make it. She took a deep breath. Maybe she was wrong, maybe he had some other destination in mind.

Then at the last second, he jerked the steering wheel and took the right after all. There could be no mistaking it now. Panicked, she glanced down at his satchel.

'Father, what's in the bag? What are you planning to do?'

Outside the window, each block was progressively seedier than the last until she could see Joy's apartment building in the distance. Her mind flashed back to the last time she'd been there. The horror. Her breath quickened. She couldn't face it. She never wanted to see it again. She felt dizzy and her hands started to shake.

'Father, I can't go back there. Please don't make me go back there.' She whimpered like a kicked dog.

'Shut up. You need to face this. No child of mine is going to be humiliated like that.'

'No, no, I don't need revenge. I'm fine. I'll just avoid them. I'll be more careful. I'll come right home after school every day. It was wrong of me to try to make friends. I promise I'll never do it again. Just me and you from now on, Father, you hear? I know that's for the best.' The useless chatter was pouring out of her.

With shaking hands, she grabbed the satchel and flipped it open, rummaging inside.

Her head rang. The bag contained only three items: a hammer, a pair of gloves, and the butcher knife – the one she'd always carefully hidden from her father. He must have known where it was all along.

'Father, this is crazy. We can't go in there with this. Even if we threaten them we could end up in jail. Remember what happened in Nevada?'

'Shut up, Cora. I know what I'm doing. And I know what *you're* doing. This is your mess and you're going to fix it.'

'What are you talking about?' She was screaming now. She grabbed his arm to try to force him to turn the wheel. He shook it loose from her and smacked her hard against the head with the palm of his hand. He turned to face her, taking his eyes off the road. The truck veered wildly, nearly running onto the sidewalk as the front tire bounced off the curb. His eyes flashed and spittle dribbled from his mouth.

'You do as I say. It's him or you, do you hear me?'

She shrank back into the narrow space between the ripped vinyl seat and the door, cowering in fear. What was he planning? How had she brought this tragedy down onto her head?

And then the moment had come. They arrived at the apartment. He pulled in and ripped the bag out of her hands. Without a word, he got out of the truck, walked around back to the bed and lifted out a large coil of thin rope.

He flung the passenger door open.

Paralyzed, she couldn't – she wouldn't move. She'd have no part in this. There was still some chance she could escape, run away from her father, yell at Reed to get the hell out of there.

But he grabbed her roughly by the arm and yanked her out of the truck. He was strong and alcohol only made him stronger. He handed her the twisted circle of rope and leaned in close to her ear, his hot breath on her cheek.

'You've brought shame on us, Cora. You're a disgrace. Whatever happens here is your fault. You come with me now, or I can promise you your life won't be worth living. You think they did something to you? Wait until you see what I'll do.'

She had to ignore her fear of him. There was more at stake for her than a few bruises.

'This is a bad idea, Father. If they arrest you, they'll check your prints and match them against all those other . . . situations. You can't go to jail. What will I do?'

'That's why I'm not going to do anything. You are.'

Cora felt her whole body go cold.

He pulled out the gloves and squeezed his fingers into them.

When she wouldn't budge from her spot on the sidewalk, he drew his arm back, balling his hand into a tight fist. She winced and covered her face with her arms, terrified of it landing on her still-delicate flesh.

'Come on,' he said through clenched teeth.

She followed him, her feet like lead. Afraid to go forward, afraid to run. Maybe she could get control of things once they were inside. She had no choice but to keep letting him drag her forward. She had to think. She had to find a solution before events unfolded too quickly to stop.

Her father knocked on the door, but there was no answer.

Thank God, she thought. They usually came here every day, but maybe for once in her life things were in her favor. If she could have prayed in earnest, she would have been on her knees then and there. She counted silently in her head. One, two, three, four . . . at ten, her heart was surging. They were safe.

'There's no one here, Father. Let's go. We'll come back another time,' she pleaded.

He didn't look at her, just stared at the door, clenching and unclenching his fists as if willing himself passage.

'Please. They didn't come today.' She pulled at his sleeve.

Then suddenly the door creaked opened. And Reed Lassiter stood smiling before them.

CHAPTER 28

Cora stood in the dark over the sleeping girl, gripping her knife. She'd been there too long already, willing herself on. Her hands trembled uncontrollably, but otherwise she couldn't move.

She'd come here with a purpose, she reminded herself. *She had to do it.*

The girl rolled over onto her side, murmuring in her sleep, her face half-buried in the pillow. How Cora longed to stop up her red blooming flower of a mouth. To erase her entirely and forget this whole episode.

Yet the task had seemed easier from the other room.

She stood still for a minute more, screwing up her courage, but picturing the knife piercing that smooth pink flesh forced her mind back to that day in Stillwater. The raw grunt of pain as the knife plunged in. The metallic smell of blood as it congealed in thick, sticky pools on the floor. The shock in his eyes.

She shivered and thrust the switchblade back in her pocket, deploring her weakness.

She sighed. But what else could she do?

James would return soon and then what? What if he cast her out entirely now that the girl was giving him the child she never could?

Where would she go? How would she live?

Her two suitcases were buried at the edge of the farthest field, placed there as part of their original escape plan. They contained so little though – a few items of clothing and some canned food – only enough to keep her going for a week. Only he knew where the emergency funds were hidden.

She knew she must have faith that James would remember the Revelation in all its glorious detail. It was written that she was joined with him, their souls entwined for all eternity. She was the Wife. He would remember that, surely.

But the girl was beautiful, or rather, would be again if restored to health. She wasn't stupid like the other one. That throwaway girl would never have satisfied James. She wouldn't have lasted a day.

But this one.

Cora must make sure she understood her place. It was her only recourse.

She leaned in close to the dozing girl until their faces were mere inches apart. She held still a moment, listening to the girl's even breathing, smelling her unwashed smell, feeling the faint heat coming off her body.

'Wake up,' she said suddenly.

The girl, startled out of sleep, bolted upright, and, seeing Cora, scuttled to the corner where the wall met the bed, bundling herself into a ball.

Cora flicked on the light.

'Get into position,' she snapped, determined to keep her under total control tonight.

The girl obeyed instantly. Though dazed, she lifted her arms beside her head and crossed her ankles.

'I have something important to say to you,' she began.

The girl nodded slightly, as if she weren't sure whether such a gesture was permitted.

'You and I, we are meant to bear what comes to pass. To do our duty.' The girl's face showed no expression, yet Cora could only imagine the condemnation brewing beneath it. This girl was always judging, always plotting and scheming. 'Even now that the Revelation has gone wrong.'

'Yes, it's certainly all gone wrong,' the girl agreed sullenly.

'It's my fault. I failed James. Because of my youthful transgressions, I could not give him a child. Do you see how we are punished for our sins – though the dawn of restitution be long in coming, the punishment will arrive?'

The girl sniffed, her look suddenly steely.

'My punishment *has* arrived.'

Cora ignored her impudence.

'I know you judge me. I know what you think. My house was not supposed to be like this though. Everything was supposed to be different when we got the farm. We were to gather a new group of Followers here, to live in peace upon the land.' Cora's voice dropped as she let her mind slip back to that other time. 'Instead the Followers never came and James became impatient. He said we must grow the Divine Family another way.'

At that, the girl began to whimper.

'The Revelation came to him in the night. We would find a girl whose body was young and fertile. Through the mystery of the universe, the Divine Child would be ours.'

Cora clutched her own belly, there where her child's heart had once beaten. It was too much for her. The Revelation seemed so different from the other side of it.

Suddenly overcome by the enormity of it all, she fell to her knees, clasped her hands together, and cast her eyes up to the ceiling. In that moment, she forgot her resolve, her anger, and even her exalted role.

'If only I had not sinned, none of this would have come to pass.'

Out of the corner of her eye, she saw that the girl too had dropped to the floor, daring to defy Cora's instructions. Cora couldn't think about that. The girl crept closer to her, inching her way over, testing the waters. Cora let her do it. She was tired, worn out. Nothing mattered anymore.

The girl snaked her arm around Cora's shoulders and stroked her face. Cora jerked back, but then let her continue. It was soothing. It felt good. No one had touched her with kindness in ages. She thought of Reed's arms around her, his voice in her ear.

She'd been alone for so long.

The girl's eyes shone bright with concern, but her look made Cora uneasy. She turned away from her, her glance sweeping the space instead.

'I deserved to watch him build this room, board by board. To desecrate my house,' she mumbled, settling her gaze on the window covered in thick planks.

The girl held her tighter.

'It's okay,' she said quietly. 'It's okay.'

Cora could feel the girl's heartbeat through the layers of their clothes as she sank slightly into her embrace. So like the steady thud under Reed's warm skin that night at the dam. How nice it would be to allow herself this comfort.

But, no, not from her.

She pushed the girl away. She didn't need her. She sat up straight, smoothing her clothes.

'Reed would have laughed at all this,' she muttered. 'He and the others, if they were still alive.' She shook her head. 'If only he'd wanted the child, I could have saved them both.'

'Reed? Who is Reed?'

'Hush. Don't you dare say his name. You are not worthy.'

'What child?' the girl whispered. 'Did you and Reed have a child? What happened to them? You can tell me.'

Embarrassed to have said so much, Cora grabbed the girl by the shoulders and dug her fingers into the folds of her sweatshirt. Yanking her up to her feet, she held her face in between her hands and squeezed hard. The girl groaned.

'Forget about that. *This* child is not yours, do you hear me? You are a mere vessel with no claim. It is written that James and I are one. 'The Wife suffers, but in suffering finds her Great Reward.' Do you understand me?'

The girl nodded, the fear flashing onto her face again, restored as if by magic to its proper state.

'Yes, yes, I understand,' she said, nodding eagerly. 'I'm learning to accept, just as you say.'

Cora stood staring at her, panting. She felt calmer now that it was out there between them, now that she could see the girl begin to comply. Everything would be okay if the girl understood, if she would cooperate.

Cora pushed her roughly onto the bed and sat down next to her. She needed to calm down. She breathed slowly and deliberately, felt her pulse returning to normal. She wrapped her arms around her body and rocked gently back and forth. It was going to be fine. Nothing had happened. James didn't even know yet. There was time to sort it out.

She turned slowly to face the girl, studied her shriveled body beside her, the color drained from her face, the shine of her hair dulled. She was watching Cora intently, obviously frightened. Perhaps she was not the threat Cora feared after all.

At any rate, Cora need not make any decisions yet. She should wait for James to come. He would know what to do. He would make things right. Her mind was unruly, filled with impure thoughts but she must remember her vows, remember her duty. It was easy to forget when she thought of what she might lose. She must confess all to him and throw herself upon his mercy.

If only James would come home.

Before she strayed from the Path and killed this girl.

CHAPTER 29

Grim Stokes hadn't been that hard to track down with Deirdre's help. Turns out he'd stayed in Stillwater to take over the family business, a network of low-level drug operations and run-down strip clubs scattered along Highway 81. The elder Stokes having retired early to a comfortable spot in Cellblock A of the Minnesota Correctional Facility at Faribault, Grim had graduated from high-school weed dealer to local kingpin at a preternaturally young age. By all accounts he'd taken to it well and business was booming.

His office was in the back of the fanciest topless bar in the tri-state area, the one with an actual standalone building at the intersection of a state and county road about five miles outside of town. The corrugated plastic sign out front was plastered over with red glow-in-the-dark letters that would have said 'Scooters' had the 'c' not fallen off. It was midday on a Tuesday so Adam hadn't expected anyone to be in there, but the lot was full of late-model pickup trucks with tinted windows and off-color bumper stickers.

The transition from the bright light of day into the dark bar blinded him for a few seconds, but when his eyes adjusted he braced himself and approached the bartender, an underfed girl in white cutoffs and a tank top tied suggestively in a knot just between her breasts. She wore a cowboy hat and her hair, brown with inexpertly dyed streaks of blond, was twisted into two giant, loose curls that dripped over her shoulders. Enormous lashes framed her chocolate-brown eyes and her lips glistened with pale pink gloss.

'Hey, there, what can I do for you, mister?' She winked at him with gross exaggeration.

Adam forced a smile.

'I'm looking for Grim Stokes. I was told I could find him here?'

The woman stood up straight, looking serious all of a sudden.

'He know you're coming?' she said, pointedly returning her attention to polishing the brass taps.

'No, no, he doesn't. Will you tell him I was, um, referred to him by Joy Marcione? An old friend.'

The woman grudgingly gave up her task and turned to the regular snoozing two spots down from Adam.

'Ray, I'll be back. Can you mind the front?' she said, tossing her hair over her shoulder.

The long-haired man in the denim vest lifted his head just enough to grunt his assent, then lowered it back down onto his thick, heavily tattooed forearms.

Two minutes later she returned, shaking her head at Ray, and picked up her bar towel.

'He says he'll see you,' she said, eyeing Adam warily as she jabbed her thumb in the direction she'd come from.

Adam made his way through the maze of chrome-plated chairs and lacquered tables scattered here and there in front of the stage. A few drunk souls had pulled up close to the main catwalk, where a barely legal bottle-blond slid her naked back up and down a pole, looking bored and distracted. Her eyes followed Adam, the youngest male in the bar by a couple of decades, but he kept his own firmly on his destination, a metal door in back painted the same glossy black as the walls.

Before he got there, however, it swung open as if on its own, revealing an even darker cavern within. He took a step forward but before he could register the space he found a tightly muscled arm around his neck and the cold hard barrel of a revolver jammed up to his temple.

Defenseless and unarmed, all he could do was yelp before his throat was too constricted for sound. Panicked, he tried to get his bearings. The windowless room was richly furnished with red-and-gold Turkish carpets and an outsized mahogany desk with turned legs and an intricate inlaid design. In an oversized leather chair behind it sat a tall man with gelled-back brown hair and a long beard, a cigarette in his ring-covered fingers. The sleeves of his flannel shirt were rolled up to reveal arms covered in tattoos.

The man pinning Adam's arms back must have weighed at least two hundred and fifty pounds and was clad entirely in black leather. Another thug, virtually his twin, stood on the other side of the door. They both looked to the giant behind the desk for direction.

'What the fuck do you want?' said Grim calmly as he took a puff on his cigarette before stubbing it out in a ceramic ashtray in the shape of a swan.

'Joy Marcione thought you might be able to help me.'

The bouncer's grip on Adam's neck tightened.

'Now why would that bitch tell anyone to do that? Unless she's trying to get you killed. She trying to get you killed?'

Adam shook his head no as best he could, given the circumstances.

'Where is that sorry piece of shit these days?' Grim continued. 'I hope six feet underground, but she was just the type to squirm her way back to life even then. You can count on her to be the first to arrive at the zombie apocalypse.' He stood up and walked around to the front of the desk, revealing stick legs swathed in tight super-skinny jeans and feet snug in bright orange low-rise sneakers.

'She's in prison, actually,' he choked out.

Suddenly, Grim smiled so wide it seemed his face might split open.

'Prison. Even better. Best news I've had all day.' He made an elegant gesture with his fingers in the air, as if he were tossing a hat in the air.

'You're Grim Stokes?' Adam ventured.

'How'd you guess?' He nodded to the man to release him, but one guy felt him up for weapons first before the other would let go.

'This dapper fellow doesn't look like he can do much harm, now does he?' Grim said to his guys. Adam was suddenly ashamed of his pale blue Oxford button-down and the jeans he'd bought five years ago. 'Stick around, boys, maybe you'll learn something.

'What's your name, kid?'

'Adam Miller.' The real one slipped out.

'What business you got with Joy? Did she screw you out of a multimillion-dollar deal too? Or was she looking for fast cash?' He scanned Adam up and down, trying to assess whether he was any kind of source for fast cash.

'Neither. I've been trying to get some information about a triple murder, and I thought she could help.'

The two guys stood up, moving in on him again. Adam had clearly said the wrong thing.

'You a cop?' Grim asked, his head cocked to one side. ''Cause generally speaking, cops identify themselves right off the bat. That's only playing fair now, isn't it?'

'Not a cop. N-n-no. Not strictly speaking.' Adam thought he might be safer playing it straight with this guy. 'I used to be. Got kicked off the force.'

The goons eased off and Grim visibly relaxed.

'So now what? You're looking to make some money? Is that it? I have a couple of ex-cops working for me in fact. I happen to like them as a rule. They learn valuable skills in the academy, and then figure out I pay better.'

The image of such a future flashed through Adam's mind. Setting up house for good in Stillwater, working for a small-time drug dealer, spending weekends on a stool next to Ray out there, never calling his mother back. No, no, he'd never sink so low.

'No, thanks. I told you. I'm investigating these murders.'

'Even though you're a civilian? So this is, like, unofficial? For fun? Or are you looking for revenge?'

'It's personal.'

'Okay,' Grim said, accepting that and then seeming to mentally sort through a list, 'which one?'

'Reed Lassiter, Lila McIntyre, Johnny—'

'Let me stop you right there,' Grim said, stepping up to Adam with a finger in his face. 'Because that one's personal with me too. You know what I mean? Those were my peeps. Not just business acquaintances. This is serious territory you're getting into.'

Adam didn't know what to say. He stood there, frozen.

Grim stared at him for a moment, his eyes protruding from his sockets. Then he took a deep breath and slowly walked back to his chair. He motioned for Adam to sit in one of the wing-backs facing his desk.

'Get outta here,' Grim said abruptly to his tough guys. They cut out fast as lightning.

Grim settled back into his chair and took out another cigarette but didn't light it this time. He just held it, apparently forgotten, between his fingers.

'I don't think I can help you,' he said finally. 'I have no idea what happened.'

'Joy thinks she knows who killed them,' Adam blurted out, almost immediately regretting it.

Grim's brows knitted together.

'Joy? Does she now? She tell you it was that Laura girl?'

Adam hesitated. He didn't know what kind of waters he was wading into. Somehow he didn't think he should be providing information to his witnesses, but he'd already stepped in this one.

'Yeah, that's what she said,' he admitted.

'Laura. Now she was a special kind of character.'

'How so?' Finally, Adam might get somewhere.

'Well, I never figured her out. Though you can't say I didn't try.'

'You were friends with her?' 'Friends' sounded so childish coming out of his mouth. As if they were in a playgroup together.

'Not exactly. I mean, I knew her. She was in the crowd for a few months. We'd all hang out at Joy's place sometimes, sometimes at the dam where I kept a little office of sorts, but we weren't close. I liked to keep dibs on her, though. I had assets to protect.'

'Such as?'

'Look at it this way. I had a little operation going on. It was pretty well known and I don't deny it. Anyway, here's this new girl drops in out of nowhere. No one knew where she was from, where she lived, what her deal was. I checked it out with my friend who worked in the school's front office. No freaking records. Even had some kind of religious exemption for her medical form.

'I never liked mysteries. Even back then, I made it my business to know what was up with people. Especially those my friends were hanging around with. I had this sinking feeling she was a narc and that I was on the verge of getting busted. So I followed her.'

'And?'

He shook his head, folded his hands over his stomach and leaned back.

'She wasn't a narc. No way. If she was, that was the deepest cover I've ever seen. In fact, funny thing was she was a real goody-two-shoes as far as I could tell. Nice girl, in a way, who got herself mixed up in the wrong crowd.

'You see, I figured out where she lived, out at the RV camp on County Road 67, poked around a little bit. I had a client over there, old hippie lady who needed a steady supply of my – product, if you will, so I gave her some free samples to listen in, keep an eye on things. She moved her trailer right next door. She may or may not have gone through their garbage, looked through their mail.' He smiled. 'So I knew they were planning to skip town.'

Adam couldn't believe what he was hearing.

'I mean, I don't know if they went there in the end. They'd been packing for a while before those murders, throwing a bunch of shit out. People weren't as careful with their personal information back then, even people as careful as those two.'

He sat back, stared off over Adam's head. 'Truth is, I always thought Joy had a hand in those killings. We were tight though and I had stupid ideas about trust and loyalty back then. I guess I'd seen *River's Edge* too many times.'

He chuckled. 'So it was convenient when the rumor mill blamed a girl who was about a thousand miles away by then. I kept my mouth shut and let it roll.'

Adam could barely get the words out, his lips were trembling so with excitement.

'Don't keep me in suspense,' he said, attempting a joke. 'Where were they going?'

Grim leaned back, pulled out a pack of what appeared to be tobacco but probably wasn't and started rolling a joint.

'Now why should I tell you?'

'Why shouldn't you? If I'm able to prove she did it, what do you care?'

'That's not the right question. Question is – what do you get out of it if you aren't a cop anymore? What's your angle?'

'Maybe I get back on the force.' Adam shrugged.

Grim studied Adam's face as if pondering some great mystery of life.

'Really? You like putting people in jail that much, do you?'

Adam blushed a deep crimson, thinking how he would have liked to have done it a little more often.

'I see. Well, here's the deal. I'll tell you, but I want us to stay in touch, my friend. I never know when I might need a helping hand from one of our saviors in blue. That is, assuming you make it back into uniform. If you do, I trust you'll remember the favor.'

'I don't see how I could help you.'

'You never know, my friend. You never know.' He seemed pleased with himself.

Adam sat there for a moment, unsure. Was he willing to make a deal with the devil to keep this search going? He'd never before heard even the slightest hint about where they'd gone after the murders. He had to do it and then trust that Grim would never find him when the chips were down.

'Okay. Deal.'

Grim smiled for real this time.

'Roanoke. That's where they were off to. I remembered it because I dated a girl from there once. Laura's dad had some people out there. A sister at least. Like I said, I don't know if they went there. And whether they did or not, I'm sure they're long gone now.'

'Do you know the sister's name?'

'I heard it, I'm sure, but that was twenty years ago. Maybe if you said it I'd recognize it.'

Adam shook his head. A dead end after all.

'Would that hippie lady remember it?'

Grim laughed.

'Highly doubtful, given her daily intake of natural herb. You can give it a try though. She's still there. Old as the hills, but the pot keeps her young. Name's Jewel something-or-other. Can't miss her shack, trust me. Be extra nice to her though, she's still a steady customer.'

As Adam crossed the parking lot and slid behind the wheel of his car, he berated himself for selling his soul for nothing. Roanoke. That did him no good without a name.

He Googled it and found there were about a hundred thousand people in Roanoke. Now his entire case was in the hands of some doped-up old lady who lived in an RV park, who was never going to remember a name she'd pulled out of a garbage can twenty years ago.

CHAPTER 30

Cora crossed the creaking boards to the bureau where she'd left the scrap of paper she'd received that morning. A letter from James scribbled out on the back of a Quik-Mart receipt. His messages used to be mystical and mysterious. Now they were simple. He needed money.

No surprise there, but when she read it in full her heart sank. Her instructions were to raise two hundred and fifty dollars – minimum – in the next two weeks and send it to a Western Union address in Lewiston, Idaho. So he would not be returning soon to lead her back to the Path. He would let her run adrift.

Never mind. She knew she must do her duty, but where would she get that kind of money? Didn't she have enough to struggle with already?

She barely had what she needed to keep the farm functioning as it was, much less to set aside savings for the property taxes due in January. Once winter settled in, they'd have to buy feed for the animals. Plus, she hadn't been able to cut enough firewood on her own this year, so she'd have to buy a cord at least from the neighbors down the road.

And then there'd be the plow bill and, to make matters worse, propane prices had gone up. She could shut off the heat to most of the rooms again this winter and bundle up, but she had to have something. She couldn't freeze to death, could she? That's probably what he would expect her to do so he could pay his bar tab or whatever other trivial expenses he'd incurred out in Idaho.

But she mustn't think that way. Even now. Even as her thoughts churned in her head and her panic mounted, she had to believe in him. There was no rationale for the damage they'd done, not if he wasn't holy. Not if he wasn't answering to some higher power that justified the violence he'd been obliged to render to the Unbelievers and the Servants at Hand. Of course he was. Anything else was unthinkable.

She folded his note into a small square and then turned it over again, setting it down gently in the soft purple velvet of the jewelry box that had played 'The Blue Danube' before she'd overwound it. She walked to the closet, opened the door, and dropped to her hands and knees, pushing aside several old pairs of shoes and a couple of moth-eaten wool sweaters that had slipped off their hangers. In the far back corner behind the black garbage bag was a slim metal lock box where she kept her cash. She fished the key out from the bottom of her shoe and opened the lid.

After counting out the crinkled bills, she placed them in small, neat stacks. Taking out the worn ledger she'd found in Mrs. Johnson's study, she looked at last winter's numbers. The situation was pretty dire as it was. But two hundred and fifty more? There was no way.

If he continued to carry on like this, it could cost them the farm. She pictured the bill collectors knocking on the door for money she didn't have. And then what?

The night before she'd sifted once again through the boxes in the spare room. It was pointless really, because she couldn't go back to the thrift store on Main Street. The last time had been a disaster. She'd put the silver on the counter and Mrs. Eldridge had lifted it up to the light, squinting. Cora had panicked. She'd forgotten about the initials.

'Wait just a minute, this is the Johnson family silver.' She'd stared hard at Cora. 'This has been in that family for three generations. Now they want to sell it?'

It had been too close a call. She'd talked her way out of it that time, but that old bag would get suspicious if she came in with more of her clothes or the china set with its distinctive Wedgwood pattern.

If only James would tell her where the money was hidden. He had plenty, she knew, but he'd buried it in different spots along his planned escape route in case everything went bust. Two hundred and fifty dollars wouldn't make any difference to him. But no, of course he'd put the burden on her. He expected her to be resourceful and knew that she'd figure out a way.

For a second she let herself think about how much she could raise if she ransomed the girl. She didn't think she was brave enough to pull off such a scheme, but if she could manage it, she'd have enough to run away and live comfortably on her own for years. Of course, she'd have to be prepared to lose James and the farm in the bargain.

She stopped herself and took a deep breath. These thoughts were only more proof that she was evil, always ready to betray those close to her. Just like she'd done to her father. She was only out for herself, that was the truth she didn't want to reckon with. No, she'd prove her loyalty this time, even if James wasn't holding up his commitments exactly as she'd expected. She'd come up with something.

She sighed and put the money back in the box, sliding it into its space hidden in the long folds of Mrs. Johnson's peach wool cowl-neck coat.

There was that old console upstairs, of course, with the stereo and television in it. She'd seen one like it in the antique store on Elm Street and had asked about it. A collectible from the 1960s, they'd said. They wanted two hundred dollars for that one. Strange how people were willing to spend their money on junk that didn't even work.

The thought of it cheered her though. The one upstairs was in even better shape. They'd give her at least a hundred for her share. That would be a great start. Maybe that amount could temporarily satisfy James if he knew the rest would follow shortly. Then she shook her head in despair.

Of course there was a problem with this plan. A big problem.

The console was in the room with the girl.

Even if she tied the girl to the bed, Cora wouldn't be able to carry it by herself and she couldn't exactly pay the

Folsom boy a few bucks to help her get it out of there. What would she say, never mind the captive girl in the corner? Even that dim-witted fool wasn't so stupid as that.

Nevertheless she had to figure out a way. She had no choice.

CHAPTER 31

That afternoon Adam pulled his car slowly down the bumpy dirt road leading into Keshler's Campground and RV Resort. 'Resort' seemed like an awfully strong word for it, but maybe conditions had been better twenty years ago. At least he hoped so, shuddering as he eyed the detritus scattered around. He had to stop the car once to remove a fallen branch in his path and under it had found a dead possum that must have been decomposing for at least a couple of days, already oozing with maggots. Not a lot of traffic in and out of here apparently.

There weren't that many vehicles parked at the grounds either, maybe six or seven. It was late fall so he figured the transients had hightailed it out of there before the cold season hit. It was obvious these remaining trailers were permanent fixtures. Some had rusted-out flat tires, a couple had no means of transport attached, and one had simply given up the illusion of ever leaving and was set up on cement blocks. The weeds had grown up and around all of them. No one here appeared to be particular about lawn care.

He parked his car in the tall grass and got out, thinking of Grim's words about being able to identify her trailer easily. He glanced around and saw a wizened man of uncertain age, shirtless and fat, sprawled out in a lawn chair in front of a yellow-and-cream RV, drinking from a bottle in a crumpled brown-paper bag. He watched Adam without interest, nodding at him slightly before taking his next swig.

And then Adam saw what Grim meant, for ahead of him was a small Airstream painted in psychedelic rainbow colors. Not the kind of thing one saw much anymore since most of the old-school hippies were running investment banks or tech firms these days. This woman had clearly not gotten her generational memo.

As he approached, he saw a small fire burning in the pit of her designated patch of yard. A cast-iron pot hung from a makeshift spit and some kind of greenish-brown glop bubbled inside it. To Adam it looked like lentils mixed with mud. Her laundry hung from a string connecting the trailer to a rusted metal post stuck in the ground at an angle. Long-faded multicolored skirts and gauzy tunics swayed in the breeze like the flags of some deserted country.

Adam stepped gingerly over a pile of old Kashmiri blankets next to the fire to make his way to the trailer. He noticed that beside the rocks lining the pit was a small, carved wooden box that must contain her marijuana supply and paraphernalia.

This had to be the place. He knocked on the door more gently than he had when he held the authority of the police force behind him. He sighed.

When there was no answer he rapped at it again. A gentle voice floated up from behind, startling him.

'Peace, my brother,' she said.

He turned around to face surely the oldest person alive. Dressed in clothes identical to those hanging on the line with the addition of a pair of crude leather espadrilles, she stood smiling beatifically at him, her gray hair in two loose braids tied with rags. Three rows of long, beaded necklaces draped down over her chest. She was thin and wiry, as if years of hard living in this dump had given her the strength to survive anything. Or maybe it was the pot. Whatever it was, she gave off an air of indestructibility and showed no fear of this stranger invading her space.

'I'm looking for Jewel.'

'And so you've found her,' she smiled, her blue eyes hazily taking his measure. 'Please, join me.' She held out her open palms to him in a vague gesture of welcome and then tipped her head toward the rugs on the ground.

Adam was slightly hesitant to sit, wondering what kinds of bugs infested them. He had no choice, though, so he carefully settled himself on the edge of one. She sat down next to him and picked up the box, but then paused.

'What spiritual force has brought you to my home, sir?' In other words, she was asking if he was a cop.

'Grim Stokes, actually.'

Her shoulders tensed slightly at the name but she nevertheless felt safe enough to open the box. Nestled inside were a small intricately decorated silver pipe, a red plastic gas-station lighter, and a small Ziploc filled with weed. She lifted the pipe to him, but he shook his head. She shrugged and continued.

'What does he need?'

'I'm not here on his behalf. He only directed me to you.'

She said nothing, focused on emptying her pipe and cleaning it with a dirty rag she'd pulled out from somewhere in her skirts. Adam grimaced to himself when she wasn't looking.

'I'm searching for Laura Martin. She used to live here?'

She glanced up from her work and sat still.

'Laura –' Her gaze drifted off above the camp, over the trees, up into the clouds. 'That poor soul. A true wanderer of the earth. May she find peace traveling with the winds.'

'Yes, she moved around quite a bit,' Adam said, shifting uncomfortably onto the grass. 'That's why it's been a little difficult to track her down. But I'm investigating a triple homicide.'

'What do you want with *her* then?' She put down her pipe and fingered the beads around her neck. 'She would never have anything to do with killing. She was a good girl, that Laura. Her father, on the other hand . . .'

She peered deep into Adam's eyes. 'She needed liberation. I hope she found it,' she said quietly.

Adam had been thinking much the same thing in recent days. The old woman reached out and took his smooth hands in her rough ones.

'Will you help her or will you hurt her?' she asked earnestly.

Adam felt his face go red again. How could he answer this question without betraying his intentions? Did he even know what his intentions were?

She continued to stare at him.

'You don't need to answer. I can see it. I can see what you mean to do.' She closed her eyes, not letting go of his hands.

'How can I help?' she finally said, lifting her eyes to heaven and then releasing him. She picked her pipe up off the ground. Having cleaned it to her satisfaction, she filled and lit it. She offered it to him first, and again he refused with a shake of his head.

'I need to know the name of her aunt. The one who wrote to them from Roanoke. I know it was a long time ago, but I'm hoping you can tell me something.'

She sat back and breathed out the smoke slowly. He noticed that the whites of her eyes now took on a pinkish hue. His hope was draining away. With this amount of pot, it was unlikely this woman could remember her own name, much less one she'd read on an envelope twenty years ago.

'So you know about that, do you? I'm ashamed of what I did for Grim back then. It was wrong to be deceitful like that in the service of my consumerist desires.'

'It could be helpful now. Do you know her name? The street she lived on? Anything?'

'Oh, yes, I remember her name. Of course I do.' She took another long, slow hit, and then gazed into the crackling fire as if transfixed.

Adam stared at her in shock. This wasn't possible. Perhaps she was hallucinating.

'It was such a beautiful and poetic name that I remembered it always. A name of the earth and sky. I named my orange-and-white tabby after her. Sadly, she wandered off into the wild blue yonder.'

She was rambling.

'Can you tell me the name?' he prodded gently.

'Tomorrow.'

'You want me to come back tomorrow?'

'I mean that was her name. "Tomorrow". Magical, isn't it?'

'Tomorrow?' Adam was skeptical. She was in a drug haze after all. 'What about the last name?'

'I only remember Tomorrow. I hope that will help you with your journey.' Again she held out the pipe to him and again he shook his head. Then she set it down on a rock, and stood up to stir her strange gruel.

Adam took that as his cue to leave and rose to shake her hand. Instead, she embraced him, resting her head on his chest, much to his embarrassment.

'You will know what to do when the time comes. I can feel it,' she whispered. Adam shivered as if she'd given him a bad omen or cursed his soul.

Back in his hotel, he furiously searched the Whitepages online for someone named Tomorrow in Roanoke. No luck. It was possible that Jewel had fried so many brain cells she was entirely unreliable, or perhaps when she'd gazed into his eyes, she'd seen that his intentions were not pure after all and she'd sent him down a false trail. Either way, it didn't matter. He'd wasted all this time in Stillwater and was no closer to the truth.

Why did he think he could track her down? No documents, no criminal record, no history of government benefits, constant name changes, and stops all over the country. This was a wild goose chase and he'd never get anywhere.

He tossed and turned all night on his lumpy mattress, cold because the heating unit in his room barely functioned despite its unceasing rumbling. The streetlights outside the window shone through the unlined brown-and-beige curtains, and one of them was blinking at irregular intervals like a form of Chinese torture. He pulled the thin, stale-smelling blankets up to his chin. What would he do next? Go home? Admit he was a failure?

He rolled over, half expecting Deirdre to be there beside him. He fumbled for his phone on the bedside table. It was two a.m. He couldn't call her now. It was surprising how much he'd come to depend on her, to need her. He turned off his phone and lay there staring into the dark.

And then it suddenly occurred to him. Something had been bouncing around in his mind since he'd heard that name today. It was as if the clouds had parted and the sun's rays had burst through in his head like the painting on Jewel's trailer.

He jumped out of bed, oblivious now to the chill in the air, and threw himself down on his knees in front of his boxes of files. He pulled out the atlas and flipped through its hard, crinkled pages. He knew he'd seen it somewhere, he'd paged through this book a thousand times. Where was it?

And then, there on page 82 was the scribble. It wasn't in her handwriting, but there it was: 'Tamara, 654–7291'. The numbers had been scratched out but he was pretty sure he had them right. Perhaps the four was a nine, but that was nothing. This must be what she meant. She wasn't named Tomorrow, it was Tamara, and now he had an area code he could pair with the number. The area code for Roanoke.

CHAPTER 32

The day began with steps on the stairs at the wrong time. Julie had become accustomed to the rigid schedule of her imprisonment: the twice-daily feedings, twice-weekly bucket of soap and warm water, twice-monthly laundered clothes. Any variance pricked at her nerves, for it would inevitably require her to make spur-of-the-moment decisions and take actions that could seal her fate forever. So it was with great trepidation that she listened and counted the footfalls to her door, picturing that wretched bitch bounding clumsily up the stairs. Sure enough, she heard her trip on the last step up, stumbling back to her feet, no doubt, just in time to reach the top.

Yes, she was far too early today. Something was up.

With seconds to spare, Julie scrambled up onto the bed into position, waiting for the peephole cover to slide open so her obedience could be confirmed. This time, though, the woman didn't check in on her first. What did it mean?

The woman's altered appearance was her next tip-off that something was amiss. She'd taken extra care with her looks that day, not that it did her much good. For the first time in Julie's memory, not a stray hair spilled out of the brown bun wound tightly on the top of her head. It had been pinned with meticulous symmetry and sprayed flat, shiny with gel.

She wore makeup too, blue eyeshadow and a peachy blush that made her look even older and slightly comic, like a cheap vaudeville player who'd forgotten to wash it off after the show. Yet, in contrast to her garish face, she was dressed for hard labor in Carhartt overalls with an oversized black-and-white checked flannel shirt underneath. Nothing made sense, and that's what triggered Julie's panic.

There was something else too. Something that made Julie sit up and take notice from a different angle. The woman's daily mask of indifference had been replaced by the slightest shadow of fear. Oh, she was trying to hide it, but Julie knew better. Her animal instincts began to awaken and unfurl. Like a cat in the jungle, she sensed weakness. A twinge of hope began its slow crawl out of her heart and down through her skin. Her fingertips tingled.

The old witch barely glanced at Julie as she placed a large canvas bag in front of the bed and knelt down on the floor beside it, plunging both hands in. She lifted out a large spool of thin rope and a pair of vintage dressmaker's shears like the ones in the costume shop at school. Julie knew they'd be sharp, and she knew the damage they could do.

The woman set them next to the bed, inches from Julie's bare toes. Julie stared at those shears with a feeling approaching lust. If only she had the courage, she could pounce on them now. She pictured herself jabbing them into the woman's chest and running like mad while that harridan seized up in death throes behind her.

Just at the moment she needed to act, however, she blanched. When it came down to it, she couldn't do it. Not like that. And then the chance had passed, for the woman had taken up the shears in her calloused hands, unwound a length of rope, and snipped it off. The shears went back in the bag and were pushed far out of Julie's reach.

'Today's a big day. I'm giving you the opportunity of a lifetime.' Was it a smile or a smirk that twisted across her face?

Julie held back a sneer of contempt. Whatever 'opportunity' this woman offered wasn't likely to be to her advantage. She had to get her emotions under control but she couldn't speak, could only sit there, slack-jawed, attempting to force her vocal cords into an appropriately respectful reply, but nothing would come.

'I'm going to let you prove yourself to me today. You keep asking me to trust you and now I have a task that will show me if I can. Don't ruin it, girl, or you will never get such a chance again.'

Julie held her breath, waiting for the woman to get to the point. Her nausea had subsided but her belly had started to bulge in earnest; she had no time for long-range plans anymore. Any chance could be her last.

She'd learned her role well, however, and bowed her head deferentially.

'Thank you, ma'am.'

The room was silent for a moment. Then the woman finally unveiled her plans.

'We're going to move this console out of here.'

Julie's head jerked up in shock.

She was going to leave this room.

The one thing she knew for sure was that they'd never get her back in it alive. The thrill of it overwhelmed her as hot patches erupted all over her body and beads of sweat popped out on her flushed face, but she held her expression in check. She must not show anything, she would be a blank slate, a vessel, a projection screen for whatever crazy notion this woman had of her that led to this moment of inexplicable trust.

She would figure out the rest later. Right now, she had to get across that threshold.

'Now, don't get any ideas. I've worked it all out.' She examined the console, seeming to note its true dimensions as if for the first time.

It was enormous, alarmingly so to Julie. That heavy wooden cabinet was unexpectedly the key to her destiny, yet what if they couldn't carry it? She reassured herself, remembering the stories she'd heard of people developing superhuman strength in times of disaster, lifting cars off loved ones, fighting off bears, scaling rocky cliffs. If this wasn't an emergency, she didn't know what was. She needed her miracle. She *deserved* her miracle.

The woman sighed. 'This won't be easy but I think we can do it.'

Julie nodded slowly, hoping the woman couldn't see the fire burning in her eyes.

'Yes, ma'am,' she managed to choke out. She felt as if a fever had come on. Everything inside her started rushing at once, rivers of blood flowed, brain waves crashed, synapses fired off like lightning, riptides of cells exploded against one another.

'Hold still,' the woman was saying from someplace far away.

A sudden tightness at her ankle forced her out of her haze enough to look down. That bitch was knotting the rope and winding it around and around her leg, tugging at it hard enough to constrict the blood flow. So that was her plan. No matter, Julie would overcome these obstacles. Nothing would stop her, she thought, transfixed as she watched the rope dip around her calf for its fifth circle.

Then Julie realized the true scope of it. She was tying them together.

She suddenly felt sick again for the first time in days, but she swallowed her bile. There was no time for weakness. The other end of the rope was already wrapped halfway up the woman's calf, tied at the end with a strangely intricate knot. They were joined together all right. Irrevocably so.

That could only mean one thing then. Julie would simply have to break out with a dead weight attached. Fine, she would render that woman unconscious one way or another, and then, if she had to, she'd drag her fat, inert body behind her until she found a phone or made it down the driveway into the road where she could hail passersby. Julie would haul her carcass until her skin ripped off in shreds, all the way to the nearest town. There had to be people somewhere nearby. Someone would help her.

Apparently satisfied that they were secured together with a length of rope between them, the woman pushed Julie toward the most important object that ever existed, positioning her so that she would be the one backing down the stairs, bearing most of the weight. Julie accepted her lot with joy though, eager to begin.

The top edge of the console cabinet jutted out by about three inches. Julie slid her fingers awkwardly underneath it in a weak grip that made her hands ache. It would have to do.

'One, two, three, up,' the woman uttered, as they heaved in unison. The set rose a mere two inches off the ground. It was obviously heavier than either had expected but they could just manage it in quick baby steps, stopping to rest every few feet.

By the time they reached the door, Julie was panting from the effort of lugging it the six short paces across the room.

Superhuman strength, she chanted inwardly.

The woman pulled the key out of a patch pocket on her pants, and then there it was: the door, *open.*

The dark hallway gaped outside of it, beckoning her. And further on, she could see the top step disappearing into empty air.

Oh, God, the stairs.

They were the most beautiful things Julie had ever seen, those stairs covered in their worn red floral carpet, that oak banister that traced the route to her freedom. Her eyes could hardly bear the glory of them.

'Don't get excited, girl,' the woman said, as if reading her thoughts. 'Remember.' She lifted up her leg.

'Yes, ma'am,' Julie said softly, turning her head so the woman wouldn't see the determination on her face.

'Back it out slowly,' the woman said. 'I'll count each step so we stay in sync. No mistakes.'

Julie nodded. Her right foot crossed the threshold first and she took another step back into paradise. She couldn't help but close her eyes, the pleasure was so overwhelming.

She was outside the room.

If only she could stand there for a moment, savoring the deliciousness of it. But there was no time. She had to keep moving. And she had to calm down. The woman was right, don't get excited. Don't blow it.

How would she do it though? She could tell from their work that the woman was twice as strong as she was. Julie would lose any physical confrontation. She'd need a weapon.

'One, two, three, step,' came the woman's singsong voice, guiding them down the stairs.

Julie pretended to look behind, judging her next steps, as she desperately tried to get a glance at what waited at the bottom. She knew the kitchen was below, but her memory of its layout from the night of her abduction was foggy, and she wanted to see if there was something within reach, a knife, a hammer, a cast-iron frying pan. Anything that could do the deed. But all she could see was the landing where the stairwell turned, the kitchen still out of sight.

As they carefully lowered the set down the stairs, most of its weight settled on Julie's upper arms, shoulders and back. Her whole body shook from the strain, and pain clouded her thoughts. She needed a plan but it was impossible to think like this.

When they reached the turn, Julie was pinned to the red-papered wall with barely room to breathe, her stomach pressed hard against the bottom edge of the console. Sweat dripped down her face and her chest heaved as she gulped at the air. She slid to the right, and a framed photograph toppled off the wall over her shoulder, landing in the corner beside her, face up, balanced against the molding.

'Leave it,' the woman barked.

Julie didn't touch it, but she thought for a second she'd seen a spark of encouragement glint in the eyes of the young woman staring out at her from the sepia-toned picture beneath the cracked glass. Julie took it as a sign.

Ripping her gaze away from the image, her eyes slid over slightly to the rope that bound them together. It was too long for its task and had trailed behind them as they'd come down the stairs. Now the bulk of it had slid down in a pool on top of her feet. If she took one wrong step or moved a little too quickly, she would topple over and the set would come crashing down on her. After all she'd been through, what if it ended like this, in a freak accident, her insides crushed by a hunk of junk from 1965?

That's when she had the idea.

'Can we – can we rest for just a moment, ma'am? I can't – I need to get my bearings.' The words came out at a staccato pace between sharp breaths.

'Okay.' The woman needed to stop too. She placed the edge of the set several steps up from where Julie stood. Putting her hands on her hips, she stretched her back, her elbows pinned behind her like a resting butterfly. She panted too but was much less winded than Julie.

Julie didn't get much of a break even then, because she was still bearing the weight of her end. She placed one foot on the step and balanced the console on her bent knee for a moment, then lifted it back up to ease the strain on her leg.

Then she went into action. Without taking her eyes off the woman's face, she slid her other foot under the rope, and twirled it around her ankle until there was only a foot or so of slack left in the line. The fates were going to have to decide this one, but Julie wagered they'd be on her side.

'Enough resting. Let's go. When we get it out of the house, we'll put it in the trunk of the car. I left it open.'

'Yes, ma'am.'

The woman lifted her end and tightened her grip, her knuckles going white. Julie did the same, easing her way down a few more steps, her eyes glued to the woman's graceless feet. When the woman had taken the first step off the landing, Julie yanked her entwined foot hard, pushed the console up as much as she could over the banister and threw herself backward down the stairs.

Two birds, one stone.

Both women tumbled down and Julie's world switched abruptly into slow motion. The red walls blurred with black-and-white checks and bare skin. A crash of breaking glass filled her ears as the console landed and shattered somewhere on the hard floor behind her. Searing pain shot through her back and up her spine just before her head hit the ground and bounced back up from the impact. Something spurted down her face.

She reached up to assess the damage, but before her hand touched her skin, everything went dark.

Chapter 33

Cora was awakened by a loud knocking sound that rang in her ears, the pounding echoing in her head as if a thousand tiny hammers were pummeling her skull from the inside. She forced herself to open her eyes. Everything was bathed in a milky haze, her focus fluctuating in and out. She squinted and at last saw the ceiling fan spinning above her.

The knocking again. She couldn't tell if it was inside her head or out. And then it dawned on her.

It was the door. *Someone was at the door.*

Cora lifted herself off the floor, but her back seized up and she flopped down like a fish on the dock. Then she realized that her skin was stinging in a hundred different places. Her temple throbbed from within but little specks of pain tingled on the outside too. She raised her hand to it, and pulled it back to see that it was covered in small shards of glass.

What had happened? Where was she?

Then the memories floated back slowly. They'd fallen somehow.

With great effort, she turned her head. Sprawled out on the kitchen floor a few feet away was the girl, still

240

unconscious, thank God, and in between them, her precious collectible, utterly destroyed. The picture tube had shattered, revealing a myriad of valves and wires. Even the wooden frame was askew, splintered in part to reveal the particleboard crumbling on the edges.

It was over. She'd never raise the two hundred and fifty dollars now. James would kill her.

She let her head fall back to the floor.

The knocking again.

Oh, yes, someone was at the door. What would she do?

Her first thought was to lie perfectly still, to do nothing until they went away. But her car was out front with the trunk open. They'd know she was home, and it was likely some interfering person who would be worried for her safety. They might break in to save her, or, worse, call the cops. Unless it *was* the cops.

Either way, she had to answer it.

She was lucky she'd taken the extra precaution of locking the front door with the key. Lucky the girl hadn't been the one to wake up. The visitor, whoever it was, could have simply walked into this scene and everything would have been over.

Her heart pounded against the walls of her chest as she thought of all the possible permutations. How could she have taken this chance? All because James couldn't manage his money. This was his fault.

Those thoughts were for later. First she had to get through this.

'Hold on,' she yelled out weakly. 'Be right there.'

Her heart was racing as she forced herself to a sitting position. She held her head in her hands, grimacing from the pain. Her right arm was starting to swell. She must have sprained something, but nothing felt broken. She'd be sore for a while but she wasn't dead. Not until James got back, anyway.

She turned over, crawled to the edge of the table as far as the rope that joined them would reach, and pulled herself up slowly.

A voice spoke to her from the other side of the door.

'It's me, Ellie Rainey. From the diner? I tried to call but the phone was disconnected. I brought some chicken soup for Mrs. Johnson.'

Cora froze. She couldn't move, couldn't answer. But she knew she had to.

'Everything okay in there?' came the voice again.

'Yes, yes, it's fine. Just a moment.'

Cora forced herself to stand up straight, despite the resistance of every muscle in her body. The console would have to stay where it was for now, but she had to get the girl out of here. She glanced up at the stairs, imagining dragging her limp body all the way up. It would take too long, and she wasn't sure she could manage it with her wrist like it was. She'd have to put her in the pantry for now. And then hope.

She crossed over to the girl and placed two fingers on her neck. Her pulse beat weakly but she was alive. Cora felt a rush of relief, even though she knew it might have been better for her in the long run if the girl had died in the fall.

She slid her hands under the girl's arms and heaved her seemingly lifeless form toward the pantry. It was only five feet away but in her state it seemed like a million miles. Plus, they had to pass by a gap in the curtain of the front-door window. If this nosy woman dared to take a peek, well, Cora would have a major problem on her hands.

One foot behind the other. She had to make it there. She lifted the girl up higher in her arms, pressing her head to her breast. The girl rolled her sagging head, moaning softly.

'Shut up, shut *up*,' Cora whispered, hoping she had trained her enough to fear the sound of her voice.

The girl was a total dead weight. Even in her emaciated state, she was heavier than Cora had expected.

She sighed and inspected the route along the floor behind her. There was no choice but to lug her through some of the glass. Hopefully a few more cuts and scrapes wouldn't wake her.

One foot behind the other.

Just as she reached the pantry door, the interloper knocked again, gently this time at least.

'Are you sure everything is okay? Should I call for help? Do you need—'

'No,' Cora barked, then softened her tone. 'It's fine. I've just got to run something up to Mrs. Johnson. Five minutes.'

She hauled the girl into the pantry closet. She didn't fit lengthwise, so Cora folded her over and rolled her onto her side, her back slumped up against the large jars of pickles along the bottom shelf. The pantry had only a heavy cloth curtain but at least it touched the floor. She would be concealed for now, but this was a very temporary solution. She had to hope for the best.

Cora sat on the floor just outside the curtain, her fingers flying over the knot pressing into her leg. She'd expected to be able to cut it off, but she'd left the shears upstairs. She tugged at the rope, but the knot seemed to get tighter the more she fooled with it.

She flipped open the curtain and scanned the pantry. Wasn't there something? Her eyes lit upon a pair of scissors on the top shelf, propped up in a can jammed full of kitchen tools. She dragged the stool in the corner closer to her. The rope held her fast though. She couldn't reach it. She was six inches shy.

She climbed down and pulled the girl's legs closer to the ladder, then mounted it again. The handles of the scissors were too far away, but she could just grasp the can. She inched it closer to the edge, and then it spilled out. The can and the scissors crashed to the floor.

Standing still on the step with her shoulders hunched, Cora waited for Ellie's rap at the door again. Surely she'd heard that.

Silence though.

She peered out the small window in the pantry and saw that Ellie had stepped off the porch into the yard, her hand over her eyes shielding them from the sun as she stared at the upper windows of the house.

Damn her. Why couldn't she mind her own business?

Cora grabbed the scissors and cut herself loose, then quickly unwrapped the rope from the rest of her calf. She checked the girl's pulse again. Slow, but alive. Now she had to hope she'd stay knocked out until she could get rid of that woman. Whatever she did, Cora would have to keep this Ellie Rainey out of her house.

Checking herself in the small mirror at the foot of the stairs, Cora panicked at the sight and hurriedly wiped a smear of blood off her cheek. Her hair had tumbled out of its bun, stiff, over-sprayed bits of it erupting here and there. She quickly twisted it and shoved it back up in a knot, pulling out pins and redoing it with fingers flying. The makeup she'd put on this morning looked awful. She'd thought it would shore up her courage, make her feel powerful, but in truth it only made her look like a fool.

She was a wreck but there was nothing for it. Wiping her hands on the back of her pants, she limped her way over to the door, absently massaging her injured wrist.

She opened the door a crack, no more than three inches. She knew that seemed suspicious, but there was no choice.

Her visitor, seeing the door finally open, hastened back up the steps and lifted the steaming Dutch oven from where she'd left it on the bench by the door. She held it up to Cora like burnt offerings.

'Seems like I caught you at a bad time. Sorry to come without calling, but like I said, the phone is out. Maybe you didn't realize?'

Cora stepped out onto the porch and closed the door, holding the knob with both hands behind her.

'Oh, no. That's so strange. I'll have to get it checked out. Maybe that storm last week. I never use the landline really. We just have it for emergencies.'

The woman nodded, looking past Cora toward the door.

'Mind if I come in? I can just drop this in the kitchen. How is Mrs. Johnson? Well enough for a visit today?'

'Oh, n-no. Definitely not today. She's sleeping now. Had a rough night, but she'll love the soup. Don't worry though. I'll just take it.' She reached out for the pot, feeling that she'd dodged a bullet.

As Ellie handed it over, however, she glanced down at Cora's wrist, which was swollen now with an unmistakable bluish hue.

'Oh, my,' Ellie said, pulling back the pot. 'I can't let you carry this. Look at your wrist. What happened?'

A chill shot through Cora's heart. Everything was lost. She'd have to kill her. And then what? Her mind quickly ticked off the tasks that would be involved. Bury the body, burn her clothes, throw her jewelry in the river. Her eyes swept out over the driveway. She'd have to ditch her car somewhere in the woods, wipe it down of all traces, prints, DNA. If anyone had known she was coming—

Then Cora saw it. There was someone else in Ellie's car.

'Oh, who's that?' she asked, trying not to let the panic sound in her voice.

'Never mind him, that's just my husband, Fred. He'll read the paper while we visit. My car's been in the shop for weeks, so he's had to be my chauffeur. The truth is, we're newlyweds, so he secretly enjoys it,' she laughed, turning red. 'Third time's the charm.'

'Fred,' Cora muttered, frantically recalculating the odds of surviving this predicament.

'Well, here, let me just take the soup in and then we'll go. I don't want to take up your time. I'll come back to visit Mrs. Johnson another day. Perhaps we can schedule it now?'

'Sure, sure,' Cora said, her mind too overwhelmed to stop her.

Ellie had her hand on the doorknob. Cora would have had to openly fight her to keep her out of there. She was going to have to admit this small defeat to win the war.

The door swung open and Ellie, as Cora had expected, gasped at the scene before her. Cora closed her eyes, trying to think.

'Good grief, what's happened?' Ellie exclaimed, rushing to the counter and putting the pot down on a tea towel. She turned to Cora, a confused look on her face.

Cora stared at the floor, seeing it with fresh eyes now that she had a witness. Not only was the console smashed into a thousand bits, but there was an obvious trail of blood droplets smeared through the shattered fragments.

'Hold on, let me get Fred,' Ellie moved swiftly to the door.

'No, no, please. Don't bother him. I've already arranged for someone to come and deal with it. They'll be upset if they don't get their money, you know?' Cora laughed nervously. 'They'll be here in a bit. I was just waiting. That's who I thought was at the door, in fact. See,' she said, pointing to the path wiped through the glass, 'I was starting to mop up. Gracious, I didn't want you to see the place in such a mess.'

Ellie smiled, relaxing for the first time. She'd fallen for it completely.

'Now I understand. I thought something strange was going on. I was ready to call the police.' She paused, pushing the bits of splintered wood around with the toe of her shoe.

'How did it happen?' Ellie went on. 'You weren't trying to move this by yourself, were you?' She looked up at Cora in horror.

'Well, yes, I was. I can usually handle that sort of thing, but I guess I overestimated my strength this time.'

Cora heard the girl moan softly from her hiding spot. She had to talk louder, drown out the sound.

'It was very silly of me,' she said, moving in between Ellie and the pantry.

'Please promise me you'll call me if you need something like this again. I can have Fred help you.'

'Oh, I will, I definitely will.'

Ellie was still staring at the floor, obviously perplexed.

'Why, there's blood here.' She leaned down, wiping a bit of it with her fingertip.

Cora swallowed hard.

'Is this yours? Oh, that's what happened to your wrist. Why, you're hurt. You're really hurt,' she said, stepping over to Cora. The cut on her head was bleeding again.

'Come on, Fred and I will take you to the hospital. You need to have this checked out.'

Cora pulled back and away.

'No, no, I don't need that. I'm fine, really.'

'You aren't fine. Look at your wrist. That could very well be broken.'

Cora heard a movement in the pantry. The girl must be coming to. She was shifting around in there. In another minute, Ellie would pick up on it too.

She grabbed Ellie by the shoulder, much to her surprise, and firmly but politely walked her to the door.

'Really, I will be fine. I'll tell you what, after the guys come to help me get this out of here, I'll have them drive me over to the hospital and get checked out. I need to be here when they arrive. You know how hard it is to get people out to take care of anything.' She laughed. 'And I can't bear it another minute to have this place be such a mess. You can understand that, right?' They stood in the doorway, Ellie obviously reluctant to leave.

'Okay, well, I'll come back in a few days to get my pot. I'll check on you then.'

'No, no, we're so far out. I'll bring it to you at the diner, and then I'll let you inspect me for cuts and bruises.' She forced a smile.

'Well, all right then. We can set up a visit then too. I'm warning you though, if you don't come by there this week, I'm coming back to see how you are.'

'Don't worry. I will absolutely be there.'

Cora shut the door, sighing with relief, and then rushed to the dining room where she could get a better view of the driveway. Fred and Ellie sat there in their idling Buick, not moving. Ellie was chattering on to Fred, who listened intently. Ellie talked with her hands, waving them around frenetically. She was upset. She was worried. But it was none of her damn business.

'Come on, Fred,' Cora said aloud. 'Calm her down. Tell her to leave it well enough alone.'

Then Cora heard a thud in the kitchen. The girl. She had to get back to the girl.

As soon as she stepped into the kitchen she saw her. She was crawling along on her belly, wincing in pain, moving slowly back across the glass on the floor, the straightest path out of the house. Her face and hands were sliced up from the broken screen and her cheek was covered in a massive blue-and-purple bruise. She wasn't letting that stop her. Determined little beast.

Had Cora locked the door behind her when she'd let Ellie out? She patted her front pockets. The keys weren't there. Her eyes flew to the lock and there they were, jutting out. The girl's freedom dangled there, inviting catastrophe.

She crossed the room in two great strides, jumping over the girl. As she yanked the key out of the lock, Cora glanced quickly out of the kitchen window, checking on Ellie and Fred as best she could from this vantage point. The car was still there, but now only Fred was in it. Ellie must be coming back. But where was she?

Cora had no time to track her down though. She ran to where the girl slithered on the floor, pulling her backwards first by the hair, and then getting a grip around her torso. She flung her toward the pantry, and grabbed her by the arms, dragging her away from the door. The girl could hardly struggle, she was so weak, barely alive even, but she managed to kick her legs and twist her body so that Cora had to work hard to keep her moving in the right direction.

She had to find a better place to put her for the time being. Someplace with a door at least. She moved past the pantry farther down the hallway this time, to the bathroom they never used. The toilet was broken, so Cora mostly used it for storage. The grime had built up in the corners, and she could see a small hole in the corner of the wall shoved full of pillow stuffing. The mice had moved in.

She pushed the girl into the corner and hoisted the three cardboard boxes filled with household miscellanea out of the claw-foot tub and onto the floor. Using all her strength and force of will, she heaved the girl up waist high and dropped her in on top of the golden-brown-streaked porcelain. As she tumbled in, the girl's head hit the curved edge hard enough to knock her out again. Afraid that she was faking it, Cora slapped her face and watched the bright red spot flare up on her cheek, but the girl didn't move. Cora closed the door and propped a kitchen chair up under the knob.

She'd bought herself a few minutes at least.

She raced back out to the kitchen and stormed to the window as she tried to catch her breath. Everything looked to be in its usual state. The car was gone. The trees and grass and flowers were still as a painting.

What had Ellie been doing though? Had she peered into another window of the house? What had she seen? Had she noticed missing family heirlooms they'd sold to pay the bills? Or Mrs. Johnson's wheelchair thrown onto the scrap pile behind the barn? Were they racing off to alert the cops now?

She'd told James they shouldn't make so many changes so quickly, but he'd wanted to erase all traces of that senseless biddy, as he'd dubbed her. They'd been told she didn't have any family living and that she was such a mean old codger that there was no one left on earth to care for her, but this Ellie Rainey was exactly what she'd been afraid of. There always seemed to be a flaw in their plans, one thing they hadn't considered that changed every calculation.

Cora wouldn't be able to rest easy for days, she knew. What a stupid mistake she'd made. A stupid mistake James had made forcing her to raise that kind of money on short notice. She'd risked everything now for two hundred and fifty dollars. Everything.

Well, she certainly couldn't raise it now, she thought morosely as she scrutinized the exploded hunk of wood in front of her. She sank down to the floor, rubbing her finger along the edge of a piece of broken glass, hoping the pain of the cut would drown out the pain she felt inside.

Tomorrow she'd go to Western Union. She'd send him fifty dollars out of her savings. It was the best she could do. She would have to let James down. She'd tell him the rest would arrive as soon as she could get it together. There'd be hell to pay, even if she did eventually raise the funds. But she had no choice.

She shook her head and stood up. It was time to get to work. Nothing left but to drag the girl back upstairs and pick up the pieces of this mess.

CHAPTER 34

When Julie came to she thought she was in her bedroom at her parents' house. It took her a moment to register the absence of her four-poster bed with its pale blue ruffled canopy flanked by white bedside tables and porcelain lamps shaped like teapots. No, she realized hazily, she must not be there.

Maybe she was in the city.

She'd been dreaming the most amazing dream. There was a white sand beach with crystal-clear water reflecting an achingly blue sky. Mark was there, laughing, reaching out for her. They splashed together, dipping in and out of waves as warm as bathtub water. The sun burned bright above as she tasted the salt from the foamy water rushing up around her on its return from the coast.

They held hands and walked out of the sea, stepping across rocks that grew up, sprouting like weeds from the ocean bottom to form a path through the waves breaking against them in their wake. They walked along a gradually sloping incline toward a huge white house that stood on the pinnacle of a cliff in the distance. Its shutters clapped against ivy-covered walls, its doors flung open, inviting them home. It was her grandparents' place on Nantucket, where they'd gone every August of her childhood, except it wasn't. It was bigger, more ornate, a house lowered down from the heavens.

She and Mark stopped, their feet sinking into the sand as their eyes met and they embraced. Suddenly she wore a long white gown that clung to her with damp, and little wisps of her hair blew around her face and his.

She turned back toward the house. In each window stood someone beloved, waving to her from above, smiling, beckoning her to join them.

'They're waiting for us.'

There were her mother, her father, her brother, her best friend from middle school, her long-dead grandfather. She ran toward them, still holding Mark's warm hand.

Then the dream faded and she glided back into consciousness. She resisted it, squeezing her eyes shut, trying to recapture that vision, to rewind and play it out to the end, but it was gone, drifted away into the ether.

She rolled over, nestling into the mattress, smiling as she clung to the ephemeral threads of the dream.

It was the smell of the putrid sheets and the soft brush of the fleece blanket that brought her back to reality. She felt that familiar sinking in her chest that would inevitably be followed by the onslaught of recent memory. She opened her eyes and bolted upright, but slumped back down again immediately, her head throbbing.

'Oh, no, *no, no*,' she whispered. *She was still here.*

The room was spinning, but she could see that it remained unchanged from before except for an empty spot along the far wall where the console had stood.

It was coming back to her in bits. The last thing she remembered was crossing the threshold into the hall, the rest of it gone. How had she ended up back here, back in this room, and with every muscle of her body contorted with pain? She put her hand behind her neck. It felt worse than when she'd had whiplash from the car accident last year.

She moaned and lay back against the flattened pillow.

Then she remembered the baby. Panicked, she put her hands around her belly, splaying her fingers across it. She held perfectly still, waiting for it to move. In that moment, she was a tightrope walker, balancing a thousand feet in the air. Was it still there? Was it alive? Suddenly nothing else mattered. Not Mark, not her parents, not even getting out of there.

Why wouldn't it move?

It was in that moment that she knew she could never fulfill her plan, she could never kill this child. If only it would move, she would protect it with every ounce of energy she had until her dying day. If only it was okay, she swore, she would make any bargain with any devil to keep this child alive. It wasn't the baby's fault, she suddenly understood with perfect clarity. Evil wasn't genetic.

'Please, little one,' she whispered, 'please move.'

And then, finally, she felt it kick and could exhale at last. 'Thank God.'

For a moment after, she was the one who didn't move. She sat there clutching her stomach, picturing this precious fetus with tiny moving fingers. It floated inside her, unsuspecting and naïve. She breathed deeply in and out, eyes closed.

How could she have ever wanted to do this child harm? She was going crazy in here, succumbing to their influence. She was turning into an animal, a vicious and depraved murderer. She'd let her mind slip into these dark patterns, had allowed herself to think that the ends justified the means, and in the process had rationalized her way into planning the most despicable act possible. She had almost killed an innocent baby. She shivered, thinking how easily it could have happened.

'They are making you crazy but you can't let them, Julie. You can't.'

This child was a survivor, just like she would be. Once she got them both out of here, it wouldn't be a symbol of her suffering, but of her strength. And she would get out of here. She had to get back to Mark, to that house on the hill, to where the waves rolled freely over the earth, washing it clean of sin.

When she opened her eyes, she noticed something else, as if her vision had been directed by an outside force. Across the room, shoved up against the wall, was a canvas bag rumpled up in a ball. At first, she didn't recognize it, but something about it made Julie go numb all over, sparking some buried memory.

Then she knew.

'No fucking way,' she murmured.

The shears. She remembered the dressmaker's shears. The woman had forgotten to take this bag out of here, and with that one misstep, had sealed her doom. Whatever had happened must have been enough of a shock to rattle her at last because she had always been so careful, checking and double-checking, locking and re-locking, but now she'd made her fatal error. This was it, the miracle Julie had been waiting for.

She hurt everywhere, but she had to get up. She shifted her weight onto her right side so she could roll off the bed, but found that, for some reason, she couldn't do it. Something was wrong. Her left leg wouldn't move. And then, she realized with horror that she *couldn't feel it*.

She threw off the covers in a panic and immediately understood the problem. A rope was wrapped around her calf at least ten times, like a crude gladiator sandal, and the end of it was tied fast to the bedpost. The skin beneath the rope was blue, with bulging trapezoids of flesh pressed through the crisscross pattern. The stupid woman had tied it too tightly. There was no circulation and it had gone past the point of numbness. It was like a plastic doll part sewn onto her flesh, floppy and useless.

'Okay, Julie. Stay calm.' She wiggled her toes. 'It's not too late. It's fine. This will be fine.' But she knew in her heart it wouldn't be fine for long.

She swallowed hard and pounced on the knot, searching for a weak point, a crevice she could use to pry it loose. Then she drew back from it in despair.

She took a deep breath, leaned back against the pillow.

Why had that woman tied her up this time? Why now? Julie knew the answer. She knew why patterns changed. That woman was panicking, losing her cool. Julie could have the advantage here if she could just stay calm and think rationally.

She grabbed the knot, tearing at it anywhere she could get a grip. Her jumping hands pushed and prodded it all over to find where it began. She couldn't, no matter how furiously her fingers worked at it. Nothing would budge. In frustration, she uselessly pounded it with her fists. She might have kept going if she hadn't noticed the red marks blooming up on her skin, fresh bruises she couldn't even feel. She stopped.

She went back in, pulling and tugging at the rope, but more methodically, if with no more success. She tried a new approach, swinging her other leg over the footboard onto the floor.

'Forget the knot, just drag the whole stupid bed over there,' she muttered.

It was an awkward position, but she managed to hobble along on one foot, grab the bedframe with both hands, and lean back, pulling with her full body weight against it. It wouldn't move, not even a fraction of an inch. She leaned down to look under the bed to see why it was stuck.

When she saw the situation, she fell to her knees in abject defeat. The bedposts were bolted to the floor.

'That motherfucker. He thought of everything, didn't he?' She had no choice but to go back to the knot.

She had to focus. It was thinking that would save her, not force, not power, and certainly not delirium. She had to draw on childhood summer-camp skills she'd never properly mastered in the first place.

'There's always a trick, and when you know it, it works like magic. Come on, Julie, find the magic.'

The downside was, some knots played against you, like a devil's bargain. The more they were pulled, the tighter they got. She couldn't risk that. Any more pressure and that leg would be done for. She wouldn't let herself think about the details, the gangrene and the rot and inevitable removal. She'd read *Madame Bovary* last semester. She knew how it went.

Instead, she had to remember back to the sailing lessons she'd taken the summer between eighth and ninth grades. They'd been taught at least a dozen nautical configurations, but she hadn't paid the closest attention.

'Maybe if you hadn't been so busy flirting with Marcus Cooperman, you could be saving your life right now.' She stopped. She took a deep breath.

'Think, damn it.' There was the bowline, the cleat hitch, the clove hitch, all pointless jokes compared to this monstrosity. She peered more closely at the beast, this odd little primrose of hemp.

It looked a bit like a clove hitch, but one end seemed to have been passed under the other. She wriggled her fingers into the middle of it, and pinched. She yanked at it and it tightened up exactly as she'd feared. Okay. New strategy.

She closed her eyes again, calling on all the strength she had left. Then, unbidden, an image passed through her head, a piece of some puzzle in her subconscious. There was a yellowed photograph of a woman behind broken glass, a section of coiled rope, her bare foot.

Determination surged within her and the solution came to her in that same instant like a thunderclap. Her hands, which had been shaking, suddenly stilled. An extraordinary lucidity descended upon her and with a burst of unexpected confidence, she gently tugged the end of the rope parallel to her leg, prying it up and away, into the opposite edge. She eased it out from there. It was beginning to slip.

'Have I done it?'

As the first layer came loose ever so slowly, she could see it was a double, so she applied the same strategy again, parallel, up and through.

'Keep breathing. You got this.'

Then, just like the magic she'd been hoping for, the knot was undone and the rope fell away like a demon cast out. Her eyes flew up to the ceiling.

'Thank you, spirits. Whoever is watching over me. Star-power angel or elfin demon unicorn. Whoever you are. Thank you.'

There was no time to waste on the gods, however. Her leg was an eerie blue with white x's ridged deep into the skin and she needed it to function, *now*. She massaged her thigh until it hurt, encouraging the blood to flow again through the veins, to restore life to its contiguous parts. She slapped up and down the length of her leg.

'Come on, come on.'

Hoping for the best, she tossed the rope to one side and scrambled up out of bed. Her calf and foot were completely numb. She couldn't feel a thing, not even tingling, no pins and needles. But at least she had muscle control, even if she was limping, and as heavy and awkward as the injured leg felt, the color was returning in splotchy patches.

'It's going to have to do.'

She lumbered over to the bag, bent like an ogre, with one hand on her protruding stomach, her good leg moving too fast to carry the rest of her body along. She stumbled and dove for the canvas, jamming her hands in and feeling around to the bottom. At first she thought it was empty, that her memory was mistaken, but there in the folds of the seam, her hands hit metal. She pulled them out victoriously, clinging to the shears as she suppressed tears of joy.

She wasn't imagining this. It was real. She held her salvation in her hands.

'Fuck. *Yeah*.'

CHAPTER 35

Cora carried a small plastic garbage bag with her into the gas-station bathroom. In it were her clothes from the day before, stiff with caked blood. She and her father had driven all night, so she figured they were far enough away to ditch the evidence. As luck would have it the bin was nearly full. The night staff would have to take it out soon.

She checked the chart on the back of the door to be sure. 'Claire S.' was scheduled to empty the trash by four. Must be the half-drugged girl in flannel restocking the pain relievers she'd passed on her way in. Not a girl likely to notice much about her surroundings, even crimson-soaked sneakers from a fresh murder shoved against the plastic. Not with eyes that blotted with mascara and thrashing grunge rock blasting at that volume out of her earbuds.

Cora shoved the bag to the bottom of the garbage can, ignoring the various pieces of disgusting matter coming into contact with her skin. Then she stood in front of the mirror, studying her puffy tear-stained face, yellowed with fading bruises. No one would remember that either. It was incredible how easily one could disappear into the candy-wrapper foreground of a Sunoco at two a.m.

Her eyes, red and big as saucers, stared back at her, emptied out, hollowed. She couldn't feel anything inside. Numb to the center, her heart had apparently shriveled up into a hard nugget, resistant to all but the basest of emotions. It was better that way. She had to perfect the technique of turning everything off. Good feelings only got her into trouble. Only got people killed.

She squeezed her eyes shut tight, trying to erase the awful memory of that moment. Her father's hand had curled around hers, and she'd been unable to resist his strength as he'd plunged the knife into Reed's flesh. That was it, the end of everything.

She opened her eyes. No choice but to face facts.

They'd surely found Reed's body by now, and she tried hard not to imagine what they'd be doing to it. His soft, smooth skin would be naked, exposed on the slab, the camera flash tinting it blue. A lab tech would be charting the bruises, a thousand thumbprints of purple, and the rope burns, a half-dozen magenta lines twisting across the dragon tattoo on his left biceps. The assistant would be dipping a steel ruler into the jagged cuts they'd left in his torso, calculating their depth and width, checking for serrations. His face, that beautiful chiseled face, would be still for once under the bright lights above the exam table. No more half-smiles to tempt her into iniquity. No more whispered dirty thoughts to make her dizzy with lust. No ironic glances from his electric eyes to corrupt her to the core.

She had to stop herself. Think about the danger going forward, not the damage done. It was too late for that. She had to forget him and try to take comfort in the knowledge that at least she wouldn't be caught.

They'd never find the knife. Her father had scrubbed it clean back at the trailer and thrown it into the swirling river as they'd crossed the bridge that night. She'd watched it sail through the night air until it was merely a pinpoint above, a glint in the dark. She never saw it fall, but she imagined it must have entered the current like an Olympic diver, perfectly vertical, smooth with no splash. It was gone, she knew, safely sunk into the deep. She pictured it there, half covered by sand, jabbing into the earth as the bottom dwellers swished and dipped around it, hidden for all eternity.

Her DNA samples would be gathered up in separate plastic baggies by now, labeled but never matched. She had no records, her father had made sure of that. She'd never been to a doctor or a dentist or even the school nurse. She'd never been allowed to have school pictures taken, and when the sheriff's office had come in to gather student fingerprints in fifth grade, he'd kept her home. It was as if he'd known this day would come. She was anonymous, a ghost, a vapor. She simply didn't exist.

The backpack Reed had taken from her was the only small problem. No matter, they wouldn't be able to trace her from that. It was too bad about the letter inside, but she couldn't change facts now.

She wiped her nose with her sleeve. How was she going to go on? Her father had the shakes and she knew he'd be sitting in the truck now, swigging down forties as fast as he could swallow. They'd barely said a word since setting out the day before, the unreality of it all having left them both in shock. If he kept at it the way she expected, they wouldn't get far tonight before he'd pass out completely.

Cora's practical side was slowly kicking in. She couldn't afford to think about what had happened, couldn't begin to process her own suffering until they were safely ensconced in a new town. For tonight, they'd need to find a place to park off the road. She didn't want to wake up to flashlights flooding the trailer, searching for evidence. If only she had her atlas. It was such a stupid thing to lose in the midst of this whole mess.

She washed her face with cold water, blew her nose, and stuffed extra paper towels into the back pocket of her jeans, anticipating more tears that night.

Before she left, she bought a cup of coffee and two kielbasa sausages from the endlessly turning electric spit roaster by the counter. The meat, dried out, crinkly and dotted with spots of grease, had probably been spinning under the heat lamp for days, but it would have to do. Neither of them had eaten since breakfast the day before. They needed the protein.

The girl with the earbuds rang her up, singing along something about the killer in her as she dropped two dollars and change into Cora's open palm, not once making eye contact.

It was just as well.

She carried her quarry out to the car, dismayed to find a pile of empty bottles in the floorboard of the passenger side. She hadn't thought he could get so many down in one go. He already looked bleary-eyed and appeared to be having trouble keeping his tongue in his mouth. She shrank back from him in disgust. There was no alternative. She'd have to take over.

She got out, slamming the door behind her, and walked purposefully to the driver-side door. Getting in, she shoved him over and grabbed the cap off his head, throwing it onto hers and pulling her ponytail through the back loop, hoping it would make her look older. The cops especially liked to pull people over in the middle of the night. They guessed rightly that that's when all the bad guys were out.

She shrugged to herself in the darkness and took a sip of the steaming coffee, instantly spitting it back out onto the dashboard. Burned beyond recognition. Well, what did she expect? Cursing, she wiped up the foul liquid with her sleeve and peered over at her father. He hadn't noticed, didn't budge. He was out cold.

She lifted the cup of chicory bitterness to her lips again, this time chugging it down. Wiping her mouth with the back of her hand, she clicked open the glove compartment, rooting around until she found a jumbo-sized bottle of NoDoz. She checked the expiration date – close enough – and popped three pills, then an extra for good measure.

Suddenly she needed to be as far away as possible. She needed to put Reed Lassiter and her stupid hopes behind her. And for that, she had to stay awake and carry them forward into the distance. She'd drive until they got to their new home. She'd drive until her tears had all dried up and her bruises had faded into oblivion.

She'd drive until they fell off the face of the earth.

CHAPTER 36

It took Adam three weeks to score an audience with the elusive Tamara Barron of Roanoke, Virginia, and even that was the result of a bit of trickery. She didn't answer her phone much, and when she did, she hung up as soon as she heard Adam's name. She placed him for a cop from the get-go and no amount of denial could dissuade her from that belief. Adam was secretly pleased because it proved that the job was an integral part of him, his essential nature and his ultimate destiny.

In the end, he'd resorted to flying out to Roanoke to confront her in person. Her house was a rambling cottage perched up in the mountains, painted the same shade of green as the foliage surrounding it. He climbed the twenty-seven steps up the winding deck to the entrance and rapped at the screen door. Inside he saw a living room overfilled with two white loveseats covered in patchwork throw pillows, an array of whimsical quilts, and walls covered with framed posters of inspirational quotes. Quaint, old-fashioned, and sickeningly sweet.

Classic rock played softly in the background, one of those crooning hits from the eighties with too much sax. Somebody was doing dishes in the kitchen at the back.

The noise stopped at his knock, but no one came out.

'Hello,' he yelled. 'Anybody home?'

Still silence.

'Hi, it's Adam Miller. We spoke on the phone?'

Nothing but one last clink of glass against glass. Adam checked the number outside to make sure he had the right place. He knew she'd retired from teaching elementary school a few years ago and had never married. It had to be her in there, but why was she avoiding him like this?

Just as he was about to give up, something stirred. A door creaked open from somewhere deep within the house and a moment later, a gray-haired woman with squinting blue eyes emerged from the arched doorway at the back of the living room. She parted the beaded curtain with an upheld shotgun pointed directly at Adam. Not exactly what he'd been expecting from a kindergarten teacher.

'What do you want?' she said, walking steadily toward the door, her eyes a muddy mix of anger and puzzlement.

'I only – I only want to talk to you about your brother.' He'd told her this already. Why did everyone make everything so difficult?

'I told you before, I'm not in touch with him. I want no part in his shenanigans.' Only the screen separated Adam from the working end of that Remington double barrel. He swallowed, screwing up his courage to talk his way in.

'Can I come in? I don't bite. I promise.' He gave her what he hoped was a dazzling smile, knowing he could still pass for boyish.

She looked him up and down, then, after a moment's consideration, finally lowered the gun.

'Fine, come in. But keep in mind I know how to use this. I've practiced at the firing range every Thursday afternoon for the past thirty years.'

'Duly noted,' he said, shivering slightly, as he opened the screen door himself and followed her to a club chair in a corner of her homespun paradise.

She settled on one of the couches after tossing aside a tattered aqua-and-pink striped blanket she'd probably crocheted herself.

'I'm sorry I can't offer you any tea, but I don't think you'll be staying long enough to drink it.'

True to her word, she kept the gun close, propping it up against the sofa beside her.

'Fair enough,' he said, nodding his assent. 'Just a couple of minutes.'

'What is it you want with my brother?'

'It isn't really him I'm looking for. I'm trying to find his daughter. She used to go by Laura Martin.'

The name set her twitching. Maybe she knew about the girl's origins. Maybe she was an accomplice. She crossed her legs at the ankles, which were bare beneath the edge of her white capris, and stared at her unvarnished nails, not daring to glance back up at him. It figured. He'd keep a close eye on this one, kindergarten teacher or not.

'You'll have to discuss that with my brother. If you can find him.' He thought she seemed a little too nonchalant, a little too coy.

'I'd like to. That's just the point. I need to find him so I can find her.'

'Maybe you can, maybe you can't. Me? I haven't seen her since she was seven.'

Seven. Just like Abigail. He stared at her, as if his penetrating gaze would be the thing that broke her. But she remained inscrutable.

'What about her mother? Do you know her?' He was determined to probe around until he hit the a-ha moment.

She only laughed at the idea.

'Her mother? No, no. She was my brother's ex and they didn't exactly have a long-term relationship. He never brought her home to the family. He didn't even know about the girl until she was two or three.'

'Then how did he end up with the child?'

'Apparently the mother had hidden the girl's existence from him – I don't exactly blame her. He found out through some old friends they had in common and lit out like a shot to get her. There was no stopping my brother when he got an idea in his head. Supposedly there was a big battle but he got full custody. Or so he said. Strange to me that the court would give that ruling, I thought. Then they went on the road. You do the math.'

Adam's pulse quickened. She was practically telling him the girl was abducted.

'He was on the run, wasn't he?'

She shrugged. 'I tried not to think about it.'

'You believed the girl was his daughter?'

The woman pursed her lips and closed her eyes for a moment, sighing.

'Believed it? Sure I did. Probably not the only bastard kid he's got out there. I couldn't see him taking responsibility though, unless he was sure. Once he started drinking, well, then it was a different story. He didn't care so much about women then. He just wanted money, money, money all the time. That's why I mostly cut ties. I was sick of working like a dog and then having him beg for every penny.'

'What about now? Is he still in Roanoke?' He'd take what he could get.

She gave a low laugh, presumably more at ease now that he'd moved away from the sore spot.

'No, thank goodness. He hasn't been here in years. They stayed in town for maybe six months and then I understand there was some . . . trouble over at the campgrounds. Don't know the details, but I gathered he and his girl had some kind of falling-out. He never mentions her in his letters now.'

Adam could feel the color draining out of his face. What if he'd gone through all this trouble to track down her father, and now they were estranged? Or worse, what if that was an excuse he'd told his sister, and in reality he had finally killed the girl? An abrupt end of the line for Adam's long quest.

'He still writes you?'

She raised an eyebrow.

'How else is he going to ask for money?'

'So you do know where he is.'

She sighed, stood up, and walked over to the window, where she stared out at the daffodils growing wild far down the hill below the house.

'Listen, the one thing I don't want to do is make my brother angry. He has a temper, still drinks. He's unpredictable. True, I haven't seen him in a few years, but I don't know when he'll turn up and what kind of havoc he'll wreak in my life. I don't want to have a mark against me in his book.' She turned to face him.

'Tell me the truth. Why do you want to find his daughter? Is she in some kind of trouble?'

Adam paused, his mind running through all the possible excuses before landing on one he thought might work. He had a feeling she wouldn't tell him anything if he mentioned murder. He needed a sob story.

'No, not at all. The truth is, this isn't a police matter. It's personal. You see, I think we might be related through her mother. I haven't been able to track her down, so now I'm looking for Laura Martin. My cousin needs a bone-marrow transplant and we can't find a match.'

She walked back to her spot on the couch, sat back down. She leaned forward with her elbows on her knees and hands clasped together. Her eyes softened.

'I see.'

'And of course the family would love to meet her after all these years.'

'Hm. Well, that girl probably would have been better off sticking with her mother's people, truth be told. Or living with me. You know, I offered to raise her.'

Adam surveyed the cozy room and his heart sank for Laura Martin. That news cast it in a different light. Things would have been so much better for her if her father had taken her up on the offer. Living here, in this peaceful, comfortable home, with this sane woman who was obviously capable of protecting them both, would have changed everything.

She stood up.

'Well, I doubt he knows anything about her current whereabouts, but hold on.' She sighed. 'I'll tell you where he is. Might make up for some of his sins to help out in this situation.'

She went over to the pale yellow painted desk in the corner of the room. It was covered with papers, which she shuffled around for a bit. She picked up a handful of envelopes and rifled through them, tossing the discarded ones into a drawer.

'Here, this is the most recent one I have. He's in New York. Way upstate, Rochester.' She leaned in, squinting at the small print on the envelope. 'Northwoods Resort.'

Adam smiled at the name as he wrote it down in his notebook that he then slid into his front shirt pocket. He stood to go.

'Thank you. Thank you so much. Do you want me to deliver any messages?'

'I'd prefer it if you kept my name out of it, to be honest. Whatever he's doing in Rochester, he should keep at it. I haven't heard from him in over three months. No telling what kind of scam he's running, and I don't want to know.'

Adam let himself out, careful to keep the screen door from slamming behind him, and drove directly to the regional airport. He'd sleep in his car that night to save money, and drive it back to the rental lot first thing before moving on. He needed to go back to Stillwater, then on to Rochester. More plane tickets, more rental cars, more rounds of scrimping on badly cooked diner meals.

Adam had checked the balance of his bank account earlier that day. For the first time, he'd dipped under five thousand dollars. That wouldn't last much longer at the rate he was spending money. If only those two had stayed in one damn place. Eventually he'd have to grovel to his mother, but even she couldn't afford to keep him going. He wouldn't be able to sustain this search much longer. He needed a breakthrough fast.

At the airport, he watched the small planes taking off and landing. It calmed him, made the world seem so orderly to see them wait their turns on the runway before tilting out into the sky, filled with the hoi polloi on their way to dull business meetings, tense family reunions, and drunken sales conferences. Normal things. While he, he the defrocked and disgraced pseudo-cop, was wasting years of his life tracing an untraceable girl who'd brought a bloodbath down on a small town twenty years ago. He'd never shake the dark side, never be ordinary. He knew that even now, as he drummed his fingers on the steering wheel, whistling the killer's tune from the old Fritz Lang film before he realized what he was doing and abruptly stopped.

He shook his head. He mustn't get discouraged. If he gave up now, everything would be for nothing. He'd never be the hero he was born to be, would never claim his birthright.

Staring at the flat asphalt expanse before him as the blue-and-white runway lights flicked on, he ran his hands through his hair in frustration.

'Laura Martin, where are you?' he whispered out to the jetway.

CHAPTER 37

They'd been at the new camp in Virginia for three weeks and Cora still hadn't spoken to a soul there. She refused to go to school, figuring that by the time someone reported her to the truant officers, the academic year would be over anyway. For the most part she barely left their tiny kitchenette, spending the bulk of her days hugging her knees in the corner by the sink going over the events of the previous year in minute detail. She was looking for the mistake, trying to figure out how everything had gone so wrong. It was her own fault, she knew, and now she had to puzzle out a way to tame this destructive power of hers.

Meanwhile her father left her alone. He didn't want to face their day-to-day practical concerns any more than she did. They were trapped in the nuclear halo of what happened, still disoriented and confused. He watched her quietly out of his watery, blinking eyes, waiting to see who would make the first move in this delicate dance of theirs. They simply didn't know how to relate to one another now. Neither seemed able to decide whether to address the murders head on or to tacitly agree to let those horrors lay buried in Stillwater.

Cora knew that same set of memories must be swirling in both their heads. Tying them to the chairs, the panic and screams and tears. Surely he thought of that same moment that played for her on repeat: her father's hand gripped around her own, forcing the blade into Reed's flesh. She hadn't wanted to do it, but she was guilty just the same. She hated herself for her weakness, for her stupid missteps that had led them straight to catastrophe.

Her father too must wake with a start each day, ripped from sleep by violent images of blood and bone and flesh. He must be feeling the same sinking regret that flooded into Cora's heart with every sunrise. The 'if onlys' that tried to erase it, but never could, bubbling up like foam in a flooded stream. Those three faces, floating before them at night, when they wanted sleep. Maybe that was why their eyes couldn't meet, why they took their meals at different times, why one left the trailer as soon as the other entered.

Through all of it, she was surprised to find she missed the old place. As much as she'd tried to avoid making friends at that camp, she'd taken comfort in the familiarity of the hippie lady next door and the autistic kid three trailers down. They hadn't exactly been family. Not exactly, no. But they were constant, and that kind of regularity was something she'd never had before Stillwater.

She stopped herself. There was the name again. It echoed in her head because she knew she was supposed to have wiped it clean from her memory. The killings had made national headlines, if only for a day or two, but it had been enough to make her father paranoid. He'd traded their brand-new, though stolen, jumper cables for a beat-up transistor radio, and he spent half the day sitting out front with his ear glued to its speaker as it churned out static-y weather reports and news on the half-hour.

The story had only been a brief mention at first and then it was gone, lost in a sea of other, more significant, tragedies. Domestic terrorism, chemical-plant explosions, hurricanes, avalanches, wars. No one cared about a few lower-middle-class kids stabbed to death in some forgotten mining town in the flyover part of America. At least not without a particularly diverting narrative to attach to it, like a pedophile ring or a cult killing or a known serial killer with a twisted M.O. Theirs looked by all accounts like an ordinary drug deal gone bad, so the media lost interest fast. Lucky for them.

Her father started to breathe easier as time wore on without fresh news. They'd outrun it, it seemed, just like all his other more trivial crimes. She could tell it was bothering him though. He kept to himself more and even made sporadic yet feeble attempts to stay sober, attempts that sometimes lasted all the way until nightfall. Still, it had affected him deeply, she knew, and so she braced herself for the inevitable breakdown that would set their worlds rocking.

Once the camp started to liven up after hours, he couldn't help himself though. The warm weather came early in Virginia, and so did the campfire drinking. Lively shifted to rowdy and then to chaos by midnight, and her father seemed determined to be the drunkest of them all. It was how he could forget. Cora was envious of him for having that escape, but when, without a word, he passed her an open bottle of gin one night, she shook her head with regret. In truth, she wanted to remember. She deserved her punishment and wanted to feel its full effects, however painful and for however long it took.

The heat got to her in a different way. Forced outside to escape the unbearable swelter of the trailer, Cora moved her sleeping bag over to one end of their patch of yard and built a provisional shelter out of their last garbage bag. She enjoyed staying there all night under the stars, reciting the names of the constellations when she had trouble sleeping. Ursa Major, Cassiopeia, Cepheus. They sparkled above her the same way night after night, wherever she'd lived and whatever had happened, unchangeable, unfeeling, without regrets of their own.

If sleep proved to be especially elusive, she'd get up and walk, sometimes for hours. The place grew still in the early hours of the morning when the partying finally subsided. She loved it there then, alone with her thoughts and the chirping crickets and the black night, stepping over the passed-out bodies of these forgotten souls who littered this dirty corner of nowhere.

It was on one of those midnight rambles that she noticed a glowing light a few hundred yards from the edge of the camp, in the woods that were strictly off-limits. An orange sign posted on a black locust tree designated that area as private property, but somebody had strayed over the line nevertheless. Something was happening.

A flicker of light shone through the twisted trunks. A rumbling voice mumbled quietly and a chorus of answering 'amen's called out from the shadows.

She crept closer and crouched down behind the thick underbrush just outside the clearing. There were about ten scraggly-looking men and women of varying ages gathered around a blazing fire, sitting cross-legged on the ground, their eyes closed and their hands clasped in prayer. One ethereal-seeming man stood at the edge of the ring in a filthy long white robe. Their leader, she presumed. A golden amulet the size of a half-dollar hung from a bright red ribbon around his neck. His long hair and beard covered his face except for his glittering eyes, which avidly studied his flock.

His expression was stern as he muttered under his breath and made his way slowly around the circle. By his side was a thin girl, not much older than Cora, who trailed behind him with a large silver bowl in her arms. She wore a robe similar to his except hers was a faded army green. Her thick hair was wound into a demure bun topped by a coronet of flowers. She had a skittish air about her. Her eyes were locked on his, as if waiting for a secret signal. Every now and then he dipped his hands into the bowl she carried and then touched the forehead of one of his supplicants.

Then his voice boomed out, 'Though the world may judge you, I have foretold that the universe has its place for each of you, my Followers. A place where only the Spirits may distinguish between true rights and wrongs.'

Cora rolled her eyes. She'd seen this sort of nonsense before. Missionaries were always roaming around the camps, handing out pamphlets, talking about God's love, the kingdom of heaven, and the renunciation of earthly sin. Cora and her father had always ignored them, slamming the door in their faces if they dared to knock. They knew the drill. Half the time these wanderers were just trumped-up beggars with a well-practiced scam.

With that in mind, Cora decided to leave before she was caught spying on them. She didn't want to have to explain herself or fend off the inevitable offers of redemption and perfect peace.

His voice rose up again: 'Destiny! It is our destiny to differentiate between the sacred and the profane.'

His congregation, such as it was, rose at his words, lifting their hands in mute joy. He gestured for them to sit, so he could continue in peace.

'The earth is filled with both pleasure and pain. But we, the Chosen Ones, shall rule over all.'

Cora had had enough but as she turned to go, she had to do a double take. She gasped, unable to believe her eyes.

Her father sat in the circle, as enraptured as any of them. The preacher's hands were crossed over his face as he chanted some ridiculous prayer or incantation.

She realized then that she hadn't actually laid eyes on him in at least two days. She hadn't thought much of it, figuring he'd gone on one of his patented benders and had been crashing at that guy Leroy's camp but apparently not. She stared at the scene, in awe this time, noticing how her father's shoulders shook ever so slightly, the telltale sign that he hadn't had a drink in several hours. And at this time of night? It made no sense.

And lo and behold, there was Leroy beside him, looking up at their leader with what could only be called religious fervor.

Had those two actually fallen for this? It was the last thing on earth she would have expected.

She had to get closer.

'The Visions have revealed the truth. They have sorted the mystical from the mundane. Hear the Words, and be glad.'

Squatting down, she crept a few feet toward the circle under cover of the brambles. She didn't recognize this man. He must have moved into the camp within the last week. There'd only been one spot over on the north side left with a proper RV hook-up, so he must have taken it.

He was tall, late twenties she guessed, and, while he wasn't handsome exactly, she could see his appeal to the crowd. He had a charismatic, seductive quality to him that she could read even at this distance. His voice had a soothing undercurrent, comforting and lilting until it would suddenly burst into a deep-throated thunder.

Cora didn't like this. No, she didn't like it one bit. Her father wasn't one to fall prey to these shysters. There was something dangerous about this man, something to watch and fear. Every nerve in her body was on high alert. Instinct told her to run, get out of there, get her father and move on to another camp.

The hot night air shifted and blew her hair around her face. She pulled it out of her eyes and crossed her arms, rubbing away the goosebumps that had popped up. There was a strange energy surrounding her like a mist. She could feel it pulsing under the earth, flowing around her, carried by this wind. It wouldn't let go unless she shook it off with force, unless she outpaced it, but she was rooted to the spot, immobilized by a strange sense of dread.

Suddenly the man looked up in her direction. She was certain he couldn't see her there in the dark, hidden by the thick forest, but she held perfectly still just in case. He paused in his sermon. Her heart beat faster.

Could he see her?

It couldn't be the case but it seemed as if he was staring right at her, right through her, with eyes aflame. Then his voice bellowed out, exploding in a barrage of unintelligible words, a terrifying and mystical gibberish, some kind of dark, archaic spell in a long-lost language.

'And so it is written in the dark book of Time,' he ended with a wave of his arms.

Everything was dead silent. Cora blinked once. Twice.

Then, with that booming voice rising up at the end of each word, he called out her name.

CHAPTER 38

Cora didn't hesitate. She turned and broke into a hard run, forcing her way through a netting of branches that seemed to close in around her, pulling her backwards toward the circle. She ignored the scratches on her arms and face and hands. She felt she was running for her life. Something there had scared her, shaken her to the core, and her fear drove her on, to get far, far away from it.

Damn her father for getting involved with that man. Damn him for dragging her to this camp in the backwoods of hell. Damn them both for leaving Stillwater in the first place.

She ran on until she couldn't breathe, stumbling back into the camp and flying up the steps into their trailer. She slammed the door behind her, trying to catch her breath, trying to figure out a way to protect herself from the evil lurking on the other side of the door. The lock was useless and she had nothing to barricade herself in with. Even in that enclosed sealed space she felt vulnerable and exposed.

She peered through the cheap plastic blinds they'd put on the back window. The camp was still. A few fires burned here and there, but mostly there were only trickles of smoke climbing their way to the heavens. To her left, a shirtless man with his shorts unbuttoned flopped over in his sleep, rubbing his eyes until his hand slowed to a stop and slipped to the ground. To the right, a lone squirrel had come out of hiding to steal some scraps of food before the humans stirred at daybreak.

No one had followed her. He'd let her go. It didn't matter if he'd followed her then or not though. He would come for her. She felt it.

The worst of it was that he'd known her name. Her new one anyway – Caroline – the one she'd picked out randomly from a dime-store thriller she'd read last winter. It meant her father was blabbing about her when he had no cause to. Had he volunteered the information or had the devil asked?

Still panting, she crossed the few feet to the sink and filled a glass with water. It had a metallic taste here that people blamed on bad pipes, but everything was wrong in this place. It was a sinister omen, water that tasted like blood. She spat it back out, letting half of it run down her chin as she leaned over the drain.

Cora wiped her mouth with a small towel and then buried her face in it. She couldn't explain her feelings about this man. Maybe she was being irrational, maybe she'd lost her mind, but she couldn't help but feel her father had betrayed her by joining in that absurd ritual. If he couldn't be counted on, then what did she have left?

She curled up on the bed in the back and threw her arm over her eyes. Her father could take the sleeping bag outside tonight. She had to forget what she'd seen. She'd try to concentrate on her memory of Reed's face, hoping that he'd come to her in her dreams tonight. Maybe he'd been false, only pretending to care for her, but she'd convinced herself she couldn't be sure of that. Whatever the true story, in her dreams he loved her and that was all she had left anyway. She closed her eyes, wishing the outside world away, and must have eventually drifted off.

The next thing she knew she was awakened by a gentle knocking at the door, as the light flooded in across her face. It wasn't her father out there. He would have been beating the door down, kicking it until he dented it in. The marks already there showed clearly enough what he could do. No, this was a new sound. And Cora knew exactly who it was.

He'd come for her after all.

She didn't move. Maybe he would go away.

But he didn't. The outline of his hands and lips showed through the frosted glass of the door. She shivered, scooting farther back onto the bed.

He used the soothing voice.

'Caroline, I know you're in there.'

Yes, he knew. She knew something too. That there would be no escaping him. She slowly rose from her perch, throwing off the dirty sheet, and limped over to the sink to wash her face. She looked in the mirror at her disheveled hair and red face. She combed down her hair and straightened her clothes, the ones she'd been wearing continuously for the last two days. Hopefully she smelled.

She wanted to repel him, to drive him away like an exorcised spirit.

She opened the door and stepped out into the yard without a glance in his direction. It was the eyes that held the power, like a Medusa who would surely turn her to stone.

From her periphery, she could see he wasn't wearing his robes today. Just a cheap pair of jeans and a Western-style plaid shirt, the kind with snaps instead of buttons. Salvation Army, for sure. He wore beat-up leather shoes at least one size too big. His feet swam in them. And the smell. Acrid body odor mixed with the burnt embers of last night's events. He was a nobody, a thief, a villain. He was looking for trade.

She sat down on a log in front of their empty fire pit. Her father must have left without breakfast, or more likely didn't come home at all.

The man reached up to the maple next to them and twisted off a small branch. He knelt down on one knee, took out his knife, and started whittling. His hands were expert, deftly carving off tiny splinters and flicking them into the pit.

Her heart raced.

'Caroline.' His knife paused in mid-air, as he turned to look at her slyly. 'Tell me. Is that your real name?'

He cocked his head to one side. So sure of himself, wasn't he? Had her father tipped him off? She'd kill him if he'd let this man in on their secrets. They both had too much to lose.

'Yes,' she said firmly. 'Named after my grandmother.'

He chuckled quietly.

'Exactly.' He paused. 'Well, I'm James.'

Her face was numb. With nothing else to do with her hands, she worked at the fabric at the edge of her shirt, kneading it with her thumbs. *A tell*. She dropped it like a burning coal.

Hold still. Give nothing away.

'Why did you run from me last night?'

'I didn't – I didn't want to disturb whatever it was you were doing. It's not my business.'

'You wouldn't disturb us. It's open to all, Caroline. You should have come closer. Heard what I had to say.'

'No. It's okay. No offense or anything. I'm just not cut out for religion.'

'But this isn't like any other religion.'

She nodded, staring into the ashes of yesterday's fire, unable to speak.

'Caroline, look at me.'

She resisted. She wouldn't look at him. That was one thing she could still do, not look at him.

'Car-o-line.' He said it teasingly, in singsong, as if she were being a petulant child avoiding his face.

'I think you know already how much you need me. I can feel a strong power emanating from you. And I'm sure you can sense my own force reaching out to you across the cosmos. You have been through many trials. I can help you. I understand you. Will you please look at me?'

No, she wouldn't. She stubbornly gazed down at the ashes, even as she felt her skin going hot and cold. She would never look at him. There was something wrong with him. Something bad.

'When you change your mind, you know where I'll be. Come to me. Tell me your real name and then I'll know you are ready. That will be the sign between us.'

To her relief, he stood to go, tossing the finely pared-down stick at her feet.

She didn't move after he'd gone. He was right. His presence did exert some kind of force over her. He was the flame, she the moth, but she could resist now because she *knew* he would burn her up in an instant.

She'd made her mistakes already and now she knew better. She picked up his whittled stick, lifted it up to eye level, and snapped it in two.

CHAPTER 39

Julie sat up in bed, as close to being in position as she could manage with her foot touching the bedpost, posing as if it were still secured there. Sweat coated her skin despite the cold of the room.

In the few seconds she had before the woman entered, she slid one hand under the blanket to touch the shears and reassure herself once again that they were real, not another hallucination. She jabbed the center of her palm onto their tip, relieved at once by the pain.

'Go time,' she whispered.

The footsteps were closer now. She was right outside. Julie took a deep breath and put both hands up in the air. She knew she could do it. She mustn't imagine what it would feel like, must not overthink it, but simply act the moment she had a decent line of attack. She had no choice but to kill.

The window cover slid open and slammed shut in seconds and the door opened. Julie trembled, unable to look at her full on, as she put the tray of food on the edge of the bed and gave Julie the usual signal to begin.

Julie choked down the food. The dry crusts of bread were barely edible to begin with, but now her throat was constricted under the stress of the occasion.

'What's wrong?' the woman taunted. 'Aren't you hungry? Or is the food not to your liking?'

'Thank you, ma'am. It's delicious.' She swallowed hard, hoping the soggy broccoli would stay put.

'As you can see, I've tied you down for now. Didn't want you hurting yourself anymore after the accident.' Julie couldn't tell if she was being serious.

'Accident?'

'With the console.'

'I don't remember.'

The woman stared at her hard.

'Are you – is the baby –?'

Julie automatically put her hand on her stomach.

'The baby's moving but I don't know if it's hurt. I should see a doctor.'

The woman took a deep breath.

'You seem fine. A couple of bumps and bruises won't kill·you.'

'My leg though. I can't feel it. I think there may be something wrong.'

Check it. Pull off the blanket.

If she could only get one clear view of her back.

She slid her hand under the edge of the blanket as the woman's eyes flicked to her covered leg. She was moving toward it, reaching out one hand. Inch by precious inch, she moved into Julie's target zone, oblivious to the danger.

Julie grabbed the shears, her fingers shaking as she wrapped them around the cold metal handles. The woman whipped off the cover and gasped as she processed Julie's ruse.

Rage coursing through her, Julie drew back her arm, poised to strike. So she could do it after all.

But the woman was fast, her survival instinct unerring, as she twisted around and grabbed Julie's arm mid-air. She squeezed the flesh between her fingers, her nails cutting into it. With her other hand, she held Julie's wrist, pressing hard into the center of her bones.

Julie screamed.

One by one, she pried Julie's fingers off the shears. Julie clenched her teeth, sweat pouring off her now. Their arms shook as they gripped one another, struggling for control. Julie leaned her head forward ready to bite wherever her teeth could make contact. In that instant though, the woman gave a final hard jerk and ripped the shears from her hand.

They clattered against the tiles as the woman shoved Julie onto the bed. Her head hit the wall and Julie gaped up at the woman in terror. She'd surely kill her now. She'd never talk her way out of this one.

'I wouldn't have done it,' she said through tears. 'You frightened me and I couldn't let go but I could never have done it.'

The woman stepped back, panting. She picked up the shears and pointed them at Julie.

'You tried to kill me,' she said between clenched teeth.

Julie had to talk fast. Paint a picture.

'I had – I had planned to use the shears but when the time came, I knew I couldn't. You've been—'

'You tried to *kill* me.' This time she seemed more incredulous than anything else.

'I wasn't going to do it,' Julie screamed, pulling the sheet up under her chin as if that would protect her.

'You set it up. You made a plan. You *were* going to do it. You *tried*.'

The woman shook her head in disbelief.

'You disgusting ingrate. Don't you know I could have killed you when I found out about that baby? James would never have known. But I didn't. I took care of you. I've done everything for you. You would *die* without me.'

'I'm so grateful – so grateful for everything you've done.'

'All your sweet words and your fake pity. Now I see how it really is. Now I know you.'

'I'm sorry, I'm so sorry.'

'You should be. You're going to have a long time to think about it all alone up here. I've been too indulgent with you. That stops now. It's over. Whatever foolish sympathy I might have felt, whatever I'd imagined about you, it's all over. Forget it. Now I know. You aren't giving in. You aren't accepting anything. You are a deceiver.'

She headed to the door. Julie tried again.

'It isn't like that. Please don't leave me. I'm sorry. I'll make amends.'

She wouldn't listen though. As she stormed out of the room, Julie dissolved in tears. How could she have done this? She'd blown it. The hours of studying, thinking, plotting, planning – all for nothing. She'd thought she was so smart, as usual. A veritable mastermind. But now, with one simple false move, everything was in ruins.

CHAPTER 40

For months Cora watched from a distance while her father attended James's midnight rituals with the rest of his ragtag bunch of losers. She followed them out most nights, scoffing at James's ridiculous words even as they sank ever deeper into her psyche. They were absurd, inane, sometimes obviously concocted on the spot. He contradicted himself over and over again. Yet there was a compelling element to it that Cora could not deny. Perhaps it was his voice, his stance, his blazing eyes, or his fiery tongue. Whatever it was, it drew her in even as she pushed it away.

To make matters worse, the camp buzzed with talk about this newfangled cult. It brought excitement to their dreary mundane lives and at once bound the small community together and split it apart over whether to join or to dismiss it as a joke. Cora's ears perked up when she heard the talk, but she wouldn't engage in it, shrugging her shoulders and moving away when asked directly what she thought.

Two of the older women had sewn the congregants robes made from fabric scraps collected door-to-door. Everywhere she turned, the patchwork drones were poking around, distributing pamphlets or silently handing out lit candles with a show of earnestness. Her father looked like an idiot rendering these servile tasks, but what came out of his mouth was worse, a garbled mix of half-baked religious notions formed with a weak understanding of theology and a misplaced reliance on astrology. Cora wasn't buying any of it.

And yet.

James had come around to their trailer a few times after his initial visit. It was always the same.

'Come tonight, Caroline. Hear me lecture. I promise you won't be disappointed.' She shook her head.

As much as she resisted, though, it felt as if they were connected by an endless length of rope that tightened up when he came near, drawing her down into a fathomless hole that would swallow her up. Her heart felt sick when he approached, even as she played the deaf mute, focusing on insignificant acts, repairing their generator, hanging out washing, skimming the self-help book she'd borrowed from the woman next door. In short, using any and every ploy to avoid him. She'd lose herself if she weren't careful.

She needed to think. She needed to get away. And so she walked, for hours, for miles, as far away from his orbit as she could go.

One hot August day she strayed farther than usual when black clouds began to gather in the sky above. A storm was coming, the routine afternoon drenching that would move on after half an hour. She stole into a crumbling shed at the edge of a freshly mown field to wait it out, nearly jumping out of her skin at the first clap of thunder.

Across the landscape, a shape moved toward her. She swallowed, recognizing his loping gait and the tic of his twitching right hand. She tucked her body into the shed away from the doorframe, making herself as small as possible. He would head for the same shelter. It was inevitable. She cursed herself for not timing it better.

He picked up the pace as huge droplets fell from the sky, spattering against the tin roof above her. Then he ran.

She braced herself for confrontation.

He ducked his head in beneath the low entryway and found a clear spot on the dirt floor. He didn't even glance in her direction because he knew exactly who was here. He'd been following her. Of course, she should have known. He probably shadowed her every day, waiting for his moment. She knew then that it had been a mistake to resist him so openly. It only tantalized him, turned her into bait. Now he would never rest until he had her.

She looked away from him, one hand in her mouth as she chewed on her fingernails, the other twisting at her hair.

'That's a disgusting habit,' he said sharply. Not his usual teasing tone.

She jumped and sat up straight.

'I didn't ask you,' she replied as she dropped the offending hand to her lap, staring directly ahead at the deteriorating boards, wondering if she should pick up and run despite the storm. But something compelled her to stay. Something weak and terrible within her.

'I've been wanting to talk to you.' His voice was so sure. He knew he had her full attention.

'No kidding.'

'It's serious, Car-o-line.'

She said nothing, but relaxed a bit now that the cajoling tenor of his voice had returned. He sat, leaning against the opposite wall, his knees bent in front of him.

'I've been picking up strong vibrations from you,' he said with utter seriousness.

She could feel him staring.

'Right,' she replied, rolling her eyes.

'And I understand something about you.' He waited for a minute, but when she steadfastly failed to respond, he carried on.

'I wouldn't be so cavalier, Caroline. Not when you've done what you've done. I know who you are. You've committed a terrible act, and you can't live with yourself.'

She twisted to face him, her eyes squinting in disgust. She didn't want to let him rile her but she could feel her temper flaring out of her control.

'Leave me alone. Can't you just get out of here? The rain is stopping.' She peered through the doorway. It poured down harder than ever.

He glanced out at the deluge and smiled a slow smile.

'You're feeling very guilty. Wondering what kind of horrible person you are. But at the same time, mostly hoping you'll never get caught. Feeling that you might be, just maybe, a little bit –' He paused for effect.

She glanced up at him, unable to overcome her curiosity.

'Evil,' he completed.

She shivered. It was the damp that made her cold.

'You see, Car-o-line, this is where I can help you. My philosophy – let's call it that since you are not "cut out" for religion – can help you put your acts into perspective. Help you understand what you were destined for and what you weren't. I think once you have absorbed my Revelation, you'll feel much better. It will be an enormous . . . relief.'

'I haven't done anything wrong. You're mistaken.' On the outside she was icy, but inside the emotions were flooding her sensory capacity, threatening overload. Had her father told him what had happened? She'd kill that useless old man if he'd spilled their secret.

James moved closer and took her hand in his, flipped it over and stared down at her palm. She was afraid of what he would see there and tried to tug it away from him, but his grip was strong.

'You have a long lifeline. And important work to do. You are called to greatness, whoever you are. I can help show you the way.'

He stared deep into her eyes.

'I know how you feel, Caroline. Perhaps no one else has ever tried to understand you.'

She blinked.

'I know you feel alone. Because I know what that feels like. You see, I was orphaned when I was twelve. I lived on the streets, begging for scraps of food, running away from the social workers. I did what I had to do. I stole. I hurt people, Caroline. I had to. It was me or them in this world, and I chose me. And I wasn't wrong. It was the most noble thing I could have done. We have lived alone for a reason, to form ourselves out of the weak putty of human flesh into something divine. Now we don't have to live in solitude. Together we can form a new covenant. I will show you the way.'

He stroked her hair with one hand, then ran his finger along her lower lip. She couldn't move.

'You are only resisting me because you feel how strongly this force is between us. It scares you. I understand that. I am here to help you in your time of need.'

Cora pulled her hand free and stood up.

'You know nothing about me. Stay away from me. I don't want your help.'

She stumbled over him and out of the shed into the rain. The drops hit her like hail. It was one of the seven plagues to be sure, punishing her for her multiple transgressions.

He called after her, his hand cupped around his mouth.

'Caroline, come back to me. I am the only one who can help you. Don't wander alone in the desert. Let me be your refuge and strength.'

She ran hard, pushing the wet strands of hair out of her face. The clouds parted and forks of white lightning shot from the sky, hitting the earth at the edge of the horizon in front of her. She tripped and fell to the ground, spitting out rain. She clawed at the dirt beneath her, throwing it away in fistfuls as she dragged herself up and fled across the open landscape. She looked back: he was behind her, walking at his usual pace through the torrents. No matter how fast she went, he'd catch up with her eventually.

She couldn't run forever.

CHAPTER 41

A week had passed since the girl had tried to kill her. Cora did her duty even then, keeping her alive though she couldn't bear to look at her. She'd never felt so alone. She couldn't believe this is where everything had led – trapped with this pregnant girl, desperate for money, waiting for the authorities to find her and take her away to prison, the asylum, the electric chair. Her life was a ticking time bomb, a vise that had no release.

She thought she might burst open.

With these pressures mounting inside her, she had no patience for the girl's constant entreaties.

'I want to tell you again how sorry I am. I have been tortured by guilt ever since that day.' There she was, blathering as usual. Her glittering green eyes cast about frantically for any hold on Cora.

But Cora stared straight ahead, carelessly dropping the tray to the floor, letting it clatter against the tiles as flecks of mush hit the wall. She folded her arms, waiting impatiently for the girl to begin.

'You've done so much for me.' Sure enough, she was off. 'I'm so grateful. You feed me, care for me, talk to me. You've been like a mother to me.'

Liar. So many lies.

'I know this isn't your doing. It's him. I don't blame you. He brought me in to torture you. Don't let him use me as an instrument. Let us unite.'

Cora couldn't listen to her.

'Eat your food, girl, before I take it away.'

The girl fell to the floor at last, but ignored the tray. She beat her chest with her fist.

'Haven't you ever done anything that made you regret your whole existence? Haven't you ever felt guilt like this?'

Cora saw Reed's face, felt his warm blood running out over her hand.

'Shut up. I've had enough of your nonsense.'

The girl shoved aside the plate of uneaten food and crawled across the floor, prostrating herself at Cora's feet. She touched the edges of Cora's scuffed work boots with her grimy fingertips and looked up at her with imploring eyes. Cora wanted to stomp on her hands, to pull her hair out at the roots.

'I know you have regrets, too,' the girl cried. 'I can see it. I've spent every second of this last week thinking about our . . . situation and what I've come to realize is this – we are exactly the same.'

Cora clenched her teeth, felt her jaw set. What was she talking about?

'Don't you see it? You and I, we're in identical positions.'

Cora's anger flared.

'How dare you say that? I'm his *wife*.' The girl should know better. She should watch her mouth.

'We're both captives, though. You may be able to leave this room, but you can't get out of this place. He has a grip on your mind and you can do nothing but serve him.'

Cora's heart raced. That was exactly how it was. How could this girl know what it was like?

'He has you working night and day to keep me alive, to take care of this house and the farm—'

The girl stopped suddenly.

'To raise two hundred and fifty dollars,' Cora finished without thinking. She hadn't meant to say it aloud.

The girl, her eyes locked on Cora, struggled to her knees and clasped Cora's hands in hers. With shaking fingers she tried to pull Cora toward her, but she resisted.

'We can only make it if we are together,' the girl whispered urgently. 'We could be like the Followers once were, toiling together, side by side. We can make this house a home.'

Their shadowy outlines flashed in Cora's mind, walking side by side in their coarse cotton robes, arms lifted to the skies in holy ecstasy. She shook the image away. How dare this girl invoke them? *How dare she?*

'You told me once that I was a gift. Perhaps I am, but not the way you thought. Maybe I've been sent to build a family – the Divine Family – with you. Not with him.'

Cora jumped back, startled.

What fresh blasphemy was this?

And yet.

Was there any chance they had misinterpreted the Revelation? Could the Servant at Hand have been sent to *her*? To help her? Could this be the reward for her suffering?

The Wife shall suffer, but in suffering shall find her Great Reward.

'I am ready to accept my fate now. No more fighting it. I want –' the girl looked down at her belly, holding it with both hands – 'I want the baby to have a family. You've shown me that, despite everything, there is love in your heart. What I haven't told you is that the child responds to your presence, to the sound of your voice – I can feel it move when you enter the room. *It wants you.*' She paused and looked up at Cora's face. 'Together we can make things right. All of it.'

Cora gaped at the girl's protruding stomach. Could it be true? Was it *her* child tucked in there? The one she'd lost, reborn through the mystery of the Word. With a little pixie face and Reed's eyes.

'Consider the facts. He's been gone so long,' the girl went on. 'I don't think he's coming back. It's just the two of us now, plus the child. Why live apart when we can co-exist in peace and harmony, as you did with the Followers, sharing the burdens, rejoicing in a common vision?'

Maybe he wouldn't come back if she didn't send the money. She shouldn't think that way, but the truth was, she had been. The girl's words only echoed her own shameful thoughts. What would it be like if he never returned?

The girl paused and took a deep breath. She rose to her feet and approached Cora with slow, halting steps. This time Cora let her take her hands. The girl gently placed them on her stomach and Cora felt the child shift within her. Her child.

'*We are the same.*' The girl's chapped lips trembled. 'We've both lost everything. I've lost my family and Mark. You've lost Reed and your child from long ago. Think about it.'

Cora *was* thinking.

'Together you and I can restore your family and build a home,' the girl said. 'We can pick up the pieces. We can . . . we can fulfill the unfulfilled.'

Cora listened, she imagined.

'Let me come downstairs and I'll prove it. Housework. Farm work. I'll do anything you need. Please let me *help* you. Let us toil together.'

Cora felt confused. Images jammed up in her head of life on the road, in the camps, on the farm. She'd always felt alone. The family she'd been looking for had never materialized anywhere.

The girl squeezed her hands and lifted them to her chest. She closed her eyes as if making a wish, then opened them, beseeching Cora with her steady gaze.

'Would you please call me Julie? That's my name. Julie.'

Could this girl hold the answer, a spell to weave together the finished and the unfinished? With James gone, perhaps they could rebuild what she'd lost. If the girl had been sent to bring back her child, then the meaning of it all was suddenly clear. It was more than the girl even realized. It could be a final chance for her, a new Path in the dark wilderness of fate. She finally understood the true Revelation.

She shook her head, her mind on fire.

'No,' she said, pulling away from the girl and moving toward the door, dizzy with emotion. 'No, your name is not Julie. Forget that name. Your name is Laura.'

CHAPTER 42

It amazed Cora to see that her father had broken away so cleanly from James's cult. He must have grown bored with it. Or maybe he'd merely wanted an excuse to fall off the wagon. Either way, she never thought she'd be so glad to see him passed out and reeking of booze. When she'd returned to the trailer to find him that way the first time, she could hardly contain her delight. The old world was better than the new.

For a few weeks, too, she'd managed to avoid James. Her heart was light and her anxieties substantially calmed. She'd spent more time in town, buying school supplies and hitting the thrift stores to compile a dress-code-compliant wardrobe. Her hopes had risen on the thought that she'd possibly over-reacted to the threat James had posed. That summer she'd been at her most vulnerable, mourning and unstable, but she was pulling out of it now in time to forge ahead with life.

She still thought about Reed every day, but time had had a transformative effect. Now he was a sort of guardian angel, hovering over her, without blame and without regret. She'd managed to separate her feelings from their actions that day. She'd swept the blood and violence clean from her mind. It was pointless to dwell on it. Whatever had happened, had happened, and now she was lucky enough to start over in a new town, with new friends, and a new outlook. She had no choice but to embrace this fresh beginning and put the past behind her. Her survival depended on it.

All was well then, until the day she went out walking the fields again and stumbled upon James shooting at a row of cans. She should have stopped then, turned and run back to the camp. But she felt strong now and he seemed to have lost interest in her for the time being. Plus, she was curious. She'd never seen a real gun before, and he had three of them, loaded and ready for aim.

He spotted her immediately, put his weapons down in a row on the grass, and stood waiting for her, his arms folded and a cunning smile on his face.

'Have you come to tell me your name?' he said, winking.

She found herself smiling back. It all seemed so innocent now. He didn't believe all that stuff either. Why had she taken it so seriously before?

'I don't know what you're talking about,' she joked in return.

'I see,' he replied with his smile fading. He turned his back to her, lifting the rifle up to his shoulder and facing his ad-hoc firing range. He'd set up a pile of cement blocks she recognized from a deserted site at the edge of the trailer park. On top of them he'd lined a row of empties he could very well have gathered from their own garbage can.

She held still, watching him. Everything on earth paused as he concentrated on his task. He pulled the trigger and a Miller Lite can sailed up in the air and fell behind the cement blocks. He was good. A pro.

He turned to her.

'Want to try it?'

She did. But she didn't want him to know how badly.

She shrugged.

'I guess.'

He handed her the gun, and, standing behind her, foot for foot, put his arms around her with his hands over her grip. He slid his finger under hers to place it on the trigger. Her body felt electric. It was like Reed all over again. But no, he wasn't Reed. He was infinitely more sinister, infinitely more dangerous.

Nevertheless, she closed her eyes and let the warm feeling wash over her. He lingered a few seconds too long, apparently also savoring the feeling of standing so close. At last he let her go and moved to her side. She couldn't bear to look at him, to let him see the desire on her face. It would be a catastrophe.

'Focus on the target, let your eyes and hands guide you.'

She nodded.

'Stop moving your head. Let your mind merge with the gun. You must be one with the instrument of death.'

She lifted her head up from the sights.

'What?'

'Never mind. Just focus on your target. Hold still. Your whole body must be immobilized until the second you pull the trigger.'

She let her eyes drift back to the Sprite can across the field, willing herself to be one with it. Almost without realizing it, she pulled the trigger and the rifle recoiled in her arms, thrusting her backwards.

The can tipped off the edge of its block.

She'd done it. He clapped.

It had been such a rush. She felt bold, empowered, suddenly fearless.

'Well done. You're a natural. Try the pistol.'

He lifted the rifle from her hands and replaced it with the compact metal of the handgun. He showed her how to hold it, again by putting his arms around her from behind. This time his lips brushed her ear as he whispered his instructions. She felt an overwhelming urge to turn to him, but she forced herself to stare straight ahead. It wouldn't matter if she did, though, would it? She was safe from him now. She was going to school in two weeks. His spell was broken, wasn't it?

She shot and missed.

'Don't worry, Car-o-line, you'll get the hang of it. I'll give you lessons.'

She handed the gun back to him, her head clearer now. She stepped away from him into the safe zone just out of his reach as he lined the weapons on the ground in the space he'd set up for them. He opened the canteen that hung from his shoulder strap, took a drink, then offered her one.

She shook her head. She had to get out of there.

'Wait. Stay a minute. It's almost as if you've been purposefully avoiding me these past few weeks.'

She blushed.

'I've been busy. I'm going back to school this fall.'

'Oh? Where?'

'Piedmont High.'

He raised an eyebrow.

'How old are you?'

She'd turned fifteen the month before.

'Eighteen.' The lie slipped off her tongue unbidden. 'I missed some school though, so I'm behind. I want to finish up.'

He nodded, taking this in.

'Eighteen. Good.'

Her face was hot. Why had she said that?

He took her hands in his, pulling her to the ground.

'Sit with me. We need to talk.'

She felt desperate.

'I have to go. I need to see how my father is.'

'Speaking of your father. He seems to have lost his faith. Fallen back on his weaknesses.'

'That was inevitable. It's who he is.'

'But that's not who you are, Caroline. Your father is not worthy – he should tell you himself why. But I can see that you're different. You are chosen. I also know – I feel quite strongly that there is a secret in your past that's holding you back from your true potential. Voices have spoken to me in the night, from the sky, from the stars, from the unknowable darkness.'

'That's crazy.' She tried to keep the fear out of her eyes. She wouldn't be the one to give anything away.

He paused, looked up to the heavens, and then breathed in deeply, his eyes slitting as he leaned in close to her.

'I'll have to say it then. To bring the unreal to the plane of the real. You've killed someone, Caroline. Someone you loved.'

A chill rushed over her body. What had her father done? He'd seemed so earnest, so scared for his own well-being. Could he be that convincing a liar?

She struggled to keep her face a blank. She must never admit anything to this man.

'I want to tell you that you are absolved of your guilt because you are so chosen. The universe grants some of us the power, Caroline, the power to pass judgment on others, the power to act. Join me in my faith and you can see that for you there is no guilt, no shame. Together, we can walk in the shadow and be protected from all things.'

He was stroking her hair. She felt a sudden confusion. Could he be telling the truth? Did he practice some kind of dark magic, some mysterious witchcraft that had revealed her secrets to him? Her father had sworn he hadn't told anyone.

'Caroline, do not deny me. I know that you feel what I feel. You are not like the others here –' He waved a dismissive hand in the direction of the camp. 'They are lowly, mere tramps wandering through life in a haze. My followers are no different. I believe I was directed to this camp for a reason. And that reason is you. You are the only thing that matters to me right now.'

'What about that girl, your assistant? I thought that—'

He put his finger to her lips.

'Shh. Do not speak of that trifling girl. She is nothing to me. She has not been called. It's you. Remember our signal? Are you ready?'

She pulled away from him. The lure was powerful, but she could not help the dark feeling that passed over her heart when he was near. The bad omens were potent, crowding her vision, urging her to run away.

'You've been alone for such a long time now. You've had to carry so much. No one was there to protect you, to care for you, to offer you the unconditional love you need.'

She felt something tugging inside. A part of her wanted to fall into his arms, to let him decide, to have him support her. What was he offering, in truth?

'I have to go now.'

He didn't get up.

'I understand. You are always free to choose, Caroline. You should only come to me if you are willing. If you want to be with me – to be a part of me – the choice is yours.'

She nodded, looking away.

'But I will tell you now, the choice is total. And there's no going back. To embrace me is to embrace all that I am. Ask yourself, has life so far led you to happiness? To safety? To a place of pure love, understanding, and forgiveness? If you accept me into your heart, you must accept with total abandon, or not at all. Do you understand?'

She did. She understood only too well. She turned to walk away, knowing that she must never look back.

CHAPTER 43

Adam sat in a velvet-lined booth across from the beautiful, inimitable Deirdre, in a teal sweater set, her lips outlined and filled in with a deep orangey-red. She was a living cut-out doll from 1950s Americana, but then that was her shtick. Adam had to admit the allure and evidently Deirdre read the desire on his face.

'You like?' She raised a dark-outlined eyebrow at him, turning her head from side to side.

The bartender switched the channels on the television behind her head, and Adam's eyes flicked involuntarily to the screen.

'Very nice.' But he wasn't looking.

Out of the corner of his eye, he saw the waitress bring him a second beer and put down a martini glass in front of her.

'How's the case going?' Deirdre asked. He forced his gaze back to her.

'Great. Just great.' He took a sip of his beer, wiped away the ring it left on the table, met her eyes again. 'Unfortunately this time I'll be gone for quite a while.'

The corners of her smile fell a tiny bit.

'Of course you will. Why'd you come back here anyway?'

'Ship some boxes. Clear out of the hotel.'

She nodded, stirring the drink she hadn't yet touched.

'And to say good-bye to me?' She looked up at him from under her long, heavily mascaraed lashes. Winsome. Delectable.

Adam blushed.

'Not good-bye. Come on. Not at all.'

'Yeah, I get it. Let me guess. You are "not emotionally equipped for a relationship right now".' She lifted her glass and put her lips to its edge without taking her eyes off him. 'I'm still glad you came back.'

'Deirdre, of course I want to keep seeing you. I mean it. It's just a trip.'

She didn't seem convinced.

At that moment, the bartender settled on a twenty-four hour news channel and the thud of its theme music jolted Adam to attention.

'*The search continues for Ivy Murray, who disappeared from the Westgate Shopping Mall on December seventeenth. Last seen wearing . . .*'

He was instantly riveted. It was like crack. Like the needle reaching the vein. Like the—

'Adam. Adam, stop watching that.'

The screen filled with a montage of photographs of Ivy Murray. At her high-school graduation, in lacrosse gear, with her prom date in a glittering dress and high heels.

'Shh-shh. I want to hear this.'

The camera zoomed in on her face. Long brown hair, blue eyes, straight teeth of startling whiteness. A distinctive cherry-red birthmark below her left eye.

'The twenty-six-year-old University of Minnesota student disappeared without a trace, but her family believe she is still alive and say that no matter what, they will never give up hope. Police say—'

'Yes, they will,' Adam muttered under his breath. 'Eventually they will. Around the ten-year mark.'

'You can't stop, can you? Hello, Adam.' She snapped her fingers in front of his face. 'Not your case, Adam. Why don't you take a break for once and try to have a life?'

She looked at him hard.

'Actually, I take that back, just try to have a *date* for starters.'

He shook his head, forcing himself to focus on her.

'I'm sorry. I'm just a little distracted tonight.'

She slid her drink away from her.

'Tonight and every other second of your life. It's self-destructive, you know? There's nothing noble about it, even though I know that's what you think.'

She sat with her arms folded now, leaning back against the booth. Then she propped herself up on her elbows, close to him. She took his hands in hers.

'I have one question for you, Adam. I mean this seriously. Why is it you think you don't deserve to have a life?'

The words struck him hard. He'd never thought of it like that. The truth was, he *didn't* think he deserved to have a life. Not when so many others were robbed of theirs. Not when Abigail didn't get to have hers. But he couldn't explain that. Didn't want to.

Deirdre laughed to herself and clamped her hands to her forehead.

'Of course, I'm such an idiot. I always go for guys like you. What was I thinking?'

'Guys obsessed with solving crimes?' He watched her, puzzled.

'That, or programmers launching their own tech companies, or day traders with stocks in free fall, or guys still married with three kids. You know, totally emotionally unavailable men. My specialty.'

As Adam's mind drifted back to Ivy Murray, Deirdre banged her hands on the table and he jolted upright.

'Adam, I need you to focus. I can't sit by and watch you waste your life living out this fantasy. You've spent three years on it so far – how many more are you willing to put in?' She stopped. Her tone softened. 'I'm sorry. It's just that you and I are only getting started. This could go somewhere if you let it.'

Adam stared at her. She was right. They did have something. Possibly something extraordinary.

'Stay in Stillwater,' she continued. 'Let's do something crazy. Move in with me. You don't have to be a cop. You can work at my father's textile company. You might even like it.'

For a moment, he let himself imagine that. Putting on a suit and tie, going into the office. Fulfilling requisitions, filing documents. That was valuable too, wasn't it? But no, he couldn't stray from his mission for a life so mundane, so pointless, so ordinary.

He took her hands in his.

'Life has to have a purpose, Deirdre. That's all. And mine is justice. Do you understand what I mean?'

'Not really, no.'

Her face fell and she pulled away from him, gesturing for the waitress to bring the check.

He couldn't stand seeing her disappointed like this. He had to make himself clear.

'At first I wanted to solve this case to get back on the force. But it's more than that now.' He struggled for the right words. 'I used to see the world as a binary, divided into right and wrong, evil and goodness, sin and purity. It all made sense. But this case – instead of chasing a wicked, sadistic man like the one who took my sister, I'm after a woman who was just a confused kid going through hell. That's not the plan I had in mind.'

The waitress set the bill down in front of them. Deirdre scooped it up and slid two twenties into the faux-leather folder.

'You need change?' the waitress asked. Deirdre shook her head.

Adam kept on, barely registering them.

'But it's made me see another path to justice. Bigger than the police department. More important than getting my job back.'

Deirdre only stared at him with – was it pity? Perhaps he wasn't making sense after all.

'Let's try taking a vacation,' she said, clearly not hearing him. 'I'm thinking Hawaii. Umbrellas on the beach, snorkeling?'

He couldn't even picture such an unfathomable scenario. Not when there was work to do. He had to make her understand.

'Deirdre, think about it. She was so young. What if, after these murders, she got away from her father, got her act together, and now I'm coming out of nowhere to drag her back down into that past she's trying to forget? Is that justice?' He sighed. 'I have a huge decision ahead of me.'

Deirdre looked puzzled for a moment, then she stood up abruptly and put on her coat.

'Yes, Adam. Yes, you do.'

He stared at her, finally focusing on the situation at hand. He knew she didn't mean his case.

He didn't want to lose her. If she would just give him a few more weeks – he was so close. He knew it this time.

His mother's voice echoed in his mind: *You've been saying that for years. Exactly the same words.*

For a fleeting second, he doubted his purpose. Maybe they were right. Maybe he was on a wild goose chase that would inevitably fail. Maybe he was using this case to try to fix something that couldn't be fixed. Maybe he should stay here with Deirdre and make a fresh start.

She stood waiting for an answer. She clearly wasn't giving him any more time. It was now or never. His last chance.

He shifted uncomfortably to face the empty booth in front of him. He couldn't look at her just then. The world stood still, but his head was spinning. This wasn't fair. It wasn't fair for him to have to choose.

But he'd known all along which way he'd go.

'I have to finish this. I have to find her.'

He looked back toward Deirdre in time to see the tears spring up in her eyes. She wiped them with the palm of her hand and forced a half-smile.

Everything inside him wilted when he saw her expression. He hated to hurt her this way.

'Okay, Adam. Okay. Go find her.' She looped the belt on her coat and yanked it tight. 'I hope she's worth it.'

She turned and left. He watched her disappear into the crowd at the bar as he gulped the last of his beer and then slammed the glass down on the table.

A feeling of emptiness crept over him.

It was his destiny, he reminded himself. It was out of his control.

CHAPTER 44

Her father sat outside the trailer drinking gin straight from the bottle while Leroy lay on the ground beside him, his head propped up on a faded orange rucksack, playing an old blues song on his harmonica. The music stopped abruptly though when Cora stepped into the firelight and both men stared up at her stony expression. Leroy never said much, but he was an astute judge of character and situations. Without a word, he rose, gathered his possessions, and slunk off into the woods, taking up the melody again right where he'd left off.

Her father watched him go, shaking his head in frustration.

'Well, if it isn't my sweet little spoilsport, running my friends off,' he said snidely. He lit a cigarette in the flames and shoved it in the corner of his mouth, puffing like a smokestack. Then he took a good long look at her. 'Are you sick? You look like you've seen a damn ghost.'

'I guess I have, Father. I guess I have.' She wouldn't waste time with pleasantries. 'Remember when we had our talk about what you did or didn't tell James about a certain incident?'

His face went white.

'What I remember,' he said, 'is that we agreed to stay away from him. Listen, I hear the tide has turned. Everybody left his so-called ministry. You'll be safer if you aren't seen with him.'

This was news. The last time she'd crept over to the clearing, he'd had at least twenty followers. Had it fallen apart just like that? Then she put two and two together. The guns, the target practice. Was he preparing to defend himself? Had things gotten ugly? She wondered fleetingly if it had something to do with that young apprentice who followed him around like a lost puppy. She hadn't seen her lately and knew she had family at the camp.

That was beside the point right now.

'Father, I'm only going to ask you this once more, and then we'll be done with it. But I need the truth.' She sat down next to him, yanked the cigarette out of his mouth. He'd stopped smoking last month and they couldn't afford the habit. 'Did you tell James about Stillwater?'

'Don't say that word. Honestly, Cora –' he was whispering now, peering around them to see if anyone could hear – 'you can't talk about that. No, I told you I did not tell him and that should be enough for you.'

'He knows something though,' she said more to herself than to him. Cora felt so confused. If James was telling the truth about his visions then maybe there was a larger purpose to her life after all. Maybe their union was an inevitability that she was wrong to fight.

'He doesn't know shit.' Her father interrupted her thoughts. 'Unless he sees the guilt on your face.' He smiled and pulled another cigarette out of his pocket. 'It doesn't matter anyway. He'll be moving on soon enough. I can guarantee you that.'

So her father knew something too. Cora felt every muscle in her body tense up. Were they going to hurt him? She pictured pitchforks and torches, a gathering at the castle gates. A month ago she would have marched along with them, but now? Now she wasn't so sure.

The thought of him leaving – but no, it was for the best and she had to stay out of it. She was going back to school. She'd make friends this time. Nice friends. The ones who studied and made good grades and went to football games and did all the innocent stuff regular teenagers do. No drugs this time, no sex, no weirdo outsiders.

It would be a clean slate. But James had put a doubt in her mind about her father. They had outstanding business to settle first.

'Okay, let's put that past behind us. Start fresh.'

She sat for a moment, screwing up her courage. She hadn't dared broach this topic in years, but the time had come. She took a deep breath.

'I have one more serious question I need answered before I can do that.' She paused. She hoped he was ready for this. Hoped she was too. 'I need to know about my mother.'

His face clouded over.

'Cora, come on, could you forget about her? That's ancient history.'

'Not to me. I need to know. Is she looking for me?'

'Looking for you?'

'Did you abduct me? Is that why we're on the run?'

He shook his head, muttering uncomfortably.

'She was hiding you from me, Cora, but I found you. Oh, I found you. She couldn't keep my child away from me.'

'What did you do?' she whispered, afraid to hear the answer, but knowing she couldn't be at peace until she did.

'Jesus, Cora, I've told you over and over to let it be. It doesn't matter anymore.'

'Please. Just tell me. Then we don't have to discuss it again. I can handle it, whatever it is.'

He was annoyed, but she wouldn't let him off the hook this time. Finally, he shrugged and cleared his throat.

'You don't understand. She hired some fancy lawyer to say all these abominable things in court. He didn't know me. He had no right to talk like that.

'And that judge, stupid stuck-up bitch. She was about to give your mother full custody. Do you know what that means? That means my sweet baby girl would be gone from me. Gone, gone, gone. No one has the right to do that. Maybe they'd let me visit you once a year at Christmas, but then you wouldn't even know your old Pa.'

She rolled her eyes. He would never let her call him that.

'I had to take matters into my own hands, you see.' He chuckled. 'I guess I showed her.'

I showed her. The words reverberated in her head. She stared at him, dumbfounded.

'What do you mean?'

'I mean,' he stuttered, backing away from her, 'it was all an accident.'

'An accident? Like Stillwater was an accident?'

'I didn't know my own strength. She was . . . she just stopped . . . breathing.' He looked away from her. At least he had the decency to show some shame.

He'd killed her. Like he'd probably do to her one day, if she weren't careful. She was just another accident waiting to happen.

'You were always mine, Cora. I couldn't let her take you.'

Yes, that's how he thought of it. His possession, an object for his convenience. His to take care of him when he was hungover, to cook and clean for him, to be a built-in emotional support system when situations got tough, to beat when he needed an outlet for his rage. A useful prop in his tragicomic life story. It didn't matter to him what she needed. A home, a steady life, basic love and affection. A mother.

She looked at him in disgust, then stood up to go.

'Cora, wait. You have to understand.'

'I do understand. I know what you've taken from me. It isn't fair, Father. It isn't fair.' She stepped away, intending to wander the fields alone all night if she had to, to think about what it all meant.

'Where are you going?' The anger had faded from his voice, replaced by the piteous whine he used when he was feeling sorry for himself.

She turned on him, having had enough of his manipulations for one night.

'Nowhere. How could I go anywhere? I have nowhere to go. I'm stuck and I'll always be stuck here with you. Because you've taken everything from me.'

'It wasn't like that,' she heard him say as she walked away. 'I didn't mean it to be like that.'

Yeah, she thought. *You never do.*

CHAPTER 45

Cora couldn't sleep again. She lay there on her pallet, look-ing up at the stars and wondering how she could even stand it. She was utterly alone. She hadn't spoken to her father in three days and she would never speak to James again for fear she would weaken and tell him the truth. She longed for the distraction of school, now just days away. She needed to be with people her own age, needed to get out of the stifling environment of this camp before she went stark raving mad.

Something stirred in the woods behind the trailer, and she rolled over to see a figure approaching in the dark. She sat up, grabbing the pepper spray she kept concealed in her sleeping bag, ready to protect herself or run if need be. You never knew what kind of creeps would be out wandering in the night, looking for things to steal or vulner-able young girls to take advantage of.

As the silhouette took form though, she realized it was only James. Out on the prowl, ready to make another attempt at her she figured. She pulled her blanket over her head as he crept to her side. She couldn't help herself though, she peeked out. He held a finger to his lips.

'Relax, I'm not going to hurt you. You know that, Caroline.'

He was close enough now that she could see the giant gash across his forehead. His arm was in a sling made out of a ripped-up T-shirt. She threw off the covers and crawled over to him.

'What happened to you?' she whispered, not wanting to wake her father who had the trailer door propped open for air.

'Oh, Caroline, there are Unbelievers here. There are those who cannot face up to the true facts of the universe. You must not mind them. The Chosen will prevail.' He grasped her hands in his. 'We will prevail.'

'You need to see a doctor. That wound is still bleeding. That isn't good, James.'

'No, Caroline. I need no ordinary healers of the earth. The Spirits will heal me. But I have come to you tonight with a dire message.'

'Let me at least get a wet rag,' she said, still staring at his injury. 'And some Tylenol. I need to clean that wound. It's terrible.' She reached up to touch it and he winced, pushing her hand away.

'No. There is something more urgent. You see, I am leaving this camp. Tonight. And I want you to come with me.'

Her pulse quickened. Her father had been right. The others in the camp must have come after him. They were driving him away. Suddenly her heart flooded with pity. He didn't deserve that. He was only trying to spread his beliefs. He knew about her, understood her when no one else ever had. Everything he'd said so far had been true.

Was it her destiny to be with this man? Had everything happened so that she would end up here, in this moment, faced with this choice? In a strange way it all began to make sense. Reed and the others, were they simply sacrifices that had to be made so that she could be brought to James in his hour of need?

'I couldn't. I mean, even if I were willing to do such a thing, I'd need more time to get my things ready, to pack. And then, I'm starting school soon.' She felt a pang. She did want to go to school.

'You won't need anything. We can start a new following. The universe will provide for us both. You, you don't need school. I have all the knowledge you seek.'

She looked at the belongings she'd gathered around her in her improvised shelter to see what she could take with her. Two trunks she was using for benches, but they held nothing but a bunch of worthless keepsakes. A plastic garbage bag beside her contained her thrift-store haul from the day before. Enough to make do for a few days anyway, until they got things sorted.

'And your father. I'm sure you must feel some . . . hesitation about leaving him, but the child must part from the father. It is written. It is the way of all of life.' He was whispering frantically into her ear, all the while running one hand up and down her arm. He didn't seem like his normal self. She'd never seen him so worked up.

'Caroline, you are special. So special. Your father does not understand who you are. But I do. I will treasure you. We will be partners. Helpmates. I will show you the true kingdom. The universe, the heavens, the stars will be ours. No one can stop us. This is your destiny. This is our destiny. Your father is beneath you. Are you letting your filial affections hold you back?'

She paused, taking stock of it all, her life, her father, the empty bottles of rum strewn about their yard, their poverty, her guilt, the fading memories of her mother.

'No,' she said firmly, deciding once and for all. 'No, I'm not.'

She turned to James and at last their lips met as he held her in a passionate embrace. They parted and he stroked her face, beaming.

'Help me get my things.' She stood up and they held each other there in the faint glow of the moonlight.

He pulled back from her.

'You are coming to me then freely? You know what this means, and you are accepting my terms as I have offered them? All or nothing.'

'Yes.' It was thrilling to her, taking this leap. She would let come what may. She would finally believe in something, in someone. She could put her whole heart in his hands and he would keep her safe.

'And James?'

'Yes, my darling?'

She looked deeply into his eyes, knowing she was making the choice she'd always been meant to make.

'My name is Cora.'

CHAPTER 46

The Northwoods Resort was several levels above the Stillwater RV park. Not only were the campers top-of-the-line and the hook-up stations kept in meticulously good order, but rows of small cabins stood along the stream, each with their own front porches and window boxes that had surely been filled with annuals in the summer. At the front gate, actual security personnel had directed him to Cabin 32 on the west side. The home of Silas Lowry, the name he used now. Laura Martin's father.

Adam pulled onto the patch of gravel next to a battered green Jeep with chipped paint and went to the door. He hadn't given any advance warning this time. He'd traveled without thinking, knowing he would find the right words when he came face to face with the man who could be at the root of everything. He paused for a moment before knocking on the door, trying to calm his racing pulse. This was it. The answers were on the other side.

When Silas opened the door, however, Adam was taken aback. He'd expected a ruthless villain and instead found a stooped old man with the bulging red nose of a drunk and the sad sunken eyes of the misbegotten. It would be hard to rage against this man. He was just a broken-down sop.

'Silas Lowry?' Adam asked. At first, the man didn't seem to recognize the name and Adam thought for a second, with relief, that he had the wrong place. Then he must have remembered his own alias because he begrudgingly grunted his acknowledgment.

'My name is Adam Miller. I've been searching for your daughter for three years.'

Silas stared back at Adam, his blue eyes glinting, as if he were considering his next move. He was shrewd enough to try to hide his discomfort.

'Well, you're not going to find her here. She's dead to me, that one. Gone these twenty-plus years. Run off.' He studied Adam's face. 'But you can join me for a drink.' He looked at his watch. It was ten thirty in the morning. 'It's time for gin, after all.'

Silas beckoned him into the tiny one-room cabin. In truth it wasn't significantly bigger than an RV, but it had a certain woodsy charm. The sparse furniture looked as though it came with the property, built out of the same pine as the walls. Light flooded in through windows on all sides, each draped with cheery red-and-white checked curtains. Adam wondered in passing what kind of scam 'Silas' had been operating to end up with such fancy digs.

He followed Silas into the kitchen area, divided from the rest of the space by a slab of Formica. Silas gestured to Adam to take the solitary stool in front of it, while he rummaged around in the freezer for the gin. He pulled out two foggy glasses of questionable cleanliness and poured two fingerfuls of liquor into each. Normally, Adam would have been squeamish about such hygiene, but too much hung in the balance, and he wanted Silas to drink up to loosen his tongue.

'Why are you looking for my daughter?' the old man said suddenly. He swallowed his drink in a single gulp and poured himself another.

Adam decided to use the same ruse as with his sister. Besides, he liked the way it felt to make the claim, as if he were searching for Abigail instead. He turned up his glass and took the shot to bolster his courage.

'I think we might be related. On her mother's side.' Silas snapped to attention.

'That so, eh? That good-for-nothing whore.' He paused, looking back at Adam out of the corner of his eye. 'Did they ever find her anyway? I heard she skipped town. Probably run off with somebody's husband.'

Adam gripped the edge of the counter, wondering how to answer without giving himself away.

'No, no, she never did turn up,' he dared.

Silas seemed to relax and let his guard back down. Adam had guessed right.

'Yeah, crying shame,' Silas said under his breath.

'Did Laura – excuse me, I know she went by different names – is it okay if I use Laura?'

Silas stared down into the empty bottom of his glass, rubbing his brow.

'Fine, fine.'

He poured a third gin for himself and held out the bottle to Adam, who shook his head. Any more of that and he'd lose his train of thought. And possibly never stop.

'Do you have any idea what happened to her?'

'Nope. Probably dead. Given that dirt bag she ran off with.'

'Who? What was his name?'

Adam wondered if Silas would be able to remember anything with all that booze in him.

'Some loser who went around pretending to be a preacher. James something. It wasn't, like, a proper church or anything. Just a bunch of stupid shit about the skies and powerful life forces. Real cosmic, you know? People fell under that guy's spell hard. I got into it myself for a few weeks because he'd made it out like he could solve your problems. He talked a pretty good game, but nothing changed.' He lifted the bottle of gin. 'This is the only thing that helps wash your worries and heartache away.' He sniggered.

'How old was she when she left?'

'I forget now. Fifteen, sixteen. To tell you the truth, she was a bit of a slut like her mother. Good riddance to both of them, I say.' He raised his glass. 'Oh, sorry. No offense to your family. I'm sure the rest of you are nothing like her.'

Adam resisted punching him in the face. He twisted his fingers around the glass, boring it into the counter.

'What happened to her child?'

'Child? What child?'

'I found a letter she wrote. She said she was pregnant.'

'There wasn't any child. She was a child herself, for chrissakes. A liar too.' He chugged back the gin.

He looked genuinely surprised. Maybe she'd had an abortion before her father found out.

'Why did she leave the camp in Roanoke?'

Silas shuffled around to the other side of the bar and motioned for Adam to accompany him back out to the porch. Silas plopped down in a creaky wooden rocking chair and Adam leaned up against the porch railing, hoping it would hold his weight.

'Nicer out here, isn't it?'

It was nicer. Adam needed the air.

Silas paused, taking a slim packet from his front shirt pocket. He slipped out a pinch of chewing tobacco and tucked it in his cheek, gnawing at it for a moment before spitting out a black projectile.

'It was partially my fault. When I was in that cult, I had to make a kind of "confession" to the leader. I told him a couple of things I shouldn't have. He probably used what I said, twisted my words. That's how he was, you know? I was the idiot who made it easy for him.'

'Do you know where she is now, Silas?'

He stopped rocking.

'I quit looking for her years ago. It was pretty tough on the old man here when I first discovered her missing. I worried myself sick. Ran all over them damn woods searching for her. Crying my goddamn eyes blind, wasting tears on that useless girl. I guess we really loved each other, no matter all the bullshit that happened. I stuck around for a while, hoping she'd come back, then I gave up and made my way here.'

'And you never heard from her again?'

He shook his head.

'No. A few years later I heard a rumor that the preacher had been spotted in the Hudson Valley not far from Albany, up to his old tricks again. Later they say he gave up the calling, got into construction, transport, that type of thing. Oh, how the mighty have fallen.

'By the time I heard where she might be, I didn't want anything to do with her. She was a grown woman and could do what she liked. If she wanted to be his servant, she could. She'd betrayed me, left me like that in the middle of the night. Well, I don't care about her. She's dead to me. Dead to me.' He spat out another dark stream of tobacco for emphasis.

Adam moved to the open door, his eyes sweeping the cabin one more time. He spotted a framed picture just inside on a small shelf. He lifted it, staring at the two images captured there. Only one interested him.

'Is this her?' In the photo stood a girl of about the right age with brown hair, next to a younger version of Silas looking the other way, oblivious to the camera.

Silas crossed over to him faster than Adam would have thought possible and ripped it out of his hands.

'Give me that. You've got no business looking around here. Who are you – the cops?'

'Please, just tell me, is it her?'

'It's all I've got,' he yelled.

'Okay, okay, I understand,' Adam said. 'Calm down. I'm not going to take your picture. It's just that I've never seen one of her before.'

A slight smile broke out on the old man's face. 'That's right. No pictures. Never any pictures. This is the only one.

'If you do find her –' he started, but then stopped, holding one finger to his nose as he stared down at the carpet. For a minute, Adam thought he wasn't going to finish. 'If you do find her, why don't you tell her to drop me a line?'

Then he walked back to the kitchen and poured another glass of gin, this time filling it to the rim. While Silas put the bottle back in the freezer, Adam slipped his phone out of his pocket and surreptitiously snapped a photo of her picture.

He turned back toward the kitchen.

'Was it about the murders?'

Silas froze, the glass almost to his lips.

'What? What did you say?' He put the drink down.

'The murders in Stillwater? Is that what you told the preacher about in your "confession"?'

Silas's face went blank. Adam knew he was on to something. He kept on.

'Is that how he convinced her to leave Roanoke?'

Silas squinted over at him. 'Listen, I don't know who you really are, but you'd best just get out of here.'

Adam wouldn't let this opportunity slip by.

'Did she do it, Silas? Did she murder those three kids because that boy rejected her?'

Silas stood still, glaring.

'She disgraced herself, Silas. Your own daughter. Fourteen years old and pregnant. Then this good-for-nothing kid turned her down. She wanted revenge. Maybe you did too. Did she do it alone, Silas? Did you help her? Or did you help her get away with it?'

Silas's right eye twitched.

'I had nothing to do with anything like that. Get out of my house.' He moved toward Adam, fists clenched.

Adam edged toward the door. If he left now, Silas would clear out of there by morning and Adam might never find him again. He had to push forward.

'There's physical evidence, Silas.'

'I guarantee you none of it can be traced back to me,' he replied evenly. 'And I daresay if you find any prints, they'd lead you to one person and one person only. And that person's testimony isn't worth a damn.'

'So you do know something.'

Silas shook his head and a slow smile spread across his face.

'Three years, you say you've been looking? Three years leaving no stone unturned, eh? Digging through trash, talking to lowlifes, trying to blend in with the scum of the earth until you finally tracked me down? And for what?' He threw his head back and laughed. 'After all that, there's one thing you need to learn to accept, whoever you are.'

'What's that?'

'Not knowing shit.' He took a step toward Adam, his jaw set. 'Now go.'

For a fleeting second, Adam pictured his hands around Silas's neck squeezing the life out of him. That would be one path to justice. Who knew what this guy had gotten away with and would get away with in the future? How many lives had he ruined? And yet, Adam somehow knew that nothing would ever stick to this sneaky, manipulative son-of-a-bitch.

But he wouldn't turn Adam into a killer. Adam would walk away from this poison.

'All right,' he said. 'I'll go. But if you see me again you'd better run, because it will mean I have hard evidence to put you away for the rest of your life.'

With that, he turned and left Silas staring after him.

Adam figured that in truth he'd never meet Silas Lowry again. The old man would change his name and move on, just like he always did. He was the undercurrent of evil that kept flowing through the world, destroying everyone in its path.

But Silas was wrong. Adam did know something. While he might never know exactly what happened that day in Stillwater, Silas had told him two crucial things. First, he knew now for certain that the unidentified set of prints at the murder scene was Laura's. Second, he knew how to find her.

He would waste no time either. Things were worse for her than he'd imagined. She hadn't escaped into a normal life after all, hadn't risen above her circumstances. She'd fallen prey to a cult. Adam might not be able to bring one kind of justice to the world, but he could bring another. He knew what he had to do. He'd do it for Laura and for Abigail, for the women they might have been.

And then the world could be whole again.

CHAPTER 47

The crunch of gravel sounded outside. A truck pulled into the driveway and a flush crawled up Cora's neck. She would have recognized that sound from the grave.

James was home.

She rubbed her temples, then her eyes. Some part of her had thought he wasn't coming back. The girl must have gotten to her.

She rushed downstairs and checked the state of the kitchen. Things were in order more or less, but she hurried to put away the dishes drying on the rack and wipe down the kitchen table with a wet rag. She gently stoked the fire in the hearth, then pulled the curtain aside and peered out the window.

He walked toward the house, his cowboy boots clicking against the bluestone path and his cap pulled down low over his eyes. It was dusk and the first snow fell from the sky in great white flakes between them, further obscuring his face from view, but her radar was highly attuned to his emotional state. She could tell his mood was light. Things had gone well, even without the rest of the money.

He lifted his head enough for her to see that his eyes were clear and bright. His gait was steady, without the tell-tale sway of the wayward drunk. He even looked like he'd lost a few pounds and seemed trim and healthy. Despite the positive signs, however, she knew better than to let down her defenses. Anything could happen next.

She tried to compose herself as he approached the porch, rehearsing her first lines in her mind. She had to remember what it was like to love him, to admire him, to worship him. But so much had happened since he'd left. He'd stayed gone too long and now she'd forgotten why she'd followed him here in the first place.

A cold rush of air swept into the room when the door opened and their eyes met. Surely he must be able to see that the flame of her love had inexorably burned out? She looked away, afraid he would understand that everything had changed. If he realized he didn't hold her in his absolute power, he would kill her. She knew him well enough for that.

He hung his keys on the rack by the door and began to empty the contents of his pockets onto the table. Crumpled tens and twenties, a fifty here and there.

'What's this?' Cora dared. 'I thought you needed money.'

He sat down, leaned back in the chair and sighed with satisfaction.

'A bet came in. Plenty to take care of my issues and then get me back home. I missed this place.'

This place, Cora noted. Not her.

He gave her a broad smile. It was the old smile, the charming, winsome, little-lost-boy smile. He must have picked up on her lack of enthusiasm. He always thought it was so easy to return her to the fold. And why wouldn't he? It had happened so many times before, when she was reluctant or doubtful or dared to be petulant. A word or a kiss or the touch of his hand had made all her love come tumbling back, coupled with tears and regrets and heartfelt apologies.

But not this time. He had left her for so long and then sent her into a frenzy for money he hadn't even needed. All her sleepless nights, her worries about the girl and the money, and to top it off, having Ellie right here in their kitchen with the girl not ten feet away? Didn't he understand how worn down she was?

Not only tired, though, but afraid. For he would inevitably go upstairs and see the girl's condition. What then? What if he'd forgotten the Revelation entirely? Would he want the child or would he kill the girl to get rid of it? He mustn't do that, though. He mustn't hurt that child. The child belonged to Cora.

'Come on over here.' He grabbed her by the arm and sat her down in his lap. It was as close as they'd been in months. His sensitivities were unerring. He knew exactly when to pull out all the stops.

'Why the long face? I'm back. And we have some cash. We'll live it up for a bit, shall we? Have something nice to eat. I have plans for us, Cora. No more separations.'

She stared at him, not sure how to respond.

'You seem good, James. You look so healthy. Did you – did you stop taking those pills?' she ventured warily, never sure what would set him off.

And indeed a dark shadow clouded his face, but he quickly recovered his composure.

'Forget about that, Cora. That was the past. I have purified myself. The drugs and booze were a terrible weakness, but they are behind me. I have cast them out like the demons they were and will live purely now.' He paused, as if remembering something of vital importance. He grasped her hands. 'The girl, how is the girl?'

Now it would come out, the real source of his desires.

Cora turned away from him, fixing her eyes onto the toaster across the room.

'She's alive,' she said without emotion.

He breathed a sigh of relief. 'Good, then there is still time. I have something important to tell you.' He motioned for her to move to the chair opposite him. When she was settled he took her hands across the table and held them in his, his eyes beseeching her to understand.

'While I was gone, I went out into the wilderness. I was lost there for twelve days and nights, the Twelve Days of Infinite Discovery. My hunger went unsatisfied, my thirst unquenched. I nearly died. But that matters not. For I had visions, Cora, just like in the old days. Powerful visions that have directed me to the Answer.'

Cora was frightened. The visions had never worked in her favor. She tried to pull her hands away but he jerked them closer to him, moving her chair a few inches in the process, its legs creaking across the floor. His face was flushed, his lips trembling.

'What, James, what have they told you?' Her voice quivered.

'The girl has to go.' He looked at her, as if she would surely understand his deeper meaning.

'What do you mean "go"? Do you mean kill her?' Cora felt the panic mounting in her chest. *The child.*

He squeezed his thumbs into the centers of her palms, nearly crushing her fingers in his grip.

'That's what I thought at first, but subsequent over-powering dreams led me to the Path of Righteousness.' He let go of her hands and sat up straight, raising his arms, palms to the ceiling.

'Cora, we will let her go,' he whispered, not without melodrama.

He put down his hands. Cora couldn't breathe. She picked at the ruffled sleeve of her dress.

'We will follow a new path. We will stay here the rest of the winter, release the girl, and then in the spring we will leave everything as we found it. We will move to a purer destiny out west, to the wonderful land of bounty from whence I have come.'

Cora's heart pounded in her ears.

'But James, how can we release the girl? They will find us. She will lead them back to us.'

'How, Cora? How? We will blindfold her. I'll take her in the truck. I'll drive far, far away from here, and we'll dump her on the road. She doesn't know our names or where she is. They will never find us. Then we'll be gone anyway. They'll be looking for a farm and yet we – we will be out in the trailer again, roving the great lands, acting as the wandering spirits we were meant to be.' He spoke triumphantly, paying no heed to her.

Cora's mind was spinning. She couldn't live like that again, not after all this. And she'd seen him this way before and knew the redemptive phase never lasted long. Inevitably he'd go back to his vices, usually worse than before, but when he was convinced of something there was no arguing. Now they would lose everything they'd worked so hard for because of his stupid visions.

Outwardly, she tried to stay calm. She couldn't let him see what he was doing to her.

But inside, Reed's words came back to haunt her: *You are the prisoner . . . You can never see the truth. Not until you are well and truly blinded by it.*

James stood, pulling her up with him, and took her into his arms. How she would have longed for this before. Now his touch only repulsed her.

'Cora,' he whispered into her ear, 'we must rejoice and celebrate. The past is behind us now and a new dimension has opened up. The universe has told us to be grateful and to rise to its challenge.'

Cora forced a smile. Her body had gone rigid. He let her go and she took a step back. The girl's words echoed in her head: *We're both captives.*

'And now,' he went on, his hands folded decorously over his chest, 'let us go inform the girl of her imminent release. We must hold a cleansing ritual. I must seek her forgiveness for my wickedness.' He looked up at the heavens. 'The vices of the world took over me and changed me into a devil from a man. I have sunk low, lower than the worms that eat the earth, but I have received the message that I am to be forgiven. That I can right my ways and I will once again be privileged to carry on the mission of the universe.'

Her fury was raging. *Now* he chooses this?

He moved toward the stairs. She stared at his broad back, his saggy pants, his graying brown hair, as greasy and uncombed as ever.

She hated him. *You don't even fight back.*

Once the girl knew she was to be released, she would never want a family with Cora. She would want her own people again. She'd take the child away from here and fold it into the loving arms of those strangers. There wouldn't be any family. No one would want Cora.

You have all the power. You can save yourself.

James took another step forward and, without thinking, Cora pulled her knife out of her apron pocket and flicked it open. The blade glinted in the firelight.

She wouldn't leave this farm. She wouldn't give up her child.

'James,' she called quietly, her voice steady and calm. 'There's one thing I have to tell you. Remember what you've always said? Well, you're right. I guess I'm no better than you.'

He had barely turned around before she lunged. She jabbed the blade into the soft spot on his neck where his pulse beat, sliding it slowly across the skin where it sank into the crease. She felt it rip across flesh and tear the artery. Bright red blood spurted out at her.

James's eyes bulged at her in shock.

'Cora?' He mouthed it, no longer capable of speech. He clutched at his throat, his hands drenched with the blood that poured out of him.

He fell to his knees, struggling to grab the table with one hand, but he missed and fell to the floor, his head thudding against the boards. She jumped back from him in horror. She still held the knife in her hand, and flung it away, watching it spin and land under the cabinet ledge.

It had happened so quickly. She'd acted on impulse when she saw all she would lose, her destiny changed forever and she couldn't – she just couldn't let that happen. She wouldn't lose everything now, not after all her suffering.

But she hadn't intended to kill James.

She dropped to her knees beside him and covered his face with her hands. He wasn't breathing. Ripping off her apron, she tried to fashion it into a tourniquet to staunch the bleeding. It was useless though. Even his sputtering had stopped.

What had she done?

His eyes were frozen marbles staring blankly ahead and his body lifeless. He was gone, just like Reed; the essential James of him had gone from his body, leaving only this. Blood still oozed out of his neck, pooling around her, soaking her dress, and filling the cracks between the boards on the floor.

She had to clean it up. She had to get him out of here or else the blood would cover everything and Ellie would come and see it all. She'd be under inspection. That woman would notice even the smallest traces and the faintest stains. She would come back, kneeling over this spot, eyeing it for clues.

And Cora knew from experience that he would be harder to move once rigor mortis set in. She needed him out of there now. She'd have to drag him out to the field and bury him later, when she'd calmed down and could breathe again.

He was heavier than she'd expected, though, and she wasn't sure how far she could lug him on her own. They'd always worked together. She might not be able to handle the body by herself. With short bursts of energy, she managed to drag him through the kitchen and out the back door into the freezing air.

Though it was undignified, she bumped his body along the back steps to the pea-stone-covered area at the bottom. In one show of force, she pulled him onto the grass, where he slid more easily. When they reached the gazebo, the snow started coming down harder. She dropped his arms, watching with horror as they fell lifelessly to the ground, and she ran back into the house for her coat and gloves.

When she returned, his lips were blue. That was what broke her. The memories flooded in from the early days when she'd been a true believer. His blazing eyes across the table as they joined hands with the Followers for prayers. His warm hand enveloping hers as they processed through the fields, chanting. Before the killings. Before the madness had set in and the pills and the drinking had taken over his life.

Had he ever been a good man? Did all the forces of the universe – all his powerful guides – lead him to this end on purpose, at just the moment he'd chosen to change his ways? Cora's eyes filled with tears at the thought. It had to end like this. Neither of them could have escaped. Now she was only doing what he would have done.

She leaned over him and kissed his stiff mouth one last time.

'I'm sorry, James. I'm sorry it had to be this way.'

She dragged him only as far as the open space behind the gazebo before her strength gave out. She could rest there and no one would see him even if they came around back looking for her. She wasn't expecting anyone but she knew her own luck well enough.

She attempted to pull his arms down onto his chest to arrange them into a position of respectful repose, but the right one couldn't settle over the bulk of his jacket so she propped it up against the gazebo's base instead.

She tried to think of some appropriate words to say over him. She'd heard a thousand such eulogies coming from his mouth, but now, in her hour of need, nothing would come. She could only stare as the snow rapidly covered his body, little white specks slowly erasing what was left of his existence.

The wind blew harder. It was coming up a blizzard. Two inches of snow had already accumulated and she figured there would be six to eight more if she waited until morning. She'd never get him out to the back field in this weather. She'd have to wait until this storm had passed. His body would be stiff by then and it would be nearly impossible to move him through the snowdrifts.

She'd have to figure that out tomorrow when the skies were clear again and she'd recovered from the shock of it all. Right now she couldn't think. She couldn't even see five feet in front of her. She had to go back in.

She stood up. She wasn't wearing her winter boots. She fell once and felt the skin rip off her knee. It stung but she stumbled to the steps, ignoring it.

Back in the house, she stoked the fire and stood beside it, feeling the warmth return and penetrate her to the core. She poked the logs one more time and watched the sparks fly up and then slowly drift back down like tiny fairies floating to their deaths.

She sat down at the kitchen table, her head in her hands. Everything was quiet. All of it was over.

She surveyed the room. Blood was everywhere. But her cream-colored teapot sat patiently waiting for her on the stove. The high gloss of the stainless-steel toaster reflected the flicker of the fire. The cherry-blossom wallpaper was peeling at the top corner over the refrigerator. She'd have to fix that tomorrow.

She'd laid out the vegetables on the counter to cut for dinner later: a butternut squash, three potatoes, a red onion, and four carrots in a neat row. She'd roast them tonight with a drizzle of olive oil, some salt and pepper. Fry up a slab of ham and toast some whole wheat bread.

And then she'd carry up a tray to the girl.

CHAPTER 48

Julie sat in one of the lawn chairs, facing the door, with her nemesis on the bed just behind her. It made her nervous not to be able to see her face, especially in light of their last encounter. She'd thought she'd been so clever, finally figuring out the key to the woman's thinking, but now she worried that instead of getting the upper hand, she had simply dislodged the psychic bolt that had held together the woman's fractured self. She was getting stranger by the minute.

The woman touched the back of Julie's hair and ran her fingers through it. Julie's neck tingled. Something hard touched the top of her head and slid down to her shoulders, snagging on a knot.

This freak was brushing her hair. Yes, they'd gone deeper into creepyville.

Julie sat perfectly still as the child shifted inside her, trying not to shiver despite the chills that ran up and down her spine.

'Laura?' the woman asked softly.

Behind her, Julie could hear the woman fumbling about with a plastic bag, then rattling something hard in a small cardboard box.

'Yes?' She forced it out. It made her sick to play this game.

'The time has come to get serious.'

Julie couldn't take much more serious.

'What do you mean?'

Don't scream. Don't lose it.

'I've made a decision. I'm going to help you.'

Julie let out her breath slowly. It was possible she'd made progress after all. She wouldn't celebrate yet though, because this woman's idea of help was probably kind of fucked up.

'Will you let me go downstairs? To work with you?'

She had to try, didn't she?

'Eventually. But there are certain conditions that must be met first.'

'Conditions?'

'You have to learn, Laura. I will teach you the mysteries James taught me. You will resist. You will cling to the old ways. I did the same at first. But your life is here. Now. It's not that other life you have shed.'

Julie nodded.

Here we go.

'I understand.'

It was a lie. She would never forget her real life. She would hold on to her memories with all her might. She pictured her mother kissing her skinned knee when she fell off her big-girl bike in second grade. Her brother cracking everyone up during charades at the family reunion in Maine last summer. Her father scooping her up and whirling her around as her fairy princess dress inflated like a parachute at her fourth birthday party. And Mark, oh, Mark, the way he pushed away that one strand of hair that always fell in her face and kissed her forehead softly when he murmured how much he loved her.

She wouldn't forget any of it.

'The first step is to realize that there is no connection between the self of your past and the one of your present. Continuity of self is an illusion.'

Julie was nothing if not an excellent pupil. She would commit to memory this so-called philosophy so she could spout it back on command. She would win this battle of wits. She'd mastered deconstructionism, New Historicism and post-structuralism. She could take whatever these simpletons threw at her.

'You think there is continuity of self because you have memories, but you remember only the tiniest fraction of what's happened to you.'

'Yes, yes, that's true.' Julie would agree with anything if it got her downstairs.

'So how can your past actions have any bearing on the present when you have forgotten most of them?'

'I've never thought of it that way.' She had to choke out her disingenuous words.

'You can break from that past. You *must* break from it to join the Divine Family. Only then can you experience true joy.'

'I see what you mean.' Why was she telling her all this?

The woman lifted up her arms and squeezed something cold and wet on top of Julie's hair, then began kneading her scalp with her fingers.

'You have nothing but pain now, the pain of missing your family, or feeling you have done wrong. To be free you must let that go, let all of it go. You lose some pleasure, yes, but you lose all pain. And then you will be born anew.'

A lock of wet hair fell over Julie's shoulder and she dared to lift it up.

Sweet Jesus.

She was dyeing it brown.

Julie swallowed. She had to get through this. There was no other way out of this room.

'Yes. I'm ready to do that.'

The liquid felt oppressive as it dripped down the back of her head, as if it were sinking through her skull into her brain, coating her, encapsulating her.

'Good. Then our work can begin. I'll have this done in a minute and then you'll need to sit still for a while.'

The smell of chemicals permeated the room. Black blotches appeared in front of her eyes.

'This won't be good for the baby. I think we should do it downstairs, so I can get fresh air.'

The woman's hands stopped moving, but only for an instant. 'Nonsense. It will be fine. Nothing can harm this child. It is written.'

Julie shivered as the woman continued running her fingers over her head, working the dye through to the ends of each strand. When she finished, she gingerly wrapped Julie's head in a piece of plastic that crinkled against her ears.

'That concludes your first lesson. You have done well. Now don't let your hair touch anything. You don't want to go messing up your sheets.'

Julie moved slightly to face her, deciding to dare it.

'Is he coming back after all? Is that why you're doing this?'

The woman wiped her hands and took Julie's chin between her fingers, turning her head side to side to check her work.

'Hush. You don't need to know anything more. The Revelation has been restored to its proper order. You must wait for your next instructions.' She gathered up the brush, the bottle, and the box and shoved them into the bag.

'I'll be back in two hours and we'll rinse this out. It's going to be beautiful, Laura. You'll look wonderful.'

She smiled, her eyes misty.

'Like your old self again.'

CHAPTER 49

Cora took the Book down from the top of the refrigerator and placed it on the kitchen table in the center of seven white votive candles. The gold-and-red cushions were laid out beside them, a small pewter statue of the star and moon set in between. She'd unfolded the picture of the girl and spread it out on the table, the rolled edge weighted down by the heart medallion.

The cold winter darkness had descended outside, and it seeped in through the edges of the windows. She pulled her cardigan tighter and moved closer to the fire.

James had been dead for two weeks. The time had come.

She opened the Book, careful not to tear the delicate, yellowed paper. Her fingers trembled as she flipped through page after page covered in his scrawl, his orthodoxy, his rules: 'Pain has no meaning in the punishment of the impure.' 'The power of the New Dawn and the black dark night shall unfold and envelop us, only us.'

Bitterness lodged in her throat as she heard his voice echoing in her head. Once, clinging to those phrases had helped stave off her loss and loneliness, but the Words only hurt her now.

She closed the Book and ran her hand over the smooth raised leather surface of its cover, then clutched it to her chest. James would have said she'd failed, that she'd lost her way on the Path completely because her mind was unclean. Yes, it was true that she'd clung to those old memories, to those lost stories and people, and to that young self. In the end, the past had been stronger than James's vision. It had oozed out of her pores, floated from her ears and nose, surrounded her like a mist. She couldn't contain it.

And then the girl had taught her that there was another way, if you were so chosen. She understood now that she could retrieve and recover a part of herself, like a precious artifact dug out of the earth, a jewel to be polished to glimmering perfection. Laura Martin could be revived and restored. She must rejoice.

This time her story would be completed another way under Cora's careful guidance. Cora would build a new Path, would teach her to follow and endure. If only she could learn to cooperate in earnest this time, they could have a home, be a family, the two of them and the child who was always meant to be hers. The Revelation would be fulfilled.

She lifted her head and wiped a stray tear as she carefully closed the Book.

There was a sacrifice that must be made first, however.

She lifted up the creased picture of the girl and kissed it softly, thinking back to the whirlwind of images she'd seen of this girl's life. The parties, the caring family, the adoring lover.

'Good-bye, Julie Brookman.'

She tossed it into the fire and the heart medallion after it. She was sorry for this, but it must be done.

Meanwhile, James's teachings would not be wasted. Day in and day out, he'd drummed his messages into her brain. He'd taught her over the course of years, in an unending cycle of punishment and reward, criticism and praise, logic and nonsense, violence and tenderness. He'd destroyed her way of thinking and restructured it to his specifications. It was incredible the lengths to which the mind would go to rewire itself for survival.

Well, she'd use his techniques once more. A last hurrah, a final honor.

He'd taught her to forget, and now she would forget him.

She lifted the Book above her head.

'And so it is written,' she whispered as she threw it into the flames. The fire crackled, a log shifted, releasing a curtain of sparks up into the air.

She sat there, calm now, with her fingers interlaced as if in prayer. Her heart tugged against this act too as she watched the Words burn, fragments of torn paper erupting above the flames before crumbling to black, but it was right and good.

She'd learned all she needed from them.

Chapter 50

Late yesterday evening the woman had come to her room with the white silk dress that was now draped over the iron footboard. Julie picked it up gently, letting the soft folds of silk run over her hands. Tonight she was going downstairs for dinner. This was her first test and she intended to pass it.

She slipped off her filthy sweats. The woman had left her with a sponge, a bucket of warm water, a bar of triple-milled lavender-scented soap, and a tube of shea butter body lotion. Julie held the soap to her nose and breathed deeply. She'd forgotten what pleasure felt like.

Leaning over the bucket, she washed herself slowly, enjoying the feel of the warm water against her skin. She squeezed out the sponge and watched the soapy suds drip back in. This was heaven.

Perhaps things would be better for her from now on. Perhaps she could tolerate the situation as long as he stayed away.

She picked up the Pooh blanket from the bed and rubbed soap onto a spot in the corner in case she took the bar away after tonight. Pooh could use a good cleaning.

She lifted the dress over her head and let it fall down over her shoulders in a shimmer of softness.

She felt like a real person again.

Downstairs, things were buzzing. Pots and pans clanged together and water rushed from the spigot in fast bursts, setting off a cacophony of sounds in the pipes in the walls around her.

Eventually, she heard the footsteps on the stairs, the window slid open, and she got into position. The woman wore a nice dress too, made of pale blue Swiss dot, but there the celebration ended.

'I'm sorry it has to be this way, Laura.' She held a glistening pump-action shotgun pointed at Julie's face. 'Trust must be built slowly.'

Julie swallowed hard and nodded. Of course, the changes would progress over time. Even still, she felt grateful for this opportunity. She would leave the room after all, and there was a promise of more freedoms down the road if she only behaved. And she would. She would behave. She'd wasted her opportunities before, and this time she would be careful. She could still wait a few weeks before her belly would grow too large to run. She needn't try anything tonight.

The two of them walked in a tight bundle side by side toward the stairs, the barrel of the shotgun nestled under Julie's ribs. Before they reached the first step, though, the woman swung them around to look at the mirror on the wall behind them.

'What do you think, Laura?'

Julie stood, stunned. She didn't recognize herself. Her hair was brown, her cheeks were sunken, and her skin had lost its natural flush. Her body was emaciated except for the bulging belly with the fabric stretched tight across it. There was fear in the eyes of the girl in the mirror, her expression pinched and worn. She reached out to touch the image.

She was transformed. Had they managed to turn her into this other person, this Laura, after all? Julie closed her eyes, wanting to disappear.

The woman pulled her back and they started down the stairs.

Julie's resolve faltered. If she'd changed so much, would her family recognize her, would Mark still want her? She wasn't just different on the outside either. She'd never be the same. Maybe this was the only place she was fit for anymore. This house of horrors, this torture chamber.

Julie slumped down the stairs, feeling defeated, but as they passed the photographs on the landing, she stopped in front of one. The tip of the gun dug deeper in between her bones, yet she couldn't move on. Why was this old photo so familiar?

Then she knew. It was the image that had come to her when she struggled with the knot. This was her guiding star, her guardian angel. Even now, this long-dead woman's eyes seemed to be shining out just for Julie, urging her on. Telling her not to lose hope.

It was the reminder she needed.

Hold onto yourself. Don't let them twist your mind.

She was Julie Louise Brookman from Mamaroneck, New York, majoring in English, with a minor in History. The girl who won the regional spelling bee in eighth grade. The girl who knew the words to every song by Amy Winehouse and who'd danced the Sugar Plum Fairy last year at the Westchester Ballet. She had eleven hundred followers on Instagram and fourteen hundred friends on Facebook.

These people couldn't take any of that away from her.

She had to escape, whatever the price. She couldn't lose her focus because of a few comforts and soothing words. She had to get the fuck out of here.

As they crossed the kitchen, Julie surreptitiously scanned the room for a weapon. The room was spotless, the counters and sink bare. She'd hidden the cutlery, the ice picks, the mallets.

Giving up on that front, Julie quickly assessed the security. There was a keyed deadbolt on the inside of the kitchen door, but none visible on the windows. A small anteroom divided the kitchen from the dining room, with a French door leading off to the backyard. As they passed she studied it for vulnerabilities. It too had a keyed lock, but the sash bars appeared delicate enough to break with a baseball bat. Or, better yet, with the butt of a shotgun if she could only get her hands on it.

Through the glass, she could see the snow piling up outside and further on, a gazebo. To the left she could see the corner edge of a large red barn with a silvery tin roof, and behind all of it, a huge open field enclosed by a split-rail fence with woods in the far distance.

Okay, so the property was enormous and the neighbors far away. That only meant she had to make exactly the right choice when the time came. She had to run in the right direction. It was too cold out there for mistakes.

As they reached the dining room, the tantalizing smell of roasted meat nearly overcame Julie's senses. Real food. For a second the thought of it drowned out any strategy. She should eat, after all, to build up her strength and courage.

The woman poked the gun in the direction of a chair on the side of the table farthest from the door. The place was set with fine patterned china and frilly lace napkins, but no silverware.

Julie's plate was already filled with meat and vegetables, cut up into finger-food-sized bites. Steam rose from the perfect rectangles of steak, red potatoes, and baby carrots. Julie couldn't help but salivate.

'Thank you. This looks so – so amazing.' Her eyes had filled with tears. The smell nearly made her faint with desire.

The woman gave her the usual signal and sat next to her with her elbows on the table, the shotgun poised to fire.

'Aren't you having any?' Julie asked.

'I already ate.'

'You don't have to point the gun right at me. I promise I won't run.' She attempted a smile, but couldn't quite manage it. She tried another approach.

'Do you like my hair? Don't you think it turned out well?'

'Yes, Laura. It's almost exactly right.'

Julie took a bite of carrot. It stuck in her throat.

'Everything will be fine,' the woman murmured.

Julie took a sip of water and coughed.

'Yes, it will. It's going to be so much better from now on.'

The gun was only inches away. Julie could hardly keep her eyes off it. Should she dare it? The woman was talking to her, but she couldn't focus.

'I disobeyed James and everything got out of control. It was what I'd been afraid of for so long, but then it worked out for the best after all. Now we won't need Followers to make a family. You've helped me, Laura. And you can help yourself by doing exactly as I tell you.'

The woman gripped the gun tighter as if she could read Julie's mind. Julie had better answer.

'You're right. Everything has changed. We'll be a family now.' She used her gentlest tone.

It's too dangerous. Let it be. Wait until next time.

Then the woman took one hand off the gun to wipe the sweat from her palm onto her apron.

Something told her not to wait. It had to happen now.

With a jerk of her body, Julie thrust her arm forward and grabbed the stock of the gun, pulling it out of the woman's hands.

'Laura, what are you doing?'

The woman managed to grasp the barrel and yanked it hard. They struggled over it and the shotgun waved back and forth in the air until both chairs crashed to the floor.

'I'm not Laura, you crazy bitch.'

The two of them wrestled for control, their limbs entwined, faces grimacing with exertion.

Julie pinned her down for a moment, but she could tell the woman was strong as an ox. She wouldn't last long in this hold. Then with a great surge of energy, the woman flipped them both over and wrested the gun out of Julie's hands. Julie scrambled to her feet as the woman sat up and brought it back to her shoulder, aiming at her.

Julie grabbed the dining chair next to her and pulled it into the anteroom. She threw it through the door, sending glass and splintered wood flying. She could hear the woman coming up behind her as she squeezed through the opening, careful to evade the sharp shards left behind.

'Come back here, Laura,' the woman screeched.

Julie jumped over the steps as far as she could and sprinted off, landing on bits of glass, her bloody feet leaving smeared tracks in the snow. The cold would numb the pain.

She darted for the cover of the barn without turning to see how far the witch trailed behind her.

Before she reached it, a loud sound boomed in her ears. *Jesus, she was shooting at her.*

So much for family. Julie ducked down and put on speed. She had to reach shelter and a modicum of warmth fast.

Once at the barn, she slid the massive door open along its metal track, just wide enough to slip through. It was pitch black at first, but as her eyes began to adjust she took in the layout of the huge space with its stalls to the right and along the back wall, tools and storage to the left.

She raced toward a set of oak rain barrels in the corner, her feet taking solace in the warm prickly hay and thin layer of leftover manure that covered the floor. Her teeth chattered so loudly that surely she could be detected by their sound alone. She clamped down her jaw with both hands, trying to hold it still.

Then she realized that to the left of the door hung the greatest discovery of her life: a short row of heavy work coats covered in dirt and below them on the ground, miracle-like, two disintegrating pairs of work boots with broken laces. She threw on the jacket closest to her, though it swallowed her up, and stepped into a pair of tan lace-up work boots.

At just that moment, the barn door creaked open and Julie dashed into an empty horse stall, huddling low behind the feeder. She peered out between the boards to see the woman's outline as she slowly circled the open space, perhaps waiting for her eyes to adjust to the dark.

'Laura, I know you're in here.'

She'd left the barn door cracked open behind her. If Julie could slip her way over there unseen, she could squeeze out and make a run for it. Now with shoes and a coat, she could do anything.

'You're making a terrible mistake, Laura. You're ruining everything.'

Julie swiftly tied the cold, soggy bootlaces into tiny knots. She buttoned the barn coat all the way to the top and then she was ready, except for her breathing, which was loud in her ears. She couldn't believe the woman wasn't drawn to it like a radar bleeping at her on a dark sea.

'I guess that's how you are, isn't it, Laura? You always choose the wrong thing.' The woman's voice echoed in the air. A tingle went up Julie's spine. Why must she be so fucking weird? *Christ.*

Julie dropped down on all fours and crawled along the edge of the wall. Leaning up against the crumbling boards were several rusted-out iron tools of indeterminate use. She lifted one up only to decide it had to be from another century. But it was heavy and could do some damage, which was all that mattered. It was more than enough for her.

The woman searched the other stalls, poking the barrel of the gun into each one. She'd disturbed a couple of cows and the sounds of their heavy bodies shifting against the creaking stall gates masked those of Julie's footsteps.

'I'll find you, Laura. You can't get away from me. You might as well come back to the house. It will be fine. We'll make it right.'

Fine, my ass.

Just as she emerged from the shelter of her hiding place, Julie saw the woman's silhouette facing the door. She bolted toward it, hoping to get there in time. The woman followed, lifting up the shotgun as Julie slipped through the opening. The shot hit wood and ricocheted back into the barn.

Taking a hard right turn, Julie hightailed it to safety behind the building. She leaned up against the back wall, panting, trying to catch her breath as she held up the bizarre iron implement in the moonlight. It looked like a pair of giant pliers but the two prongs had rusted shut.

Now it was useless for anything other than a straight hit to the head. So be it.

Julie evaluated her position. If she ran back to the fields she'd be in the wide-open, a moving target on a blank white space. The moon was bright and it was a long way to the woods through eighteen inches of snow, especially hauling around this belly. Forget it. There had to be a better way.

On the other hand, the driveway in front of the barn was plowed and led to the road. She'd be able to run more than twice as fast on that flat, smooth surface. The problem was, the woman would expect it and was probably hiding somewhere now, behind the tractor or the chicken coop, waiting for Julie to make that exact move.

The farm was silent. The animals that had stirred in the barn must have settled back down. The woman waited somewhere for her out there, as still as she was and most likely as terrified. After all, what would that beast do to her if he found out she'd let his precious plaything escape? She couldn't imagine he'd take it well. Julie felt no pity for her though. It would serve her right. Then just wait until she brought the police back here, banging down the door to drag these degenerates off to hell.

But there was no time for revenge fantasies.

She took a deep breath, gripped her strange tool, and crept around the side of the barn to get the lay of the land.

The house was lit up, making it difficult to find cover. The driveway, however, was far enough away to be buried in dark shadow. Even better, it almost immediately led into thick woods that stood between the house and the road, which was invisible from here.

If she could cover the hundred feet between the barn and the driveway, she would be home free.

She leaned over and checked her laces, then bundled her coat tightly around her. Her legs felt like icicles, the thin silk of the dress offering less than zero protection against the cold. She needed to run soon if only to get the blood circulating again.

She peered a little farther around the corner, looking for the woman. It was quiet, the snow falling in delicate flurries and settling peacefully over the idyllic scenery that gave no hint of the evil festering within it.

She wanted to wait it out, to listen for any sign of movement that would indicate where the woman was waiting for her. Then if she could sneak up behind her, smack her in the head with her precious tool, she could make her way down the driveway at her leisure.

But there were no signs, no movements. Only silence and her freezing legs and shaking body. She had to move before the hypothermia set in. This cold couldn't be good for the baby.

It was only a hundred yards, she told herself. She wouldn't run it in a straight line so as to make for an easy target. She'd seen that trick in a movie. She could run a hundred yards before she was spotted, right?

She took a deep breath, gripped her piece of iron, and bolted out from her hiding place into the open night air. She cupped her belly with one hand for support, trying to relieve the pressure of its weight. It would only take a few seconds to reach the complete darkness of the driveway. She was almost there.

A shot rang out, echoing in the sky above her. She'd been seen but the woman had missed again.

The protection of the dark was ten feet away. She was only a few short paces from freedom. Her chest might explode but she'd make it, and once in the shadows she could slow up enough to catch her breath.

Her feet pounded the earth in time with her rhythmic gasps. One, two, three steps. She would be there in four seconds. Less.

The heavy tool slowed her down, though, off-setting her balance. Regretfully, she tossed it aside and broke into a faster run.

Then she was in the shadows. She immediately took a sharp turn off course to confuse her pursuer.

She'd done it. She was home free.

That's when the long row of bright floodlights that lined the driveway suddenly flicked on. She was completely exposed. But how?

Then she realized it. *Motion sensors.* The thought had never occurred to her.

The gun blasted again and in an instant searing pain ripped through her body and everything went black.

CHAPTER 51

Adam had spent the last month hitting every small town along the Hudson River, roaming RV parks, seeking out itinerant preachers for information on their shadier brethren, and showing the grainy picture to anyone who would stop to listen. Nothing had turned up, no leads. As he sat in the Chatham Diner nursing his stale coffee and trying not to think about Deirdre, he mapped out his plans for that day with a sense of foreboding. He had to make it count because this was the last Main Street he could ramble down, searching for a lost woman who might not want to be found.

No matter what she thought though, Adam knew what was best for her. He would save her. It was true that she'd committed a terrible act in her youth, he was satisfied of that now, but she had been driven to it, led down a path of destruction. He'd made his decision and knew exactly what to do if he found her.

A few files were spread over the table and he flipped through them mindlessly. They were useless now. All his hard work – the collected data, his careful notes, pages and pages of typed-up theories, all of it tabulated in his elaborately color-coded system – were for nothing. He'd reached it now. The end of the line.

'Looks like somebody's working hard.' The waitress's voice came out of nowhere, summoning Adam back to reality. She refilled his cup and stood smiling expectantly. Adam wasn't sure what she wanted of him.

'Um, yes. Busy week.'

'I've never seen you in here before. Just visiting?'

Now he got it. He knew this type. She wanted the gossip, which he was willing to provide in exchange for something more valuable.

'Right, yes. Visiting. You lived here long?'

'All my life.'

'So you're pretty familiar with the comings and goings in this town? You've got your finger on the pulse, so to speak?' He gave her his most dazzling smile.

She smiled back, obviously proud of herself. She rested the coffee pot on the table, prepared to settle in a while.

'I suppose you could say that.'

'Then maybe you can help me. You see –' he leaned toward her conspiratorially, whispering – 'I'm an investigator.' He'd learned not to say cop. Too many times he'd found himself talking to the wife of the local police chief, and they always wanted to stick their nose into everything, not liking to have their jurisdiction challenged.

'Like on television? A P.I.?'

'Exactly. Yes. A P.I.' He took a sip of the bitter coffee. 'This is delicious, by the way.'

'Fresh brewed,' she chirped.

He reached out to shake her hand.

'Adam Miller.'

She took it.

'Ellie Rainey. Pleased to meet you. What can I tell you?'

'I guess my first question is whether you've noticed any revivalist-type preachers around here?'

'You mean, like at the church? They have a revival usually every spring, but not this time of year.'

'No, not that. More like ones that would be out on the streets or the homeless shelters or campsites. That kind of thing.'

'Oh, you mean the nut jobs? They come through now and then, but the police handle them. They shuffle them off.'

'Hold on. I want to show you something.' He took out his phone and pulled up the image of Silas and his daughter.

'See this girl here. This picture is about twenty years old, so it's kind of a tough one. But I'm looking for a preacher – an on-again, off-again type – who's married to this woman.'

She lifted the picture and enlarged it with her fingers. She studied it for a full minute.

'I don't know. I mean, we all change a lot in twenty years.' She patted her hips. 'Know what I mean?'

He smiled weakly and took his phone back.

'I know it's a long shot. But I have to check.'

'And you say she's married to a minister now? Certainly narrows it down, but I can't say I know anyone who fits that description. Something familiar about her maybe, but that's probably wishful thinking because I'd love to help out an investigation.' She leaned closer and shielded her mouth with a hand.

'What did they do?'

He pursed his lips.

'That's confidential, of course.'

'Oh, right, of course.'

'Well, here's my cell number in case anything comes up.'

She glanced at his card.

'I guess this is pretty top secret, huh? You don't even put a company name on here.'

He smiled and returned pointedly to his files. She took the hint and wandered off to the rest of the customers.

He sighed. Another dead end. This was the last town on his list. He'd sacrificed everything for this search. And now, was this it? After all these years of work, of tormenting himself, of letting Deirdre slip away, would he fail at his mission?

Out of the corner of his eye, he saw the waitress returning, her face brimming with excitement. He resigned himself to another pointless conversation.

'Oh, my goodness. I just realized I know exactly who that is in your picture.'

Adam sat upright.

'You do?'

'Can I see it again?'

He pulled out his phone, his hands trembling. Could this be it?

She picked it up and held it close to her face, this time lifting up her clear-rimmed glasses with her fingertips to view it with her naked eye.

'Well, I'll be damned. I think that *is* her.'

'Who? What's her name? Where is she?'

'If that isn't Cora Jenkins. Lives up at the old Johnson place.'

He scribbled down the name and got the directions.

'Yes, yes, I'm sure of it. Obviously she doesn't look quite like that anymore but I can see it about the eyes. That's her. Definitely.' She handed his phone back.

'Her husband isn't a preacher though.'

His hopes fell a bit at that.

'Oh, no?'

'He's a truck driver. Does construction here and there too.'

Of course. Her father had mentioned that.

He'd done it. He'd found her.

'You're positive it's her? And that she still lives there?'

Adam could barely contain himself.

'Oh, yes. I was at the house not too long ago. To see Mrs. Johnson, the woman she does home-healthcare work for. I didn't get in though.' She shook her head, lips pursed. 'I knew something was up. I knew it. I told Fred we should follow up, but he said to mind my own business.'

She leaned toward him conspiratorially.

'I admit I poked around a bit when I was there, looked in through a couple of windows until Fred dragged me back to the car. I didn't see anything, but you never know, do you? And now you're here.'

She gave him a pointed look, but Adam stayed mum.

'Well, I really shouldn't gossip,' she continued, still eyeing him. 'They're nice enough folks. I don't want to get them in any trouble?' She clearly wanted to know the gory details, but Adam would never reveal anything to this motor mouth.

'Oh, no, nothing like that. They just might have some information for me, that's all.'

When she finally accepted that he wasn't giving her the real scoop, she went on about her business, but he knew the word would be spread all over town by that evening that a private investigator was looking for Cora Jenkins. He had to hurry now. He gulped down the last of the coffee, gathered his things together and went to the parking lot. He had something to take care of.

Back at his motel, he wasted no time packing everything up into the trunk of his rented white Nissan sedan. It had been a huge expense to ship these files out here, but now he realized it was worth every penny. Everything was here, in one place. His interview notes, the marked evidence bags he'd stolen years ago, the backpack, the atlas – all of it. It came to twelve boxes, all chronologically ordered and practically memorized.

The sun was going down. He had to get things moving.

He drove along County Route 32 until he was out of the town jurisdiction, stopping once for gas at a Stewart's. Eventually there was nothing left along the road but snow-covered fields and the occasional roadside farm stand closed for the season. He'd located this deserted spot a few days earlier, knowing that whether he found her or not, he had to do this one thing.

He'd take care of these files and scope the house tonight. Tomorrow he'd go in. She was the one who needed saving and his mission was clear. He would rescue her from that cult leader. They all doubted him, but they'd see.

The dirt road he'd chosen hadn't been plowed since the last snowfall, so the Nissan skidded dangerously around on it. He put it in low gear and hit the gas. He had to make it over the hill to the next field, which was tucked into a valley, invisible to prying eyes for miles around.

The guy at the rental agency had sworn these were snow tires, but Adam was beginning to think he'd been taken in. The back wheels were stuck and try as he might they spun uselessly in the snow. He got out and fell to his hands and knees, digging them out. He tried again and the car finally bumped up out of the hole it had slipped into. He gunned it, nearly sending the car into a tailspin, but at the last second he jerked the steering wheel and got back on track.

His heart soared. He was doing the right thing after all.

When he reached the valley, he stopped the car and got out. He stood there in silence, savoring the profundity of this moment. He'd done it. All these years had finally added up to something. His mother had doubted him, but his daring rescue would prove to her that he could make things right. Deirdre would see, too, that his obsessions had meant something. Maybe she'd give him another chance when she understood what he'd done.

He hurried back to the trunk and started unloading the boxes, piling them up haphazardly in the snow. Grabbing the file that contained the old newspapers he'd collected, he wadded up bits of it and stuck them in between the boxes here and there.

He went back to the trunk and got out the gasoline tank he'd filled at the station, thoroughly doused the pile, and lit a match. The cardboard instantly erupted in flames that leapt up to the sky.

He watched it burn, his eyes dancing as he saw the tongues of fire lick the air. All of it would burn. The atlas, the blood samples, his meticulous notes. All of it would be gone.

Silas was right: that evidence only led to her. But after all these years, Adam knew no judge or jury could understand the complicated moral calculus of her story. Only he did. And he'd made sure no one could ever prove anything now. He had exonerated her for her childhood sins. She could start over.

'That's for you, Laura Martin. That's just for you.'

CHAPTER 52

Cora put the cool cloth to the girl's forehead once more, watching with a sort of fascination as she writhed in pain on the bed. There wasn't much more to do for her. After several taxing hours, she'd managed to get the pieces of shot out of her shoulder – though it had been a messy and complicated proedure – and had finally stopped the bleeding, but the girl had not returned to consciousness.

It was a shame it had come to this.

Why did she have to betray Cora like that? Why couldn't she have done what she was supposed to? After all Cora had sacrificed. No one could say she hadn't tried. They would have had something together, a family. The girl could have been reinvented as a new and improved Laura Martin, a better version of the person Cora had been so long ago before everything went sour.

Things would have been different for this new Laura with Cora there to protect her, support her, and treasure her. She would have had Cora as the mother the old Laura never had, the one she'd longed for and spent years expecting to appear. It wasn't the life the girl thought she wanted, but she could have come to appreciate it if she had only been able to accept.

That version of the girl would have been so extraordinary, so special.

But it was ruined. Now Cora knew better than to believe anything that came out of the mouth of that deceitful, wicked girl. She could never be trusted again no matter how cleverly she wheedled and cajoled and spun her devious lies. That girl wasn't part of the Revelation after all.

How had it taken Cora so long to learn that everyone would betray her? Everyone she'd ever known had used her for their own purposes, manipulated her to do their bidding. Her father and Reed and James, they'd just wanted to control her, each in their own way. They never cared about her, never asked her how *she* felt or what *she* wanted. No more though. Her needs would come first.

The girl would be more trouble this way, of course, locked up inside the room for the rest of her life. She wouldn't be able to do her fair share of the cooking and cleaning, as Cora had once imagined. As usual she'd be left with the heavy lifting.

Maybe James had been right after all, and, once the child was born, she should drop the girl off at some distant location and relieve herself of the burden. But would she ever rest easy again if she did that? The girl knew what she looked like, had seen too much. She could just picture the police sketch they'd come up with. It was a risk she could not take. It was unfortunate, but it wasn't her fault.

She didn't create this situation. She was merely doing her best with what she'd been handed.

Cora sighed as she opened the prescription bottle she'd found in the hall bathroom, poured three Vicodin pills into her palm, and crumbled them into a glass of water that she held to the girl's lips, watching to make sure it went down. That would help settle her sleep, lessen the pain a bit.

She put her hands on the girl's stomach and waited. Yes, her baby was still kicking, still alive. Cora closed her eyes with relief, reassured.

After tucking the covers around the girl and switching off the light, she closed the door gently behind her and locked and double-checked it with great care. No more chances with this one.

In the morning she'd give the wound a thorough cleaning to avoid infection. Eventually the girl would wake, and she'd put her through a series of exercises to keep the muscles from stiffening up. It would help her heal. Cora knew best.

As her foot hit the first stair though, she stopped, steadying herself with one hand on the rail. She'd heard a sound from outside. She was sure of it.

Well, it had happened at last. She'd been expecting something like this ever since Ellie and that feeble-looking husband of hers had come over. She'd probably been checking in on Cora daily since that fateful visit, had maybe even heard the gunshots the other night. What if they'd been crouching in the shadows, spying on her all this time, waiting for that perfect moment to storm the house and apprehend her?

After flicking off the hall lights, she crept down the stairs in darkness, prowling silently through each of the unlit rooms, peering through the windows looking for movement. If she kept quiet, maybe they'd think everyone had gone to sleep. Sick old ladies like Mrs. Johnson need their rest after all. They'd get bored waiting it out. They'd go home. Maybe start minding their own damn business.

Her ears perked up at a scraping sound by the landing off the back door. At least they wouldn't see anything over there, for she'd boarded up the broken panes with two pieces of plywood from the basement, intending to leave it that way until spring when she could replace the window.

There, she'd heard it for sure that time, the tinkling of broken glass that lay outside the door. She hadn't cleaned it up and now she was grateful it was there to warn her of impending danger.

The shotgun leaned against the cabinets in the butler's pantry. She reached on top of the refrigerator where she kept the cartridge case and prepared to reload and defend her home.

Her chest tightened as she remembered James's body under the snow behind the gazebo, stiff and frozen, a macabre mannequin posed for the grave. It wasn't visible, but a meddling snoop could happen upon it easily enough. She'd meant to deal with it earlier, but then so much had happened. And now someone was traipsing around back there, looking for trouble.

It had to be Ellie. No one else had any inkling that things were amiss at the old Johnson place. She was sure of it.

Unless it was the FBI. Maybe Ellie had called the hotline or they'd been able to trace the girl's computer when Cora had gone online. What if they'd been working with Ellie all this time? Maybe she'd worn a wire when she'd brought the chicken soup. She'd been inside the house after all. She could have drawn them a floor plan so they could work up an elaborate rescue scheme. They could be surrounding the house right now.

Cora slunk into the living room and stealthily crossed over to the window on the northeast corner, positioning herself with her back to the wall and the shotgun ready. The back porch light shone dimly but it was enough for her to see the extra set of footprints in the snow.

Her heart went to her throat. It wasn't her imagination. Someone was definitely out there.

She gripped the gun tighter, placed her finger squarely on the trigger, not breathing, just listening. A gust of wind blew hard for a moment, stirring the fallen snow, whipping it up like smoke before it drifted back down to settle in place again.

Someone was out there who wanted to take everything away from her. If it was just Ellie and her husband, she could handle them. She'd lived with James long enough to know people can disappear. One by one, she could dispose of anyone who dared to disturb her family. But if they sent in the troops, if they overwhelmed her, then it was all over.

If only she hadn't printed out that picture.

Everything was silent now. Cora strained to hear, but only her heart beat in her ears.

Had they gone, satisfied they could learn nothing more that night? Or were they in position, waiting for her to make one false move? Perhaps they'd only been scoping the place out and would return later, armed and ready to raid.

She took a hand off the gun long enough to wipe the sweat beading on her brow. Her legs were growing stiff, so she slid down the wall to the floor, steadying the shotgun between her bent knees. She'd sit there all night – every night – if she had to, waiting for the sound of breaking glass and the leather-gloved hand of the intruder reaching through the open pane, the scream when Ellie came across James's body in the snow, the quiet knock at the door when they would claim they were 'just stopping by to say hi'. She'd die fighting them off, protecting what she had here. This farm was her only reason to live, without it she was nothing.

Why couldn't they leave her alone? James was gone. There'd be no more trouble if they let her live in peace. She'd finish out her days simply, with a steady routine, without bothering anyone.

She glanced out the window again. She could see the stars from that vantage point: Ursa Major. Cassiopeia. Cepheus. They comforted her.

Everything would work out just fine. It had to.

She only wanted a home after all. That's all she'd ever wanted, she thought as she drifted off to sleep clutching the shotgun. That was the only thing that mattered.

A home for her and her precious child.

CHAPTER 53

Adam stood on the front porch of the house the next morning, screwing up his courage to knock. It looked empty but there was a truck in the driveway. Someone must be here. If her husband were home, he'd say he had the wrong house. But if he found Laura there alone, he'd talk his way in. He'd get her attention with her picture and then explain what he knew about her past. Once she realized he'd destroyed the evidence from Stillwater, she would see that she didn't need this hidden life with James. No one could hold anything over her head anymore. She could be free. He'd save her.

The snow had finally stopped falling but the farm was blanketed with it. He pulled his coat tighter against the frigid air, then took off a glove and knocked. No one answered. He put his ear up to the glass but heard nothing. Quiet as the grave.

Peering through the window, he could see a fire burning in the hearth. They couldn't have gone for long.

Putting his glove back on and stuffing his hands in his coat pockets for good measure, he walked around to the back of the house, thinking there might be someone out at the barn. Stomping through the deep snow, he followed the tracks he'd made last night, realizing with dismay that his boots had left distinctive marks. He wondered if anyone had noticed, but in the end it wouldn't matter, because today was the day he would act.

He circled the barn and the chicken coop, but all was silent and still except the squawk of the birds.

He looked around, trying to decide his next move. He remembered the poorly repaired back door and decided to see if there was a way in. As he approached, however, he thought he caught a glimpse of something moving in a window upstairs. Was it his imagination or was someone there after all? If so, why didn't they come to the door? He thought of the old woman then, a detail he hadn't reckoned with. Perhaps she'd been left there alone and couldn't make it downstairs.

Adam hoped she hadn't spied him. What if the sight of a strange man lurking about the property put her into cardiac arrest? Or what if at that very moment she was on the phone with the police, ruining his plan?

He ran to the gazebo to hide while he sussed out the situation. He needed a minute to think.

As he squatted behind the wide post of the gazebo's frame, he noticed that his knee didn't sink as far into the snow as he'd expected. The snow formed a mound tucked up against the edge of the boards. There was something under there.

He kicked at the spot to figure out what he'd landed on.

As the snow scattered, he hit upon something hard, like a prong with blunt edges. As he brushed away the last bits of snow, four fingers stuck out at him, curled up, rigid and blue.

Jesus Christ.

With a sharp cry, he pulled back, then quickly glanced up at the house to make sure he hadn't been heard. Nothing stirred.

He looked over at the stiff hand, marshaled his courage, and burrowed further into the area above the fingers. Finally he uncovered the brass buttons of a work coat and the stiff collar of a flannel shirt. He knew exactly where the head would be now, but he paused, reluctant to reveal the empty face of death he'd seen so many times before.

He sat down and closed his eyes, picturing the newspaper copy describing his bravery and the medal they would pin to his chest.

He took a deep breath and kept going.

And then the snow gave up its secret. There it was, the blue face, morgue-ready and perfectly preserved by the cold, its eyes staring straight ahead and its frozen hair clinging to it like tentacles. The neck had been slit and black ice clung around the edges of the parted flesh.

Adam, stunned, turned away with a jerk.

'Shit,' he said quietly, wiping his mouth with the back of his hand. This wasn't what he'd expected. His fingers itched for his gun, but they'd taken it when he'd left the force.

A whirl of wind disturbed the even snow between him and the house, then everything went still again. He peered carefully into the dark windows, but they were empty. He pulled his cell out of his pocket and glanced down at it. No signal.

He knew what the rational decision was. He should leave immediately and come back with the local cops. That was the smart move.

He started back toward his car, but something stopped him. That body wasn't going anywhere and the farm was quiet now. Whatever had happened here seemed to be over. It wasn't an emergency.

He'd worked on this case for three long years of his life. He wasn't ready to share the glory until he'd gotten to the bottom of this.

No, he had to go in there. Laura Martin was *his* to save.

Turning away from the corpse, he trudged to the back door. He tentatively pulled at the plywood nailed up over it and found that it came off in his hands, leaving a gaping hole in front of him with sharp glass and wood framing the opening. Did the dead man make that hole? Was he an intruder and Laura Martin had been forced to defend herself? But no, the glass and wood splinters pointed in the other direction. Someone had broken *out* of that house.

Adam crawled through the hole and stepped into a small room that led to the kitchen, where he'd seen the fire burning. Everything was neat as a pin. The violence couldn't have been that recent.

He grabbed a butcher knife from the block and continued on down the hall, peering into a small well-organized pantry filled with canned goods and jars of pickled vegetables.

Next came a bathroom at the end that was being used for storage, boxes piled nearly to the ceiling.

He opened another door, which led to the living room. No one was in there either. It was a room out of time, with its yellow velveteen-covered loveseat, the curved mirror over the fireplace, and a rug spattered with sprays of flowers and entwined vines. He opened a drawer of the Chippendale-reproduction sideboard to find it filled with framed family photos. He lifted out one of a stern-looking bespectacled woman with an enormous bouffant, taken, he would guess, in the 1950s. Possibly Mrs. Johnson. His eyes went to the ceiling. Was she up there? Was she hurt? He was certain he'd heard another groan just above him.

He replaced the photo and carefully closed the drawer. His next stop was the dining room, where all seemed in order except for a broken chair tossed into a corner. He lifted it up, running his finger along the edge of the damaged leg. The bottom half of it lay on the floor a few feet away. A break that clean would have required serious force.

Something very strange was going on in this house.

Adam returned to the kitchen and took a deep breath. His heart thumped in his chest. This was his moment.

As he mounted the stairs, the photographs along the walls grew progressively more ancient. The history of a family now reduced to one lonely soul who was caught up in a story she was likely too decrepit to understand.

At the top, there were four doors along the hall, two closed and two open. The farthest one on the left had a row of deadbolt locks on the outside and a small slit had been cut into it.

His heart pounded harder. Did Laura Martin's husband keep her locked in the bedroom when he was out? If so, things were worse than he'd thought.

He hurried to the door, slid the window open, and peered into the room.

What he saw made him sick inside.

The room was unlike the rest of the house. It was not a room at all, but a cell, stripped down so that it was now nothing more than four bare walls and a boarded-up window, furnished sparsely with a bed, a sink, and a toilet of some kind. On the bed lay a pregnant woman in a white dress with long brown hair streaming out beside her. She was far too young to be either Laura Martin or Mrs. Johnson.

'Hey,' he called out.

She didn't move.

'Hey, you there.' He said it louder, looking back over his shoulder to make sure no one below had heard him.

After another long pause, she finally swung her head around. Adam was horrified. Gaunt and pale, with her face screwed up in pain, she looked like a skeleton, like the walking dead. She shifted toward him with what appeared to be an extraordinary effort. Her right shoulder was wrapped in a bandage and a spot of blood the size of a fist had leaked through.

What had been done to this poor girl?

Adam's heart raced. It was something out of a horror movie.

The girl struggled to sit up. She seemed dazed and her head wobbled up and down. Slowly, but with a look of determination on her face, she swung her feet around to the floor and gripped the side of the bed to steady herself. Her thin dress appeared to be some kind of old-fashioned evening gown. None of this made any sense. How did it connect with the dead body outside or the broken window and chair?

'Who – who are you?' She was obviously trying to concentrate through excruciating pain.

'I'm the police. I've come to get you out of here.' The words came out by instinct.

Her lips trembled.

'Am I dreaming you? Are you another one of those hallucinations?'

'I'm real. I'm here to help you.' He couldn't believe it. He could save two of them. In fact, maybe there were other women hidden elsewhere in this house. He had to check behind the closed doors, the basement, the attic. What had he stumbled upon?

The girl began to breathe heavily, possibly hyperventilating. He was afraid she might faint.

'It's okay. Just stay calm. I'm going to get you out.'

She stood up shakily and stumbled to the door, pressing her hand up to the slit of the window.

'Please hurry. Before she comes back.'

'She?'

'That horrible bitch. She tried to kill me. Look at me, damn it.'

Adam attempted to pry open the locks with the butcher knife, with no luck. The girl's forehead pressed up against it, her panicked eyes staring up at him.

'What the fuck are you doing? *Shoot the fucking locks*.' Adam needed to talk her down but the truth was, he was freaking out now too. They didn't run workshops to cover this particular circumstance.

'Okay, well, I—' he began, flustered.

'Well, you *what*? Just shoot.' She was screaming now.

'I can't, I can't,' he yelled back, running his fingers through his hair. 'I don't have a gun.'

'*What?*' she screeched. 'You people finally find me, and they send in a cop who *doesn't have a gun*? Are you kidding me?'

'I wasn't exactly expecting this.'

She looked puzzled. 'Weren't you looking for me?'

There was no time to explain.

'The keys. Do you know where they keep the keys?'

'*How the fuck am I supposed to know where they keep the keys?*' The girl was out of her mind. Maybe he should just leave her there and come back with reinforcements.

'Listen, I'm going to get some help.'

'No, no, I'm sorry I said that. Look for the keys. Check the kitchen. Do not leave me in this house. Do not leave me,' she said through clenched teeth.

'Okay, okay. Hold on.'

'Keep talking to me. I want to hear your voice.'

'Okay, okay.' He ran down the stairs, gripping the knife tighter as he turned the corner.

'I'm in the kitchen. I'm looking for the –' and then he saw them. A ring of keys, hanging on a little brass hook by the door. He grabbed them and raced back up the stairs.

He held them up to her through the window.

'These might be the ones.'

'*Hurry.*'

He put the knife on the floor at his feet. His hands shook as he tried different combinations of keys and locks.

'Come on. She could be back any minute. And *she* has guns.'

'Listen, isn't another woman being kept here? Older than you, mid-thirties?'

'Oh, no fucking way do you think you are saving her. She's the enemy, you idiot. She's the one keeping me here.'

Adam shook his head, puzzled. He paused in his efforts and stepped away from the door.

'I think you must be mistaken.'

'Mistaken?' She looked down at his hands. 'What are you doing? Don't stop.'

He went back to the locks, his fingers fumbling nervously as he tried each key.

'Do you know how long I've been here?' She stepped back and pointed to her belly. 'At least this long. See? Even longer. Get it? Do you get it?'

'Shut up. I need you to be quiet right now,' he yelled back at her. He knew he was losing his cool but this stupid girl was impossible to deal with. She didn't seem to understand that he was a hero. Her hero, for chrissakes.

'I'm getting you out,' he muttered.

The girl wailed. Tears streamed down her flaming red cheeks.

'Why are you crying? I'm saving you,' he bellowed at her.

She pounded on the window in obvious disgust. She should be grateful. He'd found the right keys for two of the locks, and there, there was the third. One more to go.

The girl pressed her face against the window again to watch his hands work at the final lock. He wished he could keep them from shaking. It was embarrassing.

'How can there only be one of you? Where's your partner or your backup or whatever? I've watched television and they don't ever send in just one guy.'

He stopped in his work again. This was enough. Fine, he'd tell her the truth and she could deal with the same reality he was dealing with. Maybe that would shut her up.

'Okay, I'm not really a cop.' Her eyes went wide. 'But don't worry. I used to be. I'm just on – leave.'

'So it's just the two of us? And you don't have a gun?' Her face went from red to white, but his words had the desired effect. She got quiet all right.

At that moment, the last lock clicked and he swung open the door. She flew out of the room and pushed him out of her way with her one good arm. Spotting the knife at his feet, she dove for it and carried it off down the stairs.

'Damn it,' he muttered.

He ran down the hall and flung open the first door. A linen closet. The second opened onto a makeshift hospital room, the air stale from disuse. Surely for Mrs. Johnson. But where was she?

Finding the last bedroom deserted too, he headed toward the stairs to check the basement.

He caught up with the girl just at the bottom of the stairs where she stood stock-still, panting. He bumped into her hard and the knife in her hand flew across the room and clattered to the floor.

He looked up and saw immediately why she'd quit running. Standing in the middle of the room was a wild-eyed woman, her hair in a tangled mess of a bun and clothes that looked like a cheap costume from the Depression Era.

She held a shotgun pointed right at them.

CHAPTER 54

As she stared down the barrel of the gun that had shot her once already, Julie wanted to kill the ridiculous man who had come to save her. Why would he have tried to rescue her without a gun?

The knife would have been something, but there it lay on the floor, out of reach under the table.

But she couldn't panic. She had to think.

She could barely function as it was – the room spun, her stomach heaved, and the pain in her shoulder thudded at her like a hammer – and now she had to figure out how to get them out of this situation too?

Part of her wanted to crumple up in a ball on the kitchen floor and give up. Beg the woman to kill her and put her out of this misery. She couldn't try and fail again. She didn't have the heart.

Then she remembered the child inside her.

When she'd been lying on that bed drowning in her delirious, fevered dreams of the past two days, she'd thought she'd blown everything with her premature escape attempt. Now, even though the effort so far had been thoroughly botched, she had to take this one final, fucked-up chance. Moron fake cop or not, there were at least two of them now. Her odds had to be improved.

If only her head didn't feel so thick and her body so weak. How was she going to manage this?

Behind her, she heard him call out to the woman.

'Are you Laura Martin?'

Julie couldn't understand.

She was Laura?

'I mean, I know you go by another name now,' he went on. 'Cora, right? But in Stillwater, you were Laura Martin?'

Whatever he was talking about was having an incredible effect on her. The woman's face had gone slack and the gun dropped an inch, then two. It was a distraction at least. He'd gotten her attention.

The woman gestured with the gun's barrel for them to move to the left of the fireplace.

'What do you know about that?' she said, her eyes glued to his.

'I know everything about it, Laura. About Reed Lassiter and Joy Marcione and all of it.'

The woman jumped at the names.

'Who are you? What are you doing here?' She glanced out the window. 'Who else is here?'

'They're coming. A whole lot of them,' Julie interjected. 'He told me the rest of the force is on its way. You'd better let us go.'

Instead the woman moved in closer to them, positioning the tip of the gun less than a foot from the cop.

'That true? Tell me.'

His image swam before Julie's eyes. If only she hadn't been given those pills. Everything was hazy and disconnected. How was she supposed to think like this?

'Y-yes. They're on their way,' she heard him say from far away.

Julie took a deep breath. At least he got the picture.

'You're lying. You don't have a gun. Or a uniform. You're not a cop at all, are you? I know who you are. You're the one who was snooping around here last night, scaring the daylights out of me. A petty thief, I'd wager.' The woman laughed quietly. 'Well, look what you've wandered into.'

A shadow fell over her face.

'But who told you about Stillwater?'

'I'm telling you, I'm a cop. I've been investigating you for three years. I know what happened. I know you killed those three people – Reed and the others.'

The shock of this news brought Julie back to her senses. She'd killed Reed? The one whose name Julie wasn't allowed to say because she wasn't worthy? The one the woman had clearly loved? And what about the baby the woman had mentioned? *What was this woman capable of?*

'Don't worry, Laura,' the man continued. 'You don't have to worry about Stillwater anymore. I've taken care of it.'

'What are you talking about?'

'All the evidence is gone. Destroyed. I burned it. I've come to save you, you see?'

Julie looked on in disbelief.

'Save me? I don't need saving. This is *my* house.' Julie thought she had a point.

'Laura, let me explain. My sister Abigail was abducted from a parking lot when she was seven. She would have been about your age.'

'What does that have to do with anything?'

'I know you were abducted too. So you see, it was fate that I found you, because I understand what you've gone through.'

She shook her head.

'You don't understand. Don't even try.'

'I came here to help you. Your father told me –'

She squinted her eyes at him, her jaw muscle twitching.

'You didn't talk to my father. Now I know you're lying.'

'I can prove it. I have a picture of the two of you together. It's on my phone. Can I just – will you let me show it to you?'

Julie watched them, thinking maybe this guy was a genius after all. He didn't make any sense, but at least his story was sucking the woman in. Julie followed their movements carefully, straining to focus, and trying hard not to pass out as she waited for an opportunity to grab the gun.

Keep talking, little fake cop. Keep talking.

'I'll get it out. You keep your hands up.' The woman edged over to him, the gun in his face now. She reached around to his back pocket and as she slid his phone out, Julie made her move.

She lunged for the gun. Julie's shoulder throbbed and the room blurred before her but she fought for it with everything in her. The woman was strong though, so strong. Julie thought of the baby, Mark, her parents, her guardian angel in the photo on the stairs, and she mustered up every last bit of strength she had.

With a final burst of wild energy, she wrenched the shotgun free of the woman's hands and whipped around to face her.

She'd done it.

'Get over there,' she screamed. 'Get in the corner.'

The woman growled with frustration, but did as she was told.

Julie stood there panting, the adrenaline coursing through her.

Then something gripped her arm. Julie twisted left. The stupid fake cop was trying to snatch the gun away from her.

'Leave her alone. Don't hurt her. Not after all this,' he yelled.

Julie was having none of it. She spun around and pushed the barrel of the gun against his chest, shoving him back. It went off, the blast echoing in her ears. She squeezed her eyes shut, nearly falling over, but forced herself back to consciousness in time to see the man fall to the floor clutching his leg.

Oh my God, I shot him.

'I'm sorry,' she blurted out. 'I didn't mean to. But what the hell were you thinking?'

He lay on the floor groaning in agony as blood soaked through his jeans.

'I can't believe it. You shot me.'

Julie kept the gun trained on the woman even as she scanned the room frantically trying to figure out what to do. She grabbed a tea towel hanging on the back of one of the kitchen chairs and tossed it down to him.

'Here,' she said. 'Don't worry. We'll get out of here. Give me your phone.'

'Forget it. There's no signal,' he groaned.

She turned to the woman with eyes blazing. 'Where's the landline?'

The woman just stared.

Julie scanned the room and saw it on the wall. It was killing her to balance the gun against her injured shoulder and hold it with the same hand. The butt of it was inches from her healing wound, and the jolting pain nearly made her swoon. She bit her lip and gripped her fingers tighter around it, reaching for the receiver.

She put it to her ear. No dial tone.

'Naturally,' she muttered, throwing it down in a fit of rage. It dangled uselessly by its cord, swinging back and forth against the cherry-blossom wallpaper.

Julie screamed in frustration and kicked the table leg.

What were her options?

She could take the gun and his car, and leave them there. But if she did that, the woman would get away. She obviously couldn't trust Fake Cop to hold her there until the cops came. He cared more about saving that awful bitch than her.

She could lock the woman in the room. Julie glanced over at the stairwell and felt sick to her stomach. She couldn't do it. She couldn't go back up those stairs ever again. Plus, this woman was devious. What if she managed to turn the tables and Julie ended up back in there? No way.

The walls seemed to be closing in. She struggled to get control of her thoughts.

What else?

She could shoot the woman in the leg too to keep her from running. But what if she missed and that was the last shell? She couldn't risk it.

There had to be another way.

Her eyes scoured the room and landed on a smoke detector up in the corner. Those lines would be cut along with the phone, but it gave her an idea. Eventually someone would come if there were a fire.

If it were big enough.

'Give me that towel,' she yelled at the man.

He looked at her with a puzzled expression but threw it back to her.

Keeping the gun steadily pointed at the two of them, Julie backed up to the hearth and dipped the blood-smeared towel into the flames, watching it slowly ignite.

'What are you doing?' asked the woman, her terror evident.

Julie turned to her with fury in her eyes.

'I'm going to burn this evil house to the ground, that's what I'm going to do.'

'No,' the woman cried, 'not the house.' Her eyes flew from wall to wall, panicked. Julie saw in that glance just how much it meant to her and so with great relish, she tossed the burning towel at the curtains. They lit up like a torch, the flames shooting to the ceiling.

Fake Cop screamed.

'This old house?' Julie said with venom in her voice. 'It's going to go up like a box of matches.'

Smoke began to fill the room and Julie realized that it might kill them before her rescuers arrived. No way would she risk death when she was this close to escape. They had to get out of here. She looked down at her bare feet and then through the window at the snow. She aimed the gun back toward the dining room.

'Move. In there.'

The woman walked backwards, her eyes on Julie, and Fake Cop crawled his way there, unable to bend the injured leg. They needed to get to the safety of the barn, but she wasn't sure he could make it. By the time they reached the dining room, the roar of the flames was over-whelming as they lapped at the disintegrating framework of the old house. The wires must be ancient. Julie pictured the flames racing along them to the four corners of the house, eating up its poison. But this would have to do for the moment.

Then there was a loud pop and the sound of the fire grew even more deafening. Through the windows, she could see a column of black smoke trailing out into the backyard. The rescue squads would surely arrive in minutes.

The man started blabbering again.

'I don't think you meant to do it, Laura.'

Why wouldn't he quit talking?

'Shut up,' Julie muttered as she leaned against the dining-room table for support.

He kept looking over at the woman. Why was he so fixated on her? He had to be watched carefully or else he'd still try to save this witch.

'It wasn't the real you,' he raved. 'Like my Abigail, you didn't have the life you were supposed to have. Your real life was stolen from you. Horrible circumstances can twist a person and make you do terrible things. You can't be held accountable for that.'

The woman swung her head back and forth from one to the other, looking confused.

'Make him shut up,' she said to Julie. 'He doesn't know anything about me. Shoot him again.'

'He's defending you. You should say thank you,' Julie said. Then turning to him, 'Go on. I'm dying to hear how you justify what she's done to me.'

'She's done things *for* you too. What you don't know is that James Jenkins is lying out behind that gazebo. Dead.'

Julie spun around to look at her.

'You killed him?'

The woman stammered back, 'You can't prove that. You don't know what happened.'

'He's dead?' Julie asked again.

'That's him, isn't it, Laura? Out in the snow with his throat slit?'

'Stop calling me that. My name is Cora. My name is Cora.'

'You killed him, didn't you?'

She hesitated, but then answered boldly, her chin up.

'Yes, I killed him.'

Julie felt suddenly cold. What did this mean? The Evil One was dead? Why? To help her? Because she truly meant for them to be a family? Or because he had manipulated and abused her and it had made her crazy? Time shifted and warped in Julie's mind, the scene before her veiled in a gray haze. She couldn't tell how long she'd been standing there, her arm stiff and pulsing as she forced herself to keep the gun trained on this woman. At last, the sirens sounded from afar. She turned her head toward the window. Eventually a line of rescue vehicles charged up the driveway, spinning to a stop as they spread out on the plowed area.

Her heart surged. She was almost out of here.

Then spots of black blotted out the scene before her. She was dangerously close to unconsciousness. She knew she must stay awake, but her head was heavy and her eyelids were drooping closed against her will.

Meanwhile the red, white, and blue spinning lights shone brightly against the snow, their colors refracted through the windows and projected onto the ceiling above her. She would be saved if she could just hang on a few more minutes. The Evil One was dead. The woman would be locked in jail forever and ever. But only if she kept going.

Then something clicked in her brain and suddenly brought her back to life.

'Why didn't you let me go?' she said.

The woman stared out at the line of fire trucks, ambulances, and squad cars, her face blank.

'What?' she asked as if she'd barely heard Julie.

'After you killed him. You kept me here. Why didn't you set me free?' Julie turned to Fake Cop. 'If she'd done it for me, as you say, she would have let me go. She didn't.'

Fake Cop seemed distracted by the commotion outside as well. His eyes followed the rescue workers as they jumped out of the trucks, unrolled the hoses, and dragged them over to the front of the house where the flames burned brightest.

'Give her another chance,' he said as the first burst of water hit the boards. 'Let her go.'

'Are you crazy? Did you hear what I just said? She may have killed him but – are you registering this, mister? – she wasn't just a pawn doing his bidding. *She* didn't let *me* go. *Even after he was dead.*'

'You have to understand, she wasn't supposed to have the life she had. Imagine it. She was taken from her mother, lived out of some dump of a trailer going from town to town, subjected to beatings and who knows what else, and then brainwashed into subservience by her husband. Don't you understand how extreme circumstances can change you? How they can turn you into something you aren't supposed to be?'

It flashed in Julie's mind how she'd planned to kill the baby, how prepared she was to snap its little innocent neck. She shuddered. Yes, she did know. But that didn't excuse the woman for what she did.

'Not everybody turns evil just like that. Some people do the right thing, even in the wrong situation.'

'Listen to yourself. The right thing in the wrong situation. Like now. That's what I'm asking you to do. This isn't the person she was meant to be.'

The woman jerked her head up at Adam's words, her face suddenly animated again.

'Don't tell me who I'm meant to be. People are always informing me of who I am "inside", or what the "universe holds" for me. But you – whoever you are – you don't know who I am. And none of the rest of them did either. I'm the only one who knows.'

Adam stared at her, apparently stunned into silence at last. He dragged himself to the wall, propping himself up against it, as if he needed an upright position to regain his dignity.

'I'm only trying to help you. I'm trying to save your life,' he said. 'But don't worry, I've learned my lesson. I'm going home after this, to Deirdre. I don't need to be a hero. Apparently nobody wants one.'

Julie felt a pang of guilt at that. She'd been too hard on the guy. He *had* gotten her out of that room after all.

'That's not true,' she blurted out. 'You may not be able to save her, but you saved me. I won't forget it and neither will my family. Trust me, you're a hero now, even if it was by accident.'

With that, Julie turned to the woman, searching her face for any small sign of humanity. Over these long months, she'd seen glimpses of it. She'd watched her slowly come out from under his control, little by little, like pebbles breaking free from the mountain to form an avalanche. Even as she'd lost her mind, she'd transformed. And Julie had helped her. They'd done it together.

But no, no. She knew who this woman was, whether anyone else could see it or not. Julie *knew*. She was a murderer and an accomplice to worse. She was pure evil. She didn't deserve another chance. She deserved to be punished.

'You've done something terrible to me,' she said, fighting through the fog in her brain to say what she hadn't been able to for months. 'Something really terrible. You, not just him.'

The woman stared right back at her and finally spoke, a trace of sadness in her voice that Julie didn't understand.

'You've betrayed me too, Laura. You were weak. You should never have let any of this happen. If only you hadn't gone down to the caves.'

Julie shook her head in disgust. Her words made no sense. One thing was clear, though. This woman would never take responsibility for anything.

The firemen broke down the outer door of the house to the kitchen and smashed through the windows to release the pressure inside. Water gushed against the walls. The men barked orders to one another just a few feet away.

They'd be in there in seconds.

Julie moved so her back was against the entry to the kitchen. The broken French door was in front of her, the section missing plywood letting in cold air that whooshed around her.

All she had to do was open that kitchen door and they'd rush in. She'd hand over that horrible shrew and explain all the things she'd done. At a minimum, they'd lock that hateful woman up forever, just as she'd intended to do to Julie. But perhaps that wasn't enough. She deserved the chair, the noose, lethal injection, the firing squad. The faster the better.

In fact, she could kill this woman herself. *Right now.*

Julie could just picture the life draining slowly out of her face as she begged for mercy. The image set fire to her heart. She burned with revenge, the taste of death on her tongue. Visions of retribution swam in her head. She lifted the gun. Justice at last.

By God, she would have it.

Julie drew in her breath, surprised by the force of her hatred. Now it was in her. Like a virus that could possibly never be cured, curdling her insides, killing her from within.

What had happened to her in there? Who was she now that she was capable of this murderous desire?

The world stood still. The firemen's axes hacked at the walls, red and blue disks of light spun around them, the smell of smoke filled her nostrils. All of it swirled around her as she tried to think, tried to stay afloat in the fluctuating tides of her consciousness. Then everything went silent and the scene before her seemed far away, distant, unreachable.

It hit her then and she knew without a doubt that there was only one solution. As horrible as it was, as unjust as she felt it to be, there was only one way to reverse this curse. She knew what she had to do, no matter how much it would kill her to do it. It wasn't fair. It simply wasn't fair.

She climbed out of the murky depths she'd been slipping into, to force herself to act.

Her eyes met the woman's from across the room and Julie tightened her grip on the barrel of the shotgun. The woman's face registered her powerlessness, her defeat. She was prepared to accept the verdict.

Julie squinted, clenched her teeth, and said the words as clearly and distinctly as she could, her heart breaking with each syllable.

'Run, you stupid bitch. Run.'

Now read on for the first chapter of Koethi Zan's thriller

THE NEVER LIST

Also published by Vintage

CHAPTER 1

There were four of us down there for the first thirty-two months and eleven days of our captivity. And then, very suddenly and without warning, there were three. Even though the fourth person hadn't made any noise at all in several months, the room got very quiet when she was gone. For a long time after that, we sat in silence, in the dark, wondering which of us would be next in the box.

Jennifer and I, of all people, should not have ended up in that cellar. We were not your average eighteen-year-old girls, abandoning all caution once set loose for the first time on a college campus. We took our freedom seriously and monitored it so carefully, it almost didn't exist anymore. We knew what was out there in that big wide world better than anyone, and we weren't going to let it get us.

We had spent years methodically studying and documenting every danger that could possibly ever touch us:

avalanches, disease, earthquakes, car crashes, socio-
paths, and wild animals—all the evils that might lurk
outside our window. We believed our paranoia would
protect us; after all, what are the odds that two girls so
well versed in disaster would be the ones to fall prey to
it?

For us, there was no such thing as fate. *Fate* was a
word you used when you had not prepared, when you
were slack, when you stopped paying attention. Fate
was a weak man's crutch.

Our caution, which verged on a mania by our late
teens, had started six years earlier when we were twelve.
On a cold but sunny January day in 1991, Jennifer's
mother drove us home from school, the same as every
other weekday. I don't even remember the accident. I
only recall slowly emerging into the light to the beat of
the heart monitor, as it chirped out the steady and comforting rhythm of my pulse. For many days after that,
I felt warm and utterly safe when I first woke up, until
that moment when my heart sank and my mind caught
up with time.

Jennifer would tell me later that she remembered the
crash vividly. Her memory was typically post-traumatic:
a hazy, slow-motion dream, with colors and lights all
swirling together in a kind of operatic brilliance. They
told us we were lucky, having been only seriously injured
and living through the ICU, with its blur of doctors,

nurses, needles, and tubes, and then four months recovering in a bare hospital room with CNN blaring in the background. Jennifer's mother had not been lucky.

They put us in a room together, ostensibly so we could keep each other company for our convalescence, and as my mother told me in a whisper, so I could help Jennifer through her grief. But I suspected the other reason was that Jennifer's father, who was divorced from her mother and an erratic drunk we had always taken pains to avoid, was only too happy when my parents volunteered to take turns sitting with us. At any rate, as our bodies slowly healed, we were left alone more often, and it was then that we started the journals—to pass the time, we said to ourselves, both probably knowing deep down that it was in fact to help us feel some control over a wild and unjust universe.

The first journal was merely a notepad from our bedside table at the hospital, with JONES MEMORIAL printed in Romanesque block letters across the top. Few would have recognized it as a journal, filled as it was only with lists of the horrors we saw on television. We had to ask the nurses for three more notepads. They must have thought we were filling our days with tic-tac-toe or hangman. In any event, no one thought to change the channel.

When we got out of the hospital, we worked on our project in earnest. At the school library, we found almanacs, medical journals, and even a book of actuarial tables from 1987. We gathered data, we computed, and we recorded, filling up line after line with the raw evidence of human vulnerability.

The journals were initially divided into eight basic categories, but as we got older, we learned with horror how many things there were that were worse than PLANE CRASHES, HOUSEHOLD ACCIDENTS, and CANCER. In stone silence and after careful deliberation, as we sat in the sunny, cheerful window seat of my bright attic bedroom, Jennifer wrote out new headings in bold black letters with her Sharpie: ABDUCTION, RAPE, and MURDER.

The statistics gave us such comfort. Knowledge is power, after all. We knew we had a one-in-two-million chance of being killed by a tornado; a one-in-310,000 chance of dying in a plane crash; and a one-in-500,000 chance of being killed by an asteroid hitting Earth. In our warped view of probability, the very fact that we had memorized this endless slate of figures somehow changed our odds for the better. Magical thinking, our therapists would later call it, in the year after I came home to find all seventeen of the journals in a pile on our kitchen table, and both my parents sitting there waiting with tears in their eyes.

By then I was sixteen, and Jennifer had come to live with us full time because her father was in jail after his third DUI. We visited him, taking the bus because we had decided it wasn't safe for us to drive at that age. (It would be another year and a half before either of us got a license.) I had never liked her father, and it turned out she hadn't either. Looking back, I don't know why we visited him at all, but we did, like clockwork, on the first Saturday of every month.

Mostly he just looked at her and cried. Sometimes he would try to start a sentence, but he never got very far. Jennifer didn't bat an eye, just stared at him with as blank an expression as I ever saw on her face, even when we were down in that cellar. The two of them never spoke, and I sat a little away from them, fidgeting and uncomfortable. Her father was the only thing she would not discuss with me—not one word—so I just held her hand on the bus back home each time, while she gazed out the window in silence.

The summer before we went to off to Ohio University, our anxieties reached a fever pitch. We would soon be leaving my attic room, which we shared, and go into the vast unknown: a college campus. In preparation, we made the Never List and hung it on the back of our bedroom door. Jennifer, who was plagued by insomnia, would often get up in the middle of the night to add to it: never go to the campus library alone at night, never park more than six spaces from your destination, never trust a stranger with a flat tire. Never, never, never.

Before we left, we meticulously packed a trunk, filling it with the treasures we had collected over the years at birthdays and Christmases: face masks, antibacterial soap, flashlights, pepper spray. We chose a dorm in a low building so that, in the event of fire, we could easily make the jump. We painstakingly studied the campus map and arrived three days early to examine the footpaths and walkways to evaluate for ourselves the lighting, visibility, and proximity to public spaces.

When we arrived at our dorm, Jennifer took out her tools before we had even unpacked our bags. She drilled a hole in our window sash, and I inserted small but strong metal bars through the wood, so it couldn't be opened from the outside even if the glass was broken. We kept a rope ladder by the window, along with a set of pliers to remove the metal bars in the event we needed a quick escape. We got special permission from campus security to add a deadbolt lock to our door. As a final touch, Jennifer gingerly hung the Never List on the wall between our beds, and we surveyed the room with satisfaction.

Maybe the universe played out a perverse justice on us in the end. Or maybe the risks of living in the outside world were simply greater than we had calculated. In any event, I suppose we stepped out of our own bounds by trying to live a semblance of regular college life. Really, I thought later, we knew better. But at the same time the lure of the ordinary proved to be too irresistible. We went to classes separately from each other even if we had to go to opposite ends of the campus. We stayed in the library talking to new friends well after dark sometimes. We even went to a couple of campus mixers sponsored by the university. Just like normal kids.

In fact, after only two months there, I secretly began thinking we could start living more like other people. I thought maybe the worries of our youth could be put away, packed safely in the cardboard boxes back home where we stored our other childhood memorabilia. I thought, in what I now see as a heretical break from everything we stood for, that maybe our juvenile obsessions were just that, and we were finally growing up.

Thankfully, I never articulated those thoughts to Jennifer, much less acted on them, so I was able to half forgive myself for them in those dark days and nights to follow. We were just college kids, doing what college kids do. But I could comfort myself knowing we had followed our protocols to the bitter end. We had, almost automatically, executed our protective strategies with a military precision and focus, every day a continuous safety drill. Every activity had a three-point check, a rule, and a backup plan. We were on our guard. We were careful.

That night was no different. Before we had even arrived on campus, we had researched which car service in town had the best record for accidents, and we'd set up an account. We had it billed directly to our credit cards just in case we ever ran out of cash or had our wallets stolen. "Never be stranded" was number thirty-seven on the list, after all. Two months into the semester, the dispatch guy recognized our voices. We only had to give him a pickup address, and moments later we would be safely shuttled back to our dormitory fortress.

That night we went to a private party off campus—a first for us. Things were just getting going at around midnight when we decided we'd pushed the limit far enough. We called the service, and in record time, a beat-up black sedan arrived. We noticed nothing out of the ordinary until we were in the car with our seat belts fastened. There was a funny smell, but I shrugged it off, deciding it was within the realm of the expected for a local livery company. A couple of minutes into the ride, Jennifer dozed off with her head on my shoulder.

That memory, the last of our other life, is preserved in my imagination in a perfect halo of peace. I felt satisfied. I was looking forward to life, a real life. We were moving on. We were going to be happy.

I must have drifted off too because when I opened my eyes, we were in total darkness in the backseat, the lights of the town replaced by the dim glow of stars. The black sedan was hurtling forward on the now-deserted highway, with only the faint trace of the horizon ahead. This was not the way home.

At first I panicked. Then I remembered number seven on the Never List: Never panic. In a flash, my mind retraced our steps that day, pointlessly trying to figure out where we had made a mistake. Because there had to have been a mistake. This was not our "fate."

Bitterly, I realized we had made the most basic and fundamental error of all. Every mother taught her child the same simple safety rule, the most obvious one on our own list: Never get in the car.

In our hubris, we'd thought we could cheat it—just a little—with our logic, our research, our precautions. But nothing could change the fact that we'd failed to follow the rule absolutely. We'd been naïve. We hadn't believed other minds could be as calculating as ours. We hadn't counted on actual evil as our enemy rather than blind statistical possibility.

There in the car, I drew three deep breaths and looked at Jennifer's sweet sleeping face for a long, sad moment. I knew as soon as I acted that, for the second time in her young life, she would wake up into a life utterly transformed. Finally, with great dread, I took her shoulder in my hand and shook it gently. She was bleary-eyed at first. I held my finger to my lips as her eyes focused and she began to process our situation. When I saw the look of realization and fear dawning on her face, I whimpered almost audibly, but stifled the sound with my hand. Jennifer had been through too much and suffered so hard. She could not survive this without me. I had to be strong.

Neither of us made a sound. We had trained ourselves never to act impulsively in an emergency situation. And this was definitely an emergency.

Through the thick, clear plastic partition dividing us from the driver, we could see very little of our abductor: dark brown hair, black wool coat, large hands on the wheel. On the left side of his neck, partially hidden by his collar, was a small tattoo that I couldn't quite make out in the dark. I shivered. The rearview mirror was angled up so we could see almost nothing of his face.

As quietly as we could, we tested the door handles. Safety-locked. The window mechanisms were disabled as well. We were trapped.

Jennifer slowly leaned down and picked up her bag from the floor, keeping her eyes on me as she rummaged in it silently. She pulled out her pepper spray. I shook my head, knowing it was of no use to us in our sealed-off space. Still, we felt safer having it.

I dug into my own purse at my feet. I found an identical canister and a small hand-held alarm with a panic button. We would have to wait it out, in silence, in terror, with our shaking hands clutching our pepper sprays and sweat beading our foreheads despite the October chill outside.

I scanned the interior of the car, trying to come up with a plan. And then I noticed it. There were small open air vents in the partition on my side, but those in front of Jennifer were connected to some kind of homemade metal and rubber contraption. Valves were connected to a pipe that disappeared from our view into the front floorboard. I sat very still, gaping at this intricate mechanism, my mind racing but unable to grasp a coherent thought for a moment. Finally, it sank in.

"We'll be drugged," I said at last, whispering to Jennifer. I looked down at the pepper spray in my hand with regret, knowing I'd never be able to use it. I stroked it almost lovingly, then let it drop to the floor, as I stared back up at the source of our impending doom. Jennifer followed my glance and registered at once what it meant. There was no hope.

He must have heard me speak, for just seconds later, a slight hissing sound told us we were about to get very sleepy. The air vents on my side slid shut. Jennifer and I held hands tightly, our other hands gripping the outer sides of the faux leather seat as the world slipped away.

When I came to, I was in the dark cellar that was to be my home for more than three years. I roused myself from the drugs slowly, trying to focus my eyes in the sea of gray that swam before them. When they finally cleared, I had to shut them tightly again to stop the panic that threatened to take over. I waited ten seconds, twenty, thirty, and opened again. I looked down at my body. I was stripped naked and chained to the wall by my ankle. A chill prickled up my spine, and my stomach lurched.

I was not alone. There were two other girls down there, emaciated, naked, and chained to the walls beside me. In front of us was the box. It was a simple wooden shipping crate of some sort, maybe five feet long by four feet high. Its opening was angled away from me, so I couldn't tell how it was secured. There was a dim bulb hanging from the ceiling over us. It swayed just slightly.

Jennifer was nowhere to be seen.